HOW MARRIED LIFE IS TREATING US . . .

"THE FOURTH ALARM"

John Cheever's wry commentary on a suburban husband whose wife takes a nude role in an avant garde Off-Broadway play

"GETTING ON"

Roxanna Robinson's portrayal of an elderly wife coping with the inevitability of her husband's death

"SAY YES"

Tobias Wolff's brilliant, on-target recreation of a stupid quarrel that ends up exposing the fundamental problems in a marriage

"FIREWORKS"

Richard Ford's tale of an out-of-work house husband whose bartending wife bumps into her ex

"DEATH OF A LESSER MAN"

Gina Berriault's story of a young husband's sudden illness and a pretty wife's shocking reaction

and fifteen more modern masterpieces of short fiction about the lives we see around us and the ones we lead—

WIVES AND HUSBANDS
20 Short Stories About Marriage

MICHAEL NAGLER and teach creative writin Redwood City, Calif also teaches humanities at De Anza College in Cupertino, California. Both are married.

Wives and Husbands

20 Short Stories About Marriage

Edited and with an Introduction by
Michael Nagler and William Swanson

A MENTOR BOOK

NEW AMERICAN LIBRARY

A DIVISION OF PENGUIN BOOKS USA INC., NEW YORK
PUBLISHED IN CANADA BY
PENGUIN BOOKS CANADA LIMITED, MARKHAM, ONTARIO

PUBLISHER'S NOTE

NAL BOOKS ARE AVAILABLE AT QUANTITY DISCOUNTS WHEN USED TO PROMOTE PRODUCTS OR SERVICES. FOR INFORMATION PLEASE WRITE TO PREMIUM MARKETING DIVISION, NEW AMERICAN LIBRARY, 1633 BROADWAY, NEW YORK, NEW YORK 10019.

Library of Congress Catalog Card Number: 89-60750

Permissions Acknowledgments:

From ROUGH STRIFE by Lynne Sharon Schwartz. Copyright © 1980 by Lynne Sharon Schwartz. Reprinted by permission of Harper & Row, Publishers, Inc.

From ROCK SPRINGS by Richard Ford. Copyright © 1987 by Richard Ford. By permission of the Atlantic Monthly Press.

From THE INFINITE PASSION OF EXPECTATION, Copyright © 1982 by Gina Berriault. Published by North Point Press and reprinted by permission.

Copyright © 1970 by John Cheever. Reprinted from THE COLLECTED STORIES OF JOHN CHEEVER, by permission of Alfred A. Knopf, Inc.

Copyright © 1976 by Raymond Carver. First appeared in *Esquire* and published by McGraw-Hill in a collection of Carver's stories entitled WILL YOU PLEASE BE QUIET, PLEASE? Reprinted by permission of ICM.

From AMATEUR'S GUIDE TO THE NIGHT, by Mary Robison. Copyright © 1983 by Mary Robison. Reprinted by permission of Alfred A. Knopf, Inc.

From WORLD'S END AND OTHER STORIES by Paul Theroux. Copyright © 1980 by Paul Theroux. Reprinted by permission of Houghton Mifflin Company.

From PASTORALE by Susan Engberg. Copyright © 1982 by Susan Engberg. Reprinted by permission of University of Illinois Press.

From GREASY LAKE AND OTHER STORIES by Thomas C. Boyle. Copyright © 1985 by T. Coraghessan Boyle. All rights reserved. Reprinted by permission of Viking Penguin, a division of Penguin Books USA Inc.

From SHILOH AND OTHER STORIES by Bobbie Ann Mason. Copyright © 1982 by Bobbie Ann Mason. Reprinted by permission of Harper & Row, Publishers, Inc.

From IN AND OUT OF NEVER-NEVER LAND by Maeve Brennan. Copyright © 1969 Maeve Brennan. (Originally appeared in *The New Yorker* 7/27/63.) Reprinted with the permission of Charles Scribner's Sons, an imprint of Macmillan Publishing Company.

(The following pages constitute an extension of the copyright page.)

SIGNET, SIGNET CLASSIC, MENTOR, ONYX, PLUME, MERIDIAN
and NAL BOOKS are published *in the United States* by New American Library,
a division of Penguin Books USA Inc.,
1633 Broadway, New York, New York 10019,
in Canada by Penguin Books Canada Limited,
2801 John Street, Markham, Ontario L3R 1B4

First Printing, October, 1989

1 2 3 4 5 6 7 8 9

PRINTED IN THE UNITED STATES OF AMERICA

To
JoAnne and Lynda

ACKNOWLEDGMENTS

The editors wish to thank Tom (Pride and Poise) Parker, Kathi Paton, Ira Sadoff, Lynda Swanson, and Gary Luke, whose encouragement, support and assistance were indispensable in the completion of this book.

Contents

Introduction
Marriage and Fiction

A couple of years ago, Ted, one of the guys we work with—a family man, father of two children—told us quietly over lunch that he had been in Rogerian therapy for three months and had decided to get a divorce. Both of us were surprised and puzzled. We had never seen any signs of discord between him and his wife at any of the seasonal social gatherings that inevitably bring couples together. She was a technical writer, an open-faced, outgoing sort of person. She had played the piano rather well at a Christmas party one year. Though neither of us knew her in any personal way, she didn't seem as if she would be a difficult person to get along with.

One of us asked him what had happened.

Usually reluctant to discuss personal problems, he now seemed eager to talk. They did not fight much, he said; neither was having an affair. But he was bored. He said they never talked about anything except domestic problems. The roof needed repair; their daughter needed a ride to her soccer game on Wednesday afternoon; the rug needed to be shampooed.

He said his decision would have made more sense if his wife had been sneaking off to bed with one of the engineers at work or become unreasonably jealous. But it was simply that after fifteen years, he was tired of her and the routine patterns of their marriage. He admitted that they had never had much in common except the children, and now the children were adolescents and would soon be gone. He wanted to make a change before it was too late.

Ted's feelings had crystallized one day while he was walking through a local mall. It occurred to him that he would probably never make love to a young woman again, and this thought now obsessed him. In spite of restlessness, he had never been unfaithful to his wife during their marriage; it would not have seemed fair. But while his conscience would not permit him to take a lover, it would permit him to get a divorce, to break up his family, to put his wife and children through the inevitable acrimony and trauma. All this would come to pass just so he would no longer be bored, and would be allowed once more to pursue available women. His therapist, he said, had helped him see what he had to do.

Was he wrong to be doing this? Would he feel guilt for years to come for making this break? Or would his life suddenly change for the better? Did he deserve another chance to fulfill himself in another kind of relationship? "Sure I thought about the consequences," he said unhappily at one point. "That's all I think about, but I need to do this."

The next year was a rough one for our friend. His wife responded with a combination of grief and cooperation at first. In a strained but outwardly amicable atmosphere they agreed to separate. Ted got his own apartment. His daughter refused to visit or, sometimes, even to speak to him. She began to skip days, then whole weeks of high school; she dyed her hair chrome silver, took up smoking Marlboro 100's, and listening to albums by Twisted Sister in her room. His son, the younger of the two, reacted in the opposite way. He would call his father late at night and beg to come over, or would come for a visit early in the day and, without much explanation, want to go back to his mother's. He was by turns moody, nervous, clingy, and short-tempered. Ted and his wife tried living together again, but this only made things worse. His edginess and restlessness grated on her; she criticized everything he did. They just could not stop arguing.

Finally, she got angry and hired her own lawyer. Meanwhile Ted had begun going around with a twenty-seven-year-old aerobics instructor who was also a tap dancer. His daughter liked the new young woman and told him so. His wife's lawyer canceled all previous agreements and decided to play hardball in divorce court.

The family home had to be sold to divide up the community property. The daughter, now sixteen, dropped out of high school and moved in with her boyfriend. She got along well with her father, but said she'd had it with school. His ex-wife married the owner of a vitamin-store chain and quit her job. The son got a personal computer and began to spend all of his free time in his room.

Ted has since broken up with his aerobics instructor, and lives in the new condo he bought with his half of the community property. He is dating a divorced woman who shares his enthusiasm for jazz and bicycling.

From time to time we talk about this couple, unsure of whose side to take, or who was behaving well or who behaving badly. Appearances might make one side more appealing than the other, but the details of their intimate life are unknown to us, and we are in no position to pass judgment.

Matters of this sort were once clearer. Not too many years ago whole families could be found sitting around the living room eating dinner off TV trays and watching a television program called *Divorce Court*. A disclaimer prefaced the weekly episodes and said the names had been changed, but the shows were based on testimony taken in the divorce courts of Los Angeles County. Actually, *Perry Mason* was more plausible. Every week, the villain was either a husband with oily hair and a pencil-thin mustache who would admit that he had had "extramarital relations" with his secretary, a pouty-lipped former dancer from Hermosa Beach, or a wife with a platinum blonde wig who would admit, after a tough grilling on the witness stand, that she had "intimate knowledge" of her husband's business partner, a broad-shouldered former USC running back in a checked sports coat and string tie.

The message required little interpretation. Divorce was only supposed to happen to people who were already a little sleazy. It was associated with moral aberration, base motives, and deceit.

To remember watching that show as a child is also to recall the anxiety of realizing, for reasons then beyond our comprehension, that our parents, too, might somehow be drawn into this awful world of betrayal, anger, and tearful antagonism. In some episodes of *Divorce Court* the children would be brought in to briefly testify or even, most gut-wrenching of all, be asked to choose between their parents. Sitting in front of the TV, we children were shaken by this stuff. Just knowing it could happen was upsetting. And on some subterranean level it still is.

Somehow in the last twenty-five years marriage has changed. Talk radio and afternoon TV shows stir up a daily debate on the nature of this shift in rules and expectations. American couples have more and more difficulty reconciling their desire for marriage with their belief in individual freedom. The traditional definition of marriage, based on religious sanction and personal obligation, has ceased to have the power it once did to inspire commitment. Self-sacrifice, once the ideal of married love, is now viewed as unnecessary martyrdom. Less and less does marriage resemble a personal bond; more and more it resembles a business merger or a therapeutic process. Marriage partners, like business partners, make an agreement based upon future growth potential. For many people, love has apparently ceased to have either a religious or social meaning. Instead, we have a system of emotional laissez-faire, where individuals cultivate their own personal resources, and sell them in the marketplace. A marriage is considered good to the extent that it allows both partners maximum self-realization. If children happen to be involved in a conflict between a husband and wife, then the children are expected to understand that their parents' personal needs for growth and self-actualization take precedence. Children and adults alike are supposed to treasure this form of self-reliance; to do otherwise is "unhealthy."

How to explain this change in marriage? Is it a consequence of the consumer economy, which emphasizes what you spend and not what you save? Have marriages, too, become temporary and disposable conveniences? Perhaps the cause is the narcissistic craving for novelty, new sensations, and new experiences that is endemic to a TV generation with a short attention span.

Pop psychologists (those who write books with titles like *What a Woman Really Wants to Know About a Man* and *What a Man Really Must Know About a Woman*) deal with the dilemma of marriage by doling out advice in prepackaged servings. A constant flood of books and magazine articles has left us up to our knees in trendy platitudes, commercial catch phrases, and debased social science jargon. Just look at the language, a hodgepodge of second-hand information, stale formulas, and homilies for better living. Somehow these psycholgists' "case studies" never seem quite real; their language produces more glitz than substance.

The stories collected here are after much more. With rigorous accuracy, they attempt to reveal, illuminate, and refresh. They connect imagination to thinking and feeling. This is hard to do. We can all supply our own images from the family we were born into, from the husbands and wives we have known, from our own experience of marriage. Still, what is a good marriage? What happens from moment to moment, from day to day? As readers, we should discover the secrets of other people's lives, what they say to one another when we are not around.

This book is like the apartment building in John Cheever's story "The Enormous Radio"; like Jim and Irene Westcott we can tune in on the conversations, arguments, and passions of these couples whose lives have, for better or worse, become inseparably inter-twined. We become voyeurs not for the sake of titilla-tion but to learn the truth. The media frequently reiterates what a good marriage is supposed to be—the conventional wisdom—but John Cheever or Doris Lessing or Raymond Carver can tell us some-thing we would never hear from Leo Buscaglia or Phil Donahue or Dr. Ruth.

Consider the anxiety of the husband in Raymond Carver's "What Is It?" Out of work and depressed, he gets a call from his wife, who is at a bar with a car salesman and slightly drunk. He wants to trust her but isn't sure he can. What does he have a right to expect? Is his anxiety a sign of loving concern or a fear that his wife will give in to the pleasure of the moment? Carv-er's story shows how self-indulgence, the quick cure for ennui, constantly tests the bonds of marriage. By contrast, consider Gina Berriault's "Death of a Lesser Man," in which Claudia, a wife of nine years, watches her husband collapse at a party and fall into a seizure. In the day that follows, she contemplates her own and her husband's mortality. The strength of their interde-pendence, their ability to help each other, and their need for each other become, not a source of restric-tion, but a compassionate bond of devotion.

Today, couples often use the language of psy-chotherapy to define themselves and their relation-ships. They want communication, growth, and mutual respect. In practice, they frequently get restlessness, uncertainty, and divorce. The authors of "Rough Strife," "The Fourth Alarm," "Shiloh," and "Shifting" dra-matize different aspects of this conflict, showing how the need for growth can stretch the bond between husband and wife to breaking. In each of these four stories a wife decides to make a change that will help her grow: one gets pregnant, one joins a sex show on Broadway, another starts taking classes at a community college, and another learns how to drive a stick shift, presumably to make her getaway. This tension between the genuine need for change and the equally genuine need for continuity and stability defines the central dilemma of marriage.

These stories create some new images of marriage and reflect on some traditional ones. They look at marriage from different angles; they come to different conclusions. We see men and women who no longer trust one another ("World's End," "Say Yes"), or no longer believe in one another ("Shiloh," "Separating," "What Is It?"), who want to look elsewhere ("Shifting," "Caviar"), who want to try something new ("The Fourth Alarm"). We see husbands and wives drawn together by restlessness ("The Girl Who Sang with The Beatles"), intimacy ("Sundays") and death ("Yours"). We see elaborate deceptions ("To Room Nineteen") and compassionate reconciliations ("Rough Strife"). Finally, we see the way men and women puzzle one another, the way their perceptions, intentions, and needs become muddled in the daily routines that make intimacy both a boon and a trap.

This anthology reveals the circumstances of particular lives that suggest possibilities more than solutions. Unlike social scientists, who make descriptive statements about the varying divorce rates between, say, middle-class blacks and blue-collar whites, short-story writers seek to strip away these labels and create characters whose lives are contradictory and unfinished and do not possess the coherence of a psychological theory. Writers reveal instead the unpredictability of human beings, caught between the lack of consciousness or conviction or certainty and the need to make decisions and get on with their lives. Fiction writers give us this vision we do not get anywhere else. We live, by force of habit and necessity, in a world of disembodied concepts, but these commonplace abstractions—"middle-class husband" or "unmarried woman"—distort our perceptions. We may want to have this kind of knowledge, but none of us wants to have our own identity reduced to a type. A short-story writer uses words to break this spell cast by words, to awaken the reader to the interior life of particular characters who must strike us as real, as palpably human, while we inhabit the writer's fictional world. This humanness must come through the writing and determines to what degree a story is either an artistic success or a failure.

The stories that follow are about the unexpected turns of events and sudden reversals that we experience when the rug is swept from beneath our feet and, finding ourselves suspended suddenly in mid-air, the surprise and danger we feel at the mystery and magnetism of life. Good stories live in us and make familiar places we have never been. They let us know who we are and how we got there; and, having arrived, we see things differently. Always on the lookout for the most passionate and revealing fictive moments, we find in the best short stories the brief but enduring order that these moments can bring to our lives and our marriages. Amidst the words, we discover ourselves.

—MICHAEL NAGLER AND WILLIAM SWANSON

Rough Strife

LYNNE SHARON SCHWARTZ

Lynne Sharon Schwartz was born in March, 1939, in Brooklyn. She attended Barnard, Bryn Mawr, and New York University. She told an interviewer several years ago, "When I was seven I thought I'd be a writer, and in college when I was taking all those writing courses I still thought so. But I got married very young, and—I don't know, I stopped thinking. Then I went to graduate school, and I was about to get a Ph.D. in comparative literature, which was the last thing I wanted or needed, but I didn't quite know what else to do. I had babies, and graduate school is nice when you have babies. I was just about to write my thesis, in 1972, and I couldn't face it; every topic I thought of was no good, and every time I went down in the N.Y.U. stacks I'd just get sick. Then suddenly it dawned on me. I was a little over thirty, and if I was going to write, I'd better write. I had thought it would happen—I would wake up one day and be a writer—but I didn't do it. That has a lot to do with the way women are brought up; you expect that things will happen to you, not that you should go and pursue them." She has published three novels, Rough Strife *(1980), which was nominated for an American Book Award,* Balancing Acts *(1981),* Disturbances in the Field *(1983), and two books of short stories,* Acquainted with the Night *(1984), and* The Melting Pot and Other Subversive Stories *(1987).*

In the following story, "Rough Strife," she focuses a relentless eye on the complex intense nature—the emotional fluctuations, unspoken anxieties, and hopeful expectations—of pregnancy upon a married couple, Ivan and Caroline, who have delayed the plunge into parenthood until both are established in their careers. The story is filled with the edgy self-awareness of a woman on the brink of a profound change who must balance her desires against her fears, her need for her husband against her need for strength and selfhood. "I have regrets," Lynne Sharon Schwartz has remarked, "not over having my children, they're wonderful, but over not seeing earlier that life could be lived in a more original way. I was very conventional—not anymore. I stopped at about thirty-two. It came to me when I dropped out of the Ph.D. program that I didn't have to live 'the way it was done.' I don't want to do anything anymore the way it's done. I don't want to be married the way it's done, I don't want to raise my children or do my writing that way. I've got to find another way or else I can't do it. And when I saw that, then I was fine." She lives in New York City.

Now let us sport us while we may;
And now, like am'rous birds of prey
. . . tear our pleasure with rough strife
Through the iron gates of life.
                  —*Andrew Marvell*

Caroline and Ivan finally had a child. Conception stunned them; they didn't think, by now, that it could happen. For years they had tried and failed, till it seemed that a special barren destiny was preordained. Meanwhile, in the wide spaces of childlessness, they had created activity: their work flourished. Ivan, happy and moderately powerful in a large foundation, helped decide how to distribute money for artistic and social projects. Caroline taught mathematics at a small suburban university. Being a mathematician, she found, conferred a painful private wisdom on her efforts to conceive. In her brain, as Ivan exploded within her, she would involuntarily calculate probabilities; millions of blind sperm and one reluctant egg clustered before her eyes in swiftly transmuting geometric patterns. She lost her grasp of pleasure, forgot what it could feel like without a goal. She had no idea what Ivan might be thinking about, scattered seed money, maybe. Their passion became courteous and automatic until, by attrition, for months they didn't make love—it was too awkward.

One September Sunday morning she was in the shower, watching, through a crack in the curtain, Ivan naked at the washstand. He was shaving, his jaw tilted at an innocently self-satisfied angle. He wasn't aware of being watched, so that a secret quality, an essence of Ivan, exuded in great waves. Caroline could almost see it, a cloudy aura. He stroked his jaw vainly with intense concentration, a self-absorption so contagious that she needed, suddenly, to possess it with him. She stepped out of the shower.

"Ivan."

He turned abruptly, surprised, perhaps even annoyed at the interruption.

"Let's not have a baby any more. Let's just . . . come on." When she placed her wet hand on his back he lifted her easily off her feet with his right arm, the razor still poised in his other, out-stretched hand.

"Come on," she insisted. She opened the door and a draft blew into the small steamy room. She pulled him by the hand toward the bedroom.

Ivan grinned. "You're soaking wet."

"Wet, dry, what's the difference?" It was hard to speak. She began to run, to tease him; he caught her and tossed her onto their disheveled bed and dug his teeth so deep into her shoulder that she thought she would bleed.

Then with disinterest, taken up only in this fresh rushing need for him, weeks later Caroline conceived. Afterwards she liked to say that she had known the moment it happened. It felt different, she told him, like a pin pricking a balloon, but without the shattering noise, without the quick collapse. "Oh, come on," said Ivan. "That's impossible."

But she was a mathematician, after all, and dealt with infinitesimal precise abstractions, and she did know how it had happened. The baby was conceived in strife, one early October night, Indian summer. All day the sun glowed hot and low in the sky, settling an amber torpor on people and things, and the night was the same, only now a dark hot heaviness sunk slowly down. The scent of the still-blooming honeysuckle rose to their bedroom window. Just as she was bending over to kiss him, heavy and quivering with heat like the night, he teased her about something, about a mole on her leg, and in reply she punched him lightly on the shoulder. He grabbed her wrists, and when she began kicking, pinned her feet down with his own. In an instant Ivan lay stretched out on her back like a blanket, smothering her, while she struggled beneath, writhing to escape. It was a silent, sweaty struggle, interrupted with outbursts of wild laughter, shrieks and gasping breaths. She tried biting but, laughing loudly, he evaded her, and she tried scratching the fists that held her down, but she couldn't reach. All her desire was transformed into physical effort, but he was too strong for her. He wanted her to say she gave up, but she refused, and since he wouldn't loosen his grip they lay locked and panting in their static embrace for some time.

"You win," she said at last, but as he rolled off she sneakily jabbed him in the ribs with her elbow.

"Aha!" Ivan shouted, and was ready to begin again, but she quickly distracted him. Once the wrestling was

at an end, though, Caroline found her passion dissi-
pated, and her pleasure tinged with resentment. After
they made love forcefully, when they were covered
with sweat, dripping on each other, she said, "Still,
you don't play fair."

"I don't play fair! Look who's talking. Do you want
me to give you a handicap?"

"No."

"So?"

"It's not fair, that's all."

Ivan laughed gloatingly and curled up in her arms.
She smiled in the dark.

That was the night the baby was conceived, not in
high passion but rough strife.

She lay on the table in the doctor's office weeks
later. The doctor, whom she had known for a long
time, habitually kept up a running conversation while
he probed. Today, fretting over his weight problem,
he outlined his plans for a new diet. Tensely she
watched him, framed and centered by her raised knees,
which were still bronzed from summer sun. His other
hand was pressing on her stomach. Caroline was nau-
seated with fear and trembling, afraid of the verdict. It
was taking so long, perhaps it was a tumor.

"I'm cutting out all starches," he said. "I've really
let myself go lately."

"Good idea." Then she gasped in pain. A final,
sickening thrust, and he was out. Relief, and a sore
gap where he had been. In a moment, she knew, she
would be retching violently.

"Well?"

"Well, Caroline, you hit the jackpot this time."

She felt a smile, a stupid, puppet smile, spread over
her face. In the tiny bathroom where she threw up,
she saw in the mirror the silly smile looming over her
ashen face like a dancer's glowing grimace of labored
joy. She smiled through the rest of the visit, through
his advice about milk, weight, travel and rest, smiled
at herself in the window of the bus, and at her moving

image in the fenders of parked cars as she walked home.

Ivan, incredulous over the telephone, came home beaming stupidly just like Caroline, and brought a bottle of champagne. After dinner they drank it and made love.

"Do you think it's all right to do this?" he asked.

"Oh, Ivan, honestly. It's microscopic."

He was in one of his whimsical moods and made terrible jokes that she laughed at with easy indulgence. He said he was going to pay the baby a visit and ask if she had any messages she wanted delivered. He unlocked from her embrace, moved down her body and said he was going to have a look for himself. Clowning, he put his ear between her legs to listen. Whatever amusement she felt soon ebbed away into irritation. She had never thought Ivan would be a doting parent—he was so preoccupied with himself. Finally he stopped his antics as she clasped her arms around him and whispered, "Ivan, you are really too much." He became unusually gentle. Tamed, and she didn't like it, hoped he wouldn't continue that way for months. Pleasure lapped over her with a mild, lackadaisical bitterness, and then when she could be articulate once more she explained patiently, "Ivan, you know, it really is all right. I mean, it's a natural process."

"Well I didn't want to hurt you."

"I'm not sick."

Then, as though her body were admonishing that cool confidence, she did get sick. There were mornings when she awoke with such paralyzing nausea that she had to ask Ivan to bring her a hard roll from the kitchen before she could stir from bed. To move from her awakening position seemed a tremendous risk, as if she might spill out. She rarely threw up—the nausea resembled violent hunger. Something wanted to be filled, not expelled, a perilous vacuum occupying her insides. The crucial act was getting the first few mouthfuls down. Then the solidity and denseness of the hard unbuttered roll stabilized her, like a heavy weight thrown down to anchor a tottering ship. Her head ached. On the mornings when she had no classes she would wander around the house till almost noon clutching the partly eaten roll in her hand like a talisman. Finishing one roll, she quickly went to the breadbox for another; she bought them regularly at the bakery a half dozen at a time. With enough roll inside her she could sometimes manage a half cup of tea, but liquids were risky. They sloshed around inside and made her envision the baby sloshing around too, in its cloudy fluid. By early afternoon she would feel fine. The baby, she imagined, claimed her for the night and was reluctant to give up its hold in the morning: they vied till she conquered. She was willing to yield her sleeping hours to the baby, her dreams even, if necessary, but she wanted the daylight for herself.

The mornings that she taught were agony. Ivan would wake her up early, bring her a roll, and gently prod her out of bed.

"I simply cannot do it," she would say, placing her legs cautiously over the side of the bed.

"Sure you can. Now get up."

"I'll die if I get up."

"You have no choice. You have a job." He was freshly showered and dressed, and his neatness irritated her. He had nothing more to do—the discomfort was all hers. She rose to her feet and swayed.

Ivan looked alarmed. "Do you want me to call and tell them you can't make it?"

"No, no." That frightened her. She needed to hold on to the job, to defend herself against the growing baby. Once she walked into the classroom she would be fine. A Mondrian print hung on the back wall—she could look at that, and it would steady her. With waves of nausea roiling in her chest, she stumbled into the bathroom.

She liked him to wait until she was out of the shower before he left for work, because she antici-

pated fainting under the impact of the water. Often at
the end she forced herself to stand under an ice cold
flow, leaning her head way back and letting her short
fair hair drip down behind her. Though it was torture,
when she emerged she felt more alive.

After the shower had been off a while Ivan would
come and open the bathroom door. "Are you O.K.
now, Caroline? I've got to go." It made her feel like a
child. She would be wrapped in a towel with her hair
dripping on the mat, brushing her teeth or rubbing
cream into her face. "Yes, thanks for waiting. I guess
this'll end soon. They say it's only the first few months."

He kissed her lips, her bare damp shoulder, gave a
parting squeeze to her toweled behind, and was gone.
She watched him walk down the hall. Ivan was very
large. She had always been drawn and aroused by his
largeness, by the huge bones and the taut legs that felt
as though he had steel rods inside. But now she watched
with some trepidation, hoping Ivan wouldn't have a
large, inflexible baby.

Very slowly she would put on clothes. Selecting
each article seemed a much more demanding task than
ever before. Seeing how slow she had become, she
allowed herself over an hour, keeping her hard roll
nearby as she dressed and prepared her face. All the
while, through the stages of dressing, she evaluated
her body closely in the full-length mirror, first naked,
then in bra and underpants, then with shoes added,
and finally with a dress. She was looking for signs, but
the baby was invisible. Nothing had changed yet. She
was still as she had always been, not quite slim yet
somehow appearing small, almost delicate. She used
to pride herself on strength. When they moved in she
had worked as hard as Ivan, lugging furniture and
lifting heavy cartons. He was impressed. Now, of course,
she could no longer do that—it took all her strength to
move her own weight.

With the profound sensuous narcissism of women
past first youth, she admired her still-narrow waist and

full breasts. She was especially fond of her shoulders and prominent collarbone, which had a fragile, inviting look. That would all be gone soon, of course, gone soft. Curious about how she would alter, she scanned her face for the pregnant look she knew well from the faces of friends. It was far less a tangible change than a look of transparent vulnerability that took over the face: nearly a pleading look, a beg for help like a message from a powerless invaded country to the rest of the world. Caroline did not see it on her face yet.

From the tenth to the fourteenth week of her pregnancy she slept, with brief intervals of lucidity when she taught her classes. It was a strange dreamy time. The passionate nausea faded, but the lure of the bed was irresistible. In the middle of the day, even, she could pass by the bedroom, glimpse the waiting bed and be overcome by the soft heavy desire to lie down. She fell into a stupor immediately and did not dream. She forgot what it was like to awaken with energy and move through an entire day without lying down once. She forgot the feeling of eyes opened wide without effort. She would have liked to hide this strange, shameful perversity from Ivan, but that was impossible. Ivan kept wanting to go to the movies. Clearly, he was bored with her. Maybe, she imagined, staring up at the bedroom ceiling through slitted eyes, he would become so bored he would abandon her and the baby and she would not be able to support the house alone and she and the baby would end up on the streets in rags, begging. She smiled. That was highly unlikely. Ivan would not be the same Ivan without her.

"You go on, Ivan. I just can't."

Once he said, "I thought I might ask Ruth Forbes to go with me to see the Charlie Chaplin in town. I know she likes him. Would that bother you?"

She was half-asleep, slowly eating a large apple in bed and watching "Medical Center" on television, but she roused herself to answer. "No, of course not." Ruth Forbes was a divorced woman who lived down the block, a casual friend and not Ivan's type at all, too large, loud and depressed. Caroline didn't care if he wanted her company. She didn't care if he held her hand on his knee in the movies as he liked to do, or even if, improbably, he made love to her afterwards in her sloppy house crawling with children. She didn't care about anything except staying nestled in bed.

She made love with him sometimes, in a slow way. She felt no specific desire but didn't want to deny him, she loved him so. Or had, she thought vaguely, when she was alive and strong. Besides, she knew she could sleep right after. Usually there would be a moment when she came alive despite herself, when the reality of his body would strike her all at once with a wistful throb of lust, but mostly she was too tired to see it through, to leap towards it, so she let it subside, merely nodding at it gratefully as a sign of dormant life. She felt sorry for Ivan, but helpless.

Once to her great shame, she fell asleep while he was inside her. He woke her with a pat on her cheek, actually, she realized from the faint sting, a gesture more like a slap than a pat. "Caroline, for Christ's sake, you're sleeping."

"No, no, I'm sorry. I wasn't really sleeping. Oh, Ivan, it's nothing. This will end." She wondered, though.

Moments later she felt his hands on her thighs. His lips were brooding on her stomach, edging, with expertise, lower and lower down. He was murmuring something she couldn't catch. She felt an ache, an irritation. Of course he meant well, Ivan always did. Wryly, she appreciated his intentions. But she couldn't bear that excitement now.

"Please," she said. "Please don't do that."

He was terribly hurt. He said nothing, but leaped away violently and pulled all the blankets around him. She was contrite, shed a few private tears and fell instantly into a dreamless dark.

He wanted to go to a New Year's Eve party some

close friends were giving, and naturally he wanted her to come with him. Caroline vowed to herself she would do this for him because she had been giving so little for so long. She planned to get dressed and look very beautiful, as she could still look when she took plenty of time and tried hard enough; she would not drink very much—it was sleep-inducing—and she would not be the one to suggest going home. After sleeping through the day in preparation, she washed her hair, using something she found in the drugstore to heighten the blond flecks. Then she put on a long green velvet dress with gold embroidery, and inserted the gold hoop earrings Ivan bought her some years ago for her twenty-fifth birthday. Before they set out she drank a cup of black coffee. She would have taken No-Doze but she was afraid of drugs, afraid of giving birth to an armless or legless baby who would be a burden and a heartache to them for the rest of their days.

At the party of mostly university people, she chatted with everyone equally, those she knew well and those she had never met. Sociably, she held a filled glass in her hand, taking tiny sips. She and Ivan were not together very much—it was crowded, smoky and loud; people kept moving and encounters were brief— but she knew he was aware of her, could feel his awareness through the milling bodies. He was aware and he was pleased. He deserved more than the somnambulist she had become, and she was pleased to please him. But after a while her legs would not support her for another instant. The skin tingled: soft warning bells rang from every pore. She allowed herself a moment to sit down alone in a small alcove off the living room, where she smoked a cigarette and stared down at her lap, holding her eyes open very wide. Examining the gold and rose-colored embroidery on her dress, Caroline traced the coiled pattern, mathematical and hypnotic, with her index finger. Just as she was happily merging into its intricacies, a man, a stranger, came in, breaking her trance. He was a

very young man, twenty-three, maybe, of no apparent
interest.

"Hi. I hear you're expecting a baby," he began, and
sat down with a distinct air of settling in.

"Yes. That's quite an opening line. How did you
know?"

"I know because Linda told me. You know Linda,
don't you? I'm her brother."

He began asking about her symptoms. Sleepiness?
Apathy? He knew, he had worked in a clinic. Unre-
sponsive, she retorted by inquiring about his taste in
music. He sat on a leather hassock opposite Caroline
on the couch, and with every inquisitive sentence drew
his seat closer till their knees were almost touching.
She shifted her weight to avoid him, tucked her feet
under her and lit another cigarette, feeling she could
lie down and fall into a stupor quite easily. Still, words
were coming out of her mouth, she heard them; she
hoped they were not encouraging words but she seemed
to have very little control over what they were.

"I—" he said. "You see—" He reached out and put
his hand over hers. "Pregnant women, like, they really
turn me on. I mean, there's a special aura. You're
sensational."

She pulled her hand away. "God almighty."

"What's the matter? Honestly, I didn't mean to
offend you."

"I really must go." She stood up and stepped around
him.

"Could I see you some time?"

"You're seeing me now. Enjoy it."

He ran his eyes over her from head to toe, apprais-
ing. "It doesn't show yet."

Gazing down at her body, Caroline stretched the
loose velvet dress taut over her stomach. "No, you're
right, it doesn't." Then, over her shoulder, as she left
their little corner, she tossed, "Fuck you, you pig."

With a surge of energy she downed a quick scotch,
found Ivan and tugged at his arm. "Let's dance."

Ivan's blue eyes lightened with shock. At home she could barely walk.

"Yes, let's." He took her in his arms and she buried her face against his shoulder. But she held her tears back, she would not let him know.

Later she told him about it. It was three-thirty in the morning, they had just made love drunkenly, and Ivan was in high spirits. She knew why—he felt he had her back again. She had held him close and uttered her old sounds, familiar moans and cries like a poignant, nearly-forgotten tune, and Ivan was miraculously restored, his impact once again sensible to eye and ear. He was making her laugh hysterically now, imitating the eccentric professor of art history at the party, an owlish émigré from Bavaria who expounded on the dilemmas of today's youth, all the while pronouncing "youth" as if it rhymed with "mouth." Ivan had also discovered that he pronounced "unique" as if it were "eunuch." Then, sitting up in bed cross-legged, they competed in making up pretentious scholarly sentences that included both "unique" and "youth" mispronounced.

"Speaking of 'yowth,' " Caroline said, "I met a weird one tonight, Linda's brother. A very eunuch yowth, I must say." And giggling, she recounted their conversation. Suddenly at the end she unexpectedly found herself in tears. Shuddering, she flopped over and sobbed into her pillow.

"Caroline," he said tenderly, "please. For heaven's sake, it was just some nut. It was nothing. Don't get all upset over it." He stroked her bare back.

"I can't help it," she wailed. "It made me feel so disgusting."

"You're much too sensitive. Come on." He ran his hand slowly through her hair, over and over.

She pulled the blanket around her. "Enough. I'm going to sleep."

A few days later, when classes were beginning again for the new semester, she woke early and went immediately to the shower, going through the ritual motions briskly and automatically. She was finished and brushing her teeth when she realized what had happened. There she was on her feet, sturdy, before eight in the morning, planning how she would introduce the topic of the differential calculus to her new students. She stared at her face in the mirror with unaccustomed recognition, her mouth dripping white foam, her dark eyes startled. She was alive. She didn't know how the miracle had happened, nor did she care to explore it. Back in the bedroom she dressed quickly, zipping up a pair of slim rust-colored woollen slacks with satisfaction. It didn't show yet, but soon.

"Ivan, time to get up."

He grunted and opened his eyes. When at last they focused on Caroline leaning over him they burned blue and wide with astonishment. He rubbed a fist across his forehead. "Are you dressed already?"

"Yes. I'm cured."

"What do you mean?"

"I'm not tired any more. I'm slept out. I've come back to life."

"Oh." He moaned and rolled over in one piece like a seal.

"Aren't you getting up?"

"In a little while. I'm so tired. I must sleep for a while." The words were thick and slurred.

"Well!" She was strangely annoyed. Ivan always got up with vigor. "Are you sick?"

"Uh-uh."

After a quick cup of coffee she called out, "Ivan, I'm leaving now. Don't forget to get up." The January air was crisp and exhilarating, and she walked the half mile to the university at a nimble clip, going over her introductory remarks in her head.

Ivan was tired for a week. Caroline wanted to go out to dinner every evening—she had her appetite back. She had broken through dense earth to fresh air. It was a new year and soon they would have a new baby. But all Ivan wanted to do was stay home and lie on the bed and watch television. It was repellent. Sloth, she pointed out to him more than once, was one of the seven deadly sins. The fifth night she said in exasperation, "What the hell is the matter with you? If you're sick go to a doctor."

"I'm not sick. I'm tired. Can't I be tired too? Leave me alone. I left you alone, didn't I?"

"That was different."

"How?"

"I'm pregnant and you're not, in case you've forgotten."

"How could I forget?"

She said nothing, only cast him an evil look.

One evening soon after Ivan's symptoms disappeared, they sat together on the living-room sofa sharing sections of the newspaper. Ivan had his feet up on the coffee table and Caroline sat diagonally, resting her legs on his. She paused in her reading and touched her stomach.

"Ivan."

"What?"

"It's no use. I'm going to have to buy some maternity clothes."

He put down the paper and stared. "Really?" He seemed distressed.

"Yes."

"Well, don't buy any of those ugly things they wear. Can't you get some of those, you know, sort of Indian things?"

"Yes. That's a good idea. I will."

He picked up the paper again.

"It moves."

"What?"

"I said it moves. The baby."

"It moves?"

She laughed. "Remember Galileo? *Eppure, si muove.*" They had spent years together in Italy in their first youth, in mad love, and visited the birthplace of Galileo.

He was a hero to both of them, because his mind remained free and strong though his body succumbed to tyranny.

Ivan laughed too. *"Eppure, si muove.* Let me see." He bent his head down to feel it, then looked up at her, his face full of longing, marvel and envy. In a moment he was scrambling at her clothes in a young eager rush. He wanted to be there, he said. Caroline, taken by surprise, was suspended between laughter and tears. He had her on the floor in silence, and for each it was swift and consuming.

Ivan lay spent in her arms. Caroline, still gasping and clutching him, said, "I could never love it as much as I love you." She wondered, then, hearing her words fall in the still air, whether this would always be true.

Shortly after she began wearing the Indian shirts and dresses, she noticed that Ivan was acting oddly. He stayed late at the office more than ever before, and often brought work home with him. He appeared to have lost interest in the baby, rarely asking how she felt, and when she moaned in bed sometimes, "Oh, I can't get to sleep, it keeps moving around," he responded with a grunt or not at all. He asked her, one warm Sunday in March, if she wanted to go bicycle riding.

"Ivan, I can't go bicycle riding. I mean, look at me."

"Oh, right. Of course."

He seemed to avoid looking at her, and she did look terrible, she had to admit. Even she looked at herself in the mirror as infrequently as possible. She dreaded what she had heard about hair falling out and teeth rotting, but she drank her milk diligently and so far neither of those things had happened. But besides the grotesque belly, her ankles swelled up so that the shape of her own legs was alien. She took diuretics and woke every hour at night to go to the bathroom. Sometimes it was impossible to get back to sleep so she sat up in bed reading. Ivan said, "Can't you turn the light out? You know I can't sleep with the light on."

"But what should I do? I can't sleep at all."

"Read in the living room."

"It's so cold in there at night."

He would turn away irritably. Once he took the blanket and went to sleep in the living room himself.

They liked to go for drives in the country on warm weekends. It seemed to Caroline that he chose the bumpiest, most untended roads and drove them as rashly as possible. Then when they stopped to picnic and he lay back to bask in the sharp April sunlight, she would always need to go and look for a bathroom, or even a clump of trees. At first this amused him, but soon his amusement became sardonic. He pulled in wearily at gas stations where he didn't need gas and waited in the car with folded arms and a sullen expression that made her apologetic about her ludicrous needs. They were growing apart. She could feel the distance between them like a patch of fog, dimming and distorting the relations of objects in space. The baby that lay between them in the dark was pushing them apart.

Sometimes as she lay awake in bed at night, not wanting to read in the cold living room but reluctant to turn on the light (and it was only a small light, she thought bitterly, a small bedside light), Caroline brooded over the horrible deformities the baby might be born with. She was thirty-one years old, not the best age to bear a first child. It could have cerebral palsy, cleft palate, two heads, club foot. She wondered if she could love a baby with a gross defect. She wondered if Ivan would want to put it in an institution, and if there were any decent institutions in their area, and if they would be spending every Sunday afternoon for the rest of their lives visiting the baby and driving home heartbroken in silence. She lived through these visits to the institution in vivid detail till she knew the doctors' and nurses' faces well. And there would come a point

where Ivan would refuse to go any more—she knew
what he was like, selfish with his time and impatient
with futility—and she would have to go alone. She
wondered if Ivan ever thought about these things, but
with that cold mood of his she was afraid to ask.

One night she was desolate. She couldn't bear the
loneliness and the heaviness any more, so she woke
him.

"Ivan, please. Talk to me. I'm so lonely."

He sat up abruptly. "What?" He was still asleep.
With the dark straight hair hanging down over his lean
face he looked boyish and vulnerable. Without knowing why, she felt sorry for him.

"I'm sorry. I know you were sleeping but I—" Here
she began to weep. "I just lie here forever in the dark
and think awful things and you're so far away, and I
just—"

"Oh, Caroline. Oh, God." Now he was wide awake,
and took her in his arms.

"You're so far away," she wept. "I don't know
what's the matter with you."

"I'm sorry. I know it's hard for you. You're so—
everything's so different, that's all."

"But it's still me."

"I know. I know it's stupid of me. I can't—"

She knew what it was. It would never be the same.
They sat up all night holding each other, and they
talked. Ivan talked more than he had in weeks. He
said of course the baby would be perfectly all right,
and it would be born at just the right time, too, late
June, so she could finish up the term, and they would
start their natural childbirth group in two weeks so he
could be with her and help her, though of course she
would do it easily because she was so competent at
everything, and then they would have the summer for
the early difficult months, and she would be feeling
fine and be ready to go back to work in the fall, and
they would find a good person, someone like a grandmother, to come in, and he would try to stagger his

schedule so she would not feel overburdened and trapped, and in short everything would be just fine, and they would make love again like they used to and be close again. He said exactly what she needed to hear, while she huddled against him, wrenched with pain to realize that he had known all along the right words to say but hadn't thought to say them till she woke him in desperation. Still, in the dawn she slept contented. She loved him. Every now and then she perceived this like a fact of life, an ancient tropism.

Two weeks later they had one of their horrible quarrels. It happened at a gallery, at the opening of a show by a group of young local artists Ivan had discovered. He had encouraged them to apply to his foundation for money and smoothed the way to their success. Now at their triumphant hour he was to be publicly thanked at a formal dinner. There were too many paintings to look at, too many people to greet, and too many glasses of champagne thrust at Caroline, who was near the end of her eighth month now. She walked around for an hour, then whispered to Ivan, "Listen, I'm sorry but I've got to go. Give me the car keys, will you? I don't feel well."

"What's the matter?"

"I can't stop having to go to the bathroom and my feet are killing me and my head aches, and the kid is rolling around like a basketball. You stay and enjoy it. You can get a ride with someone. I'll see you later."

"I'll drive you home," he said grimly. "We'll leave."

An awful knot gripped her stomach. The knot was the image of his perverse resistance, the immense trouble coming, all the trouble congealed and solidified and tied up in one moment. Meanwhile they smiled at the passers-by as they whispered ferociously to each other.

"Ivan, I do not want you to take me home. This is your event. Stay. I am leaving. We are separate people."

"If you're as sick as you say you can't drive home alone. You're my wife and I'll take you home."

"Suit yourself," she said sweetly, because the director of the gallery was approaching. "We all know you're much bigger and stronger than I am." And she smiled maliciously.

Ivan waved vaguely at the director, turned and ushered her to the door. Outside he exploded.

"Shit, Caroline! We can't do a fucking thing any more, can we?"

"You can do anything you like. Just give me the keys. I left mine home."

"I will not give you the keys. Get in the car. You're supposed to be sick."

"You big resentful selfish idiot. Jealous of an embryo." She was screaming now. He started the car with a rush that jolted her forward against the dashboard. "I'd be better off driving myself. You'll kill me this way."

"Shut up," he shouted. "I don't want to hear any more."

"I don't care what you want to hear or not hear."

"Shut the hell up or I swear I'll go into a tree. I don't give a shit any more."

It was starting to rain, a soft silent rain that glittered in the drab dusk outside. At exactly the same moment they rolled up their windows. They were sealed in together, Caroline thought, like restless beasts in a cage. The air in the car was dank and stuffy.

When they got home he slammed the door so hard the house shook. Caroline had calmed herself. She sank down in a chair, kicked off her shoes and rubbed her ankles. "Ivan, why don't you go back? It's not too late. These dinners are always late anyway. I'll be O.K."

"I don't want to go any more," he yelled. "The whole thing is spoiled. Our whole lives are spoiled from now on. We were better off before. I thought you had gotten over wanting it. I thought it was a dead issue." He stared at her bulging stomach with such loathing that she was shocked into horrid, lucid perception.

"You disgust me," she said quietly. "Frankly, you always have and probably always will." She didn't know why she said that. It was quite untrue. It was only true that he disgusted her at this moment, yet the rest had rolled out like string from a hidden ball of twine.

"So why did we ever start this in the first place?" he screamed.

She didn't know whether he meant the marriage or the baby, and for an instant she was afraid he might hit her, there was such compressed force in his huge shoulders.

"Get the hell out of here. I don't want to have to look at you."

"I will. I'll go back. I'll take your advice. Call your fucking obstetrician if you need anything. I'm sure he's always glad of an extra feel."

"You ignorant pig. Go on. And don't hurry back. Find yourself a skinny little art student and give her a big treat."

"I just might." He slammed the door and the house shook again.

He would be back. This was not the first time. Only now she felt no secret excitement, no tremor, no passion that could reshape into lust; she was too heavy and burdened. It would not be easy to make it up—she was in no condition. It would lie between them silently like a dead weight till weeks after the baby was born, till Ivan felt he could reclaim his rightful territory. She knew him too well. Caroline took two aspirins. When she woke at three he was in bed beside her, gripping the blanket in his sleep and breathing heavily. For days afterwards they spoke with strained, subdued courtesy.

They worked diligently in the natural childbirth classes once a week, while at home they giggled over how silly the exercises were, yet Ivan insisted she pant her five minutes each day as instructed. As relaxation training, Ivan was supposed to lift each of her legs and arms three times and drop them, while she remained perfectly limp and passive. From the very start Caroline was excellent at this routine, which they did in bed before going to sleep. A substitute, she thought, yawning. She could make her body so limp and passive her arms and legs bounced on the mattress when they fell. One night for diversion she tried doing it to Ivan, but he couldn't master the technique of passivity.

"Don't do anything, Ivan. I lift the leg and I drop the leg. You do nothing. Do you see? Nothing at all," she smiled.

But that was not possible for him. He tried to be limp but kept working along with her; she could see his muscles, precisely those leg muscles she found so desirable, exerting to lift and drop, lift and drop.

"You can't give yourself up. Don't you feel what you're doing? You have to let me do it to you. Let me try just your hand, from the wrist. That might be easier."

"No, forget it. Give me back my hand." He smiled and stroked her stomach gently. "What's the difference? I don't have to do it well. You do it very well."

She did it very well indeed when the time came. It was a short labor, less than an hour, very unusual for a first baby, the nurses kept muttering. She breathed intently, beginning with the long slow breaths she had been taught, feeling quite remote from the bustle around her. Then, in a flurry, they raced her down the hall on a wheeled table with a train of white-coated people trotting after, and she thought, panting, No matter what I suffer, soon I will be thin again, I will be more beautiful than ever.

The room was crowded with people, far more people than she would have thought necessary, but the only faces she singled out were Ivan's and the doctor's. The doctor, with a new russet beard and his face a good deal thinner now, was once again framed by

her knees, paler than before. Wildly enthusiastic about
the proceedings, he yelled, "Terrific, Caroline, terrific," as though they were in a noisy public place.
"O.K., start pushing."

They placed her hands on chrome rails along the table. On the left, groping, she found Ivan's hand and
held it instead of the rail. She pushed. In surprise she
became aware of a great cleavage, like a mountain of
granite splitting apart, only it was in her, she realized,
and if it kept on going it would go right up to her
neck. She gripped Ivan's warm hand, and just as she
opened her mouth to roar someone clapped an oxy-
gen mask on her face so the roar reverberated inward
on her own ears. She wasn't supposed to roar, the
natural childbirth teacher hadn't mentioned anything
about that, she was supposed to breathe and push. But
as long as no one seemed to take any notice she might
as well keep on roaring, it felt so satisfying and necessary. The teacher would never know. She trusted that
if she split all the way up to her neck they would sew
her up somehow—she was too far gone to worry about
that now. Maybe that was why there were so many of
them, yes, of course, to put her back together, and
maybe they had simply forgotten to tell her about
being bisected; or maybe it was a closely guarded
secret, like an initiation rite. She gripped Ivan's hand
tighter. She was not having too bad a time, she would
surely survive, she told herself, captivated by the hell-
ish bestial sounds going from her mouth to her ear; it
certainly was what her students would call a peak
experience, and how gratifying to hear the doctor ex-
claim, "Oh, this is one terrific girl! One more, Caroline, give me one more push and send it out. Sock it to
me."

She always tried to be obliging, if possible. Now she
raised herself on her elbows and, staring straight at
him—he too, after all, had been most obliging these
long months—gave him with tremendous force the

final push he asked for. She had Ivan's hand tightly around the rail, could feel his knuckles bursting, and then all of a sudden the room and the faces were obliterated. A dark thick curtain swiftly wrapped around her and she was left all alone gasping, sucked violently into a windy black hole of pain so explosive she knew it must be death, she was dying fast, like a bomb detonating. It was all right, it was almost over, only she would have liked to see his blue eyes one last time.

From somewhere in the void Ivan's voice shouted in exultation, "It's coming out," and the roaring stopped and at last there was peace and quiet in her ears. The curtain fell away, the world returned. But her eyes kept on burning, as if they had seen something not meant for living eyes to see and return from alive.

"Give it to me," Caroline said, and held it. She saw that every part was in the proper place, then shut her eyes.

They wheeled her to a room and eased her onto the bed. It was past ten in the morning. She could dimly remember they had been up all night watching a James Cagney movie about prizefighting while they timed her irregular mild contractions. James Cagney went blind from blows given by poisoned gloves in a rigged match, and she wept for him as she held her hands on her stomach and breathed. Neither she nor Ivan had slept or eaten for hours.

"Ivan, there is something I am really dying to have right now."

"Your wish is my command."

She asked for a roast beef on rye with ketchup, and iced tea. "Would you mind? It'll be hours before they serve lunch."

He bought it and stood at the window while she ate ravenously.

"Didn't you get anything for yourself?"

"No, I'm too exhausted to eat." He did, in fact, look terrible. He was sallow; his eyes, usually so radiant, were nearly drained of color, and small downward-curving lines around his mouth recalled his laborious vigil.

"You had a rough night, Ivan. You ought to get some sleep. What's it like outside?"

"What?" Ivan's movements seemed to her extremely purposeless. He was pacing the room with his hands deep in his pockets, going slowly from the foot of the bed to the window and back. Her eyes followed him from the pillow. Every now and then he would stop to peer at Caroline in an unfamiliar way, as if she were a puzzling stranger.

"Ivan, are you O.K.? I meant the weather. What's it doing outside?" It struck her, as she asked, that it was weeks since she had cared to know anything about the outside. That there was an outside, now that she was emptied out, came rushing at her with the most urgent importance, wafting her on a tide of grateful joy.

"Oh," he said vaguely, and came to sit on the edge of her bed. "Well, it's doing something very peculiar outside, as a matter of fact. It's raining but the sun is shining."

She laughed at him. "But haven't you ever seen it do that before?"

"I don't know. I guess so." He opened his mouth and closed it several times. She ate, waiting patiently. Finally he spoke. "You know, Caroline, you really have quite a grip. When you were holding my hand in there, you squeezed it so tight I thought you would break it."

"Oh, come on, that can't be."

"I'm not joking." He massaged his hand absently. Ivan never complained of pain; if anything he understated. But now he held out his right hand and showed her the raw red knuckles and palm, with raised flaming welts forming.

She took his hand. "You're serious. Did I do that? Well, how do you like that?"

"I really thought you'd break my hand. It was killing me." He kept repeating it, not resentfully but dully, as though there were something secreted in the words that he couldn't fathom.

"But why didn't you take it away if it hurt that badly?" She put down her half-eaten sandwich as she saw the pale amazement ripple over his face.

"Oh, no, I couldn't do that. I mean—if that was what you needed just then—" He looked away, embarrassed. "Listen," he shrugged, not facing her, "we're in a hospital, after all. What better place? They'd fix it for me."

Overwhelmed, Caroline lay back on the pillows. "Oh, Ivan. You would do that?"

"What are you crying for?" he asked gently. "You didn't break it, did you? Almost doesn't count. So what are you crying about. You just had a baby. Don't cry."

And she smiled and thought her heart would burst.

Fireworks

RICHARD FORD

*Born in Jackson, Mississippi, in 1944, Richard Ford
attended Michigan State University. Following the theft
of his law books, he dropped out of Washington University law school. "The only thing I ever really wanted
to do was be a lawyer," he has written. "I went to law
school for a while, quit too soon, felt desperate, and
decided to write fiction. So: chief motivation is desperation
—probably false. I might've been an average lawyer."
He has lived in California, Chicago, New Orleans,
Mexico, Mississippi, and many other places. A recipient of Guggenheim and National Endowment for the
Arts grants, he has also taught writing at Princeton and
Williams. His novels include* A Piece of my Heart
(1976), The Ultimate Good Luck *(1981) and* The Sports-
writer *(1986).* A Piece of my Heart *was runner-up for
the Ernest Hemingway Award for best first novel of the
year. A collection of stories,* Rock Springs, *was published in 1987. "I don't think much in terms of characters," he has remarked in an interview, "I collect lines
and little snippets of things somebody might say—things
I overhear, things I see in the newspaper, things I think
up, dream up, wake up with in the middle of the night.
I write lines down in my notebook. It's a fairly taxing
clerical protocol. If I can get enough of these things,
then characters begin to emerge."*

*It is not unusual for the characters in a Richard Ford
story to find themselves doing things in places that their*

*wildest dreams failed to warn them about. Ford writes
of perplexed, restless people who live on society's fringe;
his exacting cadences illuminate the messy, mysterious
accumulation of experience that has landed them where
they are. One critic has described a typical Richard
Ford hero as a decent man, kindly and always eager to
see the hopeful side of things, but often bewildered or
hurt by what he actually experiences. In an essay on
Bruce Springsteen, Ford might have been speaking about
his own work: "Through his song's complex little beaut-
ies and surprises, he dignifies small feelings with the
gravity of real emotion, defines innocence in terms new
to it, makes rote gestures seem heartbreaking, and gives
a voice of consequence to the unlistened to." Good
writing, Ernest Hemingway said, is when the reader
remembers it not as a story he has read, but as something that has happened to himself. Richard Ford brings
to his work this penetrating vividness. He and his wife
divide their time between New Orleans and western
Montana.*

Eddie Starling sat at the kitchen table at noon reading the newspaper. Outside in the street some neighborhood kids were shooting firecrackers. The Fourth
of July was a day away, and every few minutes there
was a lot of noisy popping followed by a hiss then a
huge boom loud enough to bring down an airplane. It
was giving him the jitters, and he wished some parent
would go out and haul the kids inside.

Starling had been out of work six months—one entire selling season and part of the next. He had sold
real estate, and he had never been off work any length
of time in his life. Though he had begun to wonder,
after a certain period of time not working, if you
couldn't simply forget *how* to work, forget the particu-
lars, lose the reasons for it. And once that happened,

he worried, it could become possible never to hold another job as long as you lived. To become a statistic: the chronically unemployed. The thought worried him.

Outside in the street he heard what sounded like kids' noises again. They were up to something suspicious, and he stood up to look out, just when the phone rang.

"What's new on the home front?" Lois's voice said. Lois had gone back to work tending bar near the airport and always tried to call up in good spirits.

"Status quo. Hot." Starling walked to the window, holding the receiver, and peered out. In the middle of the street some kids he'd never seen before were getting ready to blow up a tin can using an enormous firecracker. "Some kids are outside blowing up something."

"Anything good in the paper?"

"Nothing promising."

"Well," Lois said. "Just be patient, hon. I know it's hot. Listen, Eddie, do you remember those priests who were always setting fire to themselves on TV? Exactly when were they? We were trying to remember here. Was it '68 or '72? Nobody could remember to save their life."

"Sixty-eight was Kennedy," Starling said. "They weren't just setting themselves on fire for TV, though. They were in Asia."

"Okay. But when was Vietnam exactly?"

The kids lit the firecracker under the can and went running away down the street, laughing. For a moment Starling stared directly at the can, but just then a young woman came out of the house across the street. As she stepped into her yard the can went boom, and the woman leaped back and put her hands into her hair.

"Christ, what was that!" Lois said. "It sounded like a bomb."

"It was those kids," Starling said.

"The scamps," Lois said. "I guess they're hot, too, though."

The woman was very thin—too thin to be healthy, Starling thought. She was in her twenties and had on dull yellow shorts and no shoes. She walked out into the street and yelled something vicious at the kids, who were far down the street now. Starling knew nothing more about her than he did about anybody else in the neighborhood. The name on the mailbox had been taped over before he and Lois had moved in. A man lived with the woman and worked on his car in the garage late at night.

The woman walked slowly back across her little yard to her house. At the top step she turned and looked at Starling's house. He stared at her, and the woman went inside and closed the door.

"Eddie, take a guess who's here," Lois said.

"Who's where?"

"In the bar. One wild guess."

"Arthur Godfrey," Starling said.

"Arthur Godfrey. That's great," Lois said. "No, it's Louie. He just waltzed in the door. Isn't that amazing?"

Louie Reiner was Lois's previous husband. Starling and Reiner had been business acquaintances of a sort before Lois came along, and had co-brokered some office property at the tail end of the boom. Reiner had been in real estate then, along with everybody else. Reiner and Lois had stayed married six weeks, then they had gone over to Reno and gotten an annulment. A year later Lois married Starling. That had all been in '76, and Lois didn't talk about it or about Reiner anymore. Louie had disappeared somewhere—he'd heard Europe. He didn't feel like he had anything against Louie now, though he wasn't particularly happy he was around.

"Just take a guess what Louie's doing?" Lois said. Water had started to run where Lois was.

"Who knows. Washing dishes. How should I know?"

Lois repeated what Starling said and some people

laughed. He heard Louie's voice saying, "Well, *excuuuse* me."

"Seriously, Ed. Louie's an extraditer." Lois laughed. Hah.

"What's that mean?" Starling said.

"It means he travels the breadth of the country bringing people back here so they can go to jail. He just brought a man back from Montana who'd done nothing more than pass a forty-seven-dollar bad check, which doesn't seem worth it to me. Louie isn't in uniform, but he's got a gun and a little beeper."

"What's he doing there?" Starling said.

"His girlfriend's coming in at the airport from Florida," Lois said. "He's a lot fatter than he used to be, too, though he wouldn't like me to say that, would you, Louie?" Starling heard Reiner say "*Excuuuse* me" again. "Do you want to talk to him."

"I'm busy right now."

"Busy doing what, eating lunch? You're not busy."

"I'm fixing dinner," Starling lied.

"Talk to Louie, Eddie."

Starling wanted to hang up. He wished Reiner would go back to wherever he came from.

"*Helloooo dere,*" Reiner said.

"Who left your cage open, Reiner?"

"Come on down here and have a drink, Starling, and I'll tell you all about it. I've seen the world since I saw you. Italy, France, the islands. You know what an Italian girl puts behind her ears to make herself more attractive?"

"I don't want to know," Starling said.

"That's not what Lois says," Reiner laughed a horselaugh.

"I'm busy. Some other time, maybe."

"Sure you are," Reiner said. "Listen, Eddie, get off your face and come down here. I'll tell you how we can both retire in six months. Honest to God. This is not real estate."

"I already retired," Starling said. "Didn't Lois tell you?"

"Yeah, she told me a lot of things," Reiner said.

He could hear Lois say, "Please don't be a nerd, Eddie. Who needs nerds?" Some people laughed again.

"I shouldn't even be talking about this on the phone. It's that hot." Reiner's voice fell to a whisper. He was covering the mouthpiece of the receiver, Starling thought. "These are Italian rugs, Starling. I swear to God. From the neck of the sheep, the neck only. You only get tips on things like this in law enforcement."

"I told you. I'm retired. I retired early," Starling said.

"Eddie, am I going to have to come out there and arrest you?"

"Try it," Starling said. "I'll beat the shit out of you, then laugh about it."

He heard Reiner put the phone down and say something he couldn't make out. Then he heard Reiner shout out, "Stay on yur face then, cluck!"

Lois came on the line again. "Baby, why don't you come down here?" A blender started in the background, and a big cheer went up. "We're all adults. Have a Tanqueray on Louie. He's on all-expenses. There might be something to this. Louie's always got ideas."

"Reiner's just got ideas about you. Not me." He heard Reiner say to Lois to tell him—Starling—to forget it. "Tell Reiner to piss up a rope."

"Try to be nice," Lois said. "Louie's being nice. Eddie—"

Starling hung up.

When he worked, Starling had sold business properties—commercial lots and office buildings. He had studied that in college, and when he got out he was offered a good job. People would always need a place to go to work, was his thinking. He liked the professional environment, the atmosphere of money being made, and for a while he had done very well. He and Lois had rented a nice, sunny apartment in an older part of town by a park. They bought furniture and didn't save money. While Starling worked, Lois kept house, took care of plants and fish, and attended a night class for her degree in history. They had no children, and didn't expect any. They liked the size of the town and the stores, knew shopkeepers' names and where the streets led. It was a life they could like, and better than they could both have guessed would come their way.

Then interest rates had gone sky-high, and suddenly no one wanted commercial property. Everything was rent. Starling rented space in malls and in professional buildings and in empty shops downtown where older businesses had moved out and leather stores, health food, and copy shops moved in. It was a holding action, Starling thought, until people wanted to spend again.

Then he had lost his job. One morning, his boss at the agency asked him back to his private office along with a fat woman named Beverley, who'd been there longer than Starling had. His boss told them he was closing down and wanted to tell them first because they'd been there longest, and he wanted them to have a chance for the other jobs. Starling remembered feeling like he was in a daze when he heard the bad news, but he remembered thanking the boss, wishing him luck, then comforting Beverley, who went to pieces in the outer office. He had gone home and told Lois, and they had gone out to dinner at a Greek restaurant that night, and gotten good and drunk.

As it turned out, though, there weren't any other jobs to get. He visited the other agencies and talked to salesmen he knew, but all of his friends were terrified of being laid off themselves and wouldn't say much. After a month, he heard that his boss hadn't closed the agency down, but had simply hired two new people to take his and Beverley's places. When he called to ask about it the boss apologized, then claimed to have an important call on another line.

In six weeks Starling had still not found a job, and when the money ran out and they could not pay the rent, he and Lois sublet the apartment to two nurses who worked at a hospital, and got out. Lois found an ad in the *Pennysaver* that said, "No Rent for Responsible Couple—House Sit Opportunity." And they had moved in that day.

The house was a ranchette in a tract of small, insignificant houses on fenced-in postage-stamp lots down on the plain of the Sacramento River, out from town. The owner was an Air Force sergeant who had been stationed in Japan, and the house was decorated with Oriental tastes: wind chimes and fat, naked women stitched over silk, a red enamel couch in the living room, rice-paper lanterns on the patio. There was an old pony in the back, from when the owner had been married with kids, and a couple of wrecked cars in the carport. All the people who lived on the street, Starling noticed, were younger than the two of them. More than a few were in the Air Force and fought loud, regular arguments, and came and went at all hours. There was always a door slamming after midnight, then a car starting up and racing away into the night. Starling never thought he'd find himself living in such a place.

He stacked the dishes, put the grounds in the newspaper, and emptied all the wastebaskets into a plastic bag. He intended to take the garbage for a ride. Everybody in the subdivision either drove their garbage to a dump several miles away, or toured the convenience stores and shopping malls until they found a Dumpster no one was watching. Once a Negro woman had run out of a convenience store and cursed at him for ditching his garbage in her Dumpster, and since then he'd waited till dark. This afternoon, though, he needed to get out of the house, as though with the heat and talking to Reiner there wasn't enough air inside to breathe.

He had the garbage set out the back door when the phone rang again. Sometimes car dealers called during lunch, wanting to talk to the Air Force sergeant, and Starling had learned not to answer until after one, when car salesmen all left for lunch. This time it might be Lois again, wanting him to come by the bar to see Reiner, and he didn't want to answer. Only he didn't want Lois going off somewhere, and he didn't want Reiner coming over. Reiner would think the house with the pony was a comedy act.

Starling picked up the phone. "All right, what is it?"

An unfamiliar voice said, "Dad? Is that you?"

"No dads here, Reiner," Starling said.

"Dad," the voice said again, "it's Jeff."

A woman's voice came on the line. "I have a collect call to anyone from a Jeff. Will you pay for the call?"

"Wrong number," Starling said. He couldn't be sure it wasn't Reiner still.

"Dad," the voice said. It was a teenager's voice, a worried voice. "We're in awful trouble here, Dad. They've got Margie in jail."

"No, I can't help," Starling said. "I'm sorry. I can't help you."

"This party says you've got the wrong number, Jeff," the operator said.

"I know my own father's voice, don't I? Dad, for God's sake. This is serious. We're in trouble."

"I don't know any Jeffs," Starling said. "It's just the wrong number."

Starling could hear whoever was on the line hit something against the phone very hard, then say, "Shit! This isn't happening. I can't believe this is happening." The voice said something to someone else who was wherever he was. Possibly a policeman.

"It's the wrong number," the operator said. "I'm very sorry."

"Me too," Starling said. "I'm sorry."

"Would you like to try another number now, Jeff?" The operator asked.

"Dad, *please* accept. Please, my God. *Please.*"

"Excuse the ring, sir," the operator said, and the line was disconnected.

Starling put down the phone and stared out the window. The three boys who had blown up the tin can were walking past, eyeing his house. They were going for more fireworks. The torn can lay in the street, and the woman across the way was watching them from her picture window, pointing them out to a man in an undershirt who did not look like the man who worked on his car at night. He wondered if the woman was married or divorced. If she had children, where were they? He wondered who it was who had called; the sergeant's kids were all too young. He wondered what kind of trouble Jeff was in, and where was he? He should've accepted the charges, said a word of consolation, or given some advice, since the kid had seemed at wit's end. He'd been in trouble in his life. He was in trouble now, in fact, but he hadn't been any help.

He drove toward town and cruised the lot at the King's Hat Drive-Inn, took a look in at the Super-Duper, then drove around behind a truck stop. The garbage was with him in the hot front seat and already smelled bad despite the plastic. It was at the Super-Duper that the Negro woman had yelled at him and threatened to turn his garbage over to the police. Starling stopped back at the Super-Duper, parked at the side of the lot by the Dumpster, and went inside, leaving the garbage in the driver's seat. A different Negro woman was inside. He bought some breakfast cereal, a bag of frozen macaroni, and a bottle of hot sauce, then went back out to the car. Another car had driven in and parked beside his, and the driver, a woman, was sitting in view of the Dumpster, waiting for someone who had gone inside. The woman might be another Super-Duper employee, Starling thought, or possibly the wife of someone in the back he hadn't noticed.

He got in his car and drove straight out to a campground beside the river, less than a mile from the house. He had come here and picnicked once with Lois, though the campground was empty now; all the loops and tables deserted. He pulled up beside a big green campground Dumpster and heaved his garbage in without getting out of the car. Beyond the Dumpster, through some eucalyptus, he could see the big brown river sliding swiftly by, pieces of yellow foam swirling in and out of the dark eddies. It was a treacherous river, he thought, full of perils. Each year someone drowned, and there were currents running deep beneath the surface. No one in his right mind would think of swimming in it, no matter how hot it got.

As he drove out he passed two motorcycles with Oregon plates, parked at the far end of the campground, and two hippies with long hair sitting on a rock, smoking. The hippies watched him when he drove by and didn't bother hiding their dope. Two young women were coming out of the bushes nearby, wearing bathing suits, and one of the hippies gave Starling the black power salute and grinned. Starling drove back out to the highway.

The hippies reminded him of San Francisco. His mother, Irma, had lived there with her last husband, Rex, who'd had money. When he was in community college Starling had lived there with them for six months, before moving with his first wife across the bay to Alameda near the airport. They had been hippies of a certain kind themselves then and had smoked dope occasionally. Jan, his first wife, had had an abortion in a student apartment right on the campus. Abortions were not easy to get then, and they'd had to call Honolulu to get a name out in Castroville. They had been married six months, and Starling's mother had had to lend them money she'd gotten from Rex.

When the man came, he brought a little metal box with him, like a fishing-tackle box. They sat in the living room of the student apartment and talked about this and that, and drank beer. The man was named Dr. Carson. He told them he was being prosecuted at that very moment and was losing his license for doing this very thing, performing abortions. But people needed help. He had three children of his own, he said, and Starling wondered if he performed abortions on his own wife. Dr. Carson said it would cost $400, and he could do it the next night, but needed all cash. Before he left he opened his metal box. There was nothing in it but fishing gear: a Pflueger reel, some monofilament line, several red-and-white Jitterbug lures. They had all three laughed. You couldn't be too cautious, Dr. Carson said. They had all liked each other and acted like they could be friends in happier days.

The next night Dr. Carson came with a metal box that looked exactly the same as the one before, green with a silver handle. He went into the bedroom with Jan and closed the door while Starling sat in the living room, watched TV, and drank beer. It was Christmastime, and Andy Williams was on, singing carols with a man in a bear suit. After a while a loud whirring noise, like an expensive blender's, came out of the bedroom. It continued for a while, then stopped, then started. Starling became nervous. Dr. Carson, he knew, was mixing up his little baby, and Jan was feeling excruciating pain but wasn't making noise. Starling felt sick then with fear and guilt and helplessness. And with love. It was the first time he knew he knew what real love was, his love for his wife and for all the things he valued in his life but could so easily lose.

Later, Dr. Carson came out and said everything would be fine. He smiled and shook Starling's hand and called him Ted, which was the phony name Starling had given him. Starling paid him the money in hundreds, and when Dr. Carson drove off, Starling stood out on the tiny balcony and waved. The doctor blinked his headlights, and in the distance Starling could see a small private plane settling down to the airport in the dark, its red taillight blinking like a wishing star.

Starling wondered where the hell Jan was now, or Dr. Carson, fifteen years later. Jan had gotten peritonitis and almost died after that, and when she got well she wasn't interested in being married to Eddie Starling anymore. She seemed very disappointed. Three months later she had gone to Japan, where she'd had a pen pal since high school, someone named Haruki. For a while she wrote Starling letters, then stopped. Maybe, Starling thought, she had moved back down to L.A. with her mother. He wished his own mother was alive still, and he could call her up. He was thirty-nine years old, though, and he knew it wouldn't help.

Starling drove along the river for a few miles until the wide vegetable and cantaloupe fields opened out, and the horizon extended a long way in the heat to the hazy wind line of Lombardy poplars. High, slat-sided trucks sat stationed against the white skyline, and men were picking there and beyond in long, dense crews. Mexicans, Starling thought, transients who worked for nothing. It was a depressing thought. There was nothing they could do to help themselves, but it was still depressing, and Starling pulled across the road and turned back toward town.

He drove out toward the airport, along the strip where it was mostly franchises and consignment lots and little shopping plazas, some of which he had once found the tenants for. All along the way, people had put up fireworks stands for the Fourth of July, red-white-and-blue banners fluttering on the hot breeze. Some of these people undoubtedly lived out where he and Lois lived now, in the same subdivision. That would mean something, he thought, if one day you found yourself looking out at the world going past from inside a fireworks stand. Things would've gotten far out of hand when that time came, there was no arguing it.

He thought about driving past the apartment to see if the nurses who sublet it were keeping up the little yard. The nurses, Jeri and Madeline, were two big dykes with men's haircuts and baggy clothes. They were friendly types, and in the real estate business dykes were considered A-1s—good tenants. They paid their rent, kept quiet, maintained property in good order, held a firm stake in the status quo. They were like a married couple, was the business thinking. Thinking about Jeri and Madeline, he drove past the light where their turn was, then just decided to keep driving.

There was nothing to do now, Starling thought, but drive out to the bar. The afternoon shift meant no one came in until Lois was almost ready to leave, and sometimes they could have the bar to themselves. Reiner would be gone by now and it would be cool inside, and he and Lois could have a quiet drink together, toast better cards on the next deal. They had had some good times doing nothing but sitting talking.

Lois was leaning over the jukebox across from the bar when Starling came in. Mel, the owner, took afternoons off, and the place was empty. A dark-green bar light shone over everything, and the room felt cool.

He was glad to see Lois. She had on tight black slacks and a frilly white top and looked jaunty. Lois was a jaunty woman to begin with, and he was happy he'd come.

He had met Lois in a bar called the AmVets down in Rio Vista. It was before she and Louie Reiner became a twosome, and when he saw her in a bar now it always made him think of things then. That had been a high time, and when they talked about it Lois liked to say, "Some people are just meant to experience the highest moments of their lives talking in bars."

Starling sat on a barstool.

"I hope you came down here to dance with your wife," Lois said, still leaning over the jukebox. She punched a selection and turned around smiling. "I figured you'd waltz in here pretty soon." Lois came by and patted him on the cheek. "I went ahead and punched in all your favorites."

"Let's have a drink first," Starling said. "I've got an edge on that needs a drink."

"Drink first, dance second," Lois said and went behind the bar and got down the bottle of Tanqueray.

"Mel wouldn't mind," Starling said.

"Mary-had-a-little-lamb," she said while she poured a glassful. She looked up at Starling and smiled. "It's five o'clock someplace on the planet. Here's to old Mel."

"And some better luck," Starling said, taking a big first drink of the gin and letting it trickle down his throat as slowly as he could.

Lois had been drinking already, he was sure, with Reiner. That wasn't the best he could have hoped for, but it could be worse. She and Reiner could be shacked up in a motel, or on their way to Reno or the Bahamas. Reiner was gone, and that was a blessing, and he wasn't going to let Reiner cast a shadow on things.

"Poor old Lou," Lois said and came around the bar with a pink drink she'd poured out of the blender.

"Poor Lou what?" Starling said.

Lois sat down beside him on a barstool and lit a cigarette. "Oh, his stomach's all shot and he's got an ulcer. He said he worries too much." She blew out the match and stared at it. "You want to hear what he drinks?"

"Who cares what a dope like Louie drinks out of a glass," Starling said.

Lois looked at him, then stared at the mirror behind the bar. The smoky mirror showed two people sitting at a bar alone. A slow country tune started to play, a tune Starling liked, and he liked the way—with the gin around it—it seemed to ease him away from his own troubles. "So tell me what Reiner drinks," he said.

"Wodka," Lois said matter-of-factly. "That's the way he says it. Wodka. Like Russian. Wodka with coconut milk—a Hawaiian Russian. He says it's for his stomach, which he says is better though it's still a wreck. He's a walking pharmacy. And he's gotten a lot fatter, too, and his eyes bulge, and he wears a full Cleveland now. I don't know." Lois shook her head and smoked her cigarette. "He's got a cute girlfriend, though, this Jackie from Del Rio Beach, Florida. She looks like Little Bo Peep."

Starling tried to picture Reiner. Louie Reiner had been a large, handsome man at one time, with thick eyebrows and penetrating black eyes. A sharp dresser. He was sorry to hear Reiner was fat and bug-eyed and wore a leisure suit. It was bad luck if that was the way you looked to the world.

"How was it, seeing Louie, was it nice?" He stared at himself in the smoky mirror. He hadn't gotten fat, thank God.

"No," Lois said and dragged on her cigarette. "*He* was nice. Grown-up and what have you. But *it* wasn't nice. He didn't look healthy, and he still talked the same baloney, which was all before Jackie arrived, naturally."

"All what baloney?"

"You know that stuff, Eddie. Everybody makes *themselves* happy or unhappy. You don't leave one woman for another woman, you do it for yourself. If you can't make it with one, make it with all of them. That baloney he was always full of. Take the tour. Go big casino. That stuff. Reiner stuff."

"Reiner's big casino, all right," Starling said. "I guess he wanted you to go off with him."

"Oh sure. He said he was off to Miami next week to arrest some poor soul. He said I ought to go, and we could stay at the Fontainebleau or the Eden Roc or one of those sharp places."

"What about me?" Starling said. "Did I come? Or did I stay here? What about little Jackie?"

"Louie didn't mention either of you, isn't that funny? I guess it slipped his mind." Lois smiled and put her arm on Starling's arm. "It's just baloney, Eddie. Trashy talk."

"I wish he was here now," Starling said. "I'd use a beer bottle on him."

"I know it, hon. But you should've heard what this little girlfriend said. It was a riot. She's a real Ripley's."

"She'd need to be," Starling said.

"Really. She said if Louie ran around on her she was going to sleep with a black man. She said she already had him picked out. She really knew how to work Louie. She said Louie had a house full of these cheap Italian carpets, and nobody to sell them to. That was his big deal he needed a partner for, by the way—not a very big market over here, I guess. She said Louie was thinking of selling them in Idaho. She said—and this would've made you laugh, Eddie, it would've truly—she said it's a doggy-dog world out there. Doggy-dog. She was real cute. When she said that, Louie got down on the floor and barked like a dog. He dropped his pistol out of his what-ever-you-call-it, his scabbard, and his beeper"—Lois was laughing—"he was like a big animal down on the floor of the bar."

"I'm sorry I missed it."

"Louie can be funny," Lois said.

"Maybe you should've married him, then."

"I *did* marry him."

"Too bad you didn't stay married to him instead of me. I don't have a beeper."

"I like what you have got, though, sweetheart." She squeezed his arm. "Nobody would love me like you do, you know I think that. Reiner was just my mistake, but I can laugh at him today because I don't have to live with him. You're such a big mama's boy, you don't want anybody to have any fun."

"I'd like to have a little fun," Starling said. "Let's go where there's some fun."

Lois leaned and kissed him on the cheek. "You smell awfully nice." She smiled at him. "Come on and dance with me, Ed. Justice demands that you dance with me. You have that light step. It's nice when you do."

Lois walked out onto the little dance floor and took Starling's hand. He stood close to her and they danced to the slow music on the jukebox, holding together the way they had when he'd first known her. He felt a little drunk. A buzz improved a thing, he thought, made a good moment out of nothing.

"You're a natural dancer, Eddie," Lois said softly. "Remember us dancing at Powell's on the beach, with everybody watching us?"

"You like having men think about you?" Starling said.

"Oh, sure. I guess." Lois's cheek was against his cheek. "It makes me feel like I'm in a movie, sometimes, you know? Everybody does that, don't they?"

"I never do."

"Don't you ever wonder what your ex thinks about you? Old Jan. That was a long time ago, I guess."

"Bygones are bygones to me," Starling said. "I don't think about it."

"You're such a literal, Eddie. You get lost in the lonely crowd, I think sometimes. That's why I want to be nice and make you happy." She held him close to her so her hard, flat hips were next to his. "Isn't this nice? It's nice to dance with you."

Starling saw now that the bar was decorated with red, white, and blue crepe paper—features he'd missed. Little curlicues and ribbons and stars hung from the dark rafters and down off the shaded green bar lights and the beer signs and the framed pictures behind the back bar. This was festive, he thought. Lois had fixed it, it showed her hand. Before long a crowd would be in, the lights would go up and shine out, the music

would be turned up loud. It would be a good time.
"That's nice," Starling said.

"I just love this," Lois said. Her head was on his
shoulder. "I just love this so much."

On the highway toward home, Starling passed the
hippies he had seen at the campground. They were
heading in now, the women on the backseats, the men
driving fast, leaning as if the wind blew them.

In town, a big fireworks display staged by a shopping mall was beginning. Catherine wheels and starbursts
and blue and pink sprays were going off in the twilight. Cars were stopped along the road, and people
with children sat on their car hoods, drinking beer and
watching the sky. It was nearly dark and rain had
begun to threaten.

"Everything's moved out to the malls now," Lois
said, "including the fireworks." She had been dozing
and now she leaned against her door, staring back
toward the lights.

"I wouldn't care to work in one," Starling said,
driving.

Lois said nothing.

"You know what I was just thinking about?" she
said after a while.

"Tell me," Starling said.

"Your mother," Lois said. "Your mother was a
sweet old lady, you know that? I liked her very much.
I remember she and I would go to the mall and buy
her a blouse. Just some blouse she could've bought in
Bullock's in San Francisco, but she wanted to buy it
here to be sweet and special." Lois smiled about it.
"Remember when we bought fireworks?"

Starling's mother had liked fireworks. She liked to
hear them pop so she could laugh. Starling remembered having fireworks one year in the time since he'd
been married to Lois. When was that, he thought. A
time lost now.

"Remember she held the little teenies right in her

fingers and let them go pop? That seemed to tickle her so much."

"That was her trick," Eddie said. "Rex taught her that."

"I guess he did," Lois said. "But you know, I don't blame you, really, for being such a mama's boy, Eddie. Not with *your* mama—unlike mine, for instance. She's why you're as nice as you are."

"I'm selfish," Starling said. "I always have been. I'm capable of lying, stealing, cheating."

Lois patted him on the shoulder. "You're generous, though, too."

Rain was starting in big drops that looked like snow on the windshield. It was almost dark. Lights from their subdivision glowed out under the lowered sky ahead.

"This weird thing happened today," Starling said. "I can't quit thinking about it."

Lois slid over by him. She put her head on his shoulder and her hand inside his thigh. "I knew something had happened, Eddie. You can't hide anything. The truth is just on you."

"There's no truth to this," Starling said. "The phone just rang when I was leaving, and it was this kid, Jeff. He was in some kind of mess. I didn't know who he was, but he thought I was his father. He wanted me to accept charges."

"You didn't, did you?"

Starling looked toward the subdivision. "No. I should have, though. It's on my mind now that I should've helped him. I'd just finished talking to Reiner."

"He might've been in Rangoon, for Christ's sake," Lois said. "Or Helsinki. You don't know where he was. It could've cost you $500, then you couldn't have helped him anyway. You were smart, is exactly what I think."

"It wouldn't matter, though. I could've given him some advice. He said somebody was in jail. It's just on my mind now, it'll go away."

"Get a good job and then accept charges from Istanbul," Lois said and smiled.

"I just wonder who he was," Starling said. "For some reason I thought he was over in Reno, isn't that odd? Just a voice."

"It'd be worse if he *was* in Reno," Lois said. "Are you sorry you don't have one of your own?" Lois looked over at him strangely.

"One what?"

"A son. Or, you know. Didn't you tell me you almost had one? There was something about that, with Jan."

"That was a long time ago," Starling said. "We were idiots."

"Some people claim they make your life hold together better, though," Lois said. "You know?"

"Not if you're broke they don't," Starling said. "All they do is make you sorry, then."

"Well, we'll just float on through life together, then, how's that?" Lois put her hand high on his leg. "No blues today, hon, okay?"

They were at the little dirt street where the ranchette was, at the far end. A fireworks hut had been built in the front yard of the first small house, a chain of bright-yellow bulbs strung across the front. An elderly woman was standing in the hut, her face expressionless. She had on a sweater and was holding a little black poodle. All the fireworks but a few Roman candles had been sold off the shelves.

"I never thought I'd live where people sold fireworks right in their front yards." Lois said and faced the front. Starling peered into the lighted hut. The rain was coming down in a slow drizzle, and water shone off the oiled street. He felt the urge to gesture to the woman, but didn't. "You could just about say that we lived in a place you wouldn't want to live in if you could help it. It's funny, isn't it? That just happens to you." Lois laughed.

"I guess it's funny," Starling said. "It's true."

"What'd you dream up for dinner, Eddie? I've built up hunger all of a sudden."

"I forgot about it," Starling said. "There's some macaroni."

"Whatever," Lois said. "It's fine." Starling pulled into the gravel driveway. He could see the pony standing out in the dark where the fenced weed lot extended to the side of the house. The pony looked like a ghost, its cold, white eyes unmoving in the rain.

"Tell me something," Starling said. "If I ask you something, will you tell me?"

"If there's something to tell," Lois said. "Sometimes there isn't anything, you know. But go ahead."

"What happened with you and Reiner?" he said. "All that Reno stuff. I never asked you about that. But I want to know."

"That's easy," Lois said and smiled at him in the dark car. "I just realized I didn't love Reiner, that's all. Period. I realized I loved you, and I didn't want to be married to somebody I didn't love. I wanted to be married to you. It isn't all that complicated or important." Lois put her arms around his neck and hugged him hard. "Don't be cloudy now, sweet. You've just had some odd luck is all. Things'll get better. You'll get back. Let me make you happy. Let me show you something to be happy, baby doll." Lois slid across the seat against the door and went down into her purse. Starling could hear wind chimes in the rain. "Let me just show you," Lois said.

Starling couldn't see. Lois opened the door out into the drizzle, turned her back to him and struck a match. Starling could see it brighten. And then there was a sparkling and hissing, and then a brighter one, and Starling smelled the harsh burning and the smell of the rain together. Then Lois closed the door and danced out before the car into the rain with the sparklers, waving her arms round in the air, smiling widely and making swirls and patterns and star falls for him that were brilliant and illuminated the night and the bright rain and the little dark house behind her and, for a moment, caught the world and stopped it, as though something sudden and perfect had come to earth in a furious glowing for him and for him alone—Eddie Starling—and only he could watch and listen. And only he would be there, waiting, when the light was finally gone.

Death of a Lesser Man

GINA BERRIAULT

Gina Berriault's first novel, The Descent, *was published in 1960. Other novels include* Conference of Victims *(1962),* The Son *(1966), and* The Lights of Earth *(1984). Her collections of short fiction are* The Mistress and Other Stories *(1965) and* The Infinite Passion of Expectation *(1982).* The Stone Boy, *a screenplay Ms. Berriault wrote based on one of her stories, was produced as a film starring Robert Duvall. She's appeared in the* O. Henry Best Short Story *anthologies and was a winner of the* Paris Review *Aga Khan Fiction Prize.*

"Wear your heart on the page," Gordon Lish has remarked, "and people will read to find out how you solved being alive. The subject has to possess the writer." Gina Berriault's rich, sensuous prose maps the dramatic and startling intensity of our inner lives. Obsessed with the intimate, her writing traces the intricate plight of our heart's longing to desire and to be desired. To our confusing passions, she brings clarity and comprehension.

I n the midst of several friends drinking Danish beer from tall Mexican glasses, in an apartment of red naugahyde furniture and black shag rugs, right at the moment when the hostess, who had been a Las Vegas showgirl, was leaning over to laugh something in his ear, right at that moment he threw himself off the couch and onto the rug. The others, his wife among them, thought that he was faking a fit to comically demonstrate the effect of the hostess' bosomy proximity or her words in his ear, although that sort of fakery was utterly foreign to his shy, gracious, reflective person. Then, because it *was* foreign, they realized it was a true fit, an act beyond his control. Those who were sitting near him got out of his way and stood back with the others, who had also risen, and his wife fell to her knees at his side.

For several seconds he lay rigid, eyes up, a pink-tinged froth along the lower edge of his neat, blond moustache, while his wife stroked his face and fondled his hands. The others walked around in a state of shock, conversing with mourners' voices. Someone asked her if he had ever done that before, and she said, "No, never" and repeated it to the first question asked by the young doctor who, summoned by the hostess from an apartment upstairs, knelt down at the other side of the now limp man.

Claudia, the wife, stood away while the doctor with encouraging hands and *Ah ups* assisted her husband to the couch and laid him out, long and weak. She refused a chair, feeling called upon to stand in deference to unpredictable blows. The hostess embraced her waist, but she offered no yielding to this comfort and was left alone. She watched the shocked face of her husband watching abjectly the doctor's face above his, and watched the stethoscope move over the exposed broad chest. The young doctor glanced up to ask her which arm had jerked, which leg, and replying that she had been too alarmed to notice, she saw his fleeting response to her person, the same response in the eyes of men and women seeing her for the first time—a struggle to conceal from her the emotion that a woman's beauty aroused, whatever that emotion was, whether fear or envy or desire or covetousness. The struggle in the doctor's eyes stirred an anxiety over herself—was she to be alone now?—and, at the same time, assured her that she would not be alone for long. It lasted half a second, this fear and assuaging of fear, and was followed by shame and by love for her husband, by a devotion that came over her with such force she was, again, the girl she had been for him at the beginning of their nine years together.

When he stood up, shakily, joking weakly with dry lips, someone said the pickled mushrooms were hallucinatory and someone else laughed loudly and caved in. The hostess helped him on with his overcoat, and Claudia, her arm across his back, with the host on his other side, took him down the five slow flights in the elevator and along the street.

As she drove homeward she remembered with remorse their quarrel early in the evening. She hadn't wanted to go to the party. "So they don't know who the hell Camus is," he had said, tugging the words up from his throat as he tugged unnecessarily at his socks. "Why don't you get down to the human level?" They both had got down to the human level tonight, and now he was deeply asleep, his chin sunk into his muffler, his long legs falling away from each other, his hands in his overcoat pockets where, in one, he had slipped the doctor's note with the name of a neurosurgeon. The doctor had given him no sedative, but his sleep was heavy as doped sleep.

On the bridge they were almost alone, behind them the headlights of two cars and far ahead of them, with the distance widening, the red taillights of one, and her fear of his sleep as a prelude to death changed the familiar scene of the dark bay and the jeweled, misty cities ringing the bay, changed the scene into the very strange, as if, were he to open his eyes, that would be his last sight of it. She felt, then, almost shamefully, that close affinity with Camus again, and although Camus was dead, the adoration that had taken her to Paris seven years ago was revived from her memory.

She had gone there alone and lived there for three months, the sojourn made possible by a small inheritance from an aunt, but the money had run out before the destined meeting could take place. It was true she hadn't made much of an effort to meet people who knew him. How was she to do that? She had hoped that just by wandering the street where he might wander a chance meeting would come about and he would see at first glance how far she had come to be with him. Yet in that time she had felt humiliated by her pursuit, no matter how inconspicuous it was to everyone else; she had felt her pursuit was as obvious as that of a friend of hers who, enamored of Koestler, had managed a front seat at his lecture at a university and with her transfixed gaze had caused him to stumble a time or two over his words, and, later, had accosted him in the hall and proved how deep into his work she was by criticising some points of his lecture in which he had seemed untrue to his own self. Nothing had come of her own obsessive time in Paris, and in despair—what was her life to be?—she had returned to New York. But she had refused to board the plane to San Francisco. In the waiting lounge a terrible prophetic sense had come over her: all the persons waiting to board that plane—the chic, elderly woman in black, the young mother with her small son in his navy coat and cap, the rest, all were to die that day. She had not yet left the lounge, she was still on the bench, unable to rise, unable to return to Camus and unable to return to her husband, when the plane crashed as it was taking off. She had gone back to the hotel and cried all day in her room, shaking with fear of her prophetic sense that, if she were to heed it again, would show her in old age, all beauty gone, all curiosity for life gone, all hope for a great passion gone.

On the long curving road down through the hills and into the town, only the low white fence between the car and the dropoff into space, her sleeping husband beside her, she felt again on the verge of something

more. If she had found another existence, those seven
years ago, her husband would have found another wife
and gone on living; now, another existence for her
would be the result of his dying. The sense of crisis
was followed by guilt that came on as an awful weariness, and when she waked him and was helping him
from the car, she felt in her body the same weight that
was in his.

She pulled off his shoes and his socks while he sat
on the bed, and he was asleep on his back a moment
after she had covered him to his chin. His sleep dragged
on her body as she undressed and slipped her night-
gown on. It forced her down beside him punitively,
and she lay towards him, her hand on his bare chest,
persuading him with her hand, with her heart, to stay
alive. Dear Gerald, Sweet Gerald, stay alive.

All Sunday Gerald slept, wakened every few hours
by Claudia, who was afraid he had lapsed into a coma,
and she brought him milk and toast and fruit as an
excuse for waking him. After poking around a bit that
Sunday evening, trying to recall the sensations, the
thoughts preceding the seizure, reading the papers,
showering, he returned to bed at ten o'clock and slept
until noon of the next day, when she wakened him by
stroking the smooth, veined underside of his arm that
was bent on the pillow, a half-frame for his pale,
unshaven face. She told him that the neurosurgeon
could give him an appointment no sooner than Friday
of that week, and this information liberated his eyes
from the startled frown. If the specialist was in no
hurry to see him, then nothing much could be wrong.
He flung off the covers, his legs kicking and pushing
out into air, and sat up. "I'll get up, I'll get up," he
said.

Always he was already up and about at this hour,
carving his fine wood sculptures or roaming the forest
trails or the beaches, doing what he liked to do before
he walked down the hill and caught the bus to the city
and worked at his desk until midnight on the next

day's paper. Up he got, and the moment he was on his feet again she felt again the inertia that came of her acceptance of the way her life was. The fact that he was up again, ready to return to work without having missed a day, deprived her of this crisis in her life, this crucial point of change, and alarmed by her reaction she embraced him from behind, pressing her face against his back, kissing him so many times over his back that he had to bend forward with the pleasure of conforming to her love.

Claudia was in the tub when he left, and she imagined how he looked going down the hill, under the arcade of trees, a bareheaded, strong-bodied man of thirty-six, going to work at the hour when most men were about to return home. At that moment, imagining him disappearing, she felt the emptiness of the house, and in that empty house felt her own potential for life. She was aware of herself as another person might become aware of her as so much more than was supposed. And, the next moment, afraid that a prowler was in the house, she climbed from the tub, shot the bolt on the bathroom door, and toweled herself in a fumbling hurry. After listening for a long minute for footsteps in the empty house, she unlocked the door and, holding her kimono closed, went barefoot through the rooms, knowing as she searched that there was no one in the house but herself.

Some nights she ate supper at home, alone, reading at the table, and some nights she went down into the town to one of the restaurants along the water's edge, went down with the ease of a resident in a tourists' mecca and was gazed at with curiosity—an attractive young woman dining alone. And some nights she went out later in the evening, tired of reading, restless, to the bookstore that stayed open until midnight, to sit at a little round table and drink coffee and read some more, the literary periodicals from England and France. The years her husband had worked days, she had held a few jobs. She had been a receptionist in a theatrical agency, a salesgirl in the high fashion section of a department store. But the artificiality, the anxiety of everyone, along with the obviousness of her own person when she was by nature seclusive, brought on desperate nights, and she had quit; yet she had chosen not to work in lackluster places. She wanted only to read. The only persons beside Gerald whom she could converse with were the celebrated writers and some obscure ones whose work she came upon unguided. It was always like a marvelous telepathy going on, both ways. While she read *their* thoughts, they seemed to be reading *hers*.

This night she took less care than usual with her clothes. Wherever she went she always took extreme care with her appearance, afraid of critical eyes. And always her head was bare, because the blondness of her hair was a loving gift from Scandinavian ancestors. The mauve silk blouse she put on was stained from wine and near the hem of the gray wool skirt was a small spot. To wear these clothes without embarrassment was, she felt, an acceptance of the stain on the soul of the woman who allowed herself to dream of another existence.

She left the old, raffish convertible by the small, dim park and walked along the sidewalk bordering the water that, a yard or so below, lapped the stone wall, and the reflection on the dark water of an island of low-lying fog out near the channel, and the clear, faintly starred sky, and the cluster of sea gulls floating where the waters were lit by the restaurant globes, all evoked the promise she had experienced in Paris. Just before she reached the restaurant on pilings over the water, she heard a low whistle at her back, suggestive of a hand shocked by the delight it found, and someone fell into step behind her. She felt his close gaze, she felt his bumbling, beastly obstinance, and she wanted to turn and shout at him to get away, a woman had the right to go out into the night alone, and, at the same time, she wanted to run away and escape his accusation that she had enticed him with her long, rippling, moonlit hair, her legs in black nylons, her white silk scarf with its fringed ends. On the restaurant step he spoke to her, some word to halt her or caution her about the step, and she pushed the door wildly open, banging it into a young man leaving. She chose the farthest table from the door, up close to the window over the water. The encounter with the man whose face she was afraid to see marred this night in which she had meant to be released, harmlessly, into an old dreaming of another future. She saw her hands trembling, they couldn't lift the fork without dropping food back to the plate. Able to manage only a few morsels, she waited to leave, waiting until the man must have wandered away, waiting for her heart to calm down.

But after she had gone several steps along the sidewalk, she heard his heels again. This time he did not speak, he followed as if *she* had spoken, as if they had become invitation and answer. Her heart knocking crazily, she climbed into her car, slamming the door. Her heavy skirt and coat lumped under her legs but she was afraid to take a moment to jerk them free. She swung the car around and, long before the time she intended to return, she was returning up the hill. Just before she took the first curve, her rearview mirror flashed headlights, and she took the curve too fast, almost crashing into somebody's quaint iron gate.

She stood in the unlit house, gripping the curtains, her shaking hands causing the brass rings to jangle against the rod. If Gerald had experienced a foreboding before his seizure, this sensation must be the same. The man was standing out under the gate lamp, an obscene clod out of doorways, following a woman whom he could not believe would turn him away, a woman waiting in the dark house to open the door to him and draw him down upon her. Raising his arm to fend off the branches, he came up the path. Why should he have come so far if he was not already in the arms of the woman who went out with her fringed scarf to bring a strange man back to her bed? She heard his step on the stone doorstep and heard his two raps, and heard her voice, thick with fear, shouting, "Get away! Get away!" She clung to the curtains until she heard a car's motor start up and saw the red taillights reflected on the foliage in the yard and heard the car go down the hill.

A desolation came over her, then, as she moved through the dark house. The obscene dolt must have stolen away her dream of herself in the future, the dream that was only a memory of herself in the past, that brief time in Paris, alone, desirous of a destiny, desirous of the one with a destiny, the man who would break the hull of her guilt, guide her into the intricacies of his intellect, anoint her with the moisture of his kisses. The intruder must have stolen away the past and the future, and she was nowhere else but in this dark house where she might be forever. In the dark her slender heel was caught by the grille of the floor heater in the hallway, and she left both shoes on the cold, trapping metal.

By the time Gerald came home all the lamps were lit and his late supper was on the stove, plates were set out on the table, and wine was cooling; and facing him across the small table she complained about the number of days they must wait before his appointment.

"Must be lots of people throwing fits," he said. And later, tossing the covers over himself, "Anyway, the serious things are nothing to worry about. By the time you've got a symptom you're usually too far gone to do much about it." For a minute he lay gazing up, then he switched off the lamp to conceal from her the fear in his face. She heard him mutter half a word and then he was quiet. With his few words tonight he had expressed more pessimism than in all the years of their marriage. To indulge in pessimism, as to give way to anger or criticism, was to weaken the marriage, and he did not care to weaken it. He had never appeared to be dissatisfied with his life. He had not mapped out his life for a grand endeavor and been diverted. Everything about him gave evidence of his stolidity—his deliberation over small things, his way of absorbing circumstance rather than attacking it, the almost perverse unnecessity to change his existence, to strike, to wrestle, and she had clung to him for that enduring nature. But now, lying beside him, she felt in his being the invasion of futility, she felt his resentment of the specialist for his inaccessibility, and of her, his wife, for belittling him with her other life without him. The seizure and the suspense, the possibility that he might be at the mercy of physicians and of some malady and even of the end itself, all was enough of a belittlement. The husband who had always slept with a trusting face turned up toward the coming morning lay fearfully asleep, and she was afraid to touch him. She fell asleep with her hands tucked in under her heart.

Oh God, what was going on? The obscene dolt, the faceless presence, the stranger in the night, the follower had lifted aside the hanging branches and was there, and he was cutting off her hair, crudely, with large, cold scissors. It fell in rippling, palely shining strands, moonlit, alive. It fell to the floor and the bedcovers, and her rage against the faceless presence gave way to an awful weakness as her hair was shorn. But was this really herself in a bed alone, a narrower bed? Was she really the young woman with the cropped hair, with the suffering face, the face gone beyond suffering? Was this herself? Oh God, dear God, it was herself and she was dying years before Gerald. And how young she was, this woman, herself, who was never to know that old age she had so senselessly feared. Wailing, she struck weakly at the faceless presence cutting off her hair, but he went on cutting. In the empty bed someone suddenly moved, someone beside her rose up and bent over her. It was Gerald, and her terror, her sorrow over herself was over him, instead, and into his hand that was taking her hands away from her face she wailed her anguish of love for him and his life. With both hands she gripped his wrist, wailing his name into his large, gentle hand that was soothing and calming her into waking.

The Fourth Alarm

JOHN CHEEVER

*John Cheever was born in 1912 in Quincy, Massa-
chusetts. His formal education ended when he was seventeen, following his explusion from Thayer Academy,
a prep school in Massachusetts. A year later his first
short story, "Expelled," was accepted for publication
by Malcolm Cowley and the* New Republic *magazine.
Among his many books are the short story collections*
The Enormous Radio and Other Stories *(1953),* The
Housebreaker of Shady Hill *(1958),* The Brigadier and
the Golf Widow *(1964),* The World of Apples *(1973)
and his* Collected Stories *(1978), which won the Pulit-
zer Prize. His novels include* The Wapshot Chronicle
*(1957), which received the National Book Award for
fiction,* The Wapshot Scandal *(1964),* Bullet Park *(1969),*
Falconer *(1977), and* Oh What a Paradise It Seems
*(1982). He said that his favorite definition of fiction
was Jean Cocteau's: "Literature is a force of memory
that we have not yet understood." Cheever went on to
say, "In a book one finds gratifying, the writer is able
to present the reader with a memory he has already
possessed, but has not comprehended." A member of
the National Institute of Arts and Letters, he died in
Ossining, New York, in June 1982.*

*Whether he's writing about a dinner party among the
rich suburbanites of Westchester, or a husband watching his wife simulate sex acts on a stage in New York
City, John Cheever is a graceful, tender, and humorous*

*chronicler of his characters' grief at the passage of time
and the transience of their senses. The writing is compassionate, sensuous, and celebratory. Cheever's evoca-
tion of his characters' nostalgia is never sentimental.
For these people—for us—it is always surprising, overwhelming, sad, and passionate. "Nostalgia," he noted
in an interview, "is the longing for the world we all
know, or seem to have known, the world we all love
and the people in it we love. Nostalgia is also a passion,
a longing not only for that which is lost to us, or which
has been destroyed or burned, or which we've out-
grown, it is also a force of aspiration. It is finding
ourselves not in the world we love, but knowing how
deeply we love it, enjoying some conviction that we
return, or discover it, or discover the way to it."*

I sit in the sun drinking gin. It is ten in the morning.
Sunday. Mrs. Uxbridge is off somewhere with the
children. Mrs. Uxbridge is the housekeeper. She does
the cooking and takes care of Peter and Louise.

It is autumn. The leaves have turned. The morning
is windless, but the leaves fall by the hundreds. In
order to see anything—a leaf or a blade of grass—you
have, I think, to know the keenness of love. Mrs.
Uxbridge is sixty-three, my wife is away, and Mrs.
Smithsonian (who lives on the other side of town) is
seldom in the mood these days, so I seem to miss
some part of the morning as if the hour had a thresh-
old or a series of thresholds that I cannot cross. Passing a football might do it but Peter is too young and
my only football-playing neighbor goes to church.

My wife, Bertha, is expected on Monday. She comes
out from the city on Monday and returns on Tuesday.
Bertha is a good-looking young woman with a splen-
did figure. Her eyes, I think, are a little close together
and she is sometimes peevish. When the children were

young she had a peevish way of disciplining them. "If you don't eat the nice breakfast Mummy has cooked for you before I count three," she would say, "I will send you back to bed. One. Two. *Three.* . . ." I heard it again at dinner. "If you don't eat the nice dinner Mummy has cooked for you before I count three I will send you to bed without any supper. One. Two. Three. . . ." I heard it again. "If you don't pick up your toys before Mummy counts three Mummy will throw them all away. One. Two. Three. . . ." So it went on through the bath and bedtime and one two three was their lullaby. I sometimes thought she must have learned to count when she was an infant and that when the end came she would call a countdown for the Angel of Death. If you'll excuse me I'll get another glass of gin.

When the children were old enough to go to school, Bertha got a job teaching social studies in the sixth grade. This kept her occupied and happy and she said she had always wanted to be a teacher. She had a reputation for strictness. She wore dark clothes, dressed her hair simply, and expected contrition and obedience from her pupils. To vary her life she joined an amateur theatrical group. She played the maid in *Angel Street* and the old crone in *Desmonds Acres*. The friends she made in the theater were all pleasant people and I enjoyed taking her to their parties. It is important to know that Bertha does not drink. She will take a Dubonnet politely but she does not enjoy drinking.

Through her theatrical friends, she learned that a nude show called *Ozamanides II* was being cast. She told me this and everything that followed. Her teaching contract gave her ten days' sick leave, and claiming to be sick one day she went into New York. *Ozamanides* was being cast as a producer's office in mid-town, where she found a line of a hundred or more men and women waiting to be interviewed. She took an unpaid bill out of her pocketbook, and waving this as if it were a letter she bucked the line saying: "Excuse me please, excuse me, I have an appointment. . . ." No one protested and she got quickly to the head of the line where a secretary took her name, Social Security number, etc. She was told to go into a cubicle and undress. She was then shown into an office where there were four men. The interview, considering the circumstances, was very circumspect. She was told that she would be nude throughout the performance. She would be expected to simulate or perform copulation twice during the performance and participate in a love pile that involved the audience.

I remember the night when she told me all of this. It was in our living room. The children had been put to bed. She was very happy. There was no question about that. "There I was naked," she said, "but I wasn't in the least embarrassed. The only thing that worried me was that my feet might get dirty. It was an old-fashioned kind of place with framed theater programs on the wall and a big photograph of Ethel Barrymore. There I sat naked in front of these strangers and I felt for the first time in my life that I'd found myself, I found myself in nakedness. I felt like a new woman, a better woman. To be naked and unashamed in front of strangers was one of the most exciting experiences I've ever had. . . ."

I didn't know what to do. I still don't know, on this Sunday morning, what I should have done. I guess I should have hit her. I said she couldn't do it. She said I couldn't stop her. I mentioned the children and she said this experience would make her a better mother. "When I took off my clothes," she said, "I felt as if I had rid myself of everything mean and small." Then I said she'd never get the job because of her appendicitis scar. A few minutes later the phone rang. It was the producer offering her a part. "Oh, I'm so happy," she said. "Oh, how wonderful and rich and strange life can be when you stop playing out the roles that your parents and their friends wrote out for you. I feel like an explorer.''

The fitness of what I did then or rather left undone still confuses me. She broke her teaching contract, joined Equity, and began rehearsals. As soon as *Ozamanides* opened she hired Mrs. Uxbridge and took a hotel apartment near the theater. I asked for a divorce. She said she saw no reason for a divorce. Adultery and cruelty have well-marked courses of action but what can a man do when his wife wants to appear naked on the stage? When I was younger I had known some burlesque girls and some of them were married and had children. However, they did what Bertha was going to do only on the midnight Saturday show, and as I remember their husbands were third-string comedians and the kids always looked hungry.

A day or so later I went to a divorce lawyer. He said a consent decree was my only hope. There are no precedents for simulated carnality in public as grounds for divorce in New York State and no lawyer will take a divorce case without a precedent. Most of my friends were tactful about Bertha's new life. I suppose most of them went to see her, but I put it off for a month or more. Tickets were expensive and hard to get. It was snowing the night I went to the theater, or what had been a theater. The proscenium arch had been demolished, the set was a collection of used tires, and the only familiar features were the seats and the aisles. Theater audiences have always confused me. I suppose this is because you find an incomprehensible variety of types thrust into what was an essentially domestic and terribly ornate interior. There were all kinds there that night. Rock music was playing when I came in. It was that deafening old-fashioned kind of Rock they used to play in places like Arthur. At eight thirty the houselights dimmed, and the cast—there were fourteen—came down the aisles. Sure enough,

they were all naked excepting Ozamanides, who wore
a crown.

I can't describe the performance. Ozamanides had
two sons, and I think he murdered them, but I'm not
sure. The sex was general. Men and women embraced
one another and Ozamanides embraced several men.
At one point a stranger, sitting in the seat on my right,
put his hand on my knees. I didn't want to reproach
him for a human condition, not did I want to encourage him. I removed his hand and experienced a deep
nostalgia for the innocent movie theaters of my youth.
In the little town where I was raised there was one—
The Alhambra. My favorite movie was called *The
Fourth Alarm*. I saw it first one Tuesday after school
and stayed on for the evening show. My parents worried when I didn't come home for supper and I was
scolded. On Wednesday I played hooky and was able
to see the show twice and get home in time for supper.
I went to school on Thursday but I went to the theater
as soon as school closed and sat partway through the
evening show. My parents must have called the police,
because a patrolman came into the theater and made
me go home. I was forbidden to go to the theater on
Friday, but I spent all Saturday there, and on Saturday
the picture ended its run. The picture was about the
substitution of automobiles for horse-drawn fire engines. Four fire companies were involved. Three of
the teams had been replaced by engines and the miserable horses had been sold to brutes. One team remained, but its days were numbered. The men and the
horses were sad. Then suddenly there was a great fire.
One saw the fire engine, the second, and the third
race off to the conflagration. Back at the horse-drawn
company, things were very gloomy. Then the fourth
alarm rang—it was their summons—and they sprang
into action, harnessed the team, and galloped across
the city. They put out the fire, saved the city, and
were given an amnesty by the mayor. Now on the

stage Ozamanides was writing something obscene on my wife's buttocks.

Had nakedness—its thrill—annihilated her sense of nostalgia? Nostalgia—in spite of her close-set eyes— was one of her principal charms. It was her gift gracefully to carry the memory of some experience into another tense. Did she, mounted in public by a naked stranger, remember any of the places where we had made love—the rented houses close to the sea, where one heard in the sounds of a summer rain the prehistoric promises of love, peacefulness, and beauty? Should I stand up in the theater and shout for her to return, return, return in the name of love, humor, and serenity? It was nice driving home after parties in the snow, I thought. The snow flew into the headlights and made it seem as if we were going a hundred miles an hour. It was nice driving home in the snow after parties. Then the cast lined up and urged us—commanded us in fact—to undress and join them.

This seemed to be my duty. How else could I approach understanding Bertha? I've always been very quick to get out of my clothes. I did. However, there was a problem. What should I do with my wallet, wristwatch, and car keys? I couldn't safely leave them in my clothes. So, naked, I started down the aisle with my valuables in my right hand. As I came up to the action a naked young man stopped me and shouted— sang—"Put down your lendings. Lendings are impure."

"But it's my wallet and my watch and my car keys," I said.

"Put down your lendings," he sang.

"But I have to drive home from the station," I said, "and I have sixty or seventy dollars in cash."

"Put down your lendings."

"I can't, I really can't. I have to eat and drink and get home."

"Put down your lendings."

Then one by one they all, including Bertha, picked

up the incantation. The whole cast began to chant: "Put down your lendings, put down your lendings."

The sense of being unwanted has always been for me acutely painful. I suppose some clinician would have an explanation. The sensation is reverberative and seems to attach itself as the last link in a chain made up of all similar experience. The voices of the cast were loud and scornful, and there I was, buck naked, somewhere in the middle of the city and unwanted, remembering missed football tackles, lost fights, the contempt of strangers, the sound of laughter from behind shut doors. I held my valuables in my right hand, my literal identification. None of it was irreplaceable, but to cast it off would seem to threaten my essence, the shadow of myself that I could see on the floor, my name.

I went back to my seat and got dressed. This was difficult in such a cramped space. the cast was still shouting. Walking up the sloping aisle of the ruined theater was powerfully reminiscent. I had made the same gentle ascent after *King Lear* and *The Cherry Orchard*. I went outside.

It was still snowing. It looked like a blizzard. A cab was stuck in the front of the theater and I remembered then that I had snow tires. This gave me a sense of security and accomplishment that would have disgusted Ozamanides and his naked court; but I seemed not to have exposed my inhibitions but to have hit on some marvelously practical and obdurate part of myself. The wind flung the snow into my face and so, singing and jingling the car keys, I walked to the train.

What Is It?

RAYMOND CARVER

Raymond Carver was born in 1939 in Oregon. He attended Humboldt State College in Northern California. After attending the University of Iowa in 1963 and 1964, Carver pursued a number of jobs—service station attendant, janitor, stockroom boy—followed by a period as an editor for a textbook publisher. In his essay "Fires" Carver writes: "For years my wife and I had held to a belief that if we worked hard and tried to do the right things, the right things would happen. It's not such a bad thing to try and build a life on. Hard work, goals, good intentions, loyalty, we believed these were virtues and would someday be rewarded. We dreamt when we had time for it. But, eventually, we realized that hard work and dreams were not enough." His stories began to appear during the late 1960s and early 1970s. He has been published in The Atlantic Monthly, Harper's, Antaeus, Paris Review, The New Yorker, Grand Street, *and many other magazines and journals. He has written several volumes of poetry, and his short story collections include* Will You Please Be Quiet, Please *(1976), which was nominated for the National Book Award,* Furious Seasons *(1977),* What We Talk About When We Talk About Love *(1981),* Cathedral *(1983) and* Where I'm Calling from: New and Selected Stories *(1988). He died in 1988.*

Raymond Carver's stories are characterized by their conciseness and sparseness of plot and by the tenuous-

77

*ness of human relationships. He has said, "It's possible
in a short story to write about commonplace things and
objects using commonplace but precise language, and
to endow those things—a chair, a window curtain, a
fork, a stone, a woman's earrings—with immense, even
startling power." His contemporary plots often deal
with men and women who find themselves spinning
farther and farther away from what they once held as
possible in their lives. They arrive at their revelations in
an often strange twist of events that evokes the fragility
and repressed violence that can exist between couples.
"I like it when there is some feeling of threat or sense of
menace in short stories," he has written. "There has to
be a tension, a sense that something is imminent, that
certain things are in relentless motion, or else, most
often, there simply won't be a story."*

Fact is the car needs to be sold in a hurry, and Leo
sends Toni out to do it. Toni is smart and has
personality. She used to sell children's encyclopedias
door to door. She signed him up, even though he
didn't have kids. Afterward, Leo asked her for a date,
and the date led to this. This deal has to be cash, and
it has to be done tonight. Tomorrow somebody they
owe might slap a lien on the car. Monday they'll be in
court, home free—but word on them went out yester-
day, when their lawyer mailed the letters of intention.
The hearing on Monday is nothing to worry about, the
lawyer has said. They'll be asked some questions, and
they'll sign some papers, and that's it. But sell the
convertible, he said—today, *tonight*. They can hold
onto the little car, Leo's car, no problem. But they go
into court with that big convertible, the court will take
it, and that's that.

Toni dressed up. It's four o'clock in the afternoon.
Leo worries the lots will close. But Toni takes her

time dressing. She puts on a new white blouse, wide lacy cuffs, the new two-piece suit, new heels. She transfers the stuff from her straw purse into the new patent-leather handbag. She studies the lizard makeup pouch and puts that in too. Toni has been two hours on her hair and face. Leo stands in the bedroom doorway and taps his lips with his knuckles, watching.

"You're making me nervous," she says. "I wish you wouldn't just stand there," she says. "So tell me how I look."

"You look fine," he says. "You look great. I'd buy a car from you anytime."

"But you don't have money," she says, peering into the mirror. She pats her hair, frowns. "And your credit's lousy. You're nothing," she says. "Teasing," she says and looks at him in the mirror. "Don't be serious," she says. "It has to be done, so I'll do it. You take it out, you'd be lucky to get three, four hundred and we both know it. Honey, you'd be lucky if you didn't have to pay *them*." She gives her hair a final pat, gums her lips, blots the lipstick with a tissue. She turns away from the mirror and picks up her purse. "I'll have to have dinner or something, I told you that already, that's the way they work, I know them. But don't worry, I'll get out of it," she says. "I can handle it."

"Jesus," Leo says, "did you have to say that?"

She looks at him steadily. "Wish me luck," she says.

"Luck," he says. "You have the pink slip?" he says.

She nods. He follows her through the house, a tall woman with a small high bust, broad hips and thighs. he scratches a pimple on his neck. "You're sure?" he says. "Make sure. You have to have the pink slip."

"I have the pink slip," she says.

"Make sure."

She starts to say something, instead looks at herself in the front window and then shakes her head.

"At least call," he says. "Let me know what's going on."

"I'll call," she says. "Kiss, kiss. Here," she says and points to the corner of her mouth. "Careful," she says.

He holds the door for her. "Where are you going to try first?" he says. She moves past him and onto the porch.

Ernest Williams looks from across the street. In his Bermuda shorts, stomach hanging, he looks at Leo and Toni as he directs a spray onto his begonias. Once, last winter, during the holidays, when Toni and the kids were visiting his mother's, Leo brought a woman home. Nine o'clock the next morning, a cold foggy Saturday, Leo walked the woman to the car, surprised Ernest Williams on the sidewalk with a newspaper in his hand. Fog drifted, Ernest Williams stared, then slapped the paper against his leg, hard.

Leo recalls that slap, hunches his shoulders, says "You have someplace in mind first?"

"I'll just go down the line," she says. "The first lot, then I'll just go down the line."

"Open at nine hundred," he says. "Then come down. Nine hundred is low bluebook, even on a cash deal."

"I know where to start," she says.

Ernest Williams turns the hose in their direction. He stares at them through the spray of water. Leo has an urge to cry out a confession.

"Just making sure," he says.

"Okay, okay," she says. "I'm off."

It's her car, they call it her car, and that makes it all the worse. They bought it new that summer three years ago. She wanted something to do after the kids started school, so she went back selling. He was working six days a week in the fiber-glass plant. For a while they didn't know how to spend the money. Then they put a thousand on the convertible and doubled and tripled the payments until in a year they had it paid. Earlier, while she was dressing, he took the jack and spare from the trunk and emptied the glove compartment of pencils, matchbooks, Blue Chip stamps. Then he washed it and vacuumed inside. The red hood and fenders shine.

"Good luck," he says and touches her elbow.

She nods. He sees she is already gone, already negotiating.

"Things are going to be different!" he calls to her as she reaches the driveway. "We start over Monday. I mean it."

Ernest Williams looks at them and turns his head and spits. She gets into the car and lights a cigaret.

"This time next week!" Leo calls again. "Ancient history!"

He waves as she backs into the street. she changes gear and starts ahead. She accelerates and the tires give a little scream.

In the kitchen Leo pours Scotch and carries the drink to the backyard. The kids are at his mother's. There was a letter three days ago, his name penciled on the outside of the dirty envelope, the only letter all summer not demanding payment in full. We are having fun, the letter said. We like Grandma. We have a new dog called Mr. Six. He is nice. We love him. Goodbye.

He goes for another drink. He adds ice and sees that his hand trembles. He holds the hand over the sink. He looks at the hand for a while, sets down the glass, and holds out the other hand. Then he picks up the glass and goes back outside to sit on the steps. He recalls when he was a kid his dad pointing at a fine house, a tall white house surrounded by apple trees and a high white rail fence. "That's Finch," his dad said admiringly. "He's been in bankruptcy at least twice. Look at that house." But bankruptcy is a company collapsing utterly, executives cutting their wrists and throwing themselves from windows, thousands of men on the street.

Leo and Toni still had furniture. Leo and Toni had furniture and Toni and the kids had clothes. Those things were exempt. What else? Bicycles for the kids, but these he had sent to his mother's for safekeeping. The portable air-conditioner and the appliances, new washer and dryer, trucks came for those things weeks ago. What else did they have? This and that, nothing mainly, stuff that wore out or fell to pieces long ago. But there were some big parties back there, some fine travel. To Reno and Tahoe, at eighty with the top down and the radio playing. Food, that was one of the big items. They gorged on food. He figures thousands on luxury items alone. Toni would go to the grocery and put in everything she saw. "I had to do without when I was a kid," she says. "These kids are not going to do without," as if he'd been insisting they should. She joins all the book clubs. "We never had books around when I was a kid," she says as she tears open the heavy packages. They enroll in the record clubs for something to play on the new stereo. They sign up for it all. Even a pedigreed terrier named Ginger. He paid two hundred and found her run over in the street a week later. They buy what they want. If they can't pay, they charge. They sign up.

His undershirt is wet; he can feel the sweat rolling from his underarms. He sits on the top step with the empty glass in his hand and watches the shadows fill up the yard. He stretches, wipes his face. He listens to the traffic on the highway and considers whether he should go to the basement, stand on the utility sink, and hang himself with his belt. He understands he is willing to be dead.

Inside he makes a large drink and he turns the TV on and he fixes something to eat. He sits at the table with chili and crackers and watches something about a blind detective. He clears the table. He washes the pan and the bowl, dries these things and puts them away, then allows himself a look at the clock.

It's after nine. She's been gone nearly five hours.

He pours Scotch, adds water, carries the drink to the living room. He sits on the couch but finds his shoulders so stiff they won't let him lean back. He stares at the screen and sips, and soon he goes for another drink. He sits again. A news program begins— it's ten o'clock—and he says, "God, what in God's name has gone wrong?" and goes to the kitchen to return with more Scotch. He sits, he closes his eyes, and opens them when he hears the telephone ringing.

"I wanted to call," she says.

"Where are you?" he says. He hears piano music, and his heart moves.

"I don't know," she says. "Someplace. We're having a drink, then we're going someplace else for dinner. I'm with the sales manager. He's crude, but he's all right. He bought the car. I have to go now. I was on my way to the ladies and saw the phone."

"Did somebody buy the car?" Leo says. He looks out the kitchen window to the place in the drive where she always parks.

"I told you," she says. "I have to go now."

"Wait, wait a minute, for Christ's sake," he says. "Did somebody buy the car or not?"

"He had his checkbook out when I left," she says. "I have to go now. I have to go to the bathroom."

"Wait!" he yells. The line goes dead. He listens to the dial tone. "Jesus Christ," he says as he stands with the receiver in his hand.

He circles the kitchen and goes back to the living room. He sits. He gets up. In the bathroom he brushes his teeth very carefully. Then he uses dental floss. He washes his face and goes back to the kitchen. He looks at the clock and takes a clean glass from a set that has a hand of playing cards painted on each glass. He fills the glass with ice. He stares for a while at the glass he left in the sink.

He sits against one end of the couch and puts his legs up at the other end. He looks at the screen, realizes he can't make out what the people are saying. He turns the empty glass in his hand and considers biting off the rim. He shivers for a time and thinks of going to bed, though he knows he will dream of a large woman with gray hair. In the dream he is always leaning over tying his shoelaces. When he straightens up, she looks at him, and he bends to tie again. He looks at his hand. It makes a fist as he watches. The telephone is ringing.

"Where are you, honey?" he says slowly, gently.

"We're at this restaurant," she says, her voice strong, bright.

"Honey, which restaurant?" he says. He puts the heel of his hand against his eye and pushes.

"Downtown someplace," she says. "I think it's New Jimmy's. Excuse me," she says to someone off the line, "is this place New Jimmy's? This is New Jimmy's, Leo," she says to him. "Everything is all right, we're almost finished, then he's going to bring me home."

"Honey?" he says. He holds the receiver against his ear and rocks back and forth, eyes closed. "Honey?"

"I have to go," she says. "I wanted to call. Anyway, guess how much?"

"Honey," Leo says.

"Six and a quarter," she says. "I have it in my purse. He said there's no market for convertibles. I guess we're born lucky," she says and laughs. "I told him everything. I think I had to."

"Honey," Leo says.

"What?" she says.

"Please, honey," Leo says.

"He said he sympathizes," she says. "But he would have said anything." She laughs again. "He said personally he'd rather be classified a robber or a rapist than a bankrupt. He's nice enough, though," she says.

"Come home," Leo says. "Take a cab and come home."

"I can't," she says. "I told you, we're halfway through dinner."

"I'll come for you," he says.

"No," she says. "I said we're just finishing. I told you, it's part of the deal. They're out for all they can get. But don't worry, we're about to leave. I'll be home in a little while." She hangs up.

In a few minutes he calls New Jimmy's. A man answers. "New Jimmy's has closed for the evening," the man says.

"I'd like to talk to my wife," Leo says.

"Does she work here?" the man asks. "Who is she?"

"She's a customer," Leo says. "She's with someone. A business person."

"Would I know her?" the man says. "What is her name?"

"I don't think you know her," Leo says.

"That's all right," Leo says. "That's all right. I see her now."

"Thank you for calling New Jimmy's," the man says.

Leo hurried to the window. A car he doesn't recognize slows in front of the house, then picks up speed. He waits. Two, three hours later, the telephone rings again. There is no one at the other end when he picks up the receiver. There is only a dial tone.

"I'm right here!" Leo screams into the receiver.

Near dawn he hears footsteps on the porch. He gets up from the couch. The set hums, the screen glows. He opens the door. She bumps the wall coming in. She grins. Her face is puffy, as if she's been sleeping under sedation. She works her lips, ducks heavily and sways as he cocks his fist.

"Go ahead," she says thickly. She stands there swaying. Then she makes a noise and lunges, catches his shirt, tears it down the front. "Bankrupt!" she screams. She twists loose, grabs and tears his undershirt at the neck. "You son of a bitch," she says, clawing.

He squeezes her wrists, then lets go, steps back, looking for something heavy. She stumbles as she heads for the bedroom. "Bankrupt," she mutters. He hears her fall on the bed and groan.

He waits awhile, then splashes water on his face and goes to the bedroom. He turns the lights on, looks at her, and begins to take her clothes off. He pulls and pushes her from side to side undressing her. She says something in her sleep and moves her hand. He takes off her underpants, looks at them closely under the light, and throws them into a corner. He turns back the covers and rolls her in, naked. Then he opens her purse. He is reading the check when he hears the car come into the drive.

He looks through the front curtain and sees the convertible in the drive, its motor running smoothly, the headlamps burning, and he closes and opens his eyes. He sees a tall man come around in front of the car and up to the front porch. The man lays something on the porch and starts back to the car. He wears a white linen suit.

Leo turns on the porch light and opens the door cautiously. Her makeup pouch lies on the top step. The man looks at Leo across the front of the car, and then gets back inside and releases the handbrake.

"Wait!" Leo calls and stars down the steps. The man brakes the car as Leo walks in front of the lights. the car creaks against the brake. Leo tries to pull the two pieces of his shirt together, tries to bunch it all into his trousers.

"What is it you want?" the man says. "Look," the man says, "I have to go. No offense, I buy and sell cars, right? The lady left her makeup. She's a fine lady, very refined. What is it?"

Leo leans against the door and looks at the man. The man takes his hands off the wheel and puts them back. He drops the gear into reverse and the car moves backward a little.

"I want to tell you," Leo says and wets his lips.

The light in Ernest Williams' bedroom goes on. The shade rolls up.

Leo shakes his head, tucks in his shirt again. He steps back from the car. "Monday," he says.

"Monday," the man says and watches for sudden movement.

Leo nods slowly.

"Well, goodnight," the man says and coughs. "Take it easy, hear? Monday, that's right. Okay, then." He takes his foot off the brake, puts it on again after he has rolled back two or three feet. "Hey, one question. Between friends, are these actual miles?" The man waits, then clears his throat. "Okay, look, it doesn't matter either way," the man says. "I have to go. Take it easy." He backs into the street, pulls away quickly, and turns the corner without stopping.

Leo tucks at his shirt and goes back in the house. He locks the front door and checks it. Then he goes to the bedroom and locks that door and turns back the covers. He looks at her before he flicks the light. He takes off his clothes, folds them carefully on the floor, and gets in beside her. He lies on his back for a time and pulls the hair on his stomach, considering. He looks at the bedroom door, outlined now in the faint outside light. Presently he reaches out his hand and touches her hip. She does not move. He turns on his side and puts his hand on her hip. He runs his fingers over her hip and feels the stretch marks there. They are like roads, and he traces them in her flesh. He runs his fingers back and forth, first one, then another. They run everywhere in her flesh, dozens, perhaps hundreds of them. He remembers waking up the morning after they bought the car, seeing it, there in the drive, in the sun, gleaming.

Yours

MARY ROBISON

Mary Robison was born in Washington D.C. in 1949, and grew up in Ohio. Her stories have appeared most frequently in The New Yorker *and* Esquire. *They have been included in the* Best American Short Stories of 1982 *and* The Pushcart Prize VII. *She is the author of four books: the novel* Oh! *(1981) and three collections of short fiction,* Days *(1979),* An Amateur's Guide to the Night *(1983), and* Believe Them *(1988). She is the mother of two children and has taught at the University of Ohio and at Harvard.*

Mary Robison's unadorned, dispassionate stories are little concerned with landscapes, exposition, or appearances. Her wise, humorous, and minimalist writings are usually short, subtle, and complex. There are no big scenes, no climactic moments, and everything seems to happen at the same uninflected pitch. It has been said of her stories that they are charged by confusion—not the overwhelming kind, but the kind you feel before your eyes become accustomed to the light. With Mary Robison the plot is not a succession of surprises, but as John Gardner once noted about the best sort of writing, it is an increasingly moving series of recognitions, of moments of understanding that ensnare the reader into speculating, anticipating, and caring.

She lives with her husband, the writer James Robison, in Hull, Massachusetts.

❦

Allison struggled away from her white Renault, limp-
ing with the weight of the last of the pumpkins. She
found Clark in the twilight on the twig-and-leaf-littered
porch behind the house.

He wore a wool shawl. He was moving up and back
in a padded glider, pushed by the ball of his slippered
foot.

Allison lowered a big pumpkin, let it rest on the
wide floorboards.

Clark was much older—seventy-eight to Allison's
thirty-five. They were married. They were both quite
tall and looked something alike in their facial features.
Allison wore a natural-hair wig. It was a thick blond
hood around her face. She was dressed in bright-dyed
denims today. She wore durable clothes, usually, for
she volunteered afternoons at a children's day-care
center.

She put one of the smaller pumpkins on Clark's long
lap. "Now, nothing surreal," she told him. "Carve just
a *regular* face. These are for kids."

In the foyer, on the Hepplewhite desk, Allison found
the maid's chore list with its cross-offs, which included
Clark's supper. Allison went quickly through the day's
mail: a garish coupon packet, a bill from Jamestown
Liquors, November's pay-TV program guide, and the
worst thing, the funniest, an already opened, extremely
unkind letter from Clark's relations up North. "You're
an old fool," Allison read, and, "You're being cruelly
deceived." There was a gift check for Clark enclosed,
but it was uncashable, signed, as it was, "Jesus H.
Christ."

Late, late into this night, Allison and Clark gutted
and carved the pumpkins together, at an old table set
on the back porch, over newspaper after soggy newspaper, with paring knives and with spoons and with a
Swiss Army knife Clark used for exact shaping of
tooth and eye and nostril. Clark had been a doctor, an
internist, but also a Sunday watercolorist. His four
pumpkins were expressive and artful. Their carved

features were suited to the sizes and shapes of the pumpkins. Two looked ferocious and jagged. One registered surprise. The last was serene and beaming.

Allison's four faces were less deftly drawn, with slits and areas of distortion. She had cut triangles for noses and eyes. The mouths she had made were just wedges— two turned up and two turned down.

By one in the morning they were finished. Clark, who had bent his long torso forward to work, moved back over to the glider and looked out sleepily at nothing. All the lights were out across the ravine.

Clark stayed. For the season and time, the Virginia night was warm. Most leaves had been blown away already, and the trees stood unbothered. The moon was round above them.

Allison cleaned up the mess.

"Your jack-o'-lanterns are much, much better than mine," Clark said to her.

"Like hell," Allison said.

"Look at me," Clark said, and Allison did.

She was holding a squishy bundle of newspapers. The papers reeked sweetly with the smell of pumpkin guts.

"Yours are *far* better," he said.

"You're wrong. You'll see when they're lit," Allison said.

She went inside, came back with yellow vigil candles. It took her a while to get each candle settled, and then to line up the results in a row on the porch railing. She went along and lit each candle and fixed the pumpkin lids over the little flames.

"See?" she said.

They sat together a moment and looked at the orange faces.

"We're exhausted. It's good night time," Allison said. "Don't blow out the candles. I'll put in new ones tomorrow."

That night, in their bedroom, a few weeks earlier in her life than had been predicted, Allison began to die.

"Don't look at me if my wig comes off," she told Clark. "Please."

Her pulse cords were fluttering under his fingers. She raised her knees and kicked away the comforter. She said something to Clark about the garage being locked.

At the telephone, Clark had a clear view out back and down to the porch. He wanted to get drunk with his wife once more. He wanted to tell her, from the greater perspective he had, that to own only a little talent, like his, was an awful, plaguing thing; that being only a little special meant you expected too much, most of the time, and liked yourself too little. He wanted to assure her that she had missed nothing.

He was speaking into the phone now. He watched the jack-o'-lanterns. The jack-o'-lanterns watched him.

World's End

PAUL THEROUX

Born in Medford, Massachusetts, in 1941, Paul Theroux received his B.A. from the University of Massachusetts in 1963. Following school he was a Peace Corps volunteer in Africa, and taught English in Uganda and Malaysia. He has commented that he has lived a good portion of his adult life outside the United States, ". . . mainly in equatorial places. I did not plan to be away so long but that is the way it has worked out, and, as it happens, expatriation is often my fictional subject. I am not an exile, simply a person who enjoys traveling in temptingly named places— Burma, Java, Singapore, Central Africa." Theroux has published both travel writing—The Great Railway Bazaar (1975), The Old Patagonia Express (1979), The Kingdom by the Sea (1983), Riding the Iron Rooster by Train Through China (1987)—and several novels and short story collections, among them The Consul's File (1977), Picture Palace (1978), and The Mosquito Coast (1981).

In both his fiction and nonfiction Paul Theroux favors the persona of the expatriate, the restless and uprooted seeker who must rub against other cultures in order to find the friction that sets the imagination to light. He's been praised for his ingenuity, technical assurance, and elaborate knowledge in conveying the strangeness of foreign territory. A character in one of his novels

says that fiction writing offers "the second chances life
has denied."

Paul Theroux divides his time between London and
Cape Cod.

Robarge was a happy man who had taken a great
risk. He had transplanted his family—his wife and
small boy—from their home in America to a bizarrely
named but buried-alive district called World's End in
London, where they were strangers. It had worked,
and it made his happiness greater. His wife, Kathy,
had changed. Having overcome this wrench from home
and mastered the new routine, she became confident.
It showed in her physically—she had unstiffened; she
adopted a new hairstyle; she slimmed; she had been
set free by proving to her husband that he depended
on her. Richard, only six, was already in what Robarge
regarded as the second grade: the little boy could read
and write! Even Robarge's company, a supplier of
drilling equipment for offshore oil rigs, was pleased by
the way he had managed; they associated their success
with Robarge's hard work.

So Robarge was vindicated in the move he had
made. He had considered marriage the quietest enact-
ment of sharing, connubial exclusiveness the most private way to live—a sheltered life in the best sense.
And he saw England as upholding the domestic rever-
ences that had been tossed aside in America. He had
not merely moved his family but rescued them. His
sense of security made him feel younger, an added
pleasure. He did not worry about growing old; he had
put on weight in these four years at World's End and
began to affect that curious sideways gait, almost a
limp, of a heavy boy. It was a game—he was nearly
forty—but games were still possible in this country
where he could go unrecognized and so unmocked.

Most of all, he liked returning home in the rain. The house at World's End was a refuge; he could shut his door on the darkness and smell the straightness of his own rooms. The yellow lights from the street showed the rain droplets patterned on the window, and he could hear it falling outside, the drip from the sky, as irregular as a weeping tree, which meant in London that it would go on all night. Tonight he was returning from Holland—a Dutch subsidiary machined the drilling bits he dispatched to Aberdeen.

Without waking Kathy, he took the slender parcel he had carried from Amsterdam and crept upstairs to his son's room. On the plane he had kept it on his lap—there was nowhere to stow it. A man in the adjoining seat had stared and prompted Robarge to say, "It's a kite. For my son. The Dutch import them from the Far East. Supposed to be foolproof." The man had answered him by taking out a pair of binoculars he had bought for his own boy at the duty-free shop.

"Richard's only six," said Robarge.

The man said that the older children got the more expensive they were. He said it affectionately and with pride and Robarge thought how glad he would be when Richard was old enough to appreciate a really expensive present—skis, a camera, a pocket calculator, a radio. Then he would know how his father loved him and how there was nothing in the world he would not give him. And he felt a casual envy for the man in the next seat, having a son old enough to want the things his father could afford. His own uncomprehending son asked for nothing: it made fiercer Robarge's desire to show his love.

The lights in the house were out; it was, at midnight, as gloomy as a tunnel and seemed narrow and empty in all that darkness. Richard's door was ajar. Robarge went in and fond his son sleeping peacefully under wall posters of dinosaurs and fighter planes. Robarge knelt and kissed the boy, then sat on the bed and delighted in hearing the boy's measured breaths. The breaths stopped. In the harsh knife of light falling through the curtains from the street Robarge saw his son stir.

"Hello." The word came whole: Richard's voice was wide-awake.

"It's me." He kissed the boy. "Look what I brought you."

Robarge brandished the parcel. There was a film of rain on the plastic wrapper.

"What is it?" Richard asked.

Robarge told him: A kite. "Now go back to sleep like a good boy."

"Can we fly it?"

"You bet. If it's windy we'll fly it at the park."

"It's not windy enough at the park. You have to go in the car."

"Where shall we go?"

"Box Hill's a good place for kites."

"Is it windy there?"

"Not half!" whispered the child.

Robarge was delighted by this old English expression in his son's speech, and he muttered it to himself in amazement. He was gladdened by Richard's response; he had pondered so long at the gift shop at Schiphol wondering which toy to buy—like an eager indecisive child himself—he had nearly missed his flight.

"Box Hill it is then." It meant a long drive, but the next day was Saturday—he could devote his weekend to the boy. He crossed the hall and undressed in the dark. When he got into the double bed, Kathy touched his arm and murmured, "You're back," and she swung over and sighed and pulled the blankets closer.

"I think I made a hit last night," said Robarge over breakfast. He told Kathy about the kite.

"You mean you woke him up to give him that thing?"

Kathy's tone discouraged him: he had hoped she

would be glad. He said, "He was already awake—I heard him calling out. Must have had a bad dream. I went straight up." All these lies to conceal his impulsive wish to kiss his sleeping child at midnight. "We'll fly the thing today if there's any wind."

"That's nice," said Kathy. Her voice was flat and unfocused, almost belittling.

"Anything wrong?"

She said no and got up from the table, which was her abrupt way of showing boredom or changing the subject. And yet Robarge was struck by how attractive she was; how, without noticeable effort, she had discovered the kind of glamour a younger woman might envy. She was thin and had soft heavy breasts and wore light expensive blouses with her jeans.

Robarge said, "Are you angry because I travel so much?"

"You take your job seriously," she said. "Don't apologize. I haven't nagged you about that."

"I'm lucky I'm based in London—think of the rest of them in Aberdeen. How would you like to be there?"

"Don't say it in that threatening way. I wouldn't go to Aberdeen."

"I might have been posted there." He said it loudly, with the confidence of one who has been reprieved.

"You would have gone alone." He guessed she was poking fun; he was grateful for that, grateful that things had worked out so well in London.

"You didn't want to come here," he said. "But you're glad now, aren't you?"

Kathy did not reply. She was clearing the table and at the same time setting out Richard's breakfast.

"Aren't you?" he repeated in a taunting way.

"Yes!" she said, with unreasonable force, reddening as she spoke. Then she burst into tears. "There," she stuttered, "are you satisfied?"

Robarge, made guilty by her outburst (what had he said?), approached his wife to calm her. But she turned away. He heard Richard on the stairs, and the rattle of the kite dragging. He saw with relief that Kathy had fled into the kitchen, where Richard could not hear her sobbing.

He had dropped Kathy on the Kings Road and proceeded—Richard in the back seat—out of London toward Box Hill. It was only then that he remembered that he had failed to tell Kathy where they were going. She hadn't asked: her tears had made her stubbornly silent. It was late May and once they were past Epsom he could see bluebells growing thickly in the shade of pine woods, and the pale green of the new leaves of beeches, and—already high and drooping from the weight of their blossoms—the cow parsley at the margins of plowed fields.

Richard said, "There are seagulls here."

Robarge smiled. There were no seagulls—only newly plowed fields set off by windbreaks of pines, and some crows fussing from tree to tree, to squawk.

"The black ones are crows."

"But seagulls are white," said Richard. "They follow the tractor and eat the worms when the farmer digs them up."

"You're a smart boy. But seagulls—"

"There they are," said Richard.

The child was right; at the edge of a field a tractor turned and just behind it, hovering and swooping— seagulls.

They parked near the Burford Bridge Hotel, and above them Robarge saw the long scar of exposed chalk, a whole eroded chute of it, and the steep green hill rising beside it to the brow of a grassy slope where the woods began.

"Mind the cars," said Richard, warning his father. They paused at the road near the parking lot. A motorcyclist sped past, then the child led his father across. He was being tugged by the child to the far left of a clump of boulders at the base of the hill, and then he saw the nearly hidden path. He realized he was being led by the boy to this entrance, then up the path beside the chalk slide to the gentler rise of the hill. Here Richard broke away and ran the rest of the way up the slope.

"Shall we fly it here?"

"No—over there," said Richard, out of breath and pointing at nothing Robarge could see. "Where it's windy."

They resumed, Robarge trudging, the child leading, until they were on the ridge of the hill. It was as the child had said, for no sooner had he walked to the highest point on that part of the hill than Robarge felt the wind. The path was sheltered, but here the wind was so strong it almost tore the kite from his hands. Robarge was proud of his son for leading him here.

"This is fun!" said Richard excitedly, as Robarge fixed the crosspiece and looped the twine, tightening and flattening the paper butterfly. He took the ball of string from his pocket and fastened it to the kite.

Richard said, "What about the tail?"

"This kite doesn't need a tail. It's foolproof."

"All kites need tails," Richard said. "Or they fall down."

The certainty in the child's voice irritated Robarge. He said, "Don't be silly," and raised the kite and let the wind pull it from his hand. The kite rose, spun, and then plummeted to the ground. Robarge tried this two more times and then, fearing that he would destroy the frail thing, he squatted and saw that a bit of it was torn.

"It's broken!" Richard shrieked.

"That won't make any difference."

"It needs a tail!" the child cried.

Robarge was annoyed by the child's insistence. It was the monotonous pedantry he had used in speaking about the seagulls. Robarge said, "We haven't got a tail."

Richard planted his feet apart and peered at the kite

with his large serious face and said, "Your necktie can be a tail."

"I don't know whether you've noticed, Rich, but I'm not wearing a necktie."

"It won't work then," said the child. Robarge thought for a moment that the child was going to stamp on the kite in rage. He kicked the ground and said tearfully, "I told you it needs a tail!"

"Maybe we can use something else. How about a handkerchief?"

"No—just a tie. Or it won't work."

Robarge pulled out his handkerchief and tore it into three strips. These he knotted together to make a streamer for the tail. He tied it to the bottom corner of the kite, and while Richard sulked on the grass, Robarge, by running in circles, got the kite aloft. He tugged it and paid out string and made it bob; soon the kite was steadied on the curvature of white line. Richard was beside him, happy again, hopping on his small bow legs.

Robarge said, "You were right about the tail."

"Can I have a go?"

A go! Robarge had begun to smile again. "You want a go, huh? Think you can do it?"

"I know how," said Richard.

Robarge handed his son the string and watched him lean back and draw the kite higher. Robarge encouraged him. Instead of smiling, the child was made serious by the praise. He worked the string back and forth and said nothing.

"That's it," said Robarge. "You're an expert."

Richard held the string over his head. He made the kite climb and dance. The wind beat against the paper. The child said, "I told you it needed a tail."

"You're doing very well. Walk backward and you'll tighten the line."

But Richard, to Robarge's approval, wound the string on the ball. The kite began to rise. Robarge was impatient to fly the kite himself. He said he could get

it much higher and then demanded his turn. He got
the kite very high and while it swung he said, "You're
a smart boy. I wouldn't have thought of coming here.
And you're good at this. Next time I'll get you a
bigger kite—not a paper one, but plastic. They can go
hundreds of feet up."

"That's against the law."

"Don't be silly."

"Yes. You can get arrested. It makes the planes
crash," said the child. "In England."

Robarge was still making sweeping motions with the
string, lifting the kite, making it dive. "Who says?"

"A man told me."

Robarge snorted. "What man?"

"Mummy's friend."

The child screamed. The kite was falling on its broken string. It crashed against the hill and came apart,
blowing until it was misshapen. Robarge thought: I am
blind.

Later, when the child was calm and the broken kite
stuffed beneath a bush (Robarge promised to buy a
new one), he confirmed what Robarge had feared: he
had been there before, seen the gulls, climbed the hill,
and the man—he had no name, he was "Mummy's
friend"—had taken off his necktie to make a tail for
the kite.

The man had worn a tie. Robarge created a lover
from this detail and saw someone middle aged, middle
class, perhaps prosperous, a serious rival, out to
impress—British, of course. He saw the man's hand
slipped beneath one of Kathy's brilliant silk blouses.
He wondered whether he knew the man; but who did
they know? They had been happy and solitary in this
foreign country, at World's End. He wanted to cry.
He felt his face breaking to expose all his sadness.

"Want to see my hide-out?"

The child showed Robarge the fallen tree, the pine
grove, the stumps.

"Did Mummy's friend play with you?"

"The first time—"

Kathy had gone their twice with her lover and Richard! Robarge wanted to leave the place, but the child ran from tree to tree, remembering the games they had played.

Robarge said, "Were they nice picnics?"

"Not half!"

It was the man's expression, he was sure; and now he hated it.

"What are you looking at, Daddy?"

He was staring at the trampled pine needles, the seclusion of the trees, the narrow path.

"Nothing."

Richard did not want to go home, but Robarge insisted, and walking back to the car Robarge could not prevent himself from asking questions to which he did not want to hear answers.

The man's name?

"I don't know."

Did he have a nice car?

"Blue." The child looked away.

"What did Mummy's friend say to you?"

"I don't remember." Now Richard ran ahead, down the hill.

He saw that the child was disturbed. If he pressed too hard he would frighten him. And so they drove back to World's End in silence.

Robarge did not tell Kathy where they had gone, and instead of confronting her with what he knew he watched her. He did not want to lose her in an argument; it was easy to imagine the terrible scene—her protests, her lies. She might not deny it, he thought; she might make it worse.

He directed his anger against the man. He wanted to kill him, to save himself. That night he made love to Kathy in a fierce testing way, as if challenging her to refuse. But she submitted to his bullying and at last, as he lay panting beside her, she said, "Are you finished?"

A few days later, desperate to know whether his wife's love had been stolen from him, Robarge told Kathy that he had to go to Aberdeen on business.

"When will you be back?"

"I'm not sure." He thought: Why should I make it easier on her? "I'll call you."

But she accepted this as she had accepted his wordless assault on her, and it seemed to him as though nothing had happened, she had no lover, she had been loyal. He had only the child's word. But the child was innocent and had never lied.

On the morning of his departure for Aberdeen he went to Richard's room. He shut the door and said, "Do you love me?"

The child moved his head and stared.

"If you really love me, you won't tell Mummy what I'm going to ask you to do."

"I won't tell."

"When I'm gone, I want you to be the daddy."

Richard's face grew solemn.

"That means you have to be very careful. You have to make sure that Mummy's all right."

"Why won't Mummy be all right?"

Robarge said, "I think her friend is a thief."

"No—he's not!"

"Don't be upset," said Robarge. "That's what we're going to find out. I want you to watch him if he comes over again."

"But why? Don't you like him?"

"I don't know him very well—not as well as Mummy does. Will you watch him for me, like a daddy?"

"Yes."

"If you do, I'll bring you a nice present."

"Mummy's friend gave me a present."

Robarge was so startled he could not speak; and he

wanted to shout. The child peered at him, and Robarge saw curiosity and pity mingled in the child's squint.

"It was a little car."

"I'll give you a big car," Robarge managed.

"What's he stealing from you, Daddy?"

Robarge thought a moment, then said, "Something very precious—" and his voice broke. If he forced it he would sob. He left the child's room. He had never felt sadder.

Downstairs, Kathy kissed him on his ear. The smack of it caused a ringing in a horn in his head.

He had invented the trip to Aberdeen; he invented work to justify it, and for three days he knew what madness was—a sickening and a sorrow. He was deaf, his feet and hands were stupid, and his tongue at times seemed to swell and choke him when he tried to speak. He wanted to tell his area supervisor that he was suffering, that he knew how odd he must appear. But he did not know how to begin. And strangely, though his behavior was clumsily childlike, he felt elderly, as if he were dying inside, all his organs working feebly. He returned to London feeling that a burned hole was blackened on his heart.

The house at World's End was so still that in the doorway he considered that she was gone, that she had taken Richard and deserted him with her lover. This was Sunday evening, part of his plan—a surprise: he usually returned on Monday. He was not reassured to see the kitchen light on—there was a telephone in the kitchen. But Kathy's face, when she answered the door, was blank.

She said, "I thought you might call from the station."

He tried to kiss her—she pulled away.

"My hands are wet."

"Glad to see me?"

"I'm doing the dishes." She lost her look of boredom and said, "You're so pale."

"I haven't slept." He could not gather the phrases

of the question in his mind because he dreaded the
simple answer he saw whole: yes. He felt afraid of her,
and more deaf and clumsy than ever, like a helpless
orphan snatched into the dark. He wanted her to say
that he had imagined the lover, but he knew he would
not believe words he craved so much to hear. He no
longer trusted her and would not trust her until he had
the child's word. He longed to see his son. He started
up the stairs.

Kathy said, "He's watching television."

On entering the television room, Robarge saw his
son stand up and take a step backward. Richard's face
in the darkened room was the yellow-green hue of the
television screen; his hands sprang to his ears; the blue
fibers of his pajamas glowed as if sprinkled with salt.
When Robarge switched on the light the child ran to
him and held him—so tightly that Robarge could not
hug him.

"Here it is." Robarge disengaged himself from the
child and crossed the room, turning off the television
as he went. The toy was gift wrapped in bright paper
and tied with a ribbon. He handed it to Richard.
Richard put his face against his father's neck. "Aren't
you going to open it?"

Robarge felt the child nodding against his shoulder.

"Time for bed," said Robarge.

The child said, "I put myself to bed now."

"All by yourself?" said Robarge. "Okay, off you go
then."

Richard went to the door.

"Don't forget your present!"

Richard hesitated. Robarge brought it to him and
tucked it under the child's arm. Then, pretending it
was an afterthought, he said softly, "Tell me what
happened while I was away—did you see anything?"

Richard shook his head and let his mouth gape.

"What about Mummy's friend?" Robarge was standing; the question dropped to the child like a spider
lowering on its own filament of spittle.

"I didn't see him."

The child looked so small; Robarge towered over him. He knelt and asked, "Are you telling the truth?"

And it occurred to Robarge that he had never asked the child that question before—had never used that intimidating tone or looked so hard into the child's eyes. Richard backed away, the gift-wrapped parcel under his arm.

At this little distance, the child seemed calmer. He shook his head as he had before, but this time his confidence was pronounced, as if in the minute that had elapsed he had learned the trick of it. With the faintest trace of a stutter—when had he ever stuttered? —he said, "It's the truth, Daddy. I didn't."

Robarge said, "It's a tank. The batteries are already inside. It shoots sparks." Then he shuffled forward on his knees and took the child's arm. "You'll tell me if you see that man again, won't you?"

Richard stared.

"I mean, if he steals anything?"

Robarge saw corruption in the unblinking eyes.

"You'll tell me, won't you?"

When Robarge repeated the question, Richard said, "Mummy doesn't have a friend," and Robarge knew he had lost the child.

He said, "Show me how you put yourself to bed."

Robarge was unconsoled. He found Kathy had already gone to bed, and though the light was on she lay on her side, facing the dark wall, as if sleeping.

Robarge said, "We never make love."

"We did—on Wednesday."

She was right; he had forgotten.

She said, "I've locked the doors. Will you make sure the lights are out?"

So he went from room to room turning out the lights, and in the television room Robarge sat down in the darkness. There, in the house which now seemed to be made of iron, he remembered again that he was in London, in World's End; that he had taken his family there. He was saddened by the thought that he was so far from home. The darkness hid him and hid the country; he knew that if he appeared calm it was only because the darkness concealed his loss. He wished he had never come here, and worrying this way he craved his child and had a hideous reverie, of wishing to eat the child and eat his wife and keep them in that cannibal way. Burdened by this guilty thought, he went upstairs to make sure his son was safe.

Richard was in darkness, too. Robarge kissed the child's hot cheek. There was a bright cube on the floor, the present from Aberdeen. He picked it up and saw that it had not been opened.

He put it beside Richard on the bed and leaning for balance he pressed something in the bedclothes. It was long and flat and the hardness stung his hand. It was the breadknife with the serrated blade from the kitchen, tucked beneath these sheets, close to the child's body. Breathless from the shock of it Robarge took it away.

And then he went to bed. He was shaking so badly he did not think he would ever sleep. He wanted to smash his face against the wall and hit it until it was bloody and he had torn his nose away. He dropped violently to sleep. When he woke in the dark he recalled the sound that had wakened him—it was still vibrant in the air, the click of the front gate: a thief was entering his house. Robarge waited for more, and perspired. His fear left him and he was penetrated by the fake vitality of insomnia. After an hour he decided that what he had heard, if anything, was a thief leaving the house, not breaking in. Too late, too far, too dark, he thought; and he knew now they were all lost.

Pastorale

SUSAN ENGBERG

Susan Engberg's stories have appeared in Sewanee
Review, Ploughshares, Kenyon Review, *and numerous
other literary journals. She is the author of two books of
short stories,* Pastorale *(1982) and* A Stay by the River
*(1985), and has been included in both the O. Henry
and Pushcart story collections. She is a native of Iowa.*

*Susan Engberg's writing is crisp, metaphorical, and
rich. She is always approaching the question of why we're
here. "We're not starving, we're not political prisoners,
we're not trying to escape across the mountains or the
sea. We're fortunate," a woman in her story "Lap of
Peace" says. "I would like to know what to do with
that." Her stories are ethical and moral quests, suffused
with experiences that help us to comprehend. By giving
the slightest detail significance, they prove, too, that if
we comprehend well enough, even the most normal can
be dramatic. For Susan Engberg, writing is a way of
looking at the world and being able to find meaning in it.*

She lives in Milwaukee, Wisconsin.

There was a woman who for a time loved a younger
man. Her name was Catherine, and she had lost a
child. Her daughter had been in a coma one week,
two weeks, and then one morning in October her
expression had changed slightly and she had died.

107

Hanna. She had had honey-colored hair and pale eyes with an outer rim of darker blue to the irises. Until the brain tumor she had been healthy enough and lively and competent. She had bought two goats with her own money, raised them up, rode with John to have them bred, and when they freshened, milked them herself, morning and night, and with part of the milk made yogurt for the family. Catherine took over the milking. The boys should be doing that, John said, but she wanted it for herself; the goats, at any rate, were almost dry.

She was forty; Hanna had been ten. Sometimes the rounded numbers rose up in her mind as a meaningless chant—ten, twenty, thirty, forty—and then she would look backward and forward and see nothing but inexpressive decades. Her own face, resting against the goat's fur above the stream of milk, felt used up, like a landscape of dry runnels. She cleaned the stall methodically, accepting everything—the smells of urine and dung, the impatience of the goats, the cold in her hands as she fetched the water—as she had begun to accept the death itself.

But beneath this methodical impassive continuance of life, she could feel her grief changing into something less bearable than the immediate anguish; it was a sense of absolute physical loss, of strange yearning: she wanted to touch the child again. There had been no chance to be alone with her, dead. At night Catherine would lie in the dark and think that she might be all right if only she could cradle the child's actual corpse one more time.

But of course that was impossible. Months were passing. The adolescent energy of their two boys continued on a course of its own, as if it had been a stream of water passing through the house and out again, seldom anything to hold on to, and she had the feeling that wherever they were going, they were already on their way. Childhood had never seemed to her so brief.

She and John were the maintainers. In the past they had occasionally joked to each other, companionably, about how they were merely the keepers of an establishment. A door would slam somewhere, there would be a thumping on the stairs, a call from the barnyard, and when they looked at each other, what was between them had to do with seventeen years of marriage and the pleasure they could still take in each other and the way these people who were their children had invaded their house, but only for a time. Now between them Catherine sensed a self-consciousness that it seemed discussing would only aggravate, and although they might be alone, she no longer felt the same privacy. She would lie in bed, watching him undress, and the sight of his bare back, twisting to pick up a shoe in the half-light, or of his hair and beard—how grizzled he had become!—made her want to cry out to break through this theatrical intimacy, but the sound remained voiceless. He seemed to have become gentler with her, sometimes distant. They talked, of course, and they had wept together and with Tom and Drew, and they both had their work, which was a blessing.

John had been having good success with his pottery; he would be showing at two large invitationals that early summer in addition to the usual regional exhibits, and he was working steadily now, seldom sleeping late in the morning, seldom coming in early from the shop to read or tinker with an odd repair. She herself was finishing up one commission from the nursing school, the illustrations for a handbook for expectant mothers, and on the strength of this had been given another by a biology professor, an essay on reproduction intended for high-school and college students. The coincidence between these subjects and Hanna's death she endured, because of her desire for work; she was practical and energetic by nature, and she had always handled periods of unclarity or doubt simply by applying herself to what was at hand. Several times a month she drove in to one university with her sketches, had quiet conferences in one office or another, ate lunch in one of the cafeterias around the science and medical complex, shopped a bit perhaps, or saw a friend, and then drove home.

Once she had felt drawn up to the fourth floor of the hospital past the room where Hanna had died; another child lay in the bed, and another mother sat in the green vinyl chair by the window. A shout of laughter came down the hall from the nursing station; a metal cart was clattering along a hallway out of sight. She didn't go back again.

She looked at children on the street, blond children, and at mothers who didn't seem to understand the full value of what was theirs. Once in the checkout line in a supermarket, she had rushed away in confusion, leaving behind the basket of groceries, because of her overwhelming desire to pick up the child in front of her and hold her close, perhaps even to run away with her and to keep running until she could find a quiet place to talk.

She tried to tell herself that it was natural her sorrow should be taking these different forms, and that she must simply wait and accept its evolving transformations.

One late afternoon as she drove into their lane, a thick wet February snow was beginning to fall, windless, very still, like a false oblivion, and two crows were screaming over the catalpa skeletons at the bottom of the pasture. Her body was worn down by the last stages of the flu. John too had been ill, and she found him in bed, muffled in a shawl, reading, smoking his pipe. His clay-splotched trousers hung from a chair.

"You look ravishing and creative," he said as he stretched and threw aside his book. His stiff hair was raked up and the creases beneath his eyes looked personal and contemplative.

"I'm frazzled and sick," she said. "You're just playing

the lascivious old man again; none of it is genuine."
But she went to him and sat down close, laying a hand
on his chest.

"Spending an afternoon in bed has had certain ef-
fects," he said.

"You've improved your mind and the state of your
health, I hope."

"My mind has been rotting away with carnal lust.
For you, of course, my dear," he added.

"You sound venereal," she said as she rested her
weight against him. The play of their bantering went
on by itself, remote. Outside the window the snow
continued, thicker now and bluish. "Where are the
boys?" she asked.

"I told them to go out and do the goats for you."

"That was nice." It was all distant, even the sadness, even the dried mask that was pretending to be
her face.

They were snowed in the next day, and on the
following noon Louie came with the tractor to clear
the lane. He brought in the mail, standing huge and
good-natured in the mudroom in his layers of sweat
shirts and coveralls, talking about the snow.

"That was some snow," he said.

Catherine watched him trudge out to the corncrib.
Once in the army in Alaska Louie's legs had gotten
frozen from the knees down. Watching him work made
her think of life as being a matter of putting one stolid
foot in front of another, endlessly.

"Well, he's coming," said John, holding out a letter,
"Laurits Jorgensen—that fellow I told you about. He's
taken the apprenticeship and has agreed to twenty
hours of work per week in exchange. How does that
sound?"

"For how long?" asked Catherine. She read hur-
riedly down the paragraphs.

"Six months or so—we'll how it goes." He sat in
his ragged down vest, nursing his pipe and coffee and
slowly working himself up to go out to the shop. It was

a familiar sight. He had been up until four that morning with a firing.

"This is going to be good for you, isn't it?" said Catherine. "You might actually get the new kiln finished."

"He does say he's good with tools. He's a find, I'd say."

"You'll take him sight unseen?"

"I trust Merton—he wouldn't send a slouch."

"He'll get a room in town, I suppose?" asked Catherine, returning to her dish of fruit and yogurt. She had been up at seven with the boys and for most of the morning, while John had slept with the covers over his head, had been at her drawing board in their sunny bedroom.

"He could do that," said John.

Later in the afternoon he came in for a sandwich and brought it up to the bedroom. He squeezed the back of her neck, kissed her ear, and then sat down in the old wing chair. She heard him biting through lettuce and sucking from his can of beer.

"I've been thinking," he said as he set aside his empty plate and leaned back with the beer can balancing on his chest, "that fellow Laurits could take Hanna's room, if you'd agree. It seems a waste of time for him to go back and forth to town every day when he could just as well stay right here."

Catherine turned her pencil around and around in the sharpener. She squinted at the network of mammary ducts on her paper.

"We'd have to do something about the curtains," she said at last.

"That's simple enough, isn't it? It just seems to me that it's time now to start using the room; I mean, love, we've got to do it some day."

She heard the school bus on the road and looked out to the lane where Tom and Drew were jumping down from its steps.

"All right," she said slowly, turning back to her husband. "I think we could manage that."

II

"You must be Catherine," says the voice in the barn door. She turns from the fresh straw she is forking down and sees his shape against the light. It is April.

She goes over and sees him better. He has blond hair that is parted in the middle, and it hangs straight on either side of his face. His eyebrows are black.

"Then you're Laurits."

"The master there sent me out to meet you." He tosses his head slightly toward the shop.

She smiles as he smiles. It is one of the first warm days.

"This is quite a place; it's really beautiful. What else do you have besides goats?"

"Nothing, except a hundred or so cats."

"You own it all?" He is leaning against the old timbers of the doorway and looking out towards the undulating Iowa fields.

"Just the house and the barn and the shop. Louie has the land. You'll meet Louie before long." The pregnant goats are outside the door drinking from a trough. She has filled a large pan with grain. Now she heaves up a basket of old straw and droppings.

"I'll take that," says Laurits. "Where to?"

"That dung heap over there."

"This is fantastic," he says as he jauntily brings back the basket. He tosses the hair from his eyes.

They walk together toward the shop where they find John sponging smooth the rim of a large tureen. The reddish clay glistens like a moistened lower lip. Catherine has seen John take a finished piece like this, to her eyes perfect, and slice it relentlessly apart to reveal a slight inconsistency in the thickness of the form. There are other days when he is unable to work at all; then he might lie hour after hour in the darkened bedroom, harshly humorous against himself and the world. She has understood for a long time that her strength is different from his.

"Well," he says to Catherine, screwing his face above the pipe smoke, "the slave has arrived. Have you shown him to his miserable quarters?"

"Not yet," says Catherine, "he's been helping."

"That's good, lad. I'm glad to hear you haven't wasted these precious minutes cavorting aimlessly in the barnyard. It's work we want around here. Work! do you hear?" He makes his eyes look fierce and insane.

"Yes, sir," drawls Laurits. He has propped an arm along a drying rack and seems as much absorbed in the tureen as in either of them. Catherine wonders where he has gotten his confidence.

John seems invigorated, boyish himself. He stops the wheel and draws a taut string under the base of the tureen. "That's it," he says; "let's go talk about the future."

They are very gay. Catherine sees that it is a good combination of personalities. When the boys come home, they hang on the railings beside the porch swing, fascinated. Laughter gushes out over the lawn and the beds of spring flowers and the freshly tilled garden. They are talking about the new kiln for salt glazing, about the distances to the surrounding towns, about the farm girls in the neighborhood. John allows himself a leer. "They grow up fast around here," he says.

A meadowlark is singing from the walnut tree by the lane, a piercing, slurred call that seems to contain the entire moment. Clouds are rapidly riding out of the west, fanning out into an expanse of sky and disappearing over the house. Catherine feels herself breathless at the spaciousness these approaching masses make visible. She is sitting on the steps with her coat collar up, hugging her knees. Tonight she will make a large salad with fresh mushrooms and chopped cress. Her mind is planning. She looks at her sons, and it seems weeks since she has noticed them. They are growing quickly. Their heads of identical brown curly hair are like lively, irrepressible masses of energy.

Later, in the night, she wakes and feels the house full of sleepers. Catherine turns her face into her pillow and smells her own hair. Her body is radiating heat, her cheeks feel smooth. Sometime during the night the first of the goat kids is born.

Laurits makes competent pottery, mostly smaller pieces like bowls and mugs and casseroles. He does not seem apologetic about what he has to learn. He listens carefully, and he is keeping a chart of glazing mixtures. When he sits at the kitchen table for tea, he turns the mug thoughtfully, sometimes holding it by the handle and sometimes cupping both hands around its belly.

Today he has come back from town with the onion sets Catherine has ordered. When he has made the tea, he calls up the stairs to her. He seems to like the kitchen. He talks to Catherine about an idea he has for building some shelves over the stove; getting up, he shows her how they would span, from here to here, with hooks underneath for pans and open space above for pottery. He has started to grow a blond mustache, and now when Catherine looks at his face she notices even more the darkness of his brows. She has stopped being surprised at how comfortable Laurits seems talking about these everyday household matters. He makes himself useful, but he doesn't seem to need their praise.

When they finish their tea, they go down the side yard together to the garden. They take turns making trenches with the hoe and placing the onion sets. Catherine has already planted radishes, beets, and carrots. Laurits says that when the time comes he will make some circular supports for the tomatoes from some old fencing he saw in the corncrib loft. He follows along beside her, pushing dirt onto the onions with the flat of his hoe. Catherine can feel the heat of the sun through her jacket, and she thinks that there are only seven weeks until the summer solstice. She has stopped being surprised at how comfortable she is working with Laurits; it is almost as peaceful as working alone, and yet even the simplest of motions seems to be enhanced. She is crumbling compost into the bottom of a trench, and her hands seem to be understanding exactly the nature of its richness. When she was a girl Catherine used to sketch her own hands, with wonderment, and now, remembering that, she seems to be reminded of the richness of her own nature. She straightens up to see Laurits at the edge of the garden, aiming walnuts up into the tree at the last few nuts still clinging to the branches in their green casings.

Laurits is reading in the rocking chair by the dining-room window. After lunch he always takes this rest; Catherine has told him he reminds her of her grandfather, and he has told her that he reminds himself of his own grandfather. She has come up the lane with the mail, and she taps on his window as she passes on her way to the shop. In a few minutes she returns to the house.

"You have two letters today, Laurits," she says. "I think your lovely lady must be missing you." The postmarks are from California. Laurits has said that her name is Leah and that she is studying marine biology. She is twenty years old; Laurits is twenty-three.

Laurits puts down his magazine and takes the letters. A Swedish ivy plant is hanging in the window above the library table; Laurits begins to read his letters beneath this cascade of scalloped leaves. Outside the window green maple-blossom discs drift in the sun. Catherine sees Louie in the south field beyond the garden making a sweeping turn at the end of a row with the corn planter lifted from the ground; he drives with one hand as he twists in the tractor seat to gauge the beginning of the new row. Her own hands feel empty.

She pours herself a cup of coffee in the kitchen and goes upstairs to her drawing board. The bed is unmade, and the air is warm and still, almost like a summer afternoon. She is working on a schematic frontal section of the female reproductive organs, using books and charts loaned by Maxine, the biology professor. The new women's center has inquired about the publication date of this booklet; it will be used as well by high-school family-life classes and will be among the free literature available to incoming college freshmen. Maxine is in her late fifties. One of her daughters ran way from home at the age of seventeen; it was very bad for a while, Maxine has said, but then gradually things worked themselves out. Catherine looks at her drawing and understands that what she is seeing is a section through a moment in evolution.

It is June. The boxes are packed, the van is loaded for John's Chicago fair. Today Tom is fifteen. They are having his party at lunchtime, before Catherine and John must leave, and while Tom assembles his new fishing gear, Catherine cuts down through the cake. John is at the other end of the table, waiting for the coffee to be ready. His effort the last few weeks has been tremendous. Even he has called himself a maniac. The kiln has been fired twice a week. His final project has been a series of huge vases, almost human in their forms, with gentle bellies and flared rims and handles akimbo—his vestal vessels, he has said, giving one of them a pat.

He works at his pipe and squints at Tom; Catherine can see him searching for a humorous attack: no son of his is going to come off easily from a birthday.

"That's pretty sophisticated gear for a young whippersnapper like you," he says.

"Whippersnappers are good at things like this," says Tom as he carefully fits together the sections of the rod. He is barely suppressing his excitement with the gleaming tackle and newly fitted-out box, all chosen by his father, everyone knows. Laurits has promised to take the boys catfishing and camping overnight on the river. Drew watches everything from a calculated slouch.

"So, Laurits," says John, "do you think you can keep these lads in line? No ruckuses on the Mississippi?"

"We kids will not besmirch the family name," says Laurits. "Simply think of us as young gentlemen off on a naturalistic holiday."

"Mind you look to the goats before you leave," says John to the boys.

Catherine pours the coffee in silence. She is disorganized; her bag is scarcely packed. She is remembering the long labor of her first son's birth, her partial disbelief that it was actually happening . . .

"Now there's a well got-up woman," says John to her later in the bedroom. "The brow, the bosom, the lovely thighs—a figurehead for our ship, worthy, if you pardon the expression, of breasting the crest. Together, my dear, we will navigate the evil city and bring back lots and lots of money."

"John, will you please be quiet? You're exhausting me."

"I'm exhausting you?"

"How was I exhausting you?" he asks on the highway.

"Just talk straight now, all right? We're alone, there's no one listening."

"We are alone, aren't we?" he says that night in the hotel, smiling down at her. City sirens pulsate on an eerie stratum of air, disembodied. All night there are voices and shouts, neon-light waves. Catherine does not feel that she is sleeping, but then she wakes, terrified for the safety of her children; in a moment she remembers that one child is already dead. John sleeps curved and dark.

The bathroom is white, white everywhere, but she can only think of the thousands of people who have touched its slickness without leaving a mark. She sees that her period has begun: her skin, their toothbrushes, and the brownish blood are the only colors in the room.

She sleeps again, floating on sound and the sensations of her body. Hanna is calling her on the telephone, a child's voice, difficult to make out. Yes? she says to her. Yes? Speak up! Everything but her own voice is indistinguishable; the telephone cord is slowly disintegrating. She wakes into the morning.

"This hasn't been too bad for a rickety-dinky hotel," says John, pleased with himself.

He is opening the curtains. "Will you come with me to the village square, my love, to peddle our wares?"

She puts on a large straw hat and over her swollen breasts a white blouse, open at the neck.

The week before Laurits had worked bare-chested in the garden, and she had seen that he was smooth and compact, self-contained. He had knotted a red scarf around his brow, and his back had glistened.

"Come on, lass, let's get a move on," says John.

Movement: she must move in spite of herself; she can no longer be in last week's garden, bending over vegetables.

"Are you all right, love?" asks John in the coffee shop.

Outside in the street the light is too bright; there is too much light, everywhere; even beneath the mottled plane trees at the fair she finds only an overexposed confusion of dapple. She hides beneath her hat.

"You're quiet, love," says John after he has made another sale. Year after year many of the same people return to his booth. Catherine looks up to see the face of Dr. Avakian, inviting them to dinner that night. She feels herself nodding. Dr. Avakian has greyed remarkably in the past year. He and his wife live childless in a high apartment near the lake. Catherine knows all about the evening already; she can see the iced wine, the crêpes filled with crab, the fresh strawberries, the strong coffee and pastry in the living room above the reflecting water. Each year Dr. Avakian buys two, perhaps three or four hundred dollars' worth of pottery. It is obvious that he considers himself a patron and that he must search for ways in which to spend the money of his middle age.

Catherine presses her knuckles into her eyes. The innards of her body are heavy and sinking toward the gravity of earth; within and without the world seems constructed of motion and loss. She tries to imagine her sons in a rented boat at the mouth of a Mississippi slough; what she see is Laurits, selecting bait from a bucket.

As they speed home across Illinois the next afternoon, the landscape for many miles outside the urban fringes seems tentative and barren, as if it had already lost its vigor in the face of the impending lava-creep of the city. It is not really until the Mississippi itself that Catherine begins to relax. Looking down from the bridge, she sees the wide river flowing effortlessly between its banks and feels reassured, as if she herself had caught an easier current. Inland John turns onto back gravel roads and they approach the farm into the sun, beside newly cultivated corn rows that look like giant thin-man legs running with the car. Catherine opens her window and takes a full breath of earthy air; she feels the presence of her heart.

The weather turns very warm. At the end of the month Tom and Drew prepare to take a bus out to camp in Colorado where they will ride horses, backpack, and fish for trout.

"I hope those whippersnappers appreciate this," says John as he closes the van on their gear.

Catherine takes the pipe from his mouth to kiss him. "Take care of yourself in that big-town bus station."

"I plan on being alert," says John. "Not a hussy will pass my notice."

"You sure know how to talk big," she says, feeling his arm around her. The boys are in the shop saying good-bye to Laurits. The yard is still and empty except for scattered dozing cats, and yet Catherine thinks that perhaps she and her husband are being observed. He seems charming and inscrutable, and as she lets him shuffle her through a few dance steps and lower her into an embrace of mock passion, she finds herself looking up with alarm into his grinning face.

"John," she suddenly says. "Maybe I should come along for the afternoon. Do you want company?"

"I thought you wanted some precious solitude."

"I did. I do." She looks at her watch. "There really isn't time to get ready."

"Look," he says, taking her by the shoulders, "I'll take care of our sons, and I'll take care of myself, and you take some time for yourself the way you planned, all right?"

Catherine stands silent in front of him, and for a moment his mannerisms seem to fall away, and what slams against her is his suffering.

The boys come loping across the yard from the shop.

She wants to touch him. Her throat tightens into pain. Hanna! John!

Laurits follows slowly behind the boys, wearing a rubber apron, his forearms and hands reddish.

"The troops are assembled," says John, and the moment has passed.

Catherine kisses her sons, everyone is joking, and then the doors slam and the van pulls away.

"I hope they get some good trout," says Laurits; "there's nothing in the world like mountain trout."

Catherine nods. She goes inside the back door and presses her fist to her mouth. "O, my God," she hears herself whispering. "O, my God," and she feels that her hands are being flung, taut, above her head. And then she picks up a rainjacket from the floor and puts it back on a hook. In the kitchen she watches her hands finishing the dishes. When they are done and the plants hanging above the sink have been watered, she takes down a sketchpad from the top of the refrigerator and goes out to the side porch. She draws the walnut tree and in the foreground the trunk of the wounded maple. Then she goes down to the garden and sits close to a pepper plant, letting her pencil understand the way the white blossoms are giving way to tiny green buds of fruit. She is sitting on a mulch of straw. Not far away a yellow and black spider is zigzagging a reinforcement in his web between two tomato plants. It is almost too hot to stay where she is, but she continues, turning from the peppers to the fuzzy eggplant leaves, and then to the squash vines and nasturtiums. For a long time she feels as if only the motions of her hands are keeping back the tears; then gradually she begins to forget about everything but the nature of what she is observing. At last she takes off her shoes and lies back on the hot straw.

All around her are the rustlings of insects or of plants growing. A hawk circles several times overhead and then banks out of sight. She shields her eyes with a forearm smelling of tomato leaves and herbs.

She doesn't know if she has slept, but at an indeterminate moment the air has changed; a faint cool dampness has swept the garden. She sits up. From the south a mass of round white clouds is approaching rapidly; from the north a front of blackness is bearing down with amazing speed. It is fascinating, she thinks, and the heat, thank God, will lift; then an instant later she knows the danger.

"Laur-its, Laur-its," she yells, scrambling into her shoes and running to the shop. She throws the sketchpad inside the screen door, shouting, "Laurits, a storm is coming," and without stopping further heads for the small goat-pasture behind the barn. "Here babes, here babes," she calls to the already frightened animals. She has to lift the kids over the stone sill of the barn. One door after another she runs to secure; the cloud masses converge as she is struggling with the huge double doors of the barn's central passageway. Laurits appears beside her. By the time they are running for the house, a whipping rain has begun. A trash can sails across the yard, then a tree branch.

They tend to doors and windows. The house is moaning, the windows rattling, the metal weather stripping whining above even the high-pitched fury of the storm. Outside the air is greenish through the almost horizontal slant of the rain. A bolt of lightning to the west appears to stab a nearby field; thunder shakes the house. Laurits thuds down the stairs with a blanket around his neck. He takes her by the arm—"Upstairs is all right, let's get down"—and they descend into the basement fruit cellar where the hundred-year-old lime foundation stones are damp and motionless. Laurits sinks down underneath a workbench and opens his blanketed arm like a wing for her to enter.

They are in one of Hanna's old forgotten playhouses, one of the many hideouts that she had fashioned for herself around the farm. This one consists of a few peach crates beneath the bench, set up as shelves, and on the floor a mildewed playpen pad. The child had tied some yarn around one of the crates as a sort of decoration, and inside Catherine finds a canning jar filled with rotting kernels of corn and one large spider, alive. She puts it down slowly. The mind of her child seems near enough to touch.

Catherine cannot stop the tears now; she feels that she has never been so close to her sorrow. Lowering her forehead to Laurit's knee, she lets herself become a rounded shape of grieving. "Hey," he says, "hey," as he begins to stroke her hair and back. Her body is wracked by an accumulation of feeling, as if the sobs are coming out of her bones. "Catherine," says Laurits, "here, here." He has taken her close to him in the cramped musty space; from upstairs comes the faint screaming of the wind. "Catherine, what is it, what is it? There, don't talk. Catherine." His hands over her ears are muffling all sound. Her brow is being stroked; he is kissing her eyes. They are underneath a storm, in a space made by a child. "You're having a bad time," says Laurits, holding her head against him. She is snuffling now and breathing more quietly; her brain feels as if a searing connection has been made between its two sides, leaving behind a warm fluidity. "That's better now," says Laurits. She feels herself being rocked slightly; with her eyes closed she has a slight sensation of weightlessness. Laurits is cupping her breasts with a gentle hand of comfort.

"There now," says Laurits after a time. "Let's go upstairs and see what's been happening. Do you think it's safe?" He wraps the blanket around them both and pulls her in close against him as they start up the stairs. "Catherine," he says, stopping halfway up to kiss her hair. He lowers his forehead to hers, and she lets her hands rest upon his chest.

They go from room to room, window to window. The yard and lane are strewn with tree limbs, and one huge branch has crashed down through the electrical wires to the shop. "Laurits, that's a hot line there, we should call," but when they go to the telephone, those wires are silent. They test random lights and all are dead. In the wake of the lightning and thunder and furious wind is now a heavy turbulent rain, being blown in thick curtains across the fields. The light inside the house is a brownish chiaroscuro.

Laurits sits down in a chair against a kitchen wall. Catherine goes across the room and sits beneath the useless telephone. They are being careful now. "I'm going to guess that for you there has always been only John," Laurits says quietly.

"How do you know that? Do you find it strange?"

"I think I would have expected it."

"It's not that I haven't loved others, but well, yes, there's been only John. We moved from place to place; we went through a lot together. And then, too, I've been a mother for a long time." She draws an uneven breath. "You must understand that has something to do with it."

"You don't have to apologize."

"It's different for you?"

"Literally, yes, but I've told you, Catherine, I'm my own grandfather; I'm not sure where I belong."

"And Leah?"

"Leah? Leah is like water, you could say she follows her own natural laws. She's living with someone else this summer."

"I had no idea," says Catherine. "Is that all right with you?"

"I take large chances," says Laurits. "She's a brilliant girl; she's absolutely set in her scientific interests." In the half-light Catherine watches him shrug. "We'll see," he says.

"And meanwhile, back at the farm?" she asks gently.

"God, Catherine, don't mock me—are you mocking me?" He comes and stands in front of her. "Answer me." He is smiling.

"I'm not mocking you, Laurits. It's just us, here; I'm seeing it all."

He hunkers down in front of her and circles his arms around her hips. "Why were you crying? Can you tell me that?"

She tips back her head against the wall and feels how close the tears still are. Images are welling to the surface: the face of John that noon, the layers and layers of his reality; the countless vibrant expressions of her daughter, her lovely child; her own life, obscure essence, visible movement, change, desire.

Laurits has laid his head in her lap. "Come on," he says, "we can't talk here." He lifts her to her feet. "Come on, follow grandpa." He leads her up the stairs and into Hanna's room, his room, and to the same bed where the child had first wakened in the night with the pain—a headache no mother's hand could touch.

"Laurits—"

"We'll be good. Just talk to me." He covers them both with a light blanket. "Just tell me." He opens her

blouse and lays his cheek against her breast; she can
feel the steady waves of his warm breath across her
nipple. She strokes his hair and begins to talk. She
tells him about the hospital, the days and nights that
became indistinguishable, the one resurgence of hope
when the child's eyelids fluttered and her mouth seemed
to be straining to speak; she tells him about the dreams,
how she is certain that the child's spirit is present, that
the other side of death exists even though it's untouch-
able; and then she is talking about John, about the
days when he cannot work at all and his mockery turns
inward and consumes his energy and her own as well,
about the way the death has cut through their marriage to reveal a section-view of bewilderment barely
concealed by stylized action—not that they aren't tender, not that there isn't pleasure in each other and in
life: it's just—how shall she put it—it's perhaps that a
reality has been given them that they haven't been
able to incorporate yet; it doesn't fit into the old
patterns. Does he understand, is she making sense at
all? And then she realizes that it is herself she is
talking about, grieving for: the inability of her hands
to help her child, the weakness of her mind to understand what is now happening, the confusions of her
heart. Her voice continues. She doesn't know what is
coming next, she simply doesn't know, and she is
asking herself, will she be able to live it?

When John returns at dark, they are in the kitchen
making supper in candlelight. He is drenched from
having run up through the rain from the end of the
branch-choked lane. "The survivors!" he exclaims, coming to the stove and putting an arm around each one
of them. "Did you know, my children, that you have
only narrowly escaped the fate of Louie's great-aunt?"

"We haven't had any radio, John," says Catherine.
She has laid her own cheek against his wet one.

"The tornado touched down four miles north of
here."

"That close!" whistles Laurits.

"Was anyone hurt, John?" asks Catherine.

"No one reported, but I saw damage to buildings, and lots of trees."

"What's this about Louie's great-aunt?" asks Laurits.

"You mean you haven't heard that story yet?" says John. "Catherine, love, I'll leave you to the telling while I go get dry and then may I suggest a bottle of wine for this murky night?" He shudders dramatically in his clothes.

She lays a hand on his arm. "And how were the boys? Did they seem to feel all right about leaving?"

"They couldn't wait to get away, and that's the honest truth. They said, bye, Dad—that's all, just bye old Dad." John waves his own hand in farewell and soft-shoes himself out of the kitchen.

Catherine begins to set the table.

Laurits is looking at her. "So? the story?"

"Well, once upon a time Louie had a great-aunt. I don't know her name but she lived in the days of high button shoes. Now this great-aunt was caught up in a tornado, picked up bodily; and she was finally found in a field two miles away, unhurt but covered with scratches and bruises, her hair was a mass of brambles, and—here's the crazy thing—the wind had left her absolutely stark naked except for one high button shoe."

"One high button shoe?" repeats Laurits.

"One high button shoe."

"She was lucky. But she must have been mortified."

"So to speak."

They are laughing, and it is a great relief. The thought of Louie's great-aunt being propelled naked through the air with one external item of dignity intact is exactly the image they need for the end of this day, in this world of astounding variety. "What a story," says Laurits, whooping, breathless, and then he says more quietly, "but she must have blacked out, surely the force of the wind must have knocked her out."

"I suppose so," says Catherine, and she pauses above a sliced tomato. "Tell me, Laurits, if you had your choice, would you go through a tornado like that conscious or unconscious?"

"Good God, Catherine," says Laurits, "I'm going to make you answer that one yourself."

III

One hot afternoon in September while Laurits and John were testing the new kiln, Catherine took herself for a walk along the back roads of the section. There had been no rain for weeks, and the hushed crops and weeds were coated with a film of dust from the baked roadbed. Catherine strode along in spite of the heat; her body was strong from the months of outdoor work, and she felt vital and continuous to herself beside the stretching fields. The landscape to some eyes would have seemed monotonous, she supposed, but she was coming to exult in its apparent plainness; here her eyes could spread out, rested, and her mind could empty itself, and she could be seeing nothing but straight road, fields, fences, and predominant sky until one detail—a changing of light, the thwacking up of a pheasant from a thicket, or a stream of water, invisible from a distance, cutting through the surface fertility— would simultaneously define for her both the plainness and variety of her surroundings, like the first stroke on a sheet of blank paper.

Today she was thinking how much this vast swelling land seemed to have retained its character of primordial ocean floor, and her own eyes were seeing it: the knowledge of a progression through millennia to this present moment of late-summer dry lushness and quiet was passing through her, making her a special child of the universal elements. She stepped off the road and sat down in the minimal shade of an Osage orange tree, looking up with curiosity at the globs of wrinkled greenish fruit. It was true: she felt almost like a child, and what was more, she was gradually understanding that her own lost child was being returned to her, not as she in her suffering had dreamt of the reunion, but simply as she herself was moving to the embrace.

She rested until she became thirsty, and then she got up and continued on the last two-mile stretch, lowering her eyes slightly under the sun, tasting dust on the dryness of her lips; and but for this chance direction of her gaze, she might have missed the dead frog: levelled by a car in the dust of the road, it was like the perfect shadow of a leap, yet really there, paper-thin and dried, complete with flattened eye sockets and delicately spread feet. She bent down to study the creature, her own shadow a foreshortened shape beside her on the dust; and toward this desicated carcass that like a heiroglyph said purely, *frog*, and toward the even more cryptic configuration of herself she felt a quickened outpouring of that which long ago had come to be called love.

Caviar

T. CORAGHESSAN BOYLE

T. Coraghessan Boyle was born in 1948 in Peekskill, New York. "I don't think I ever read a book until I was eighteen," he says. "I went to college as a music major and then taught high school to stay out of Vietnam. But mainly I was just hanging out, taking a lot of drugs." In 1972, he entered the Iowa Writer's Workshop and began writing stories. Since then he's published three novels, Water Music (1982), Budding Prospects (1984), and World's End (1987), as well as two books of short stories, The Descent of Man and Other Stories (1979), and Greasy Lake and Other Stories (1985). He lives in Los Angeles, teaches writing at the University of Southern California, and occasionally plays saxophone with a rockabilly band.

Near the beginning of "Stones in My Passway, Hellhound on My Trail," Boyle describes the life and times of the great blues guitarist Robert Johnson. "It is 1938, Dust Bowl, New Deal. F.D.R. is on the radio, and somebody in Robisonville is naming a baby after Jesse Owens. Once, on the road to Natchez, Robert saw a Pierce Arrow and talked about it for a week. Another time he spent six weeks in Chicago and didn't know the World's Fair was going on. Now he plays his guitar up and down the Mississippi, and in Louisiana, Texas, and Arkansas. He's never heard of Hitler and he hasn't eaten in two days." The poignancy, social history, and imagination evoked within this passage only begins to

*suggest Boyle's inventive gift of storytelling. His prose
is laced with satire, farce, even tragedy, and he has the
nerve to try anything: Idi Amin comes to New York as
the guest of honor at a dada festival; President Eisen-
hower and Nina Khruschev engage in a doomed love
affair; and in the following story a childless couple
bring a surrogate mother into their home with disturb-
ing consequences. He has been compared to writers as
disparate as S.J. Perelman, Evelyn Waugh, and Thomas
Pynchon.*

I ought to tell you right off I didn't go to college. I
was on the wrong rung of the socioeconomic ladder, if
you know what I mean. My father was a commercial
fisherman on the Hudson, till the PCBs got to him, my
mother did typing and filing down at the lumberyard,
and my grandmother crocheted doilies and comforters
for sale to rich people. Me, I took over my father's
trade. I inherited the shack at the end of the pier, the
leaky fourteen-foot runabout with the thirty-five-horse
Evinrude motor and the seine that's been in the family
for three generations. Also, I got to move into the old
man's house when he passed on, and he left me his
stamp collection and the keys to his '62 Rambler,
rusted through till it looked like a gill net hung out to
dry.

Anyway, it's a living. Almost. And if I didn't go to
college I do read a lot, magazines mostly, but books on
ecology and science too. Maybe it was the science part
that did me in. You see, I'm the first one around
here—I mean, me and Marie are the first ones—to
have a baby this new way, where you can't have it on
your own. Dr. Ziss said not to worry about it, a little
experiment, think of it as a gift from heaven.

Some gift.

But don't get me wrong, I'm not complaining. What
happens happens, and I'm as guilty as anybody, I
admit it. It's just that when the guys at the Flounder

Inn are sniggering in their beer and Marie starts looking at me like I'm a toad or something, you've got to put things in perspective, you've got to realize that it was her all along, she's the one that started it.

"I want a baby," was how she put it.

It was April, raw and wet. Crocuses and dead man's fingers were poking through the dirt along the walk, and the stripers were running. I'd just stepped in the door, beat, chilled to the teeth, when she made her announcement. I went straight for the coffeepot. "Can't afford it," I said.

She didn't plead or try to reason with me. All she did was repeat herself in a matter-of-fact tone, as if she were telling me about some new drapes or a yard sale, and then she marched through the kitchen and out the back door. I sipped at my coffee and watched her through the window. She had a shovel. She was burying something. Deep. When she came back in, her nose was running a bit and her eyes were crosshatched with tiny red lines.

"What were you doing out there?" I asked.

Her chin was crumpled, her hair was wild. "Burying something."

I waited while she fussed with the teapot, my eyebrows arched like question marks. Ten seconds ticked by. "Well, what?"

"My diaphragm."

I've known Marie since high school. We were engaged for five years while she worked for *Reader's Digest* and we'd been married for three and a half when she decided she wanted some offspring. At first I wasn't too keen on the idea, but then I had to admit she was right: the time had come. Our lovemaking had always been lusty and joyful, but after she buried the diaphragm it became tender, intense, purposeful. We tried. For months we tried. I'd come in off the river, reeking of the creamy milt and silver roe that floated two inches deep in the bottom of the boat while fifty-

and sixty-pound stripers gasped their last, come in like a wild bull or something, and Marie would be waiting for me upstairs in her nightie and we'd do it before dinner, and then again after. Nothing happened.

Somewhere around July or August, the sweet blueclaw crabs crawling up the riverbed like an army on maneuvers and the humid heat lying over the valley like a cupped hand, Marie went to Sister Eleazar of the Coptic Brotherhood of Ethiop. Sister Eleazar was a black woman, six feet tall at least, in a professor's gown and a fez with a red tassel. Leroy Lent's wife swore by her. Six years Leroy with his wife had been going at it, and then they went to Sister Eleazar and had a pair of twins. Marie thought it was worth a try, so I drove her down there.

The Coptic Brotherood of Ethiop occupied a lime-green building the size of a two-car garage with a steeple and cross pinned to the roof. Sister Eleazar answered our knock scowling, a little crescent of egg yolk on her chin. "What you want?" she said.

Standing there in the street, a runny-eyed Chihuahua sniffing at my heels, I listened to Marie explain our problem and watched the crescent of egg on Sister Eleazar's face fracture with her smile. "Ohhh," she said, "well, why didn't you say so? Come own in, come own in."

There was one big room inside, poorly lit. Old bottom-burnished pews stretched along three of the four walls and there was a big shiny green table in the center of the floor. The table was heaped with religious paraphernalia—silver salvers and chalices and tinted miniatures of a black man with a crown dwarfing his head. A cot and an icebox huddled against the back wall, which was decorated with magazine clippings of Africa. "Right here, sugar," Sister Eleazar said, leading Marie up to the table. "Now, you take off your coat and your dress, and less examine them wombs."

Marie handed me her coat, and then her tight blue

dress with the little white clocks on it, while Sister
Eleazar cleared the chalices and whatnot off the table.
The Chihuahua had followed us in, and now it sprang
up onto the cot with a sigh and buried its nose in its
paws. The room stank of dog.

"All right," Sister Eleazar said, turning back to
Marie, "you climb up own the table now and stretch
yourself out so Sister 'Leazar can listen to your insides
and say a prayer over them barren wombs." Marie
complied with a nervous smile, and the black woman
leaned forward to press an ear to her abdomen. I
watched the tassel of Sister Eleazar's fez splay out
over Marie's rib cage and I began to get excited: the
place dark and exotic, Marie in brassiere and panties,
laid out on the table like a sacrificial virgin. Then the
sister was mumbling something—a prayer, I guess—in
a language I'd never heard before. Marie looked embarrassed. "Don't you worry about nothin'," Sister
Eleazar said, looking up at me and winking. "I got
just the thing."

She fumbled around underneath the cot for a minute, then came back to the table with a piece of blue
chalk—the same as they use in geography class to
draw rivers and lakes on the blackboard—and a big
yellow can of Colman's dry mustard. She bent over
Marie like a heart surgeon, and then, after a few
seconds of deliberation, made a blue X on Marie's
lower abdomen and said, "Okay, honey, you can get
up now."

I watched Marie shrug into her dress, thinking the
whole thing was just a lot of superstitious mumbo jumbo
and pisantry, when I felt Sister Eleazar's fingers on my
arm; she dipped her head and led me out the front
door. The sky was overcast. I could smell rain in the
air. "Listen," the black woman whispered, handing
me the can of mustard, "the problem ain't with her,
it's with you. Must be you ain't penetratin' deep
enough." I looked into her eyes, trying to keep my
face expressionless. Her voice dropped. "What you do

is this: make a plaster of this here mustard and rub it on your parts before you go into her, and it'll force out that 'jaculation like a torpedo coming out a submarine—know what I mean?" Then she winked. Marie was at the door. A man with a hoe was digging at his garden in the next yard over. "Oh yeah," the sister said, holding out her hand, "you want to make a donation to the Brotherhood, that'll be eleven dollars and fifty cents."

I never told Marie about the mustard—it was too crazy. All I said was that the sister had told me to give her a mustard plaster on the stomach an hour after we had intercourse—to help the seeds take. It didn't work, of course. Nothing worked. But the years at *Reader's Digest* had made Marie a superstitious woman, and I was willing to go along with just about anything as long as it made her feel better. One night I came to bed and she was perched naked on the edge of the footstool, wound round three times with a string of garlic. "I thought that was for vampires?" I said. She just parted her lips and held out her arms.

In the next few weeks she must have tried every quack remedy in the book. She kept a toad in a clay pot under the bed, ate soup composed of fish eyes and roe, drank goat's milk and cod-liver oil, and filled the medicine chest with elixirs made from nimble weed and rhinoceros horn. Once I caught her down in the basement, dancing in the nude round a live rooster. I was eating meat three meals a day to keep my strength up. Then one night I came across an article about test-tube babies in *Science Digest*. I studied the pictures for a long while, especially the one at the end of the article that showed this English couple, him with a bald dome and her fat as a sow, with their little test-tube son. Then I called Marie.

Dr. Ziss took us right away. He sympathized with our plight, he said, and would do all he could to help

136 T. Coraghessan Boyle

us. First he would have to run some tests to see just what the problem was and whether it could be corrected surgically. He led us into the examining room and looked into our eyes and ears, tapped our knees, measured our blood pressure. He drew blood, squinted at my sperm under a microscope, took X rays, did a complete pelvic exam on Marie. His nurse was Irene Goddard, lived up the street from us. She was a sour, square-headed woman in her fifties with little vertical lines etched around her lips. She prodded and poked and pricked us and then had us fill out twenty or thirty pages of forms that asked about everything from bowel movements to whether my grandmother had any facial hair. Two weeks later I got a phone call. The doctor wanted to see us.

We'd hardly got our jackets off when Mrs. Goddard, with a look on her face like she was about to pull the switch at Sing Sing, showed us into the doctor's office. I should tell you that Dr. Ziss is a young man—about my age, I guess—with narrow shoulders, a little clipped mustache, and a woman's head of hair that he keeps brushing back with his hand. Anyway, he was sitting behind his desk sifting through a pile of charts and lab reports when we walked in. "Sit down," he said. "I'm afraid I have some bad news for you." Marie went pale, like she did the time the state troopers called about her mother's accident; her ankles swayed over her high heels and she fell back into the chair as if she'd been shoved. I thought she was going to cry, but the doctor forestalled her. He smiled, showing off all those flossed and fluoridated teeth: "I've got some good news too."

The bad news was that Marie's ovaries were shot. She was suffering from the Stein-Leventhal syndrome, he said, and was unable to produce viable ova. He put it to us straight: "She's infertile, and there's nothing we can do about it. Even if we had the facilities and the know-how, test-tube production would be out of the question."

Marie was stunned. I stared down at the linoleum for a second and listened to her sniffling, then took her hand.

Dr. Ziss leaned across the desk and pushed back a stray lock of hair. "But there is an alternative."

We both looked at him.

"Have you considered a surrogate mother? A young woman who'd be willing to impregnate herself artificially with the husband's semen—for a fee, of course—and then deliver the baby to the wife at the end of the term." He was smoothing his mustache. "It's being done all over the country. And if Mrs. Trimpie pads herself during her 'pregnancy' and 'delivers' in the city, none of your neighbors need ever know that the child isn't wholly and naturally yours."

My mind was racing. I was bombarded with selfish and acquisitive thoughts, seething with scorn for Marie—*she* was the one, *she* was defective, not me—bursting to exercise my God-given right to child and heir. It's true, it really is—you never want something so much as when somebody tells you can't have it. I found myself thinking aloud: "So it would really be half ours, and . . . and half—"

"That's right, Mr. Trimpie. And I have already contacted a young woman on your behalf, should you be interested."

I looked at Marie. Her eyes were waiting. She gave me a weak smile and pressed my hand.

"She's Caucasian, of course, attractive, fit, very bright: a first-year medical student in need of funds to continue her education."

"Um, uh," I fumbled for the words, "how much: I mean, if we decide to go along with it, how much would it cost?"

The doctor was ready for this one. "Ten thousand dollars," he said without hesitation, "plus hospital costs."

*   *   *

Two days later there was a knock at the door. A girl in peacoat and blue jeans stood there, flanked by a pair of scuffed acquamarine suitcases held shut with masking tape. She looked to be about sixteen, stunted and bony and pale, cheap mother-of-pearl stars for earrings, her red hair short and spiky, as if she were letting a crewcut grow out. I couldn't help thinking of those World War II movies where they shave the actresses' heads for consorting with the Germans; I couldn't help thinking of waifs and wanderers and runaway teenagers. Dr. Ziss's gunmetal Mercedes sat at the curb, clouds of exhaust tugging at the tailpipe in the chill morning air; he waved, and then ground away with a crunch of gravel. "Hi," the girl said, extending her hand. "I'm Wendy."

It had all been arranged. Dr. Ziss thought it would be a good idea if the mother-to-be came to stay with us two weeks or so before the "procedure," to give us a chance to get to know one another, and then maybe stay on with us through the first couple of months so we could experience the pregnancy firsthand; when she began to show she'd move into an apartment on the other side of town, so as not to arouse any suspicion among the neighbors. He was delicate about the question of money, figuring a commercial fisherman and a part-time secretary, with no college and driving a beat-up Rambler, might not exactly be rolling in surplus capital. But the money wasn't a problem really. There was the insurance payoff from Marie's mother—she'd been blindsided by a semi coming off the ramp on the thruway—and the thirty-five hundred I'd got for delivering spawning stripers to Con Ed so they could hatch fish to replace the ones sucked into the screens at the nuclear plant. It was sitting in the Country Trust, collecting five and a quarter percent, against the day some emergency came up. Well, this was it. I closed out the account.

The doctor took his fee and explained that the girl would get five thousand dollars on confirmation of pregnancy, and the balance when she delivered. Hospital costs would run about fifteen hundred dollars, barring complications. We shook hands on it, and Marie and I signed a form. I figured I could work nights at the bottling plant if I was strapped.

Now, with the girl standing there before me, I couldn't help feeling a stab of disappointment—she was pretty enough, I guess, but I'd expected something a little more, well, substantial. And red hair. It was a letdown. Deep down I'd been hoping for a blonde, one of those Scandinavian types you see in the cigarette ads. Anyway, I told her I was glad to meet her, and then showed her up to the spare room, which I'd cleaned up and outfitted with a chest of drawers, a bed and a Salvation Army desk, and some cheery knickknacks. I asked her if I could get her a bite to eat, Marie being at work and me waiting around for the tide to go out. She was sitting on the bed, looking tired; she hadn't even bothered to glance out the window at the view of Croton Bay. "Oh yeah," she said after a minute, as if she'd been asleep or daydreaming. "Yeah, that would be nice." Her eyes were gray, the color of drift ice on the river. She called me Nathaniel, soft and formal, like a breathless young schoolteacher taking attendance. Marie never called me anything but Nat, and the guys at the marina settled for Ace." Have you got a sandwich, maybe? And a cup of hot Nestlé's? I'd really like that, Nathaniel."

I went down and fixed her a BLT, her soft syllables tingling in my ears like a kiss. Dr. Ziss had called her an "oh pear" girl, which I guess referred to her shape. When she'd slipped out of her coat I saw that there was more to her than I'd thought—not much across the top, maybe, but sturdy in the hips and thighs. I couldn't help thinking it was a good sign, but then I had to check myself: I was looking at her like a horse breeder or something.

She was asleep when I stepped in with the sandwich and hot chocolate. I shook her gently and she started

up with a gasp, her eyes darting round the room as if
she'd forgotten where she was. "Oh yes, yes, thanks,"
she said, in that maddening, out-of-breath, little girl's
voice. I sat on the edge of the desk and watched her
eat, gratified to see that her teeth were strong and
even, and her nose just about right. "So you're a
medical student, Dr. Ziss tells me."

"Hm-hmm," she murmured, chewing. "First-year.
I'm going to take the spring semester off, I mean for
the baby and all—"

This was the first mention of our contract, and it fell
over the conversation like a lead balloon. She hesitated, and I turned red. Here I was, alone in the house
with a stranger, a pretty girl, and she was going to
have my baby.

She went on, skirting the embarrassment, trying to
brighten her voice. "I mean, I love it and all—med
school—but it's a grind already and really I don't see
how I can afford tuition, without, without"—she looked
up at me—"without your help."

I didn't know what to say. I stared into her eyes for
a minute and felt strangely excited, powerful, like a
pasha interviewing a new candidate for the harem.
Then I picked up the china sturgeon on the desk and
turned it over in my hands. "I didn't go to college," I
said. And then, as if I were apologizing, "I'm a
fisherman."

A cold rain was falling the day the three of us drove
down to Dr. Ziss's for the "procedure." The maples
were turning, the streets splashed with red and gold,
slick, glistening the whole world a cathedral. I felt
humbled somehow, respectful in the face of life and
the progress of the generations of man: *My seed is
going to take hold*, I kept thinking. *In half an hour I'll
be a father*. Marie and Wendy, on the other hand,
seemed oblivious to the whole thing, chattering away
like a sewing circle, talking about shoes and needlepoint and some actor's divorce. They'd hit off pretty

well, the two of them, sitting in the kitchen over coffee at night, going to movies and thrift shops together, trading gossip, looking up at me and giggling when I stepped into the room. Though Wendy didn't do much around the house—didn't do much more than lie in bed and stare at textbooks—I don't think Marie really minded. She was glad for the company, and there was something more too, of course: Wendy was making a big sacrifice for us. Both of us were deeply grateful.

Dr. Ziss was all smiles that afternoon, pumping my hand, kissing the girls, ushering us into his office like an impresario on opening night. Mrs. Goddard was more restrained. She shot me an icy look, as if I was conspiring to overthrow the Pope or corrupt Girl Scouts or something. Meanwhile, the doctor leaned toward Marie and Wendy and said something I didn't quite catch, and suddenly they were all three of them laughing like Canada geese. Where they laughing at me, I wondered, all at once feelings self-conscious and vulnerable, the odd man out. Dr. Ziss, I noticed, had his arm around Wendy's waist.

If I felt left out, I didn't have time to brood over it. Because Mrs. Goddard had me by the elbow and she was marching me down the hallway to the men's room, where she handed me a condom sealed in tinfoil and a couple of tattered girlie magazines. I didn't need the magazines. Just the thought of what was going to happen in the next room—Marie had asked the doctor if she could do the insemination herself—gave me an erection like a tire iron. I pictured Wendy leaning back on the examining table in a little white smock, nothing underneath, and Marie, my big loving wife, with this syringelike thing . . . that's all it took. I was out of the bathroom in sixty seconds, the wet condom tucked safely away in a sterilized jar.

Afterward, we shared a bottle of pink champagne and a lasagna dinner at Mama's Pasta House. My treat.

* * *

One morning, about a month later, I was lying in bed next to Marie and I heard Wendy pad down the hallway to the bathroom. The house was still, and a soft gray light clung to the window sill like a blanket. I was thinking of nothing, or maybe I was thinking of striped bass, sleek and silver, how they ride up out of the deep like pieces of a dream. Next thing I heard was the sound of gagging. Morning sickness, I thought, picking up on a phrase from one of the countless baby books scattered round the house, and suddenly, inexplicably, I was doubled over myself. "Aaaaargh," Wendy gasped, the sound echoing through the house, "aaaargh," and it felt like somebody was pulling my stomach inside out.

At breakfast, she was pale and haggard, her hair greasy and her eyes puffed out. She tried to eat a piece of dry toast, but wound up spitting it into her hand. I couldn't eat, either. Same thing the next day, and the next: she was sick, I was sick. I'd pull the cord on the outboard and the first whiff of exhaust would turn my stomach and I'd have to lean over and puke in the river. Or I'd haul the gill nets up off the bottom and the exertion would nearly kill me. I called the doctor.

"Sympathetic pregnancy," he said, his voice cracking at the far end of a bad connection. "Perfectly normal. The husband identifies with the wife's symptoms."

"But I'm not her husband."

"Husband, father: what difference does it make. You're it."

I thought about that. Thought about it when Wendy and I began to eat like the New York Jets at the training table, thought about it nights at the bottling plant, thought about it when Wendy came into the living room in her underwear one evening and showed us the hard white bulge that was already beginning to open her navel up like a flower. Marie was watching some soppy hospital show on TV; I was reading about the dead water between Manhattan and Staten Island—nothing living there, not even eels. "Look," Wendy said, an angels-in-heaven smile on her face, "it's starting to show." Marie got up and embraced her. I grinned like an idiot, thrilled at the way the panties grabbed her thighs—white nylon with dancing pink flowers—and how her little pointed breasts were beginning to strain at the brassiere. I wanted to put my tongue in her navel.

Next day, while Marie was at work, I tapped on Wendy's door. "Come on in," she said. She was wearing a housecoat, Japanese-y, with dragons and pagodas on it, propped up against the pillows reading an anatomy text. I told her I didn't feel like going down to the river and wondered if she wanted anything. She put the book down and looked at me like a pat of butter sinking into a halibut steak. "Yes,' she said, stretching it to two syllables, "as a matter of fact I do." Then she unbuttoned the robe. Later she smiled at me and said: "So what did we need the doctor for, anyway?"

If Marie suspected anything, she didn't show it. I think she was too caught up in th whole thing to have an evil thought about either one of us. I mean, she doted on Wendy, hung on her every word, came home from work each night and shut herself up in Wendy's room for an hour or more. I could hear them giggling. When I asked her what the deal was, Marie just shrugged. "You know," she said, "the usual—girls' talk and such." The shared experience had made them close, closer than sisters, and sometimes I would think of us as one big happy family. But I stopped short of telling Marie what was going on when she was out of the house. Once, years ago, I'd had a fling with a girl we'd known in high school—an arrow-faced little fox with starched hair and raccoon eyes. It had been brief and strictly biological, and then the girl had moved to Ohio. Marie never forgot it. Just the mention of Ohio—

even so small a thing as the TV weatherman describing a storm over the Midwest—would set her off.

I'd like to say I was torn, but I wasn't. I didn't want to hurt Marie—she was my wife, my best friend, I loved and respected her—and yet there was Wendy, with her breathy voice and gray eyes, bearing my child. The thought of it, of my son floating around in his own little sea just behind the sweet bulge of her belly . . . well, it inflamed me, got me mad with lust and passion and spiritual love too. Wasn't Wendy as much my wife as Marie? Wasn't marriage, at bottom, simply a tool for procreating the species? Hadn't Sarah told Abraham to go in unto Hagar? Looking back on it, I guess Wendy let me make love to her because maybe she was bored and a little horny, lying around in a negligee day and night and studying all that anatomy. She sure didn't feel the way I did—if I know anything, I know that now. But at the time I didn't think of it that way, I didn't think at all. Surrogate mother, surrogate wife. I couldn't get enough of her.

Everything changed when Marie taped a feather bolster around her waist and our "boarder" had to move over to Depew Street. ("Don't know what happened," I told the guys down at the Flounder, "she just up and moved out. Low on bucks, I guess." Nobody so much as looked up from their beer until one of the guys mentioned the Knicks game and Alex DeFazio turned to me and said, "So you got a bun in the oven, is what I hear.") I was at a loss. What with Marie working full-time now, I found myself stuck in the house, alone, with nothing much to do except wear a path in the carpet and eat my heart out. I could walk down to the river, but it was February and nothing was happening, so I'd wind up at the Flounder Inn with my elbows on the bar, watching the mollies and swordtails bump into the sides of the aquarium, hoping somebody would give me a lift across town. Of course Marie and I would drive over to Wendy's after dinner every couple of days or so, and I could talk to her on the telephone till my throat went dry—but it wasn't the same. Even the few times I did get over there in the day, I could feel it. We'd make love, but she seemed shy and reluctant, as if she were performing a duty or something. "What's wrong?" I asked her. "Nothing," she said. It was as if someone had cut a neat little hole in the center of my life.

One time, a stiff windy day in early March, I couldn't stand the sight of four walls any more and I walked the six miles across town and all the way out Depew Street. It was an ugly day. Clouds like steel wool, a dirty crust of ice underfoot, dog turds preserved like icons in the receding snowbanks. The whole way over there I kept thinking up various scenarios: Wendy and I would take the bus for California, then write Marie to come join us; we'd fly to the Virgin Islands and raise the kid on the beach; Marie would have an accident. When I got there, Dr. Ziss's Mercedes was parked out front. I thought that was pretty funny, him being there in the middle of the day, but then I told myself he was her doctor after all. I turned around and walked home.

Nathaniel Jr. was born in New York City at the end of June, nine pounds, one ounce, with a fluff of orange hair and milky gray eyes. Wendy never looked so beautiful. The hospital bed was cranked up, her hair, grown out now, was fresh-washed and brushed, she was wearing the turquoise earrings I'd given her. Marie, meanwhile, was experiencing the raptures of the saints. She gave me a look of pride and fulfillment, rocking the baby in her arms, cooing and beaming. I stole a glance at Wendy. There were two wet circles where her nipples touched the front of her gown. When she put Nathaniel to her breast I thought I was going to faint from the beauty of it, and from something else too: jealousy. I wanted her, then and there.

Dr. Ziss was on the scene, of course, all smiles, as if he'd been responsible for the whole thing. He pecked Marie's cheek, patted the baby's head, shook my hand,

and bent low to kiss Wendy on the lips. I handed him
a cigar. Three days later Wendy had her five thousand
dollars, the doctor and the hospital had been paid off,
and Marie and I were back in Westchester with our
son. Wendy had been dressed in a loose summer gown
and sandals when I gave her the check. I remember
she was sitting there on a lacquered bench, cradling
the baby, the hospital corridor lit up like a clerestory
with sunbeams. There were tears—mainly Marie's—and
promises to keep in touch. She handed over Nathaniel
as if he was a piece of meat or a sack of potatoes, no
regrets. She and Marie embraced, she rubbed her
cheek against mine and made a perfunctory little kissing noise, and then she was gone.

I held out for a week. Changing diapers, heating
formula, snuggling up with Marie and little Nathaniel,
trying to feel whole again. But I couldn't. Every time
I looked at my son I saw Wendy, the curl of the lips,
the hair, the eyes, the pout—in my distraction, I even
thought I heard something of her voice in his gasping
howls. Marie was asleep, the baby in her arms. I
backed the car out and headed for Depew Street.

The first thing I saw when I rounded the corner
onto Depew was the doctor's Mercedes, unmistakable,
gunmetal gray, gleaming at the curb like a slap in the
face. I was so startled to see it there I almost ran into
it. What was this, some kind of postpartum emergency
or something? It was 10:00 A.M. Wendy's curtains were
drawn. As I stamped across the lawn my fingers began
to tremble like they do when I'm tugging at the net
and I can feel something tugging back.

The door was open. Ziss was sitting there in T-shirt
and jeans, watching cartoons on TV and sipping at a
glass of milk. He pushed the hair back from his brow
and gave me a sheepish grin. "David?" Wendy called
from the back room. "David? Are you going out?" I
must have looked like the big loser on a quiz show or
something, because Ziss, for once, didn't have anything to say. He just shrugged his shoulders. Wendy's

voice, breathy as a flute, came at us again: "Because if you are, get me some sweetcakes and yogurt, and maybe a couple of corn muffins, okay? I'm hungry as a bear."

Ziss got up and walked to the bedroom door, mumbled something I couldn't hear, strode past me without a glance and went on out the back door. I watched him bend for a basketball, dribble around in the dirt, and then cock his arm for a shot at an imaginary basket. On the TV, Sylvester the cat reached into a trash can and pulled out a fish stripped to the bones. Wendy was standing in the doorway. She had nothing to say.

"Look, Wendy," I began. I felt betrayed, cheated, felt as if I was the brunt of a joke between this girl in the housecoat and the curly-headed hotshot fooling around on the lawn. What was his angle, I wondered, heart pounding at my chest, what was hers? "I suppose you two had a good laugh over me, huh?"

She was pouting, the spoiled child. "I fulfilled my part of the bargain."

She had. I got what I'd paid for. But all that had changed, couldn't she see that? I didn't want a son, I didn't want Marie; I wanted her. I told her so. She said nothing. "You've got something going with Ziss, right?" I said, my voice rising. "All along, right?"

She looked tired, looked as if she'd been up for a hundred nights running. I watched her shuffle across the room into the kitchenette, glance into the refrigerator, and come up with a jar of jam. She made herself a sandwich, licking the goo from her fingers, and then she told me I stank of fish. She said she couldn't have a lasting relationship with me because of Marie.

"That's a lot of crap, and you know it." I was shouting. Ziss, fifty feet away, turned to look through the open door.

"All right. It's because we're—" She put the sandwich down, wiped a smear of jelly from her lip. "Because we move in different circles."

"You mean because I'm not some fancy-ass doctor, because I didn't go to college."

She nodded. Slow and deliberate, no room for argument, she held my eyes and nodded.

I couldn't help it. Something just came loose in my head, and the next second I was out the door, knocking Ziss into the dirt. He kicked and scratched, tried to bite me on the wrist, but I just took hold of his hair and laid into his face while Wendy ran around in her Japanese housecoat, screeching like a cat in heat. By the time the police got there I'd pretty well closed up both his eyes and rearranged his dental work. Wendy was bending over him with a bottle of rubbing alcohol when they put the cuffs on me.

Next morning there was a story in the paper. Marie sent Alex DeFazio down with the bail money, and then she wouldn't let me in the house. I banged on the door halfheartedly, then tried one of the windows, only to find she'd nailed it shut. When I saw that, I was just about ready to explode, but then I figured what the hell and fired up the Rambler in a cloud of blue smoke. Cops, dogs, kids, and pedestrians be damned, I ran it like a stock car eight blocks down to the dock and left it steaming in the parking lot. Five minutes later I was planing across the river, a wide brown furrow fanning out behind me.

This was my element, sun, wind, water, life pared down to the basics. Gulls hung in the air like puppets on a wire, spray flew up in my face, the shore sank back into my wake until docks and pleasure boats and clapboard houses were swallowed up and I was alone on the broad gray back of the river. After a while I eased up on the throttle and began scanning the surface for the buoys that marked my gill nets, working by rote, the tight-wound spool in my chest finally beginning to pay out. Then I spotted them, white and red, jogged by the waves. I cut the engine, coasted in and caught hold of the nearest float.

Wendy, I thought, as I hauled at the ropes, ten years, twenty-five, a lifetime: every time I look at my son I'll see your face. Hand over hand, Wendy, Wendy, Wendy, the net heaving up out of the swirling brown depths with its pound of flesh. But then I wasn't thinking about Wendy any more, or Marie or Nathaniel Jr.—I was thinking about the bottom of the river, I was thinking about fins and scales and cold lidless eyes. The instant I touched the lead rope I knew I was on to something. This time of year it would be sturgeon, big as logs, long-nosed and barbeled, coasting up the riverbed out of some dim watery past, anadromous, preprogrammed, homing in on their spawning grounds like guided missiles. Just then I felt a pulsing in the soles of my sneakers and turned to glance up at the Day Liner, steaming by on its way to Bear Mountain, hundreds of people with picnic baskets and coolers, waving. I jerked at the net like a penitent.

There was a single sturgeon in the net, tangled up like a ball of string. It was dead. I strained to haul the thing aboard, six feet long, two hundred pounds. Cold from the depths, still supple, it hadn't been dead more than an hour—while I banged at my own front door, locked out, it had been thrashing in the dark, locked in. The gulls swooped low, mocking me. I had to cut it out of the net.

Back at the dock I got one of the beer drinkers to give me a hand and we dragged the fish over to the skinning pole. With strugeon, we hang them by the gills from the top of a ten-foot pole, and then we peel back the scutes like you'd peel a banana. Four or five of the guys stood there watching me, nobody saying anything. I cut all the way round the skin just below the big stiff gill plates and then made five vertical slits the length of the fish. Flies settled on the blade of the knife. The sun beat at the back of my head. I remember there was a guy standing there, somebody I'd never seen before, a guy in a white shirt with a kid about eight or so. The kid was holding a fishing pole.

They stepped back, both of them, when I tore the first strip of skin from the fish.

Sturgeon peels back with a raspy, nails-on-the-blackboard sort of sound, reminds me of tearing up sheets or ripping bark from a tree. I tossed the curling strips of leather in a pile, flies sawing away at the air, the big glistening pink carcass hanging there like a skinned deer, blood and flesh. Somebody handed me a beer: it stuck to my hand and I drained it in a gulp. Then I turned to gut the fish, me a doctor, the knife a scalpel, and suddenly I was digging into the vent like Jack the Ripper, slitting it all the way up to the gills in a single violent motion.

"How do you like that?" the man in the white shirt said. "She's got eggs in her."

I glanced down. There they were, wet, beaded, and gray, millions of them, the big clusters tearing free and dropping to the ground like ripe fruit. I cupped my hands and held the trembling mass of it there against the gashed belly, fifty or sixty pounds of the stuff, slippery roe running through my fingers like the silver coins from a slot machine, like a jackpot.

Shiloh

BOBBIE ANN MASON

*Bobbie Ann Mason was born in Mayfield, Kentucky,
in 1940. After graduating from the University of Kentucky, she went to New York City and worked as a
writer on a number of fan magazines—*Movie Stars,
Movie Life, *and* T.V. Star Parade. *My interest in childhood," she writes, "extends all the way from Nancy
Drew to Nabokov, whose magnificent childhood per-
meates all his works . . . He read Pushkin as a child,
whereas I read Nancy Drew. I am interested in that
contrast as a literary theme, and in the culture shock
one can experience because of geographical and eco-
nomic isolation." She received her Ph.D. from the
University of Connecticut. She has published three works
of fiction,* Shiloh and Other Stories *(1982),* In Country
(1985), and Spence and Lila *(1988) and two works of
criticism,* Nabokov's Garden: A Guide to Ada *(1974)
and* The Girl Sleuth: A Feminist Guide *(1985). In
1982 she won the PEN/Hemingway Award and was a
finalist for the National Book Critics' Book Award,
and the PEN/Faulkner Award.*

*If you picture an old stand of pine woods at dusk
with clapboard frame houses in the distance, and in the
foreground a K-Mart where the daughters of farmers
work as clerks and spend their breaks playing video
games, then you have an image of Bobbie Ann Mason's New South. It is a world of ordinary working-
class men and women where a disabled truckdriver passes*

151

*his time smoking marijuana and needlepointing, while
watching his wife firm up her pectorals with barbells.
They proceed with cautious trepidation toward the life-
style and cultural paraphernalia—New Wave music, shopping malls, Phil Donahue, and drug deals in supermarket
parking lots—of a landscape no longer rural, not yet
suburban. "You educated me, I was so out of it when I
met you," a wife who followed her Yankee husband
north says. "One day I was listening to Hank Williams
and shelling corn for the chickens, and the next day I
was expected to know what wines went with what."
Mason comments, "I think the culture I write about is
very distinctly Southern. I don't think the people I write
about are obsessed with the past. I don't think they
know anything about the Civil War, and I don't think
they care. They're kind of naive and optimistic for the
most part: they think better times are coming . . ."*

Bobbie Ann Mason lives in rural Pennsylvania.

L eroy Moffitt's wife, Norma Jean, is working on her
pectorals. She lifts three-pound dumbbells to warm
up, then progresses to a twenty-pound barbell. Standing with her legs apart, she reminds Leroy of Wonder
Woman.

"I'd give anything if I could just get these muscles to
where they're real hard," says Norma Jean. "Feel this
arm. It's not as hard as the other one."

"That's 'cause you're right-handed," says Leroy,
dodging as she swings the barbell in an arc.

"Do you think so?"

"Sure."

Leroy is a truckdriver. He injured his leg in a highway accident four months ago, and his physical therapy, which involves weights and a pulley, prompted
Norma Jean to try building herself up. Now she is
attending a body-building class. Leroy has been col-

Shiloh

153

lecting temporary disability since his tractor-trailer jack-
knifed in Missouri, badly twisting his left leg in its
socket. He has a steel pin in his hip. He will probably
not be able to drive his rig again. It sits in the backyard, like a gigantic bird that has flown home to roost.
Leroy has been home in Kentucky for three months,
and his leg is almost healed, but the accident frightened him and he does not want to drive any more long
hauls. He is not sure what to do next. In the meantime, he makes things from craft kits. He started by
building a miniature log cabin from notched Popsicle
sticks. He varnished it and placed it on the TV set,
where it remains. It reminds him of a rustic Nativity
scene. Then he tried string art (sailing ships on black
velvet), a macramé owl kit, a snap-together B-17 Flying
Fortress, and a lamp made out of a model truck, with
a light fixture screwed in the top of the cab. At first
the kits were diversions, something to kill time, but
now he is thinking about building a full-scale log house
from a kit. It would be considerably cheaper than
building a regular house, and besides, Leroy has grown
to appreciate how things are put together. He has
begun to realize that in all the years he was on the
road he never took time to examine anything. He was
always flying past scenery.

"They won't let you build a log cabin in any of the
new subdivisions," Norma Jean tells him.

"They will if I tell them it's for you," he says,
teasing her. Ever since they were married, he has
promised Norma Jean he would build her a new home
one day. They have always rented, and the house they
live in is small and nondescript. It does not even feel
like a home, Leroy realizes now.

Norma Jean works at the Rexall drugstore, and she
has acquired an amazing amount of information about
cosmetics. When she explains to Leroy the three stages
of complexion care, involving creams, toners, and mois-
turizers, he thinks happily of other petroleum products—
axle grease, diesel fuel. This is a connection between

him and Norma Jean. Since he has been home, he has
felt unusually tender about his wife and guilty over his
long absences. But he can't tell what she feels about
him. Norma Jean has never complained about his traveling; she has never made hurt remarks, like calling
his truck a "widow-maker." He is reasonably certain
she has been faithful to him, but he wishes she would
celebrate his permanent homecoming more happily.
Norma Jean is often startled to find Leroy at home,
and he thinks she seems a little disappointed about it.
Perhaps he reminds her too much of the early days of
their marriage, before he went on the road. They had
a child who died as an infant, years ago. They never
speak about their memories of Randy, which have
almost faded, but now that Leroy is home all the time,
they sometimes feel awkward around each other, and
Leroy wonders if one of them should mention the
child. He has the feeling that they are waking up out
of a dream together—that they must create a new
marriage, start afresh. They are lucky they are still
married. Leroy has read that for most people losing a
child destroys the marriage—or else he heard this on
Donahue. He can't always remember where he learns
things anymore.

At Christmas, Leroy bought an electric organ for
Norma Jean. She used to play the piano when she was
in high school. "It don't leave you," she told him
once. "It's like riding a bicycle."

The new instrument had so many keys and buttons
that she was bewildered by it at first. She touched the
keys tentatively, pushed some buttons, then pecked
out "Chopsticks." It came out in an amplified fox-trot
rhythm, with marimba sounds.

"It's an orchestra!" she cried.

The organ had a pecan-look finish and eighteen
preset chords, with optional flute, violin, trumpet, clar-
inet, and banjo accompaniments. Norma Jean mastered the organ almost immediately. At first she played
Christmas songs. Then she bought *The Sixties Songbook*

and learned every tune in it, adding variatio
with the rows of brightly colored buttons.

"I didn't like these old songs back then," s
"But I have this crazy feeling I missed somethi

"You didn't miss a thing," said Leroy.

Leroy likes to lie on the couch and smoke a joint and listen to Norma Jean play "Can't Take My Eyes Off You" and "I'll Be Back." He is back again. After fifteen years on the road, he is finally settling down with the woman he loves. She is still pretty. Her skin is flawless. Her frosted curls resemble pencil trimmings.

Now that Leroy has come home to stay, he notices how much the town has changed. Subdivisions are spreading across western Kentucky like an oil slick. The sign at the edge of town says "Pop: 11,500"—only seven hundred more than it said twenty years before. Leroy can't figure out who is living in all the new houses. The farmers who used to gather around the courthouse square on Saturday afternoons to play checkers and spit tobacco juice have gone. It has been years since Leroy has thought about the farmers, and they have disappeared without his noticing.

Leroy meets a kid named Stevie Hamilton in the parking lot at the new shopping center. While they pretend to be strangers meeting over a stalled car, Stevie tosses an ounce of marijuana under the front seat of Leroy's car. Stevie is wearing orange jogging shoes and a T-shirt that says CHATTAHOOCHEE SUPER-RAT. His father is a prominent doctor who lives in one of the expensive subdivisions in a new white-columned brick house that looks like a funeral parlor. In the phone book under his name there is a separate number, with the listing "Teenagers."

"Where do you get this stuff?" asks Leroy. "From your pappy?"

"That's for me to know and you to find out," Stevie says. He is slit-eyed and skinny.

"What else you got?"

"What you interested in?"

"Nothing special. Just wondered."

Leroy used to take speed on the road. Now he has to go slowly. He needs to be mellow. He leans back against the car and says, "I'm aiming to build me a log house, soon as I get time. My wife, though, I don't think she likes the idea."

"Well, let me know when you want me again," Stevie says. He has a cigarette in his cupped palm, as though sheltering it from the wind. He takes a long drag, then stomps it on the asphalt and slouches away.

Stevie's father was two years ahead of Leroy in high school. Leroy is thirty-four. He married Norma Jean when they were both eighteen, and their child Randy was born a few months later, but he died at the age of four months and three days. He would be about Stevie's age now. Norma Jean and Leroy were at the drive-in, watching a double feature (*Dr. Strangelove* and *Lover Come Back*), and the baby was sleeping in the back seat. When the first movie ended, the baby was dead. It was the sudden infant death syndrome. Leroy remembers handing Randy to a nurse at the emergency room, as though he were offering her a large doll as a present. A dead baby feels like a sack of flour. "It just happens sometimes," said the doctor, in what Leroy always recalls as a nonchalant tone. Leroy can hardly remember the child anymore, but he still sees vividly a scene from *Dr. Strangelove* in which the President of the United States was talking in a folksy voice on the hot line to the Soviet premier about the bomber accidentally headed toward Russia. He was in the War Room, and the world map was lit up. Leroy remembers Norma Jean standing catatonically beside him in the hospital and himself thinking: Who is this strange girl? He had forgotten who she was. Now scientists are saying that crib death is caused by a virus. Nobody knows anything, Leroy thinks. The answers are always changing.

When Leroy gets home from the shopping center, Norma Jean's mother, Mabel Beasley, is there. Until this year, Leroy has not realized how much time she spends with Norma Jean. When she visits, she inspects the closets and then the plants, informing Norma Jean when a plant is droopy or yellow. Mabel calls the plants "flowers," although there are never any blooms. She always notices if Norma Jean's laundry is piling up. Mabel is a short, overweight woman whose tight, brown-dyed curls look more like a wig than the actual wig she sometimes wears. Today she has brought Norma Jean an off-white dust ruffle she made for the bed; Mabel works in a custom-upholstery shop.

"This is the tenth one I made this year," Mabel says. "I got started and couldn't stop."

"It's real pretty," says Norma Jean.

"Now we can hide things under the bed," says Leroy, who gets along with his mother-in-law primarily by joking with her. Mabel has never really forgiven him for disgracing her by getting Norma Jean pregnant. When the baby died, she said that fate was mocking her.

"What's that thing?" Mabel says to Leroy in a loud voice, pointing to a tangle of yarn on a piece of canvas.

Leroy holds it up for Mabel to see. "It's my needlepoint," he explains. "This is a *Star Trek* pillow cover."

"That's what a woman would do," says Mabel. "Great day in the morning!"

"All the big football players on TV do it," he says.

"Why, Leroy, you're always trying to fool me. I don't believe you for one minute. You don't know what to do with yourself—that's the whole trouble. Sewing!"

"I'm aiming to build a log house," says Leroy. "Soon as my plans come."

"Like *heck* you are," says Norma Jean. She takes Leroy's needlepoint and shoves it into a drawer. "You have to find a job first. Nobody can afford to build now anyway."

Mabel straightens her girdle and says, "I still think before you get tied down y'all ought to take a little run to Shiloh."

"One of these days, Mama," Norma Jean says impatiently.

Mabel is talking about Shiloh, Tennessee. For the past few years, she has been urging Leroy and Norma Jean to visit the Civil War battleground there. Mabel went there on her honeymoon—the only real trip she ever took. Her husband died of a perforated ulcer when Norma Jean was ten, but Mabel, who was accepted into the United Daughters of the Confederacy in 1975, is still preoccupied with going back to Shiloh.

"I've been to kingdom come and back in that truck out yonder," Leroy says to Mabel, "but we never yet set foot in that battleground. Ain't that something? How did I miss it?"

"It's not even that far," Mabel says.

After Mabel leaves, Norma Jean reads to Leroy from a list she has made. "Things you could do," she announces. "You could get a job as a guard at Union Carbide, where they'd let you set on a stool. You could get on at the lumberyard. You could do a little carpenter work, if you want to build so bad. You could—"

"I can't do something where I'd have to stand up all day."

"You ought to try standing up all day behind a cosmetics counter. It's amazing that I have strong feet, coming from two parents that never had strong feet at all." At the moment Norma Jean is holding on to the kitchen counter, raising her knees one at a time as she talks. She is wearing two-pound ankle weights.

"Don't worry," says Leroy. "I'll do something."

"You could truck calves to slaughter for somebody. You wouldn't have to drive any big old truck for that."

"I'm going to build you this house," says Leroy. "I want to make you a real home."

"I don't want to live in any log cabin."

"It's not a cabin. It's a house."

"I don't care. It looks like a cabin."

"You and me together could lift those logs. It's just like lifting weights."

Norma Jean doesn't answer. Under her breath, she is counting. Now she is marching through the kitchen. She is doing goose steps.

Before his accident, when Leroy came home he used to stay in the house with Norma Jean, watching TV in bed and playing cards. She would cook fried chicken, picnic ham, chocolate pie—all his favorites. Now he is home alone much of the time. In the mornings, Norma Jean disappears, leaving a cooling place in the bed. She eats a cereal called Body Buddies, and she leaves the bowl on the table, with the soggy tan balls floating in a milk puddle. He sees things about Norma Jean that he never realized before. When she chops onions, she stares off into a corner, as if she can't bear to look. She puts on her house slippers almost precisely at nine o'clock every evening and nudges her jogging shoes under the couch. She saves bread heels for the birds. Leroy watches the birds at the feeder. He notices the peculiar way goldfinches fly past the window. They close their wings, then fall, then spread their wings to catch and lift themselves. He wonders if they close their eyes when they fall. Norma Jean closes her eyes when they are in bed. She wants the lights turned out. Even then, he is sure she closes her eyes.

He goes for long drives around town. He tends to drive a car rather carelessly. Power steering and an automatic shift make a car feel so small and inconsequential that his body is hardly involved in the driving process. His injured leg stretches out comfortably. Once or twice he has almost hit something, but even the prospect of an accident seems minor in a car. He cruises the new subdivisions, feeling like a criminal rehearsing for a robbery. Norma Jean is probably right about a log house being inappropriate here in the new subdivisions. All the houses look grand and complicated. They depress him.

One day when Leroy comes home from a drive he finds Norma Jean in tears. She is in the kitchen making a potato and mushroom-soup casserole, with grated-cheese topping. She is crying because her mother caught her smoking.

"I didn't hear her coming. I was standing here puffing away pretty as you please," Norma Jean says, wiping her eyes.

"I knew it would happen sooner or later," says Leroy, putting his arm around her.

"She don't know the meaning of the word 'knock,' " says Norma Jean. "It's a wonder she hadn't caught me years ago."

"Think of it this way," Leroy says. "What if she caught me with a joint?"

"You better not let her!" Norma Jean shrieks. "I'm warning you, Leroy Moffitt!"

"I'm just kidding. Here, play me a tune. That'll help you relax."

Norma Jean puts the casserole in the oven and sets the timer. Then she plays a ragtime tune, with horns and banjo, as Leroy lights up a joint and lies on the couch, laughing to himself about Mabel's catching him at it. He thinks of Stevie Hamilton—a doctor's son pushing grass. Everything is funny. The whole town seems crazy and small. He is reminded of Virgil Mathis, a boastful policeman Leroy used to shoot pool with. Virgil recently led a drug bust in a back room at a bowling alley, where he seized ten thousand dollars' worth of marijuana. The newspaper had a picture of him holding up the bags of grass and grinning widely. Right now, Leroy can imagine Virgil breaking down the door and arresting him with a lungful of smoke. Virgil would probably have been alerted to the scene because of all the racket Norma Jean is making. Now she sounds like a hard-rock band. Norma Jean is terrific. When she switches to a Latin-rhythm version of "Sunshine Superman," Leroy hums along. Norma Jean's foot goes up and down, up and down.

"Well, what do you think?" Leroy says, when Norma Jean pauses to search through her music.

"What do I think about what?"

His mind has gone blank. Then he says, "I'll sell my rig and build a house." That wasn't what he wanted to say. He wanted to know what she thought—what she *really* thought—about them.

"Don't start in on that again," says Norma Jean. She begins playing "Who'll Be the Next in Line?"

Leroy used to tell hitchhikers his whole life story—about his travels, his hometown, the baby. He would end with a question: "Well, what do you think?" It was just a rhetorical question. In time, he had the feeling that he'd been telling the same story over and over to the same hitchhikers. He quit talking to hitchhikers when he realized how his voice sounded—whining and self-pitying, like some teenage-tragedy song. Now Leroy has the sudden impulse to tell Norma Jean about himself, as if he had just met her. They have known each other so long they have forgotten a lot about each other. They could become reacquainted. But when the oven timer goes off and she runs to the kitchen, he forgets why he wants to do this.

The next day, Mabel drops by. It is Saturday and Norma Jean is cleaning. Leroy is studying the plans of his log house, which have finally come in the mail. He has them spread out on the table—big sheets of stiff blue paper, with diagrams and numbers printed in white. While Norma Jean runs the vacuum, Mabel drinks coffee. She sets her coffee cup on a blueprint.

"I'm just waiting for time to pass," she says to Leroy, drumming her fingers on the table.

As soon as Norma Jean switches off the vacuum,

Mabel says in a loud voice, "Did you hear about the datsun dog that killed the baby?"

Norma Jean says, "The word is 'dachshund.' "

"They put the dog on trial. It chewed the baby's legs off. The mother was in the next room all the time." She raises her voice. "They thought it was neglect."

Norma Jean is holding her ears. Leroy manages to open the refrigerator and get some Diet Pepsi to offer Mabel. Mabel still has some coffee and she waves away the Pepsi.

"Datsuns are like that," Mabel says. "They're jealous dogs. They'll tear a place to pieces if you don't keep an eye on them."

"You better watch out what you're saying, Mabel," says Leroy.

"Well, facts is facts."

Leroy looks out the window at his rig. It is like a huge piece of furniture gathering dust in the backyard. Pretty soon it will be an antique. He hears the vacuum cleaner. Norma Jean seems to be cleaning the living room rug again.

Later, she says to Leroy, "She just said that about the baby because she caught me smoking. She's trying to pay me back."

"What are you talking about?" Leroy says, nervously shuffling blueprints.

"You know good and well," Norma Jean says. She is sitting in a kitchen chair with her feet up and her arms wrapped around her knees. She looks small and helpless. She says, "The very idea, her bringing up a subject like that! Saying it was neglect."

"She didn't mean that," Leroy says.

"She might not have *thought* she meant it. She always says things like that. You don't know how she goes on."

"But she didn't really mean it. She was just talking."

Leroy opens a king-sized bottle of beer and pours it into two glasses, dividing it carefully. He hands a glass to Norma Jean and she takes it from him mechanically. For a long time, they sit by the kitchen window watching the birds at the feeder.

Something is happening. Norma Jean is going to night school. She has graduated from her six-week body-building course and now she is taking an adult-education course in composition at Paducah Community College. She spends her evenings outlining paragraphs.

"First you have a topic sentence," she explains to Leroy. "Then you divide it up. Your secondary topic has to be connected to your primary topic."

To Leroy, this sounds intimidating. "I never was any good in English," he says.

"It makes a lot of sense."

"What are you doing this for, anyhow?"

She shrugs. "It's something to do." She stands up and lifts her dumbbells a few times.

"Driving a rig, nobody cared about my English."

"I'm not criticizing your English."

Norma Jean used to say, "If I lose ten minutes' sleep, I just drag all day." Now she stays up late, writing compositions. She got a B on her first paper—a how-to theme on soup-based casseroles. Recently Norma Jean has been cooking unusual foods—tacos, lasagna, Bombay chicken. She doesn't play the organ anymore, though her second paper was called "Why Music Is Important to Me." She sits at the kitchen table, concentrating on her outlines, while Leroy plays with his log house plans, practicing with a set of Lincoln Logs. The thought of getting a truckload of notched, numbered logs scares him, and he wants to be prepared. As he and Norma Jean work together at the kitchen table, Leroy has the hopeful thought that they are sharing something, but he knows he is a fool to think this. Norma Jean is miles away. He knows he is going to lose her. Like Mabel, he is just waiting for time to pass.

One day, Mabel is there before Norma Jean gets

home from work, and Leroy finds himself confiding in her. Mabel, he realizes, must know Norma Jean better than he does.

"I don't know what's got into that girl," Mabel says. "She used to go to bed with the chickens. Now you say she's up all hours. Plus her a-smoking. I like to died."

"I want to make her this beautiful home," Leroy says, indicating the Lincoln Logs. "I don't thinks she even wants it. Maybe she was happier with me gone."

"She don't know what to make of you, coming home like this."

"Is that it?"

Mabel takes the roof off his Lincoln Log cabin. "You couldn't get *me* in a log cabin," she says. "I was raised in one. It's no picnic, let me tell you."

"They're different now," says Leroy.

"I tell you what," Mabel says, smiling oddly at Leroy.

"What?"

"Take her on down to Shiloh. Y'all need to get out together, stir a little. Her brain's all balled up over them books."

Leroy can see traces of Norma Jean's features in her mother's face. Mabel's worn face has the texture of crinkled cotton, but suddenly she looks pretty. It occurs to Leroy that Mabel has been hinting all along that she wants them to take her with them to Shiloh.

"Let's all go to Shiloh," he says. "You and me and her. Some Sunday."

Mabel throws up her hands in protest. "Oh, no, not me. Young folks want to be by theirselves."

When Norma Jean comes in with groceries, Leroy says excitedly, "Your mama here's been dying to go to Shiloh for forty-five years. It's about time we went, don't you think?"

"I'm not going to butt in on anybody's second honeymoon," Mabel says.

"Who's going on a honeymoon, for Christ's sake?" Norma Jean says loudly.

"I never raised no daughter of mine to talk that-a-way," Mabel says.

"You ain't seen nothing yet," says Norma Jean. She starts putting away boxes and cans, slamming cabinet doors.

"There's a log cabin at Shiloh," Mabel says. "It was there during the battle. There's bullet holes in it."

"When are you going to *shut up* about Shiloh, Mama?" asks Norma Jean.

"I always thought Shiloh was the prettiest place, so full of history," Mabel goes on. "I just hoped y'all could see it once before I die, so you could tell me about it." Later, she whispers to Leroy, "You do what I said. A little change is what she needs."

"Your name means 'the king,' " Norma Jean says to Leroy that evening. He is trying to get her to go to Shiloh, and she is reading a book about another century.

"Well, I reckon I ought to be right proud."

"I guess so."

"Am I still king around here?"

Norma Jean flexes her biceps and feels them for hardness. "I'm not fooling around with anybody, if that's what you mean," she says.

"Would you tell me if you were?"

"I don't know."

"What does *your* name mean?"

"It was Marilyn Monroe's real name."

"No kidding!"

"Norma comes from the Normans. They were invaders," she says. She closes her book and looks hard at Leroy. "I'll go to Shiloh with you if you'll stop staring at me."

On Sunday, Norma Jean packs a picnic and they go to Shiloh. To Leroy's relief, Mabel says she does not want to come with them. Norma Jean drives, and

Leroy, sitting beside her, feels like some boring hitch-hiker she has picked up. He tries some conversation, but she answers him in monosyllables. At Shiloh, she drives aimlessly through the park, past bluffs and trails and steep ravines. Shiloh is an immense place, and Leroy cannot see it as a battleground. It is not what he expected. He thought it would look like a golf course. Monuments are everywhere, showing through the thick clusters of trees. Norma Jean passes the log cabin Mabel mentioned. It is surrounded by tourists looking for bullet holes.

"That's not the kind of log house I've got in mind," says Leroy apologetically.

"I know *that*."

"This is a pretty place. Your mama was right."

"It's O.K.," says Norma Jean. "Well, we've seen it. I hope she's satisfied."

They burst out laughing together.

At the park museum, a movie on Shiloh is shown every half hour, but they decide that they don't want to see it. They buy a souvenir Confederate flag for Mabel, and then they find a picnic spot near the cemetery. Norma Jean has brought a picnic cooler, with pimiento sandwiches, soft drinks, and Yodels. Leroy eats a sandwich and then smokes a joint, hiding it behind the picnic cooler. Norma Jean has quit smoking altogether. She is picking cake crumbs from the cellophane wrapper, like a fussy bird.

Leroy says, "So the boys in gray ended up in Corinth. The Union soldiers zapped 'em finally, April 7, 1862."

They both know that he doesn't know any history. He is just talking about some of the historical plaques they have read. He feels awkward, like a boy on a date with an older girl. They are still just making conversation.

"Corinth is where Mama eloped to," says Norma Jean.

They sit in silence and stare at the cemetery for

the Union dead and, beyond, at a tall cluster of trees. Campers are parked nearby, bumper to bumper, and small children in bright clothing are cavorting and squealing. Norma Jean wads up the cake wrapper and squeezes it tightly in her hand. Without looking at Leroy, she says, "I want to leave you."

Leroy takes a bottle of Coke out of the cooler and flips off the cap. He holds the bottle poised near his mouth but cannot remember to take a drink. Finally he says, "No, you don't."

"Yes, I do."

"I won't let you."

"You can't stop me."

"Don't do me that way."

Leroy knows Norma Jean will have her own way. "Didn't I promise to be home from now on?" he says.

"In some ways, a woman prefers a man who wanders," says Norma Jean. "That sounds crazy, I know."

"You're not crazy."

Leroy remembers to drink from his Coke. Then he says, "Yes, you *are* crazy. You and me could start all over again. Right back at the beginning."

"We *have* started all over again," says Norma Jean. "And this is how it turned out."

"What did I do wrong?"

"Nothing."

"Is this one of those women's lib things?" Leroy asks.

"Don't be funny."

The cemetery, a green slope dotted with white markers, looks like a subdivision site. Leroy is trying to comprehend that his marriage is breaking up, but for some reason he is wondering about white slabs in a graveyard.

"Everything was fine till Mama caught me smoking," says Norma Jean, standing up. "That set something off."

"What are you talking about?"

"She won't leave me alone—*you* won't leave me

alone." Norma Jean seems to be crying, but she is looking away from him. "I feel eighteen again. I can't face that all over again." She starts walking away. "No, it *wasn't* fine. I don't know what I'm saying. Forget it."

Leroy takes a lungful of smoke and closes his eyes as Norma Jean's words sink in. He tries to focus on the fact that thirty-five hundred soldiers died on the grounds around him. He can only think of that war as a board game with plastic soldiers. Leroy almost smiles, as he compares the Confederates' daring attack on the Union camps and Virgil Mathis's raid on the bowling alley. General Grant, drunk and furious, shoved the Southerners back to Corinth, where Mabel and Jet Beasley were married years later, when Mabel was still thin and good-looking. The next day, Mabel and Jet visited the battleground, and then Norma Jean was born, and then she married Leroy and they had a baby, which they lost, and now Leroy and Norma Jean are here at the same battleground. Leroy knows he is leaving out a lot. He is leaving out the insides of history. History was always just names and dates to him. It occurs to him that building a house out of logs is similarly empty—too simple. And the real inner workings of a marriage, like most of history, have escaped him. Now he sees that building a log house is the dumbest idea he could have had. It was clumsy of him to think Norma Jean would want a log house. It was a crazy idea. He'll have to think of something else, quickly. He will wad the blueprints into tight balls and fling them into the lake. Then he'll get moving again. He opens his eyes. Norma Jean has moved away and is walking through the cemetery, following a serpentine brick path.

Leroy gets up to follow his wife, but his good leg is asleep and his bad leg still hurts him. Norma Jean is far away, walking rapidly toward the bluff by the river, and he tries to hobble toward her. Some children run past him, screaming noisily. Norma Jean has reached the bluff, and she is looking out over the Tennessee River. Now she turns toward Leroy and waves her arms. Is she beckoning to him? She seems to be doing an exercise for her chest muscles. The sky is unusually pale—the color of the dust ruffle Mabel made for their bed.

The Drowned Man

MAEVE BRENNAN

Maeve Brennan was born in 1917 in Dublin. She began secretly writing a journal and poems as a girl in convent school. "But," she later remarked, "the nuns found them." She moved with her family to America when she was seventeen. Her first writing job was at Harper's Bazaar. In the 1940s her work caught the notice of New Yorker *editor William Shawn, who asked her to write the Long-Winded Lady pieces for the magazine's Talk of the Town section. She has published two books of fiction,* In and Out of Never-Never Land *(1969), and* Christmas Eve *(1974). Most of the stories contained in these books first appeared in* The New Yorker *between 1953 and 1973. She has said that she works best under deadline and that after she has set one for herself, she writes straight through, turning out patches of prose that she then sticks together in various ways with scotch tape to find the order she likes best.*

Maeve Brennan's narratives are set mainly in Dublin and around New York City. Lower-middle-class Dubliners are as familiar to her as the fashionable set of East Hampton. She writes of childhood, family, life, marriage, and even, on occasion, animals. One reads her with the complete assurance that this is what we always thought writing should be: that it should listen and watch for the significant things, pay

*heed to the important moments, intuit and understand
the vagaries of the human heart. In Maeve Brennan's
stories we have, in place of words, raw and radiant
emotion.*

After his wife died, Mr. Derdon was very anxious
to get into her bedroom, to have a look around on
his own with the door closed and with no one there to
watch him and wonder how he was feeling. It was not
anxiety or grief or any painful sensation, not longing
or yearning or anything like that, that drew him to the
room, but curiosity. He wanted to look at it. The
room, that had hardly existed for him while she was
alive, and that he had seldom entered, although he
had occasionally stood in the doorway or at least paused
in the doorway to call something in to her on his way
out of the house—the room now seemed mysterious to
him the way an empty house will suddenly seem mysterious and even frightening to children who never
noticed it when it was occupied, and the way a bird's
nest lying empty on the ground after a summer storm
will crowd the mind with thoughts that have nothing to
do with wings and food and warmth and song: thoughts
of vacancy, and thoughts of winter, and of winds that
are too violent and nights that are too dark, and
thoughts of stony solitude, endured in silence, and of
landscapes that are too cold and flat and where no one
cares to walk. The little nest, cast to the ground,
contains an emptiness that is too big for us to understand. We cannot imagine how it must feel. It is a
limitless emptiness, and beyond us, although we would
like to be able to understand it, and examine it from
all angles, and mark its limits, and bring it under
control, and then put it away in a comfortable place
and forget about it. But the nest is nothing, no more
than a scrap. The empty nest is only a brazen image of

the fear that is so commonplace that we cannot merely walk through it every day pretending we do not notice it but can walk through it and pretend it is not there. As long as the nest is there empty, we look into it, but then it is gone and we think no more about it.

As long as the door of his wife's bedroom, in which she had died, remained closed and the room behind it empty, Mr. Derdon thought of nothing else. The emptiness beyond the door excited him, and he began to dream about it at night, and in his tired mind the door was open to him, and then—mistake—it was not open to him, and it expanded and contracted, being first a very big room and then a very little room, but never its own size, and it developed extra doors, strange doors that frightened him. And after these dreams he awoke in the morning exhausted as though he suffered nightmares, when all he had done was to dream of his wife's bedroom. His sister, his maiden sister, had come to Dublin to keep house for him, and on the very few occasions when she went out the woman who cleaned was there fussing around him and looking after him. They felt he should not be left alone at this time. He wondered what they did mean, "at this time." It was not a case of this, that, or the other time. At the moment, it was simply *before* Rose died and *after* Rose died, and when they said to him "at this time," did they mean that he was never to be left a minute to himself for the rest of his life? They bothered him, always hovering around him, and he wondered, in bewilderment, at all the freedom he had had only a month, even ten days, ago, all the freedom he had had and had not valued. Then, before, he had been immeasurably free. He marveled at the freedom he had had. He wondered at it. He had been free as a bird. Then, while Rose was alive, he could have wandered up and down the hall in front of that closed door, if he had wanted to. He could have walked up and down there all day long, passing up the hall, and passing back, and no questions would have been asked of him.

She would never have thought of questioning him. He could have wandered there at will, for as long as he liked. Of course, he would probably have said something. He might have said, "I just thought I'd take a little exercise," or something like that. And then she would have said nothing. She might have smiled or nodded in that awkward way she had, as though her neck was not accustomed to little gracious gestures, as indeed it was not, but she would not have said anything. She would have gone on to do whatever she was doing and she wouldn't have asked him any questions. She might have said—there was just a chance she might have said—"Oh, exercising yourself, if that's what you want to do," meaning to sound casual and easy, and managing only to sound clumsy, like a shy child trying to be smart. But it was more than likely that she would have given him only a shamefaced smile, as though she had no right to see what he was doing at all, and gone away, off, on to whatever little job she had in hand. She would have gone and he would have been left with that silence of hers that gave him unlimited freedom, or what he knew now to be unlimited freedom, although then it had seemed to be only a burden, that burden of indefiniteness that left him always wondering what it was he had not done that he should have done, or had not said that he should have said. He never knew where he was with her. He never knew exactly what he had done or how he had spent his time, since there was no definite point where he could stop and measure what he had done, or how he had spent the time he had spent. Indefinite, now she made him indefinite to himself, and how could he mourn her, when there was hardly anything he could remember about her apart from the obvious facts that she had been gentle, quiet, uncomplaining, beautiful—or at least more or less beautiful in her youth—things like that. He literally could not remember very much about her. He began to believe that she had been invisible, but when he thought that, he felt that he might cry with fear, because how could he even think that, when *they* were there talking about his dead wife and he knew he had a wife for more than forty years and they had had a son and the son had vanished into the priesthood, and here he was now and he could hardly remember one solitary thing about her and not really remember seeing her very much. And how could he grieve for what he could not define, or mourn for what had vanished without a trace. That was it—she had made no impression. Somehow or another, however she had done it, she had managed to live with a man, a sensitive, kindhearted man, for more than forty years without making the slightest impression on him. She had always been impossible. Several times, long ago, he had said as much to her. "You are impossible," he had said to her. And she had said *nothing*. She had said nothing and she had given him nothing, nothing to be angry about and nothing to be sad about and nothing to laugh at and nothing to wonder at and nothing at all to remember. She had given him nothing and she had left him nothing, and by leaving him nothing she had taken away from him the one thing that might have been a rock of strength to him now—that rock of grief where he might have rested in blessed isolation, not able to see or hear or speak or think with the sorrow that filled and destroyed him. But the monumental grief would now remain as it was, only a dream of grief that seemed from where he sat to be a dream of peace, because he knew that in that dreadful suffering he would find peace at last, and then he could rest himself, knowing he had done the right and proper thing, and had felt the right and proper emotions, those that represent the just tribute we must pay to death. But it was no use. He felt nothing. He could see and hear and so on, the same as usual, and he even had a little appetite for his food.

If they would only let him stand and watch her garden, he might be able to see her there, she had spent so much time there. If they would only let him stand at the back window and look at her garden, and it was well worth looking at, he might be able to find her there, and then he might be able to begin missing her—it was the least he could do, to miss her. But he didn't miss her, he didn't miss her at all; everything was just the same, he didn't miss her at all, and if he tried to stand by the window looking out into her garden, his sister or the other one would come clucking around, trying to take him out of himself. Then, before, when he had his freedom, he could have stood by that window forever without being interfered with. Then, before, he could have sat all day long in his armchair by the fire, dreaming about nothing, thinking peacefully of nothing at all, immersed in memories so confused and so alike that they were warmth to him; it was like thinking about warmth to sit there like that doing nothing and remembering, really, nothing. Then, when she was alive and he didn't know the freedom he had, he could have sat in his chair for as long as he liked, not holding a book or a newspaper or anything, and no one would have come up talking at him and telling him he mustn't be morbid and that he must keep busy and interested. How could they know that what was in his mind was morbid, when he did not really know himself what was in his mind. They were training him as if he were a dog, a poor unfortunate dog that had to do as he was told, and not ask any questions, because he was a *dog* and for no other reason. Poor dog. Poor animal. It made no sense. He had to move briskly or they sighed. He had to talk distinctly and with some vivacity or they gazed at him in worry and surmise. He had to take his walk every day, not in the garden, because that was her garden and so morbid, but out—he had to go out by the front for his walk. They seemed to believe that there was no air at the back of the house any more, but only in the front, beyond the front door, where the neighbors would come trotting up to him, people he only knew by sight, and say things to him that he hardly understood and did not want to hear, although through some miracle he kept making the correct sorrowful responses to all their sorrowful platitudes. And he felt that every word he said was a lie, and when he returned to the house he returned worn out.

He would have loved to make a clean breast of things to his sister and the others. He would have liked to confess to them—he longed to confess to them—that he felt no grief. He wanted to tell the truth. He wanted them to know what a sham, what a sham he was, or at least show them that they were making him into a sham. But if he told them the truth they would think him a monster, and he would rather know he was a sham than be thought a monster. He was a man who could feel no grief, an empty man. Even so, he would have liked to be let do as he liked, but he hesitated to hurt their feelings. There were plenty of sharp remarks that came into his head, but he did not want to say them unless he was really pushed to the wall. He knew the women meant well. He could tell them to go, of course. They would protest, but they would go, and then he would be alone and then he could be quiet. If he ordered them out, and they saw he meant business, they would have to go. But he could not do that, when they meant so well, and then, it was something to keep in mind, that he could be rid of them in a minute, any minute. It was something to look forward to, the minute when he would order them out once and for all, and he did look forward to it. Once he made up his mind, they would go, and no ifs or buts. Once his mind was made up he would take no nonsense from them, but for the time being he let them have their way in the house and he did what they told him to do and he would go on doing as he was told for as long as it suited him and not one minute longer. But it was good to look forward to, the moment when he would turn them out. He would let them have their way, he would let them have their head, they would imagine themselves entrenched, and suddenly, all of a sudden, he would turn on them and show them who was master. The moment would come. He was sure of that. They would drive him too far. He was sure of that. He would turn when they least expected it, and he would blast them. He would send them packing. He had to smile, thinking of the surprise on their faces, and his sister caught him smiling, and he caught her catching him, with that sympathetic expression on her that meant she imagined he was thinking kind sweet gentle happy thoughts about his dearest departed, and he was so annoyed that he could have hit her, and he turned down the corners of his mouth and began to look gloomy again.

They thought it was a sign of grief that he had ordered them to leave Rose's room as it was, but it was not a sign of grief at all. It had been an impulse that had made him tell them to shut that door and leave it shut. He had simply wanted to assert himself and to give a reasonable order and be obeyed, and they had obeyed him, but it had not been an important matter until all of a sudden, in some mysterious way, the closed door had become extremely important.

He thought that once he got into that empty room by himself with the door closed, he would be able to think more clearly and to know something that he did not now know. Once in there, he might be able to remember more of her than—as she was now in his mind—something humble and busy about the house. Once in there, he might be able to find more to think of than that eternal acquiescence. Even the very last word she had said to him was, "Yes." There was nothing strange about that, she had always said yes, but unbroken acquiescence had not been indefinite enough for her; she had always, until that last yes, had to qualify even her yes—"Yes, all right," "Yes, if you want to," "Yes, I don't mind, if you like. If you want to, I suppose so, yes." But that final "Yes," when he asked her should he send for the doctor, stood alone in his mind. He could hear her voice now, saying, "Yes," and he recalled that even as troubled as he had been he felt surprised, and maybe even pleased, that she was definite. It had been as though he heard her voice once again after a very long time, when she said "Yes" like that to him.

As he looked forward to the day when he would order his sister and the other woman to leave his house, now he looked forward to the opportunity to slip into the empty room and be alone there, but without anybody knowing he was there. He waited for the chance when they would both be out of the house together. He schemed. He played up to them. He did not sit dreaming in his chair by the fire, but held his book in front of him and read it with attention. He asked them to bring him the evening paper, as though he was interested in what was in it. He did not look out of the back window into her garden. He ate what was put in front of him, and even suggested that if they both thought hard, and put all their brains together, they might be able to remember that he liked the eggs just lightly boiled, and that he liked them hot, because cold boiled eggs were bad for people, especially first thing in the morning. He grew bolder. He told them that when the conventional period of mourning was past they would all get dressed in their best clothes and go into town in a taxi and see a play or something. At that, they looked at him in astonishment, and then they turned their faces away, like disappointed cats who see that their prey has ceased to move and who hope that by pretending to remove their attention from it they will trick it into life again, and into movement again, and so find it still within their power. Mr. Derdon's sister and the lady who cleaned looked away, startled, and then they looked back again, but he knew their ways and he was still smiling. "We're not doing poor Rose any good, sitting around here with long faces," he said.

*   *   *

A couple of days after that, or it might even have been the very next day, through some miracle that was carefully explained to him, while he pretended to listen, he found himself alone in the house in the afternoon. He hesitated a short time before opening the door of Rose's room. He walked up and down the hall awhile as he had longed to do, and he thought about going into the room. He did not want to go blundering in. After all, once he had gone in, the emptiness that had been increasing in there since her death would be destroyed forever, and he was anxious to catch some impression of it while it still lingered. He walked up and down a few times, thinking intently and rubbing his hands together, and then without thinking any more about it he turned the knob and opened the door and went in and closed the door behind him. There was nothing. There was not even a perceptible emptiness. It was her room, or it had been her room, but she was not in it any more. The room said nothing. The emptiness, what emptiness he felt there, was not particular, and he could not pretend to himself that he could identify it as a special and individual emptiness that she had left and that she and she alone could have left. It was a general emptiness that filled her place—he might as well have been looking into a fallen nest to try to discover the nature of what was not. He grew tired trying to press himself into what was not there and therefore could not or would not resist him. There was no resistance in the room. There was nothing he could pit himself against. He felt let down, as he had when he was a child and Christmas was over, and at the same time he felt keyed up, as though he was going to have to face an examination, *take* an examination that he had not been warned about, that he had never known people had to take, that he was not prepared for and could not prepare for, since he had no idea of the nature of the questions that would be asked him or of the tests he might be called upon to perform. He had always felt uneasily that there was something other people knew, something everybody knew and took for granted, but that he did not know. He had sometimes hoped that he might come upon this bit of common knowledge, by luck, as he might come upon a touchstone that would guide him to the secret whose existence he felt, the secret that others had and that remained closed to him. What he had thought out loud in his own mind always was, "There must be more than this to life, there must be more to life than this." Oh, indeed, indeed, yes, there must be more than this to it all, he used to think, and then, at such incredulous moments, he used to look into the faces of the people who passed him in the street, to try to read in their faces what he was sure they must know that kept them going every day—because it was not everybody that had his strength, and it was not everybody—there was hardly anybody who could have the fortitude to keep on going day in day out in the bewilderment in which he himself lived. It was not possible that others could go from day to day, as he did, for no real reason, or that others could put up the brave front that he put up, the brave, respectable front that was a front for nothing, and nothing but a front. At such moments, when he felt that he must make one more attempt to discover the secret, he used to glance, just glance, into Rose's face when he felt she would not notice him looking at her. He remembered that at such times, on those evenings, he used to hang his hat and coat in the hall as usual, and put his umbrella in the stand, and walk down the hall to where she sat, and he would sit down opposite to her and open his evening paper, but at such times he would use the evening paper only to camouflage himself as a reader while he watched her, not as a husband, not even as a man, but as a supplicant who hoped she might be able to tell him what had kept them together all these years, or what kept any two people together, or what kept people going and doing as they had been told they ought to do. When had all this obedience begun and who had marked out the appointed way where men and women walked without protest and most of the time without complaining? Most important of all, what reason had been given that guaranteed this obedience and why had the reason not been given to him as well as to everybody else? There was a common secret that he had not been allowed to share, and now it seemed that grief must also remain a secret to him, because even now, sitting in the room in which she had spent a good part of her time, and in which she had slept in her bed, he felt no grief. He was sitting on the straight chair she had kept handy to her sewing machine. The sewing machine was closed and made a flat smooth surface that was faintly marked by whitened circles, where she had kept some of her plants when the machine was not in use. She could have got herself a little plant table. He would not have minded the expense. He would have given her the money for a table, if she had asked him for it, but she had not asked. She had preferred to play the martyr and so, contemptuously and in despair of ever coming to any terms with her, he had ignored her or, as you might put it, let her have her way. She had preferred to clear the top of her chest of drawers when she wanted to do any sewing on the machine. Then to the top of the chest of drawers she would lift the plants, some of them big and heavy, and when they were all safely arranged she would open the sewing machine and go to work, bending very close to it. And with the work finished, she would go through the whole laborious process of transferring the plants back to the machine again. The machine was a makeshift plant table for her, as much in her life had been makeshift. Take, for example, that arrangement of old chocolate boxes on the blanket chest under the shelf where she had kept her few books. You would think, to see those chocolate boxes, and to note the careful order in which they were arranged, by size and also by shape, a rectangular one set straight and centered on top of a larger rectangle, the square ones built up like a child's blocks on top of the squares, and the two long equal ones set apart from the rest, completing the design of even lines and sharp angles, all of it speaking of neatness and care and of overpowering concern with order— you would think, looking at such an arrangement, that the boxes contained something of interest or of value. And what did they contain? Old bills marked paid thirty years before. Receipts for dinners she had never cooked, dinners so elaborate that she must have been dreaming of a visit from the king and queen of England when she cut the menus out of the magazines in which she had found them. Directions for making dresses that she would never in her life have had occasion to wear—there was a whole pamphlet that gave instructions, measurements, etc., for the construction of a satin ball gown. It would have been laughable if it was not so pathetic. One box contained cards of tailors' samples—bits of tweed, bits of serge, bits of velvet, bits of suiting and coat materials. He knew how she had come by those cards. She had never told him, but he had known her so well that he knew very well how she had come by those cards. He could see her now, standing in front of the tailor's window, one tailor one time, another tailor another time, admiring the bolts of cloth in the window and the pictures displayed of suits and coats, and imagining to herself that she would order something, a costume, as she would have called it, and making up her mind how she would like it made and out of what material. He could see her making up her mind, and opening the door of the shop, and going inside with that timid air of consequence that she affected in public and that had nearly driven him mad with irritation. And he could see her approaching the tailor, and speaking in the accents of a lady who may or may not bestow her custom here, and discussing with the tailor the cut and style of this coat or skirt or whatever it was she imagined she was going to buy for herself. And he could see her, in all her seriousness, taking the card of samples from the tailor and bringing it home and sitting down by herself in the afternoon to dream over it, carrying it to the window so that she could look at the scraps of fabric in a better light, and only lifting her eyes from it to look at the flowers in her garden, and all the time dreaming, dreaming, dreaming, always dreaming, and what was it that she had dreamed about, all her life? She had never said. She had never even admitted how she dreamed her time away. If you had asked her what she was "thinking" about, she would have said, "Oh, nothing," and then quickly turned her hands to something to divert attention from herself. Or she might have replied, in answer to any question at all, "There is a bad scratch on the linoleum near the door there. I was wondering what I could do to cover it." She was all indirection.

The contents of the chocolate boxes revealed a mind given over entirely to trivialities and makeshift, always makeshift, making do, making last, and putting to use somehow, wasting nothing except her time and her life and his time and his life. Even so, those times when he watched her secretly, he had had hopes that she possessed and would reveal to him the common secret that had been given to everybody except him. She had been weak, and it was simply impossible that she had lived alone like that unless she was held by something, some truth, or some belief, some magic word, some comfort that she might have shared with him, if she had been willing to speak and able to speak. But the times grew rarer when he was able to watch her, because as he grew older he grew less and less able to bear the uneasiness that trembled all over her face when she felt his eyes on her. She would be sitting there knitting or sewing or mending or looking through one of the household magazines she loved, her face all intent on what was in her hands, and in the space of an instant she would become aware that he was looking at her, and the change in her expression would be terrible to see. Her face would become destroyed with shame and apprehension. And what it all amounted to, the beginning and the end of it, was that she was afraid of him. Once long ago he had been driven to challenge her. "Am I a monster or something?" he had shouted at her. "What's the matter with you? What's wrong with you? Why are you afraid to look at me? Am I a monster?" But she had trembled so violently that he had left her alone. She was afraid of questions. He left her alone. But it was no use going over all that again, no use thinking about it, better to put it out of his mind.

Still, he could not believe that even a human being as ineffectual as she had been could vanish from life without leaving any trace of herself at all. Any trace would be a sign that might guide him to the grief he wanted to suffer for her. But there was no sign.

He got up from the chair and went and stood by her bed. It was narrow. He stood there as he had stood on her last morning. Of course, looking at her that morning, he had had no idea how bad she was. He had gone into her room when she had not turned up as usual at nine o'clock sharp with his breakfast tray, which he liked to have in his own room, by himself. He went into her room in his dressing gown and slippers, and she was lying there in bed doing nothing, not even looking, although her eyes were open, and he was so surprised to see her, it had been so long since he had seen her lying in bed, that he said, "What are you doing in bed, Rose?" And she said, "Nothing." Her voice had been perfectly normal. He started to make some little joke that would lead him around to reminding her of the breakfast tray, when she said, in the same perfectly normal voice, "I have a terrible pain in my chest." And the minute she had said those words he felt the pain in his own chest, but with him it was not new but too familiar. He had often told her that pain was familiar to him, and here it was now again, his message from that treacherous old heart of his that was going to be the death of him someday, and he put his hand up to his own chest and said, "Will I call the doctor? He can have a look at me too as long as he's here." But Rose had not answered him. Instead, she began looking at him, and her eyes that he had always considered frightened and not direct, even furtive, preoccupied and worried—those shaded green eyes suddenly seemed to belong to her, as though she had taken command of them for the first time, and was asserting her right to see for herself, and to look, and not to look at just anything but to look at everything, and then to choose what she really wanted; not that she would not see all the rest, but that she would look at and possess what responded to her, and if what responded was joy she would look at joy, and if what responded was pain, then she would look at pain, and if what responded was cruelty she would look at cruelty, until cruelty, like pain and joy, turned again and turned again and turned at last to show her what she had chosen to see in the first place, a face that was disposed to smile on her, eyes that seemed to recognize her, a heart that was inclined to value her, and hands that knew her but that wanted her just the same, just as she was, whatever she was.

She had lain there looking at him like that, and still she had not answered his question, and he said again, still stroking his dressing gown over his heart to signify his pain, "Will I call the doctor then, or not? I think I'll call him anyway, for myself. Do you want me to call him?" And Rose had said, "Yes." "Yes," she said, and the one word came out quickly, like a sigh or a laugh, like a sound of recognition and acceptance and mockery. "Yes," she said, but only once, as though she was finally giving in to something and accepting something that she had not wanted to give in to or accept yet.

He had gone then and called the doctor, and he had sat down in the sitting room to wait, and he had wished there was someone to bring him a cup of tea, and of course, when the doctor arrived and went into the room, all there was left to say was that it was over for Rose.

Now, Mr. Derdon thought, there was no use staying in that room any longer. There was nothing to be found there. He opened the door and went out into the hall and he left the door open behind him. His sister and the woman who cleaned could go in there now and do what they liked in the way of tidying up and sorting out her clothes and the rest of it. He didn't care what they did. He went into the kitchen and looked around, and then he left the kitchen and stood in the hall a minute, and then he went into the sitting room and sat down in his chair by the fire. He was too tired to read, and too tired to think, but he could not stop himself thinking. It was all a mystery, where their life together had gone, or why they had come together in the first place. He remembered the night he asked her to marry him. They were standing together on a small stone bridge that overlooked a river outside the town where she lived. He had not intended to ask her that night—he had meant to keep her wondering a little longer, not to let her get too sure of herself—but all of a sudden he turned to her and said, "I thought we might get married." She continued looking down into the flowing water and she did not answer him. He said, "I was wondering if you had thought of me at all." Still she said nothing and had not raised her head. Then he said, "Rose, please, for God's sake, will you marry me?" And she raised her head and looked at him—her eyes were still clear in those days— and she said, "Yes," and that was all she said. "Yes," she had said, in a voice that was definite and that at the same time seemed to have been forced out of her, as though she had wanted to say yes, and expected to say yes, but at the same time would have liked to put off saying yes for just a little while longer, just a little while. Her face, turned up to him that night, had been the face of one who finds herself fallen into the middle of a deep lake, and who does not know how to swim, but would rather hope for help than scream for it. "It was careless of me to fall into this deep water," her face seemed to say, "and I am all to blame for not having learned to swim, but even though I was stupid, not learning to swim, and even though the water is deep, I do not want to drown." And he had put his arms around her and told her he would always take care of her. Sitting by the fire now, thinking of that night, he found he could see her face quite clearly, as she had looked then. He could see her face, and in her face all the promises that her face had shown him, the promises that had not been fulfilled. Her walk, her step, had been brave and free and definite, and it occurred to him now, as it had before, that he had fallen in love with her for the exact qualities that were not hers at all. It was not Rose's fault that he had been mistaken in her. She had shone at a distance, but close to she had ceased to shine. Still, she was gone, she had been good, and he wished he could miss her.

When his sister returned home and found the door of Rose's room standing open, she hurried into the sitting room and confronted Mr. Derdon where he sat before the fire.

"I see the door of the room is open," she said.

"I thought it had been closed long enough," he said. "We can't make a shrine out of her room."

"Did you go into the room?" she asked.

"Yes," he said. "I went in there."

He looked up at her.

"There's nothing in there," he said, and he put his hands up in front of his face and started to cry. His sister started to cry, too, and she went out of the room and was back in a minute with a cup of tea for him. He refused the tea, and when she suggested calling the doctor he refused to see the doctor. He would not take his hands from his face and he would not get up and go into his bedroom and lie down and he would not do anything except cry. The tears hurt him. They hurt his chest and his eyes and they seemed to be tracing sticky wooden lines all over his face and neck and they hurt his brain and made it ache. The tears did not run down his face and away. They poured all over him and stayed on him and encased him, and when he tried to stop crying, because he was afraid he might smother in them, imprisoned in them, they poured out all the more and there seemed to be no end to them. The tears had him in a strait jacket, and he could not speak. Now that he could not speak, he wished he could speak, because he longed now to tell his sister the truth and have the matter cleared up once and for all. The tears hurt him and covered him with a pain that seemed to grow more unbearable every minute, but what hurt most of all was his inability to tell his sister that he was not crying for Rose, because he really and truly felt no grief for Rose, but that he was crying for the lack of grief, because surely poor Rose had deserved more than a casual dismissal from life, and that most of all he was crying simply and solely because he was sad. He was sad and he was crying, and that is all there was to it. But he could not speak to tell his sister that, and she continued to watch him, helpless with tears herself and murmuring about how happy Rose was in Heaven, and he could not speak to her to tell her that it was all only a masquerade and that he was only a sham of a man, and after a long time, when he finally got command of himself, it no longer seemed worthwhile to tell her, and the way it worked out he never told her, and never told anybody.

The Girl Who Sang
with the Beatles

ROBERT HEMENWAY

*Robert Hemenway was born in 1921 in South Haven,
Michigan, and attended the University of Chicago. He
began to write fiction at the age of thirty-seven while he
was drawing unemployment checks. The second story
he wrote was published in* The New Yorker; *the eighth,
"The Girl Who Sang with the Beatles," won the 1970
O. Henry Prize. Hemenway has worked as a teacher
and editor; from 1956–1971 he was a fiction editor at*
The New Yorker. *He has written two books,* The Girl
Who Sang with the Beatles *(1970) and* At The Border
(1984).

*The people in Hemenway's writings are detached from
themselves, adrift in uncertain, fragile couplings. "Happiness," a character in* At the Border *remarks, "is like
one of those ideas at the university: too difficult to
grasp, and therefore best evaded." Love, in Hemenway's
stories, once firmly possessed, once thought to last a
lifetime, has quietly slipped away, revealing to the reader
unfulfilled secrets of his character's lives.*

Of course their tastes turned out to be different.
Cynthia was twenty-eight when they married, and
looked younger, in the way small, very pretty women
can—so much younger sometimes that bartenders would

ask for her I.D. Larry was close to forty and gray, a
heavy man who, when he moved, moved slowly. He
had been an English instructor once, though now he
wrote market-research reports, and there was still
something bookish about him. Cynthia, who was working as an interviewer for Larry's company when he
met her, had been a vocalist with several dance bands
for a while in the fifties before she quit to marry her
first husband. She had left high school when she was a
junior to take her first singing job. She and Larry were
from different generations, practically, and from different cultures, and yet when they were married they
both liked the same things. That was what brought
them together. Thirties movies. Old bars—not the
instant-tradition places but what was left of the old
ones, what Cynthia called the bar bars. Double features in the loge of the Orpheum, eating hot dogs and
drinking smuggled beer. Gibsons before dinner and
Scotch after. Their TV nights, eating delicatessen while
they watched "Mr. Lucky" or "Route 66" or "Ben
Casey," laughing at the same places, choking up at the
same places, howling together when something was
just too *much.* And then the eleven-o'clock news and
the Late and Late Late Shows, while they drank and
necked and sometimes made love. And listening to
Cynthia's records—old Sinatras and Judys, and Steve
and Eydie, or "The Fantasticks" or "Candide." They
even agreed on redecorating Cynthia's apartment, which
was full of leftovers from her first marriage. They
agreed on all of it—the worn (but genuine) Oriental
rugs; the low carved Spanish tables; the dusky colors,
grays and mauve and rose; the damask sofa with its
down pillows; and, in the bedroom, the twin beds,
nearly joined but held separate by an ornate brass
bedstead. Cynthia's old double bed had been impracti-
cal; Larry was too big, and Cynthia kicked. When they
came back from their Nassau honeymoon and saw the
apartment for the first time in ten days, Cynthia said,
"God, Larry, I *love* it. It's pure *Sunset Boulevard* now."

The place made Larry think of Hyde Park Boulevard in Chicago, where he had grown up in a mock-Tudor house filled with the wrought iron and walnut of an earlier Spanish fad. Entering the apartment was like entering his childhood. "Valencia!" sang in his head. "Valencia! In my dreams it always seems I hear you softly call to me. Valencia!"

They were married in the summer of 1962 and by the spring of 1963 the things they had bought no longer looked quite right. Everyone was buying Spanish now, and there was too much around in the cheap stores. Larry and Cynthia found themselves in a dowdy apartment full of things that looked as if they had been there since the twenties. It was depressing. They began to ask each other what they had done. Not that either of them wanted out, exactly, but what had they done? Why had they married? Why couldn't they have gone on with their affair? Neither had married the other for money, that was certain. Larry had made Cynthia quit work (not that she minded) and now they had only his salary, which was barely enough.

"We still love each other, don't we? I mean, I know I love you." Cynthia was in Larry's bed and Larry was talking. It was three in the morning, and they had come back from their usual Saturday-night tour of the neighborhood bars. "I love you," Larry said.

"You don't like me."

"I *love* you, Cynthia."

"You don't like me." Propped up by pillows, she stared red-eyed at a great paper daisy on the wall.

"I love you, Cindy."

"So? Big deal. Men have been telling me they loved me since I was fourteen. I thought you were different."

Larry lay flat on his back. "Don't be tough. It's not like you," he said.

"I *am* tough. That's what you won't understand. You didn't marry *me*. You married some nutty idea of your own. I was your secret fantasy. You told me so." Cynthia was shivering.

"Lie down," Larry said. "I'll rub your back."

"You won't get around me that way." Cynthia said, lying down. "You tricked me. I thought you liked the things I liked. You won't even watch TV with me anymore."

Larry began to rub the back of Cynthia's neck and play with the soft hairs behind one ear.

"Why don't you ever watch with me?" Cynthia said.

"You know. I get impatient."

"You don't like me." Cynthia was teasing him by now. "If you really liked me, you'd watch," she said. "You'd *like* being bored."

Larry sat up. "That isn't it," he said. "You know what it is? It's the noise. All the things you like make *noise*."

"I read."

"Sure. With the radio or the stereo or the TV on. I can't. I have to do one thing at a time," Larry said. "What if I want to sit home at night and read a book?"

"So read."

"When you have these programs you quote have to watch unquote?"

"Get me headphones. That's what my first husband did when he stopped talking to me. Or go in the bedroom and shut the door. I don't mind."

"Well do something," Larry said, lying down again. "Now let's make love."

"Oh, it's no use, Larry," Cynthia said. "Not when we're like this. I'll only sweat."

And so it went on many nights, and everything seemed tainted by their disagreements, especially their times in bed. After they had made love, they would slip again into these exchanges, on and on. What Cynthia seemed to resent most was that Larry had not been straightforward with her. Why had he let her think he cared for her world of song and dance? She knew it was trivial. She had never tried to make him think she was deep. Why had he pretended he was something he wasn't?

How was Larry to tell her the truth without making her think he was either a snob or a fool? There was no way. The thing was, he said, that when they met he *did* like what she liked, period. Just because she liked it. What was wrong with that? He wanted to see her enjoying herself, so they did what she wanted to do— went to Radio City to see the new Doris Day, or to Basin Street East to hear Peggy Lee, or to revivals of those fifties musicals Cynthia liked so much. Forget the things he liked if she didn't—foreign movies and chamber music and walks in Central Park, all that. She must have known what he liked, after all. She had been in his apartment often enough before they were married, God knows. She had seen his books and records. She knew his tastes.

"I thought you gave all that up," Cynthia said. "I thought you'd changed."

"I thought you *would* change," Larry said. "I thought you wanted to. I thought if you wanted to marry me you must want to change."

"Be an *intellectual?*" Cynthia said. "You must be kidding."

No, he was serious. Why didn't she get bored with the stuff she watched and the junk she read? *He* did. When you had seen three Perry Masons, you had seen them all, and that went for Doris Day movies, the eleven-o'clock news, and "What's My Line?"

"I know all that," Cynthia said. She *liked* to be bored. God, you couldn't keep thinking about *reality* all the time. You'd go out of your mind. She liked stories and actors that she knew, liked movies she had seen a dozen times and books she could read over and over again. Larry took his reading so seriously. As if reading were *life*.

Larry tried to persuade himself that Cynthia was teasing him, but it was no use. She meant what she said. She *liked East of Eden, Marjorie Morningstar,*

Gone with the Wind. She liked Elizabeth Taylor movies. She found nourishment in that Styrofoam. He could see it in her childlike face, which sometimes shone as if she were regarding a beatific vision when she was under the spell of the sorriest trash. What repelled him brought her to life. He could feel it in her when they touched and when, after seeing one of her favorite movies, they made love. How odd that he should have married her! And yet he loved her, he thought, and he thought she loved him—needed him, anyway.

Sometimes they talked of having a child, or of Cynthia's going back to work or of attending night classes together at Columbia or the New School, but nothing came of it. They were both drinking too much, perhaps, and getting too little exercise, yet it was easier to let things go on as they were. Larry did set out to read Camus, the first serious reading he had done since their marriage, and in the evenings after dinner he would go into the bedroom, shut the door, turn on WNCN to muffle the sounds from the living room, put Flents in his ears, and read. Although the meaningless noises from the TV set—the not quite comprehensible voices, the sudden surges of music—still reached him, he was reluctant to buy Cynthia the headphones she had suggested. They would be too clear a symbol of their defeat.

Cynthia often stayed up until three or four watching the late movies or playing her records, and Larry, who usually fell asleep around midnight, would sometimes wake after two or three hours and come out of the bedroom shouting "Do you know what *time* it is?" and frighten her. Sometimes, though, he would make a drink for himself and watch her movie, too, necking with her the way they used to do, without saying much. They were still drawn to each other.

Sometimes, very late at night when she was quite drunk, Cynthia would stand before the full-length mirror in their bedroom and admire herself. "I'm beautiful," she would say. "Right now, I'm really beautiful and who can see me?" Larry would watch from the bed. Something slack in her would grow taut as she looked in the mirror. She would draw her underpants down low on her hips, then place her hands on her shoulders, her crossed arms covering her bare breasts, and smile at her reflection, a one-sided smile. "I'm a narcissist," she would say, looking at Larry in the mirror. "I'm a sexual narcissist. How can you stand me?" Then she would join Larry in his bed.

Larry couldn't deny Cynthia anything for long. If he insisted on it, she would turn off the set, but then she would sulk until he felt he had imposed upon her, and he would turn the set back on or take her out for a drink. How could he blame her? They had so little money. What else was there for her to do?

One Saturday night after their tours of the bars, Cynthia changed clothes and came out of the bedroom wearing a twenties black dress and black net stockings and pumps. The dress was banded with several rows of fringe and stopped just at the knee. She had had to add the last row of fringe, she told Larry. Her first husband had made her, just before they went to a costume party, because the dress showed too much of her thighs. Larry knelt before her and tore off the last row. Cynthia danced for him (a Charleston, a shimmy, a Watusi) and after that she sang. She had sung to him now and then late at night before they were married—just a few bars in a soft, almost inaudible voice. Tonight the voice seemed full and touching to Larry, and with a timbre and sadness different from any voice he had ever heard. "*Like* me. Please like me," the voice seemed to say. "Just like me. That's all I need. I'll be nice then." She might have been the star she wanted to be, Larry thought. She had the charm and the need for love, but perhaps, the voice was too small and her need too great. She had told him that twice while she was singing with a band in Las Vegas she had been "discovered" by assistant directors and offered a movie audition, and that each time she had been sick in the studio—literally sick to her stomach—and unable to go on. She had been too scared. Yet she still might have a career somehow, Larry thought. He could encourage her to practice. It would be an interest for her—something to do. She was barely past thirty and looked less. There was time.

Larry decided to read Camus in French and to translate some of the untranslated essays, just for practice, into English. One night he came home with the headphones Cynthia wanted, the old-fashioned kind made of black Bakelite, and hooked them up to the TV set through a control box that had an off-on switch for the speaker. Now that he could blank out the commercials, Larry would watch with Cynthia now and then—some of the news specials, and the Wide World of Sports, and the late-night reruns of President Kennedys press conferences, one of the few things they both enjoyed. They could both acknowledge his power, pulsing in him and out toward them—that sure, quick intelligence and that charm.

Cynthia was happier now, because with the headphones on and the speakers off she could watch as late as she wanted without being afraid of Larry. When the phone rang, she would not hear it. Larry would answer, finally, and if it was for her he would stand in front of the set gesturing until she took the headphones off. She would sit on the sofa for hours, dressed as if for company, her eyes made up to look even larger than they were, wearing one of the at-home hostessy things from Jax or Robert Leader she had bought before they were married, which hardly anyone but she and Larry had ever seen. Looking so pretty, and with those radio operator's black headphones on her ears.

The sight made Larry melancholy, and he continued to work lying on his bed, propped up with a writing board on his lap. He would hear Cynthia laughing sometimes in the silent living room, and now and then, hearing thin sounds from her headphones, he would come out to find her crying, the phones on her lap and the final credits of a movie on the screen. "I always cry at this one," she would say. With the headphones, Cynthia was spending more time before the set than ever. Larry encouraged her to sing—to take lessons again if she wanted. But she did sing, she said, in the afternoons. She sang with her records, usually. There were a few songs of Eydie's and Peggy's and Judy's she liked. She sang along with those.

In spite of everything, when Larry compared his life now with his first marriage or with the bitter years after that, he could not say that this was worse. Cynthia seemed almost content. She made no demands upon him and left him free to think or read what he pleased. But there were nights when he would put his book aside and lie on his bed, hearing Cynthia laugh now and then or get up to make herself another drink, and ask himself why he was there. Little, in his job or in his life, seemed reasonable or real.

Why had he fallen in love with Cynthia? It was just because she was so *American*, he decided one night. She *liked* canned chili and corned-beef hash, the Academy Awards, cole slaw, barbecued chicken, the Miss America contest, head lettuce and Russian dressing, astrology columns, *Modern Screen*, takeout pizza pies. She liked them and made faces at them at the same time, looking up or over at him and saying, "Oh, God, isn't this awful? Isn't this vile?" Everything he had turned his back on in the name of the Bauhaus and the Institute of Design, of Elizabeth David and James Beard, of Lewis Mumford, Paul Goodman, D. H. Lawrence, Henry Miller, Frank Lloyd Wright—here it all was dished up before him in Cynthia. All the things that (to tell the truth) he had never had enough of. He had lost out on them in high school, when he had really wanted them, because he was studious and shy. He had rejected them in college, where it was a matter of political principle among his friends to reject them, before he had the chance to find out what they were like. At thirty-eight, when he met Cynthia, what did he know? Weren't there vast areas of the American experience that he had missed? Why, until Cynthia he had never shacked up in a motel. Nor had he ever been in a barroom fight, or smoked pot, or been ticketed for speeding, or blacked out from booze.

What had he fallen in love with, then, but pop America! One more intellectual seduced by kitsch! He could almost see the humor in it. It was the first solid discovery about himself he had made for years, and he lay back in his bed, smiling. How glittering Cynthia's world had seemed, he thought. The sixties—this is what they *were!* Thruways, motels, Point Pleasant on a Saturday night, twisting on the juke! That trip to Atlantic City in winter where, at the Club Hialeah, the girls from South Jersey danced on the bar, and in the Hotel Marlborough-Blenheim he and Cynthia wandered through the cold deserted corridors and public rooms like actors in a shabby *Marienbad.* And the music! Miles, Monk, Chico, Mingus, the M.J.Q., Sinatra and Nelson Riddle, Belafonte, Elvis, Ray Charles, Dion, Lena Horne—all new to him. He had stopped listening to music before bop, and with Cynthia he listened to everything. Progressive or pop or rhythm and blues, whatever. Did he like it all—how was it possible to like it *all*?—because Cynthia did, or did he fall in love with Cynthia because she liked it all? What difference did it make? It was all new—a gorgeous blur of enthusiasms. For the first time in his life he had given himself away. How wonderful it had been, at thirty-eight, on the edge of middle age—*in* middle age—to play the fool! This was experience, this was *life*, this was the sixties—*his* generation, with his peers in charge, the Kennedys and the rest. Wasn't that coming alive, when you were free enough to play the fool and not care? And if there had been enough money, he and Cynthia might have kept it up. . . . They might.

Yet hardly a moment had passed during the first months with Cynthia when he did not know what he was doing. He had got into a discussion of pop culture one night in the Cedar Street Tavern not long after he and Cynthia were married. "You don't know what you're talking about," he had said to the others while Cynthia was on a trip to the head. "You only dip into it. Listen. You don't know. I've *married* it. I've married the whole great American *schmier*."

But how nearly he had been taken in! Cynthia never had. She knew show business from the inside, after all. She dug it, and liked it, and laughed at herself for liking it. She knew how shabby it was. Yet it did something for her—that trumpery, that fake emotion, that sincere corn. Once he found out something was bad, how could he care for it any longer? It was impossible. If he had gone overboard at first for Cynthia's world, wasn't that because it was new to him and he saw fresh energy there? And how spurious that energy had turned out to be—how slick, how manufactured, how dead! And how dull. Yet something in it rubbed off on Cynthia, mesmerized her, and made her glamorous, made her attractive to him still. That was the trouble. He still wanted her. He was as mesmerized as she. Wasn't it the fakery he despised that shone in Cynthia and drew him to her? Then what in their marriage was real? He felt as detached from his life as a dreamer at times feels detached from his dream.

Quiet and sedentary as it had become, Larry's life continued to be charged with a forced excitement. The pop love songs, the photographs of beautiful men and women in the magazines Cynthia read, the romantic movies on TV, Cynthia herself—changing her clothes three or four times a day as if she were the star in a play and Larry the audience—all stimulated him in what he considered an unnatural way. He recognized in himself an extravagant lust that was quickly expended but never spent when he and Cynthia made love, as if she were one of the idealized photographs of which she was so fond and he were returning within her to the fantasies of his adolescence, their intercourse no more than the solitary motions of two bodies accidentally joined.

"We shouldn't have got married," Cynthia said one hot Saturday night in the summer of 1963 as they were lying on their beds trying to fall asleep.

"Maybe not," Larry said.

"Marriage turns me off. Something happens. I told you."

"I didn't believe you," Larry said. "And anyway we're married."

"We sure are."

"I picked a lemon in the garden of love," Larry said. Cynthia laughed and moved into Larry's bed.

Late that night, though, he said something else. "We're like Catholics and their sacrament," he said. "When you're married for the second time, you're practically stuck with each other. You've almost got to work it out."

"You may think you're stuck, but *I'm* not," Cynthia said, and moved back to her own bed. The next Saturday night she brought up what Larry had said about being "stuck." Why had he said it? Didn't he know her at all? Whenever she felt bound she had to break free—right out the door, sooner or later. That was what had always happened. Was he trying to drive her away? He knew how independent she'd been. That's what he liked about her, he'd said once. All that talk about protecting each other's freedom! What a lot of crap. Look at them now. Two birds in a cage, a filthy cage.

Cynthia's anger frightened Larry, and, to his surprise, the thought of her leaving frightened him, too. But nothing changed. There wasn't much chance of her breaking away, after all. They didn't have enough money to separate, and neither of them really wanted to—not *that* routine, not again.

More and more often now Larry would sit in the living room reading while Cynthia watched her programs, headphones on her ears. He would look over at her, knowing that at that moment she was content, and feel some satisfaction, even a sense of domestic peace. At times he would lie with his head on Cynthia's lap while she watched, and she would stroke his hair.

One payday Larry came home with a second pair of headphones, made of green plastic and padded with foam rubber, the sort disc jockeys and astronauts wear, and plugged them into the stereo through a box that permitted turning off the speakers. Now he, like Cynthia, could listen in silence. He stacked some of his records on the turntable—the Mozart horn concertos, a Bach cantata, Gluck. It was eerie, Larry thought, for them both to be so completley absorbed, sitting twenty feet apart in that silent living room, and on the first night he found himself watching Cynthia's picture on the TV screen as the music in his ears seemed to fade away. Finally, he took off his earphones, joined Cynthia on the sofa, and asked her to turn on the sound. After a few nights, however, the sense of eeriness wore off, and Larry was as caught up in his music as Cynthia was in her shows. The stereo sound was so rich and pure; unmixed with other noises, the music carried directly into his brain, surrounding and penetrating him. It was so intense, so mindless. Listening was not a strong enough word for what was happening. The music flowed through him and swallowed him up. He felt endowed with a superior sense, as if he were a god. Yet there was something illicit about their both finding so intense a pleasure in isolation. He was troubled, off and on, by what they were falling into, but their life was tranquil and that was almost enough.

One night when Larry was reading (something he rarely did now) and there was nothing on TV she cared for, Cynthia put some of her records on the turntable and Larry's headphones on her ears and listened to Eydie and Judy and Frank, dancing a few steps now and then and singing the words softly. "Why didn't you tell me!" she said. It was *fantastic*. She could hear all the bass, and the color of the voices, and things in some of the arrangements she had never known were there. More and more often as the summer wore on, Cynthia would listen to her music instead of watching the tube, and Larry, thinking this a step in the right direction—toward her singing, perhaps —turned the stereo over to her several evenings a week and tried to concentrate again on his reading. But music now held him in a way books no longer could, and after a few weeks he bought a second stereo phonograph and a second set of headphones. By the fall of 1963, he and Cynthia had begun to listen, each to his own music, together. "This is really a kick," Cynthia would say. The intensity of it excited them both.

On the day President Kennedy was assassinated, Larry and Cynthia were having one of their rare lunches in midtown at an Italian place near Bloomingdale's, where Cynthia planned to go shopping afterward. There was a small television set above the restaurant bar, and people stood there waiting for definite news after the first word of the shooting. When it was clear that the President was dead, Larry and Cynthia went back to their apartment. Larry didn't go back to work. They watched television together that afternoon and evening, and then they went to bed and began to weep. When Larry stopped, Cynthia would sob, and then Larry would start again. So it went until after four in the morning, when they fell asleep. Until the funeral was over, Cynthia sat before the set most of the day and night. Much of the time she was crying, and every night when she came to bed the tears would start. Larry, dry-eyed sooner than she was, was at first sympathetic, then impatient, then annoyed.

"He was such a *good* man," Cynthia would say, or

"He was *ours*. He was all we had," and after the burial she said, half smiling. "He was a wonderful star." Nothing in her actual life could ever move her so deeply, Larry thought. How strange, to feel real sorrow and weep real tears for an unreal loss! But she was suffering, no question of that, and she could not stop crying. The Christmas season came and went, and she still wept. She had begun to drink heavily, and often Larry would put her to bed. On the edge of unconsciousness, she would continue to cry.

What was she, he thought, but a transmitter of electronic sensations? First she had conveyed the nation's erotic fantasies to him, and now it was the national sorrow, and one was as unreal as the other. But there was more to it than that. John Kennedy had been a figure on her own erotic fantasies. She had told Larry so. She wept for him as a woman would for her dead lover. She was like a woman betrayed by Death, Larry thought, when what had betrayed her was the television set she had counted upon to shield her from the real. It had always told her stories of terror and passion that, because they were fictitious, might be endured, and now it had shown her actual death and actual sorrow. There was no way to console her, because her loss was not an actual loss, and Larry began to think her suffering more than he could endure. He began to wonder if she might not have lost her mind.

Cynthia read nothing for weeks after the assassination but articles on it, and so she did not hear of the Beatles until Larry, hoping to distract her, brought home their first album. She thought little of it at first, but after the Beatles appeared on the Ed Sullivan Show in February she became an admirer and then a devotee. Larry brought her the new Beatles 45's as they came out and, he stood in line with teen-age girls at the newsstands on Forty-second Street to buy the Beatles fan magazines. "I guess the period of mourning is over," Cynthia said one Saturday night. She still saved articles about the assassination, though, and photographs of Jacqueline in black.

When Cynthia began to sing as she listened to the Beatles, late one night, Larry, listening from the bedroom, was pleased. She would play their records over and over, accompanying them in a voice that seemed flat and unresonant, perhaps because with the headphones on she could not hear the sounds she made. She no longer wept, or Larry was asleep when she did.

One night, Larry woke around three to the tinny noise of "I Want to Hold Your Hand" spilling from Cynthia's phones and found he was hungry. On his way to the kitchen, he stopped in the dark hall to watch Cynthia, who stood in the center of the living room with the astronaut headphones on, singing what sounded like a harmonizing part, a little off-key, holding an imaginary guitar, swaying jerkily, and smiling as if she were before an audience. Her performance, empty as it was, seemed oddly polished and professional. Afraid of startling her, he stood watching until the end of the song before he entered the room.

"How much did you see?" Cynthia said.

"Nothing," Larry said. "I was going to get a glass of milk, that's all." The look on Cynthia's face as she stood before him with those enormous headphones clamped to her ears troubled him, as if he had discovered her in some indecency better forgotten. "After this I'll flick out the lights and warn you," he said.

And he said no more about it, though often now he awoke during the night to the faint sounds from Cynthia's headphones and wondered what she was doing that held her so fast. He was jealous of it in a way. She was rarely in bed before four, and always in bed when he left for work in the morning. In the evening, though, as she watched television, she seemed happy enough, and much as she had been before Kennedy's death.

For some time after the assassination, she gave up their Saturday nights in the bars, but by April they

were again making their rounds. Once, when they
came home higher and happier than usual, Cynthia
danced and sang for Larry as she had before, and for a
while Larry danced with her, something he did not do
often. They were having such a pleasant time that
when Larry put on a Beatles album and Cynthia began
her performance for him, she explained. "We're at the
Palladium in London, you see," she said. "The place
is mobbed. . . . The Beatles are onstage. . . . I'm singing with them, and naturally everybody loves us. I
work through the whole show . . . playing second guitar. I back up George." And then she sang, a third or
so below the melody. " 'She was just seventeen if you
know what I mean. . . .' "

"I never sing lead," Cynthia said when the number
was over. "I play a minor rôle."

"Is this what you do at night?" Larry asked her.

Cynthia was breathing heavily. "Sure," she said. "It
sounds silly, but it's not. Besides, it's possible, isn't it?
It *could* happen. I can sing." She looked at Larry, her
eyes candid and kind. "Don't worry," she said. "I'm
not losing my grip."

"It's a nice game," Larry said later when they were
in bed.

"Oh, it's more than a game," Cynthia said. "When
I'm with them in the Palladium, I'm really *there*. It's
more real than here. I know it's a fantasy, though."

"How did you meet the Beatles?" Larry asked her.

"D'you really want to hear?" Cynthia said. She
seemed pleased at his interest, Larry thought, but then
she was drunk. They both were.

"It's not much of a story," she said. "The details
vary, but basically I am standing on Fifth Avenue
there near the Plaza in the snow waiting for a cab at
three in the afternoon, dressed in my black flared coat
and black pants and the black boots you gave me, and
I have a guitar. No taxis, or they're whipping right by,
and I'm *cold*. You know how cold I can get. And then
this Bentley stops with a couple of guys in front and in

back is George Harrison all alone, though sometimes
it's Paul. He gives me a lift and we talk. He's completely polite and sincere, and I can see he likes me. It
seems the Beatles are rehearsing for a television special at Central Plaza and they'll be there the next day,
so he asks me to come up and bring my guitar. I go,
naturally, and it turns out they are auditioning girls,
and I'm the winner. What would be the point if I
wasn't? They want a girl for just one number, but
when they see how terrific I am, of course they love
me, and when they find out I've already worked up all
their songs I'm in."

"You join them."

"Sure. They insist. I have to leave you, but you
don't mind, not anymore. In one year, we're The
Beatles and Cynthia and we're playing the Palladium,
and Princess Margaret and Tony are there, and Frank,
and Peter O'Toole, and David McCallum, and Steve
McQueen, and Bobby Kennedy. And all those men
want me, I can feel it, and I'm going to meet them
afterward at the Savoy in our suite."

" 'Our'?"

"I'm married to a rich diamond merchant who lets
me do whatever I want. Played by George Sanders."

"I thought you were married to me," Larry said.

"Oh, no. You divorced me, alleging I was mentally
cruel. Maybe I was once, but I'm not anymore, because the Beatles love me. They're my brothers. They're
not jealous of me at all."

"Are you putting me on?" Larry said.

"No. Why should I? I made it all up, if that's what
you mean, but I *really* made it up."

"Do you believe any of it?" Larry said.

Cynthia smiled at him. "Don't you? You used to say
I had a good voice and you used to say I was pretty.
Anyway, I don't have fantasies about things that
couldn't possibly happen. I could get a job tomorrow
if you'd let me."

Cynthia's voice had the lilt Larry remembered from

the days before they were married. The whole thing was so convincing and so insane. He began to indulge her in it. "I'm going to Beatle now," Cynthia would say nearly every night after dinner, and Larry would go into the bedroom. Whenever he came out, he would flick the hall lights and she would stop. She was shy and did not let him watch often at first. She seemed embarrassed that she had told him as much as she had—if, indeed, she remembered telling him anything at all.

Larry liked the Beatles more and more as the nights went by, and often he would listen to their records with the speakers on before Cynthia began her performance. "Listen, Cynthia," he said one Saturday night. "The Beatles are filled with the Holy Ghost." He was really quite drunk. "Do you know that? They came to bring us back to life? Out of the old nightmare. Dallas, Oswald, Ruby, all of it, cops, reporters, thruways, lies, crises, missiles, heroes, cameras, fear—all that mishmash, and all of it dead. All of us dead watching the burial of the dead. Look at *you*. They've brought you back to life. I couldn't—not after November. Nothing could."

"You're right," Cynthia said. "I didn't want to tell you. I thought you'd be jealous."

"Jealous? Of the Beatles?"

"They're very real to me, you know."

"I'm not jealous," Larry said.

"Then will you read to me the way you used to? Read me to sleep?"

"Sure."

"Can I get in your bed?"

"Sure."

Before Larry had finished a page, he was asleep, and Cynthia was asleep before him.

For her birthday in September, Larry gave Cynthia an electric guitar. Though she could not really play it and rarely even plugged it in, she used the guitar now in her performances, pretending to pluck the strings. She began to dress more elaborately for her Beatling, too, making up as if for the stage.

She was a little mad, no question of it, Larry thought, but it did no harm. He no longer loved her, nor could he find much to like in her, and yet he cared for her, he felt, and he saw that she was too fragile to be left alone. She was prettier now than he had ever seen her. She *should* have been a performer. She needed applause and admirers and whatever it was she gave herself in her fantasies—something he alone could not provide. Their life together asked little of him at any rate, and cost little. By now he and Cynthia rarely touched or embraced; they were like old friends—fellow-conspirators, even, for who knew of Cynthia's Beatle world but him?

Cynthia discussed her performances with Larry now, telling him of the additions to her repertoire and of the new places she and the Beatles played—Kezar Stadium, the Hollywood Bowl, Philharmonic Hall. She began to permit him in the living room with her, and he would lie on the sofa listening to his music while her Beatling went on. He felt sometimes that by sharing her fantasies he might be sharing her madness, but it seemed better for them both to be innocently deranged than to be as separate as they had been before. All of it tired Larry, though. He was past forty. He felt himself growing old, and his tastes changing. Now he listened to the things he had liked in college—the familiar Beethoven and Mozart symphonies, and Schubert, and Brahms, in new stereophonic recordings. Often as he listened he would fall asleep and be awakened by the silence when the last of the records stacked on the turntable had been played. Usually Cynthia's performance would still be going on, and he would rise, take off his headphones and go to bed.

One night Larry fell asleep toward the end of the "Messiah," with the bass singing "The trumpet shall sound . . ." and the trumpet responding, and woke as usual in silence, the headphones still on his ears. This time, he lay on the sofa looking at Cynthia, his eyes barely open. She had changed clothes again, he saw, and was wearing the silver lamé pants suit, left over from her singing days, that she had worn the first night he had come to her apartment. He saw her bow, prettily and lightly in spite of the headphones on her ears, and extend her arms to her imaginary audience. Then he watched her begin a slow, confined dance, moving no more than a step to the side or forward and then back. She seemed to be singing, but with his headphones on Larry could not hear. She raised her arms again, this time in a gesture of invitation, and although she could not know he was awake it seemed to Larry that she was beckoning to him and not to an imaginary partner—that this dance, one he had never seen, was for him, and Cynthia was asking him to join her in that slow and self-contained step.

Larry rose and sat looking at her, his head by now nearly clear. "Come," she beckoned. "Come." He saw her lips form the word. Was it he to whom she spoke or one of her fantasies? What did it matter? She stood waiting for her partner—for him—and Larry got up, unplugged his headphones, and walked across the room to her. The movement seemed to him a movement of love. He plugged his headphones in next to Cynthia's and stood before her, almost smiling. She smiled, and then, in silence, not quite touching her in that silent room, with the sound of the Beatles loud in his ears, Larry entered into her dance.

Getting On

ROXANA ROBINSON

Roxana Robinson was born in Harlan County, Kentucky, and grew up in Bucks County, Pennsylvania. She was brought up a Quaker and studied at Bennington under Bernard Malumud and Howard Nemerov. She has worked as an art dealer and curator in New York City and Westchester County. Her stories have appeared in The New Yorker, McCall's *and* The Southern Review. *"Getting On" was her second published story and was selected for* Best American Short Stories 1984. Summer Light, *her first novel, was published in 1988, and she is currently at work on a biography of Georgia O'Keefe.*

"Ordinarily," the following story says of Priscilla, a wife whose husband is dying, "she could feel Edward's day travelling along next to hers. He might spend the morning reading, or writing letters, or out in the car doing errands, but she could feel the pace of it; she knew she would meet him for lunch, and for dinner. Now she felt him hidden and distant, his day unknown. This was the other part of his being in the hospital. The first part, grief and fear, she thought she could deal with, but this absence was more difficult, as it did not lessen. There was something at the back of her mind, but she did not seek it out." With poignancy and tenderness Roxana Robinson relentlessly pursues the essence of Priscilla's experience and with graceful understanding makes her experience—however unfamiliar to

our own—something, finally, that we know. "Getting On" is not only about one woman's gallantry and commitment, but also about the deep, abiding faith the author places in human love and its profound affirmative spirit.

Roxana Robinson lives in Katonah, New York.

Priscilla's husband began bleeding very late on New Year's Eve. This was not the result of wild partying: they had been in bed by ten. Mary McDougal had served them an elegant meal: smoked trout, roast veal, lemon soufflé, and two very nice wines. Edward had toasted Priscilla, lifting his glass and inclining his head courteously. "Priscilla, dear," he said. "Edward," Priscilla said, lifting hers, and they drank together.

"Well, what shall we do with this one?" Priscilla asked, leaning back as though she could see the year standing before her like an old cabinet, each drawer full of possibilities. She was seventy-three years old.

"I plan to do a lot of errands. Catch up on sleep. Find God. Things like that."

"I have *lots* of plans," Priscilla said grandly. "I want to put in white iris, all along those granite rocks. I have a vision of a great drift of white against that dour gray stone. And I think this is the year for the rose garden. I want it along the bottom lawn, against the fence. I plan to become known as the first great blind landscape designer." Priscilla had, in spite of three operations, lost almost all of her sight two years earlier. She now wore thick glasses, which made her eyes look bleary and enormous beneath her short, tufty white hair.

"Purr," Edward said, "why don't we just have roses sent out by limousine from New York every day all year? It would be much cheaper."

"Edward—"

"A rose garden would cost the earth," Edward said. "It really would. You'd have to bring in nearly two tons of topsoil, and gravel and things. I looked into it once. And here's Mary with the champagne, which I'd much rather have than topsoil and gravel."

Every year Edward asked Mary McDougal to sit down and have dessert and champagne with them. She had been with them in the house in Connecticut for sixteen years. He always drank a toast to her.

"To Mary," Edward said, raising his glass. He was small-boned and frail, and dry as a cricket. "We could not do without you." He was a kind man, gentle, but not sentimental.

Mary McDougal, neat, sandy-haired, and Scottish, dipped her head.

"We *adore* you," Priscilla announced. She took a long drink of champagne and raised her glass again dramatically. "Having you here makes it *pure* heaven. Being without you is impossible to imagine—pure hell, I'm sure." Priscilla had been outspoken since she had learned, early, to talk.

"To both of you," Mary said, raising her glass and nodding, with a small frown to show her seriousness. They were all three rather formal people.

"What I love about you, Mary, is the way you *learn* things," Priscilla said. She looked at Edward. "Take Mary's birds. She knows a hundred times more birds than I've ever thought of. And she's only been at it about a minute."

"Eight years," Mary said.

Priscilla waved her hand. "I've been at it for thirty," she said, "or meant to. The way I go after things like that is to put the book under my pillow and sleep on it, hoping that something will seep through during the night. Mary really learns all the different calls, and the colors of the mates, and every little thing. It's *quite* extraordinary. I'm still stuck on crows and robins."

Edward smiled. He would not be drawn into his

wife's hyperbole. He was a dry counterpoint. "Quite extraordinary," he said.

"Do you know we had two downy woodpeckers at the feeder this morning," Mary said, uncomfortable at the praise.

"They're cold," Edward said. "We should be putting suet out for them."

"I have been," Mary said. "It was four below zero this morning."

"Dear God," Priscilla said, "why didn't anybody tell me!" She was six feet tall, and had been lean and rangy until her forties, when she was attacked so violently by arthritis that she considered suicide. Instead, cortisone had been discovered, and Priscilla had chosen relief over vanity. Her body was now bloated and blurred by the disease and the drugs, and she shuffled about the house with a walking stick. She went outside rarely during the winter.

"It's bitter," Edward said, looking at his wife. Edward's skin was a very pale tan, and his eyes were a dark bright brown. He spoke flatly, without inflection, and he seemed to be in possession of some quiet secret that other people did not have. Calm and complete, he watched other people steadily as they spoke.

It was just before ten when the three of them went off to bed—Mary McDougal to her room off the kitchen, Edward and Priscilla to the other end of the house. Edward went alone up to the big square bedroom he and Priscilla had shared for thirty years. Priscilla now slept in the guest room off the library, which had become her room when she could no longer manage the stairs. Neither slept immediately. Edward was rereading "War and Peace," and he looked forward to the thin strip at the end of each day—distant turbulence, remote passion—before he slept. Priscilla watched the news on a television set perched right next to her bed. She could see very little of it, but she knew each of the voices, and she could see gestures and make out some of the closeups. It comforted her

to find this familiar group available to her night after
night. She turned off the television after the news and
slept, her thickened body a large mass beneath the
peach-colored covers.

In the middle of the night, Mary McDougal knocked
gently on her door. Priscilla was a light sleeper and
awoke immediately It's come, she thought calmly,
though she did not know what she meant by that.

"What is it, Mary?" she asked, sitting up.

"It's Mr. Green," Mary said. "he's bleeding. From
the nose. I've tried ice, but it won't stop."

"Have you called the doctor?" Priscilla asked. She
struggled to disentangle her feet from the bedclothes.

"They're sending an ambulance," Mary said.

"Would you hand me my wrapper?" Priscilla had
gotten free, and swung her heavy feet onto the rug.

"Are you going up to him, then," Mary said, her
accent strong.

"Of course I'm going up to him. Would you hand
me my cane, please?"

When she reached the bottom of the big front stairs,
Priscilla called up, "Whoo-oo! Edward! I'm coming
up!" She put her foot onto the bottom step, gave her
cane to Mary, and took hold of the bannister.

By the time she had reached the landing the ambulance had arrived. Four men in pale-blue shirts and
dark-blue pants carried a long stretcher up the stairs,
angling around the corner. "Excuse me," one of the
men said as they stepped smoothly past her. Priscilla
wavered and turned toward Mary.

"It's the men with the stretcher," Mary said loudly.
"Let me help you down. We'll wait in the hall."

The two women made the trip down carefully, step
by step. By the time they reached the hall, the men in
blue had caught up with them. They carried the stretcher
as though it weighed no more than before, as though it
were worth no more than before. They started to go
by the two women, but Priscilla, leaning forward onto
her cane, stopped them.

"Just one moment," she said loudly, as though she had caught them stealing something from her house. The men stopped; Priscilla shuffled to the stretcher. "Edward?" she asked, as if hoping that he were still upstairs, unconnected with these strange, crisp men.

"I'm here, Priscilla," Edward said, and he reached out a hand and touched her forearm in the woolly robe. The rest of him lay passive: he had given other people responsibility for his movement.

"*There* you are," said Priscilla, as though she were reassuring him of that. She could not make out her husband's face; the stark white of the sheets seemed uninterrupted. She patted his hand. "Don't worry," she said, her voice strong.

"Don't *you* worry," Edward said. His wife peered toward his voice, trying to discover his face. It was muffled with wads of Kleenex. Edward had taken a whole boxful and pressed it to his nose; he had not wanted Priscilla to see the blood.

"We've got to get back to the vehicle," said one of the men in blue.

"Yes, all right," Priscilla said. She wished she could see Edward's face; she wished she could stoop easily and kiss him before the men carried him out the door. She patted his hand and stood back, releasing him. The men walked on with the stretcher, making no noise at all on the thick dark rugs that stretched the length of the hall.

"I'll get you some warm milk, shall I?" Mary said loudly, speaking to cover the sound of the front door closing behind the men.

Priscilla heard the worry in Mary's voice, but liked to prove people wrong about herself. "No, thank you, dear," she said briskly. "I'll just take a pill and go right off to sleep."

The doctor had said only that things were under control, and that he would talk to her in the morning. Priscilla took her pill and lay in bed in the dark, waiting for the pill to work. She had timed it: it took forty minutes to seep into her bloodstream, to quiet her thoughts. She hoped Edward had been warm enough in the ambulance—how cold had Mary said it was? But of course the ambulance would be heated.

She rolled heavily over to look at the time. She used a kitchen clock, with enormous numerals that glowed with an unholy green light. Even so, she had to turn on the lamp and reach for her glasses. Only fifteen minutes had passed. Priscilla had never thought Edward would leave first; the doctors had always been called for *her*. She had assumed he would go on looking after her: foolish, she thought now. He was six years older than she was, and there they were, three old people in a big house in the country. It could not go on forever. At least Mary would not leave her. When Mary had first come to them, she was in her early forties, and Priscilla worried that she might marry and leave them. Mary had been pert and unpredictable then, and never said where she went when she spent the night out. But that had passed. She was quieter now; the three of them would be childless forever. Priscilla had warned Edward in the very beginning that she could not have children. A clumsy doctor in Paris had settled that for her in 1932. Edward had said it didn't matter; what he wanted was her. He had never mentioned it again. She thought of her husband's kind silence. She wished she could have stooped and kissed him goodbye; she wished she could have ridden in the ambulance with him, holding him steady against the curves.

Priscilla shifted her feet under the sheets, wondering if she should take off some covers, or put some on. For a moment she could not remember what season it was, whether she should feel hot or cold. But it was cold, she remembered, with exasperation at her muddleheadedness. Edward had said it was bitter; she had worried about his being cold in the ambulance. She still could not really connect Edward with the ambulance—

it was so unlike any way she had ever known him. But she had heard the door close behind him, she had felt the cold air come in around her. Surrounded by smooth flower-printed sheets and soft blankets, she tried to imagine the night just outside the walls of her bedroom, the still cold eating into the bones of the landscape.

In the morning, Priscilla asked Mary to put a call through to the hospital even before she brought in the breakfast tray. The doctor was precise, but he did not give Priscilla what she wanted to hear. Closing her eyes while she spoke to him, she wanted a particular tone in his voice, a note that would answer the question she was not ready to ask. But the doctor's voice was low and full of moderation. Edward was in intensive care; they were doing everything they could.

"Is he still bleeding?" Priscilla asked.

"Yes," the doctor said, "but very little."

"Why did he start?"

The doctor cleared his throat. "It's hard to say exactly," he said. His voice had shifted to a higher level, as though he were talking about something he took no responsibility for, something that sailed free through the air. "With someone that age, often things just give out. Some of the veins in his nose simply gave out."

"But why doesn't it stop?"

"Your husband is taking medication for his heart which has an anti-clotting agent in it."

Priscilla thought about this. "So he's a hemophiliac."

"Practically speaking, the conditions are similar."

"Why can't you stop the heart medicine, for God's sake?"

The doctor sounded nettled. "We have, of course, considered that, Mrs. Green. We don't want to do anything drastic."

"What *have* you done!"

"We've cauterized the vessels and closed them. An-

other has opened, very slightly. We're going to give
him a massive transfusion. He's lost quite a lot of
blood."

"A transfusion, good," Priscilla said. She waited,
but the doctor had nothing more to say.

Priscilla had her breakfast on a tray in the dining
room instead of in bed. She felt she must make a show
of strength, that she must carry all this off.

It was still very cold, Mary told her. The trees were
glittering with ice. Priscilla had to ask Mary to draw
one of the curtains against the glare that fell across the
table. She had tea, then toast, and part of a sweet
green melon. She wondered what Edward had had for
breakfast. Surely he was conscious? She could not
bear to think of him with tubes entering his body.

She liked the idea of his having a transfusion. She
imagined a huge vessel of blood blooming by his side,
the steady scarlet stream flowing into his pale arm,
enriching his frail body, urging him on. She had had a
transfusion once herself, after the operation in Paris.
It had been amazingly casual. On one side of a curtain lay a dock-worker, or a grocer, with black hair
and a huge burly chest and a thick reek of garlic. She
lay on a pallet on the other side of the curtain, and his
blood flowed silently into her. She had felt wonderful
afterward, rich and strong.

Priscilla drank her second cup of tea very slowly, sip
by sip, as though the process itself were very important. She felt as though she were walking on ice of
exquisite fragility, and that every step must be super-
humanly smooth—a gliding gesture, without shock or
impact. She did not want to turn her head suddenly,
she did not want a thought to enter her mind unannounced.

It was particularly good tea. She preferred black
Lapsang souchong to the stronger Earl Grey that Edward had liked. *Likes*, she corrected herself, frightened by the past tense. The trouble with Lapsang
souchong was that it should be drunk clear and dark,

the taste untroubled by milk and sugar, but Priscilla liked milk and sugar in her tea. It was a problem. This morning she was having Earl Grey, with a little milk and a lot of sugar. She could tell from the feel that it was in one of the Herend cups, with butterflies on the sides and beetles in the bottoms of the saucers. She liked the butterflies, but had never been fond of the beetles. When Mary came in to clear away, Priscilla said, "We must send over a basket to the hospital. Some Earl Grey tea, some marmalade. What else? Should we send over whole meals, do you think?"

She tried to talk to the doctor again, but he was making his rounds. She left her name, and shuffled into the library to watch the news. The television was hidden by a pair of cupboard doors in the panelling; she sat in a leather armchair in front of it. Priscilla watched the news, then the soaps. She knew Mary was watching the soaps in the kitchen. At lunch they would compare notes. The people in the soaps were invariably badly behaved. "Wasn't it awful how he took up with his wife's sister?" Mary would ask indignantly.

Priscilla did not like the way the day was proceeding. Ordinarily, she could feel Edward's day travelling along next to hers. He might spend the morning reading, or writing letters, or out in the car doing errands, but she could feel the pace of it; she knew she would meet him for lunch, and for dinner. Now she felt him hidden and distant, his day unknown. This was the other part of his being in the hospital. The first part, grief and fear, she thought she could deal with, but this absence was more difficult, as it did not lessen. There was something at the back of her mind, but she did not seek it out.

On the third day, she had Mary drive her over to see him. She was wheeled through the long quiet corridors, as though she herself were a patient, but this did not bother her. She wanted to get to him quickly, faster than she could walk. All her life she had wanted to get on with things.

Once in the room, Mary had to point Edward out to
Priscilla, there were so many unknown shapes and
outlines before her. When finally she could see Edward, she knew she had lost him. He had been taken
over, closed off to her. There were vessels hanging
over him, with pale fluids that dripped into the secret
places inside Edward, not the direct red flow she had
imagined but a slow, relentless drip. Sheets were spread
over him, and his face—although she could not be
sure—seemed smaller, the dry, parchment skin useless
for expression or protection. Only the eyes were the
same: dark, bright, watchful.

But Priscilla was herself. She had been preparing for
this. She was a richly embroidered charmer—intricate,
lush, inexhaustible. "Darling!" she cried, as though
they were lovers meeting in front of the cameras.
"You look very uncomfortable," she went on, turning
her head, tilting it, to focus. "What can we do to make
you feel better? And what would you like us to bring
you?" The room was already bright with flowers. "I've
brought your little radio, so you can have some good
music, and some marmalade, and some Earl Grey,
and a little pillow that smells good, and your silk
pajamas . . ." Priscilla carried on as if she were in a
salon. She did not know how else to behave. Edward
smiled at her, and sometimes spoke. When Mary
wheeled Priscilla out again into the hall, Priscilla felt
as though she weighed three hundred pounds. She did
not speak to Mary until late that night, when she
asked if Mary would call the nurses' station to tell
Edward good night from her. Then Priscilla took her
pill and went to bed. The weight had not left her; she
could barely move. It was an immense relief to settle
down on the mattress and lie still.

Edward was Priscilla's second husband. She had
loved Dennis, her first, with a headlong desperation
that had not calmed in the fifty years she had known
him. She had put him out of her life entirely, but when

she thought of him it was with the fierce, remembered appetite of an addict. Dennis had stiff reddish-brown hair—they wore it short in those days—and with blue eyes, and had been as trustworthy as a kite. He had made ardent love to Priscilla in Paris, while still married to his second wife. Once divorced he had married Priscilla, and they moved back to New York. She had come home one afternoon to find him taking a steamy bath with one of her friends. She had never felt so outraged—that was really the word for it. All her love, all her high, keen passion, all that profound tenderness she felt for him, and the best he could do in response was to soap Julie Langdon's back up into a creamy lather.

Dennis had been even more ardent in winning her the second time than he had been the first, but she knew him now. During his siege, Priscilla met a friend in the middle of Park Avenue one day, and, balancing between streams of traffic, asked her friend what she was doing.

"Going to Reno to get a divorce," the friend said.

"I'm coming with you," Priscilla said, and that was that.

Edward had not swept her off her feet. He had waited for her. At parties he watched her, and he would smile, but he would not come over to speak. The first time he took her to dinner he picked up her hand and said, "These paws are enormous. Why do you have such large hands?"

"I'm six feet tall, that's why," Priscilla answered. She had been charmed: other men told her how lovely she was. Why was Edward so sure of himself? It was only from his close, silent scrutiny that she knew how he felt.

Priscilla was living then in a little apartment on East End Avenue, with windows on the river, and good rugs, and her beautiful Queen Anne highboy. Edward had sent her, carefully wrapped, a pair of shiny black galoshes with red buckles. They were huge; they must have been for a fireman, she thought. She filled them with freesias and lilies and put one on either side of the highboy. Edward smiled when he saw them, and nodded, but neither of them mentioned the boots.

It beguiled Priscilla that Edward would not be mad for her. She could not make him do what she wanted. Once, depressed and surly, she had hung up on him when he called. He had not called back. After a week she called him, anxious.

"Edward? It's Priscilla."

"I know that."

"Well, aren't you sorry?" she asked.

"For what?"

"For not calling?" Priscilla's heart pounded. What if she were going too far?

"Haven't I called?" asked Edward.

"Not enough," said Priscilla, and it was an apology. It was the end of her struggling; she liked knowing she had met her match, and she felt that Edward was kind and solid. Edward was for keeps, not for other ladies. He had been the center of her life for thirty-five years, and took all his baths alone.

When she lost most of her eyesight and stopped talking or moving, sitting like a fallen tree in the library all day, Edward had bullied her back to life. "Oh, there you are," he would say. "Still sulking. Good, good. Gets the blood going. Well, let me know if you ever want to say anything."

In the beginning, she had barely heard him. She could not spare any extra attention, with the world turned into this shifting screen of smoky images, watery colors, and unpredictable shapes; she could not remember why people had conversations at all, or what there might be to discuss. Then she began to hear him, and she got cross and answered back. "I am not sulking, Edward, for God's sake, I'd like a little peace and quiet once in a while."

"Yes, I see that. I'm very impressed. Well, anytime, you'd like a little conversation, do let me know."

She was sleeping downstairs by then, and that night he took her in his arms when they said good night to each other, holding her for a minute and breathing into her ear. She had been beautiful as a young woman; she knew why Edward had been drawn to her, but what could he now feel for the thickened, gimpy, bleary-eyed creature she had become?

Lying in bed, Priscilla realized that Edward would not come back to this house. However long it took, she could see that he had begun something which would end with his death, and that she was no longer connected with his life or even with this process of dying. She was now alone for good, in the big house with Mary. Edward would not emerge from the lemon-colored bedroom upstairs, he would not argue with her anymore about politics. Her life would be discussing the soaps with Mary, and listening to Great Books on her tape machine. Most of her friends had died, and her two brothers lived in California and Florida.

Priscilla rolled over in the dark, waiting for the pill to work. She would not think about that. Thirty years ago, she and Edward had bought twenty acres in this town and built a house. They had used it on weekends until Edward retired, and then they moved to the country altogether. The house was on a plateau. The land in front sloped gently down from the terrace, through marshes and meadows toward the road, which was hidden. In back, there were broad fields, and then the land began to rise to a wooded ridge, with glacial outcroppings of gray rock. Priscilla and Edward had planted very carefully. They had begun with a line of trees along the edge of the woods—redbuds and dog-woods and witch hazel—so that the first hint of spring was the mist of color at the end of the field, a fine haze that made Priscilla's heart lift when she saw it. She imagined the rest of the woods behind it, the oaks and ash trees building up slowly into a green breaker that would flood over the ridge and down across the meadows. The fields were full of jonquils and narcissus in the spring, and she had planted wild flowers in them for midsummer and fall: Indian paintbrush and Queen Anne's lace, chicory and sweet everlasting. Priscilla went over all of this in her mind.

Below the terrace was the lower lawn, and it was here that Priscilla wanted the rose garden. She began to plan it. She would have one long bed, the length of the lawn, with a wooden fence behind it for the climbers. She began to list the roses: Queen Elizabeth and Charlotte Armstrong, Albertine and Souvenir du Docteur Jamain. She had always wondered who Docteur Jamain was; she imagined a dark-eyed lover whose roses flourished on the strength of his passion. Along he fence she would plant New Dawn, Étoile de Hollande, Ophelia. She loved the names, and the flimsy softness of the petals. She wanted big bowls of roses, big floating pools of scent throughout the house. In the darkened room, she raised her hand above her head and opened the fingers, closed them. It was a small movement, and one that caused her no pain. She could do it easily.

Sundays

ELLEN WILBUR

Ellen Wilbur was born in Montclair, New Jersey. She was a student at Bennington College and Wesleyan University and began to publish short stories in the early 1970s in Ploughshares, The Virginia Quarterly Review, Shenandoah, *and* The Georgia Review. *A book of stories,* Wind and Birds and Human Voices, *was published in 1984. She lives in Cambridge, Massachusetts, with her husband and son.*

In the following story a woman wonders about the reasons her husband has taken to lying down on Sunday afternoons. Within several pages Ellen Wilbur touches upon the essential circumstances of a married couple in love: the depth of their companionship, the pleasures and surprises they find in each other's company, and the piercing brevity of their days together.

She couldn't remember when he'd started lying down on Sunday afternoons. He hadn't done it when they first were married. At least not regularly. Now he seemed to do it every week, each Sunday sometime after four. She'd notice the sudden quiet in the house when he lay down, but then she would forget it, lost in some task. She'd be wiping down the woodwork, washing windows, sweeping up the hall or cooking, hum-

ming to herself and peaceful in the way she only felt
when she was busy. Of all the days she liked Sundays
the best. The other days went by so fast, they jumbled
all together. But Sunday was long. The hours passed
slowly, with dignity, like time out of her childhood.
She could catch up on things she'd missed or put off
all the week while she was out at work. She liked to
bake on Sundays. She made pies and home-made breads
or muffins. All the things he liked. She'd prepare a
roast of lamb or beef or chicken with potatoes. The
kitchen windows steamed up in the winter and the
cooking smells spread through the whole of the little
house until it was so warm and homey that it seemed
to cry out for the child they'd lost, the tiny girl who'd
lived only one day, whose perfect little face was still so
real to her that when she thought of it her hand would
fly up to her mouth, and she would sometimes throw
the kitchen door wide open to the chill and let the
frigid air pour into the cheerful, steamy room.

It always took her by surprise to find him lying
down. She'd be carrying up the laundry or her sewing
when she'd pass the open bedroom door and see him
on their bed. Sometimes she'd hurry past the door
without a word as if the sight of him embarrassed her.
She couldn't imagine lying down during the day doing
nothing. Just the thought of it made her jumpy. If he'd
only sleep, it wouldn't bother her so much. But he
never did. He lay there wide awake and he looked
unlike himself. Sometimes not even gazing out the
window, but staring up at the empty ceiling in a way
that made her think of someone very old. Yet he was
only thirty-five, a burly, lively man. He looked out of
place, lying so still.

Why shouldn't the poor man rest, she told herself.
He worked hard all week long. He was up before her
every morning, wide awake the moment that he rose.
She'd wake to the sound of him whistling in the shower
and have to wrench herself up through a wall of sleep
and hurry down to fix his breakfast. She'd have his

orange juice fresh squeezed, his eggs done over light, his dark rye lightly buttered and his coffee steaming in his cup by the time he appeared with his brief-case in his hand.

"I don't know why you make yourself get up. I could just as easily eat out," he'd said hundreds of times. She didn't have to be at work till ten.

She stood at the window when he left the house. He liked to walk the mile down town to catch the train to work. Even in winter he went off through ice or heavy snow as if the weather couldn't touch him. He had a light, springy walk for someone so large. She'd never seen another man who walked exactly as he did.

He never watched t.v. or listened to the radio or read when he lay down on Sundays. His stillness and his silence fascinated her. When they went out to parties, people hurried up to greet him. They gathered all around him. He was such a talker and a story teller. She was shy in groups. She never laughed or joked or became close to people at her job the way he did. He was always calling her to see if he could bring somebody home to supper. Yet when they were alone together, he was quiet. She did most of the talking, as if there were no end to all the things she'd like to tell him.

"Tom?" she said some Sundays, stopping at the bedroom door. He'd turn and look at her with a little smile, never startled. He wasn't a nervous man, not at all like her. "What were you thinking about just then? You looked a million miles away." She stayed in the hall with her broom or dust cloth held tight, anxious to resume her work.

"Not anything really," he replied.

"You must have been thinking of *something*," she insisted. Her own mind was never still or empty. It was always focused hard on something; something bothering her or pleasing, something coming up or in the past. It never stopped. Not even at night when she lay down to sleep. Her mind was always ticking.

"Come here," he'd say. He liked to stop her in the middle of her work.

"Lie down with me a minute," he would say while she stood perplexed with the broom gripped tightly in her hand.

"Come here," he'd urge her, smiling like a cat, lazy and happy, as if her irritation were amusing to him.

"Not now," she'd argue, but drawn to him and giving him her hand.

"Just for a minute," he would say, pulling her down on the tassled spread till she rested her cheek on his great chest and felt his chin on top of her head.

"You fit against me perfectly," he'd whisper with his arm tight around her.

"I've got a million things to do," she'd say, all wiry with thoughts and wanting to jump up before the lethargy descended.

"Just lie a minute," he would say in a way that made her give in to the warmth of his shirt, his faint tobacco smell, and the silence building in the house till she could hear the birds outside so clearly and see their shapes streak by the window. The sky was violet or pink and she would feel the sweetness of the fading room begin to lull her.

"You're a devil," she would sigh, tipping back her head to gaze at him.

"I love you, May," he'd say, kissing her forehead or her hair. He never wanted to make love on Sunday afternoons. Only to hold her in the stillness for half an hour or more until it seemed to May that a spell came over them, a heavy sense of peace, as if the whole of life had swept away from them in a great wave and they'd become as motionless and changeless as the rocking chair beside the window, the tall white dresser and the row of pictures on the flowered wall that grew more dim and less distinct each minute in the dusky room. She would imagine the darkness growing in the house, filling up the unlit rooms downstairs, the empty kitchen growing desolate and grey and disappearing,

until she'd suddenly jump up from the dark bed and
with a beating heart she'd hurry like a child from room
to room snapping the lights on, her face urgent and
serious, as if she were preventing a great death.

Separating

JOHN UPDIKE

John Updike was born in March 1932 in Shillington, Pennsylvania. His writing career began at eight, when he wrote his first short story. He was graduated from Harvard—where he was an editor of the Lampoon—in 1954. He spent a year at the Ruskin School of Drawing and Fine Arts at Oxford, and from 1955 to 1957 he was on the staff of The New Yorker. Since then his prolific writing career has spanned novels, short stories, literary criticism, poetry, and essays. Among his many books are the novels Rabbit Run *(1960),* The Centaur *(1963),* Couples *(1968),* Bech: A Book *(1970),* Rabbit Redux *(1971),* The Coup *(1978),* Rabbit Is Rich *(1981),* The Witches of Eastwick *(1984); the short story collections* The Music School *(1966),* Problems and Other Stories *(1979),* Too Far to Go: The Maples Stories *(1979); and his collections of criticism and essays,* Picked-up Pieces *(1975), and* Hugging the Shore *(1983). He is a member of the American Academy of Arts and Sciences.*

The meticulous rendering of the physical world, the deftly fashioned imagery, and the highly polished prose style are the immediately recognizable signposts of John Updike's fiction. Also, the generosity of spirit: though his men and women are often exploring the sad sexual terrain between them, it's the equanimity of Updike's sympathies that remains keenly in the reader's mind. "The people in my books are often driven," he says, "by the wish to make connections, to explore their own

potential, to be both safe and free at the same time. My
characters are very fond of both safety and freedom,
and yet the two things don't go together, quite, so
they're in a state of tension all the time." In his introduction to The Best American Short Stories of 1984
which he co-edited, he writes that short stories should
". . . startle and engage me within the first few sentences,
and in their middle widen and deepen or sharpen my
knowledge of human activity, and end by giving me a
sensation of completed statement. The ending is where
the reader discovers whether he has been reading the
same story the writer thought he was writing. A narrative is like a room on whose walls a number of false
doors have been painted; while within the narrative we
have many apparent choices of exit, but when the author leads us to one particular door, we know it is the
right one because it opens."

John Updike has lived in Massachusetts since 1957.

The day was fair. Brilliant. All that June the weather
had mocked the Maples' internal misery with solid
sunlight—golden shafts and cascades of green in which
their conversations had wormed unseeing, their sad
murmuring selves the only stain in Nature. Usually by
this time of the year they had acquired tans; but when
they met their elder daughter's plane on her return
from a year in England they were almost as pale as
she, though Judith was too dazzled by the sunny opu-
lent jumble of her native land to notice. They did not
spoil her homecoming by telling her immediately.
Wait a few days, let her recover from jet lag, had been
one of their formulations, in that string of gray
dialogues—over coffee, over cocktails, over Cointreau—
that had shaped the strategy of their dissolution, while
the earth performed its annual stunt of renewal unno-
ticed beyond their closed windows. Richard had thought

to leave at Easter; Joan had insisted they wait until the four children were at last assembled, with all exams passed and ceremonies attended, and the bauble of summer to console them. So he had drudged away, in love, in dread, repairing screens, getting the mowers sharpened, rolling and patching their new tennis court.

The court, clay, had come through its first winter pitted and windswept bare of redcoat. Years ago the Maples had observed how often, among their friends, divorce followed a dramatic home improvement, as if the marriage were making one last strong effort to live; their own worst crisis had come amid the plaster dust and exposed plumbing of a kitchen renovation. Yet, a summer ago, as canary-yellow bulldozers gaily churned a grassy, daisy-dotted knoll into a muddy plateau, and a crew of pigtailed young men raked and tamped clay into a plane, this transformation did not strike them as ominous, but festive in its impudence; their marriage could rend the earth for fun. The next spring, waking each day at dawn to a sliding sensation as if the bed were being tipped, Richard found the barren tennis court—its net and tapes still rolled in the barn—an environment congruous with his mood of purposeful desolation, and the crumbling of handfuls of clay into cracks and holes (dogs had frolicked on the court in a thaw; rivulets had evolved trenches) an activity suitably elemental and interminable. In his sealed heart he hoped the day would never come.

Now it was here. A Friday. Judith was reacclimated; all four children were assembled, before jobs and camps and visits again scattered them. Joan thought they should be told one by one. Richard was for making an announcement at the table. She said, "I think just making an announcement is a cop-out. They'll start quarreling and playing to each other instead of focusing. They're each individuals, you know, not just some corporate obstacle to your freedom."

"O.K., O.K. I agree." Joan's plan was exact. That evening, they were giving Judith a belated welcome-home dinner, of lobster and champagne. Then, the party over, they, the two of them, who nineteen years before would push her in a baby carriage along Fifth Avenue to Washington Square, were to walk her out of the house, to the bridge across the salt creek, and tell her, swearing her to secrecy. Then Richard Jr., who was going directly from work to a rock concert in Boston, would be told, either late when he returned on the train or early Saturday morning before he went off to his job; he was seventeen and employed as one of a golf-course maintenance crew. Then the two younger children, John and Margaret, could, as the morning wore on, be informed.

"Mopped up, as it were," Richard said.

"Do you have any better plan? That leaves you the rest of Saturday to answer any questions, pack, and make your wonderful departure."

"No," he said, meaning he had no better plan, and agreed to hers, though to him it showed an edge of false order, a hidden plea for control, like Joan's long chore lists and financial accountings and, in the days when he first knew her, her too-copious lecture notes. Her plan turned one hurdle for him into four—four knife-sharp walls, each with a sheer blind drop on the other side.

All spring he had moved through a world of insides and outsides, of barriers and partitions. He and Joan stood as a thin barrier between the children and the truth. Each moment was a partition, with the past on one side and the future on the other, a future containing this unthinkable *now*. Beyond four knifelike walls a new life for him waited vaguely. His skull cupped a secret, a white face, a face both frightened and soothing, both strange and known, that he wanted to shield from tears, which he felt all about him, solid as the sunlight. So haunted, he had become obsessed with battening down the house against his absence, replacing screens and sash cords, hinges and latches—a Houdini making things snug before his escape.

*   *   *

The lock. He had still to replace a lock on one of the doors of the screened porch. The task, like most such, proved more difficult than he had imagined. The old lock, aluminum frozen by corrosion, had been deliberately rendered obsolete by manufacturers. Three hardware stores had nothing that even approximately matched the mortised hole its removal (surprisingly easy) left. Another hole had to be gouged, with bits too small and saws too big, and the old hole fitted with a block of wood—the chisels dull, the saw rusty, his fingers thick with lack of sleep. The sun poured down, beyond the porch, on a world of neglect. The bushes already needed pruning, the windward side of the house was shedding flakes of paint, rain would get in when he was gone, insects, rot, death. His family, all those he would lose, filtered through the edges of his awareness as he struggled with screw holes, splinters, opaque instructions, minutiae of metal.

Judith sat on the porch, a princess returned from exile. She regaled them with stories of fuel shortages, of bomb scares in the Underground, of Pakistani workmen loudly lusting after her as she walked past on her way to dance school. Joan came and went, in and out of the house, calmer than she should have been, praising his struggles with the lock as if this were one more and not the last of their long chain of shared chores. The younger of his sons, John, now at fifteen suddenly, unwittingly handsome, for a few minutes held the rickety screen door while his father clumsily hammered and chiseled, each blow a kind of sob in Richard's ears. His younger daughter, having been at a slumber party, slept on the porch hammock through all the noise—heavy and pink, trusting and forsaken. Time, like the sunlight, continued relentlessly; the sunlight slowly slanted. Today was one of the longest days. The lock clicked, worked. He was through. He had a drink; he drank it on the porch, listening to his daughter. "It was so sweet," she was saying, "during the worst of it, how all the butchers and bakery shops kept open by candlelight. They're all so plucky and cute. From the papers, things sounded so much worse here—people shooting people in gas lines, and everybody freezing."

Richard asked her, "Do you still want to live in England forever?" *Forever:* the concept, now a reality upon him, pressed and scratched at the back of his throat.

"No," Judith confessed, turning her oval face to him, its eyes still childishly far apart, but the lips set as over something succulent and satisfactory. "I was anxious to come home. I'm an American." She was a woman. They had raised her; he and Joan had endured together to raise her, alone of the four. The others had still some raising left in them. Yet it was the thought of telling Judith—the image of her, their first baby, walking between them arm in arm to the bridge—that broke him. The partition between his face and the tears broke. Richard sat down to the celebratory meal with the back of his throat aching; the champagne, the lobster seemed phases of sunshine; he saw them and tasted them through tears. He blinked, swallowed, croakily joked about hay fever. The tears would not stop leaking through; they came not through a hole that could be plugged but through a permeable spot in a membrane, steadily, purely, endlessly, fruitfully. They became, his tears, a shield for himself against these others—their faces, the fact of their assembly, a last time as innocents, at a table where he sat the last time as head. Tears dropped from his nose as he broke the lobster's back; salt flavored his champagne as he sipped it; the raw clench at the back of his throat was delicious. He could not help himself.

His children tried to ignore his tears. Judith, on his right, lit a cigarette, gazed upward in the direction of her too energetic, too sophisticated exhalation; on her other side, John earnestly bent his face to the extraction of the last morsels—legs, tail segments—from the scarlet corpse. Joan, at the opposite end of the table, glanced at him surprised, her reproach displaced by a quick grimace, of forgiveness, or of salute to his superior gift of strategy. Between them, Margaret, no longer called Bean, thirteen and large for her age, gazed from the other side of his pane of tears as if into a shopwindow at something she coveted—at her father, a crystalline heap of splinters and memories. It was not she, however, but John who, in the kitchen, as they cleared the plates and carapaces away, asked Joan the question: "*Why is Daddy crying?*"

Richard heard the question but not the murmured answer. Then he heard Bean cry, "Oh, no-oh!"—the faintly dramatized exclamation of one who had long expected it.

John returned to the table carrying a bowl of salad. He nodded tersely at his father and his lips shaped the conspiratorial words "She told."

"Told what?" Richard asked aloud, insanely.

The boy sat down as if to rebuke his father's distraction with the example of his own good manners. He said quietly, "The separation."

Joan and Margaret returned; the child, in Richard's twisted vision, seemed diminished in size, and relieved, relieved to have had the bogieman at last proved real. He called out to her—the distances at the table had grown immense—"You knew, you always knew," but the clenching at the back of his throat prevented him from making sense of it. From afar he heard Joan talking, levelly, sensibly, reciting what they had prepared: it was a separation for the summer, an experiment. She and Daddy both agreed it would be good for them; they needed space and time to think; they liked each other but did not make each other happy enough, somehow.

Judith, imitating her mother's factual tone, but in her youth off-key, too cool, said, "I think it's silly. You should either live together or get divorced."

Richard's crying, like a wave that has crested and

crashed, had become tumultuous; but it was over-topped by another tumult, for John, who had been so reserved, now grew larger and larger at the table. Perhaps his younger sister's being credited with knowing set him off. "Why didn't you *tell* us?" he asked, in a large round voice quite unlike his own. "You should have *told* us you weren't getting along."

Richard was startled into attempting to force words through his tears. "We *do* get along, that's the trouble, so it doesn't show even to us—" *That we do not love each other* was the rest of the sentence; he couldn't finish it.

Joan finished for him, in her style. "And we've always, *especially*, loved our children."

John was not mollified. "What do you care about *us?*" he boomed. "We're just little things you *had*." His sisters' laughing forced a laugh from him, which he turned hard and parodistic: "Ha ha *ha*." Richard and Joan realized simultaneously that the child was drunk, on Judith's homecoming champagne. Feeling bound to keep the center of the stage, John took a cigarette from Judith's pack, poked it into his mouth, let it hang from his lower lip, and squinted like a gangster.

"You're not little things we had," Richard called to him. "You're the whole point. But you're grown. Or almost."

The boy was lighting matches. Instead of holding them to his cigarette (for they had never seen him smoke; being "good" had been his way of setting himself apart), he held them to his mother's face, closer and closer, for her to blow out. Then he lit the whole folder—a hiss and then a torch, held against his mother's face. Prismed by his tears, the flame filled Richard's vision; he didn't know how it was extinguished. He heard Margaret say, "Oh stop showing off," and saw John, in response, break the cigarette in two and put the halves entirely into his mouth and chew, sticking out his tongue to display the shreds to his sister.

Joan talked to him, reasoning—a fountain of reason, unintelligible. "Talked about it for years . . . our children must help us . . . Daddy and I both want . . ." As the boy listened, he carefully wadded a paper napkin into the leaves of his salad, fashioned a ball of paper and lettuce, and popped it into his mouth, looking around the table for the expected laughter. None came. Judith said, "Be mature," and dismissed a plume of smoke.

Richard got up from this stifling table and led the boy outside. Though the house was in twilight, the outdoors still brimmed with light, the lovely waste light of high summer. Both laughing, he supervised John's spitting out the lettuce and paper and tobacco into the pachysandra. He took him by the hand—a square gritty hand, but for its softness a man's. Yet, it held on. They ran together up into the field, past the tennis court. The raw banking left by the bulldozers was dotted with daisies. Past the court and a flat stretch where they used to play family baseball stood a soft green rise glorious in the sun, each weed and species of grass distinct as illumination on parchment. "I'm sorry, so sorry," Richard cried. "You were the only one who ever tried to help me with all the goddam jobs around this place."

Sobbing, safe within his tears and the champagne, John explained, "It's not just the separation, it's the whole crummy year, I *hate* that school, you can't make any friends, the history teacher's a scud."

They sat on the crest of the rise, shaking and warm from their tears but easier in their voices, and Richard tried to focus on the child's sad year—the weekdays long with homework, the weekends spent in his room with model airplanes, while his parents murmured down below, nursing their separation. How selfish, how blind, Richard thought; his eyes felt scoured. He told his son, "We'll think about getting you transferred. Life's too short to be miserable."

They had said what they could, but did not want the moment to heal, and talked on, about the school, about the tennis court, whether it would ever again be as good as it had been that first summer. They walked to inspect it and pressed a few more tapes more firmly down. A little stiltedly, perhaps trying now to make too much of the moment, Richard led the boy to the spot in the field where the view was best, of the metallic blue river, the emerald marsh, the scattered islands velvety with shadow in the low light, the white bits of beach far away. "See," he said. "It goes on being beautiful. It'll be here tomorrow."

"I know," John answered, impatiently. The moment had closed.

Back in the house, the others had opened some white wine, the champagne being drunk, and still sat at the table, the three females, gossiping. Where Joan sat had become the head. She turned, showing him a tearless face, and asked, "All right?"

"We're fine," he said, resenting it, though relieved, that the party went on without him.

In bed she explained, "I couldn't cry I guess because I cried so much all spring. It really wasn't fair. It's your idea, and you made it look as though I was kicking you out."

"I'm sorry," he said. "I couldn't stop. I wanted to but couldn't."

"You *didn't* want to. You loved it. You were having your way, making a general announcement."

"I love having it over," he admitted. "God, those kids were great. So brave and funny." John, returned to the house, had settled to a model airplane in his room, and kept shouting down to them, "I'm O.K. No sweat." "And the way," Richard went on, cozy in his relief, "they never questioned the reasons we gave. No thought of a third person. Not even Judith."

"That *was* touching," Joan said.

He gave her a hug. "You were great too. Very reassuring to everybody. Thank you." Guiltily, he realized he did not feel separated.

"You still have Dickie to do," she told him. These words set before him a black mountain in the darkness; its cold breath, its near weight affected his chest. Of the four children, his elder son was most like a conscience. Joan did not need to add, "That's one piece of your dirty work I won't do for you."

"I know. I'll do it. You go to sleep."

Within minutes, her breathing slowed, became oblivious and deep. It was quarter to midnight. Dickie's train from the concert would come in at one-fourteen. Richard set the alarm for one. He had slept atrociously for weeks. But whenever he closed his lids some glimpse of the last hours scorched them—Judith exhaling toward the ceiling in a kind of aversion, Bean's mute staring, the sunstruck growth of the field where he and John had rested. The mountain before him moved closer, moved within him; he was huge, momentous. The ache at the back of his throat felt stale. His wife slept as if slain beside him. When, exasperated by his hot lids, his crowded heart, he rose from bed and dressed, she awoke enough to turn over. He told her then, "Joan, if I could undo it all, I would."

"Where would you begin?" she asked. There was no place. Giving him courage, she was always giving him courage. He put on shoes without socks in the dark. The children were breathing in their rooms, the downstairs was hollow. In their confusion they had left lights burning. He turned off all but one, the kitchen overhead. The car started. He had hoped it wouldn't. He met only moonlight on the road; it seemed a diaphanous companion, flickering in the leaves along the roadside, haunting his rearview mirror like a pursuer, melting under his headlights. The center of town, not quite deserted, was eerie at this hour. A young cop in uniform kept company with a gang of T-shirted kids on the steps of the bank. Across from the railroad station, several bars kept open. Customers, mostly young, passed in and out of the warm night, savoring summer's novelty. Voices shouted from cars as they passed; an immense conversation seemed in progress. Richard parked and in his weariness put his head on the passenger seat, out of the commotion and wheeling lights. It was as when, in the movies, as assassin grimly carries his mission through the jostle of a carnival—except the movies cannot show the precipitous, palpable slope you cling to within. You cannot climb back down; you can only fall. The synthetic fabric of the car seat, warmed by his cheek, confided to him an ancient, distant scent of vanilla.

A train whistle caused him to lift his head. It was on time; he had hoped it would be late. The slender drawgates descended. The bell of approach tingled happily. The great metal body, horizontally fluted, rocked to a stop, and sleepy teen-agers disembarked, his son among them. Dickie did not show surprise that his father was meeting him at this terrible hour. He sauntered to the car with two friends, both taller than he. He said "Hi" to his father and took the passenger's seat with an exhausted promptness that expressed gratitude. The friends got into the back, and Richard was grateful; a few more minutes' postponement would be won by driving them home.

He asked, "How was the concert?"

"Groovy," one boy said from the back seat.

"It bit," the other said.

"It was O.K.," Dickie said, moderate by nature, so reasonable that in his childhood the unreason of the world had given him headaches, stomach aches, nausea. When the second friend had been dropped off at his dark house, the boy blurted, "Dad, my eyes are killing me with hay fever! I'm out there cutting that mothering grass all day!"

"Do we still have those drops?"

"They didn't do any good last summer."

"They might this." Richard swung a U-turn on the empty street. The drive home took a few minutes. The mountain was here, in his throat. "Richard," he said, and felt the boy, slumped and rubbing his eyes, go tense at his tone, "I didn't come to meet you just to make your life easier. I came because your mother and I have some news for you, and you're a hard man to get ahold of these days. It's sad news."

"That's O.K." The reassurance came out soft, but quick, as if released from the tip of a spring.

Richard had feared that his tears would return and choke him, but the boy's manliness set an example, and his voice issued forth steady and dry. "It's sad news, but it needn't be tragic news, at least for you. It should have no practical effect on your life, though it's bound to have an emotional effect. You'll work at your job, and go back to school in September. Your mother and I are really proud of what you're making of your life; we don't want that to change at all."

"Yeah," the boy said lightly, on the intake of his breath, holding himself up. They turned the corner; the church they went to loomed like a gutted fort. The home of the woman Richard hoped to marry stood across the green. Her bedroom light burned.

"Your mother and I," he said, "have decided to separate. For the summer. Nothing legal, no divorce yet. We want to see how it feels. For some years now, we haven't been doing enough for each other as, making each other as happy as we should be. Have you sensed that?"

"No," the boy said. It was an honest, unemotional answer: true or false in a quiz.

Glad for the factual basis, Richard pursued, even garrulously, the details. His apartment across town, his utter accessibility, the split vacation arrangements, the advantages to the children, the added mobility and variety of the summer. Dickie listened, absorbing. "Do the others know?"

"Yes."

"How did they take it?"

"The girls pretty calmly. John flipped out; he shouted and ate a cigarette and made a salad out of his napkin and told us how much he hated school."

His brother chuckled. "He did?"

"Yeah. The school issue was more upsetting for him than Mom and me. He seemed to feel better for having exploded."

"He did?" The repetition was the first sign that he was stunned.

"Yes. Dickie, I want to tell you something. This last hour, waiting for your train to get in, has been about the worst of my life. I hate this. *Hate* it. My father would have died before doing it to me." He felt immensely lighter, saying this. He had dumped the mountain on the boy. They were home. Moving swiftly as a shadow, Dickie was out of the car, through the bright kitchen. Richard called after him, "Want a glass of milk or anything?"

"No thanks."

"Want us to call the course tomorrow and say you're too sick to work?"

"No, that's all right." The answer was faint, delivered at the door to his room; Richard listened for the slam that went with a tantrum. The door closed normally, gently. The sound was sickening.

Joan had sunk into that first deep trough of sleep and was slow to awake. Richard had to repeat, "I told him."

"What did he say?"

"Nothing much. Could you go say goodnight to him? Please."

She left their room, without putting on a bathrobe. He sluggishly changed back into his pajamas and walked down the hall. Dickie was already in bed, Joan was sitting beside him, and the boy's bedside clock radio was murmuring music. When she stood, an inexplicable light—the moon?—outlined her body through the nightie. Richard sat on the warm place she had indented on the child's narrow mattress. He asked him, "Do you want the radio on like that?"

"It always is."

"Doesn't it keep you awake? It would me."

"No."

"Are you sleepy?"

"Yeah."

"Good. Sure you want to get up and go to work? You've had a big night."

"I want to."

Away at school this winter he had learned for the first time that you can go short of sleep and live. As an infant he had slept with an immobile, sweating intensity that had alarmed his babysitters. In adolescence he had often been the first of the four children to go to bed. Even now, he would go slack in the middle of a television show, his sprawled legs hairy and brown. "O.K. Good boy. Dickie, listen. I love you so much, I never knew how much until now. No matter how this works out, I'll always be with you. Really."

Richard bent to kiss an averted face but his son, sinewy, turned and with wet cheeks embraced him and gave him a kiss, on the lips, passionate as a woman's. In his father's ear he moaned one word, the crucial, intelligent word: *"Why?"*

Why. It was a whistle of wind in a crack, a knife thrust, a window thrown open on emptiness. The white face was gone, the darkness was featureless. Richard had forgotten why.

Sweet Talk

STEPHANIE VAUGHN

Stephanie Vaughn was born in Millersburg, Ohio, and grew up on army posts in the United States and abroad. She attended Ohio State University, The University of Iowa Writer's Workshop, and Stanford University. Her work has been included in the O. Henry Prize story collections, and has appeared in Antaeus, Redbook, The New Yorker, *and other literary journals.*

In "Sweet Talk" a young couple, overeducated and unemployed, embark on a journey in their van. Their guidebooks take them across an unfamiliar landscape, but stranger still is the uncharted realm of their own feelings for each other. Jealousy, sexual impulse, intellectual competition, and general friskiness enliven their days and darken their nights.

Sometimes Sam and I loved each other more when we were angry. "Day," I called him, using the surname instead of Sam. "Day, Day, Day!" It drummed against the walls of the apartment like a distress signal.

"Ah, my beautiful lovebird," he said. "My sugar sweet bride."

For weeks I had been going through the trash trying to find out whether he had other women. Once I found half a ham sandwich with red marks that could have been lipstick. Or maybe catsup. This time I found five slender cigarette butts.

"Who smokes floral-embossed cigarettes?" I said. He had just come out of the shower, and droplets of water gleamed among the black hairs of his chest like tiny knife points. "Who's the heart-attack candidate you invite over when I'm out?" I held the butts beneath his nose like a small bouquet. He slapped them to the floor and we stopped speaking for three days. We moved through the apartment without touching, lay stiffly in separate furrows of the bed, desire blooming and withering between us like the invisible petals of a night-blooming cereus.

We finally made up while watching a chess tournament on television. Even though we wouldn't speak or make eye contact, we were sitting in front of the sofa moving pieces around a chess board as an announcer explained World Championship strategy to the viewing audience. Our shoulders touched but we pretended not to notice. Our knees touched, and our elbows. Then we both reached for the black bishop and our hands touched. We made love on the carpet and kept our eyes open so that we could look at each other defiantly.

We were living in California and had six university degrees between us and no employment. We lived on food stamps, job interviews and games.

"How many children did George Washington, the father of our country, have?"

"No white ones but lots of black ones."

"How much did he make when he was Commander of the Revolutionary Army?"

"He made a big to-do about refusing a salary but later presented the first Congress with a bill for a half million dollars."

"Who was the last slave-owning president?"

"Ulysses S. Grant."

We had always been good students.

*   *   *

It was a smoggy summer. I spent long hours in air-conditioned supermarkets, touching the cool cans, feeling the cold plastic stretched across packages of meat. Sam left the apartment for whole afternoons and evenings. He was in his car somewhere, opening it up on the freeway, or maybe just spending time with someone I didn't know. We were mysterious with each other about our absences. In August we decided to move east, where a friend said he could get us both jobs at an unaccredited community college. In the meantime, I had invented a lover. He was rich and wanted to take me to an Alpine hotel, where mauve flowers cascaded over the stone walls of a terrace. Sometimes we drank white wine and watched the icy peaks of mountains shimmer gold in the sunset. Sometimes we returned to our room carrying tiny ceramic mugs of schnapps which had been given to us, in the German fashion, as we paid for an expensive meal.

In the second week of August, I found a pair of red lace panties at the bottom of the kitchen trash.

I decided to tell Sam I had a lover. I made my lover into a tall, blue-eyed blond, a tennis player on the circuit, a Phi Beta Kappa from Stanford who had offers from the movies. It was the tall blond part that needled Sam, who was dark and stocky.

"Did you pick him up at the beach?" Sam said.

"Stop it," I said, knowing that was a sure way to get him to ask more questions.

"Did you have your diaphragm in your purse?"

We were wrapping cups and saucers in newspaper and nesting them in the slots of packing boxes. "He was taller than you," I said, "but not as handsome."

Sam held a blue and white Dresden cup, my favorite wedding present, in front of my eyes. "You slut," he said, and let the cup drop to the floor.

"Very articulate," I said. "Some professor. The man of reason gets into an argument and he talks with broken cups. Thank you Alexander Dope."

That afternoon I failed the California drivers' test again. I made four right turns and drove over three of the four curbs. The highway patrolman pointed out that if I made one more mistake I was finished. I drove through a red light.

On the way back to the apartment complex, Sam squinted into the flatness of the expressway and would not talk to me. I put my blue-eyed lover behind the wheel. He rested a hand on my knee and smiled as he drove. He was driving me west, away from the Vista View Apartments, across the thin spine of mountains which separated our suburb from the sea. At the shore there would be seals frolicking among the rocks and starfish resting in tidal pools.

"How come you never take me to the ocean?" I said. "How come every time I want to go to the beach I have to call up a woman friend?"

"If you think you're going to Virginia with me," he said, "you're dreaming." He eased the car into our numbered space and put his head against the wheel. "Why did you have to do it?"

"I do not like cars," I said. "You know I have always been afraid of cars."

"Why did you have to sleep with that fag tennis player?" His head was still against the wheel. I moved closer and put my arm around his shoulders.

"Sam, I didn't. I made it up."

"Don't try to get out of it."

"I didn't, Sam. I made it up." I tried to kiss him. He let me put my mouth against his, but his lips were unyielding. They felt like the skin of an orange. "I didn't, Sam. I made it up to hurt you." I kissed him again and his mouth warmed against mine. "I love you, Sam. Please let me go to Virginia."

"George Donner," I read from the guidebook, "was sixty-one years old and rich when he packed up his family and left Illinois to cross the Great Plains, the desert, and the mountains into California." We were driving through the Sierras, past steep slopes and the deep shade of an evergreen forest, toward the Donner Pass, where in 1846 the Donner family had been trapped by an early snowfall. Some of them died and the rest ate the corpses of their relatives and their Indian guides to survive.

"Where are the bones?" Sam said, as we strolled past glass cases at the Donner Pass Museum. The cases were full of wagon wheels and harnesses. Above us a recorded voice described the courageous and enterprising spirit of American pioneers. A man standing nearby with a young boy turned to scowl at Sam. Sam looked at him and said loudly, "Where are the bones of the people they ate?" The man took the boy by the hand and started for the door. Sam said, "You call this American history?" and the man turned and said, "Listen, mister, I can get your license number." We laughed about that as we descended into the plain of the Great Basin desert in Nevada. Every few miles one of us would say the line and the other one would chuckle, and I felt as if we had been married fifty years instead of five, and that everything had turned out okay.

Ten miles east of Reno I began to sneeze. My nose ran and my eyes watered, and I had to stop reading the guidebook.

"I can't do this anymore. I think I've got an allergy."

"You never had an allergy in your life." Sam's tone implied that I had purposefully got the allergy so that I could not read the guidebook. We were riding in a second-hand van, a lusterless, black shoebox of a vehicle, which Sam had bought for the trip with the money he got from the stereo, the TV, and his own beautifully overhauled and rebuilt little sports car.

"Turn on the radio," I said.

"The radio is broken."

It was a hot day, dry and gritty. On either side of the freeway, a sagebrush desert stretched toward the hunched profiles of brown mountains. The mountains were so far away—the only landmarks within three hundred miles—that they did not whap by the windows like signposts, they floated above the plain of dusty sage and gave us the sense that we were not going anywhere.

"Are you trying to kill us?" I said when the speedometer slid past ninety.

Sam looked at the dash surprised and, I think, a little pleased that the van could do that much. "I'm getting hypnotized," he said. He thought about it for another mile and said, "If you had managed to get your license, you could do something on this trip besides blow snot into your hand."

"Don't you think we should call ahead to Elko for a motel room?"

"I might not want to stop at Elko."

"Sam, look at the map. You'll be tired when we get to Elko."

"I'll let you know when I'm tired."

We reached Elko at sundown, and Sam was tired. In the office of the Shangrila Motor Lodge we watched another couple get the last room. "I suppose you're going to be mad because I was right," I said.

"Just get in the van." We bought a sack of hamburgers and set out for Utah. Ahead of us a full moon rose, flat and yellow like a fifty-dollar gold piece, then lost its color as it rose higher. We entered the Utah salt flats, the dead floor of a dead ocean. The salt crystals glittered like snow under the white moon. My nose stopped running, and I felt suddenly lucid and calm.

"Has he been in any movies?" Sam said.

"Has who been in any movies?"

"The fag tennis player."

I had to think a moment before I recalled my phantom lover.

"He's not a fag."

"I thought you made him up."

"I did make him up but I didn't make up any fag."

A few minutes later he said, "You might at least sing something. You might at least try to keep me awake." I sang a few Beatle tunes, then Simon and Garfunkel, the Everly Brothers, and Elvis Presley. I worked my way back through my youth to a Girl Scout song I remembered as "Eye, Eye, Eye, Icky, Eye, Kai, A-nah." It was supposed to be sung around a campfire to remind the girls of their Indian heritage and the pleasures of surviving in the wilderness. "Ah woo, ah woo. Ah woo knee key chee," I sang. "I am now five years old," I said, and then I sang, "Home, Home on the Range," the song I remembered singing when I was a child going cross-country with my parents to visit some relatives. The only thing I remembered about that trip besides a lot of going to the bathroom in gas stations was that there were rules which made the traveling life simple. One was: do not hang over the edge of the front seat to talk to your mother or father. The other was: if you have to throw up, do it in the blue coffee can, the red one is full of cookies.

"It's just the jobs and money," I said. "It isn't us, is it?"

"I don't know," he said.

A day and a half later we crossed from Wyoming into Nebraska, the western edge of the Louisiana Purchase, which Thomas Jefferson had made so that we could all live in white, classical houses and be farmers. Fifty miles later the corn began, hundreds of miles of it, singing green from horizon to horizon. We began to relax and I had the feeling that we had survived the test of American geography. I put away our guidebooks and took out the dictionary. Matachin, mastigophobia, matutolypea. I tried to find words Sam didn't know. He guessed all the definitions and was smug and happy behind the wheel. I reached over and put a hand on his knee. He looked at me and smiled. "Ah, my little buttercup," he said. "My sweet cream pie." I thought of my Alpine lover for the first time in a long while, and he was nothing more than mist over a distant mountain.

In a motel lobby near Omaha, we had to wait in line for twenty minutes behind three families. Sam put his arm around me and pulled a tennis ball out of his jacket. He bounced it on the thin carpet, tentatively, and when he saw it had enough spring, he dropped into an exaggerated basketball player's crouch and ran across the lobby. He whirled in front of the cigarette machine and passed the ball to me. I laughed and threw it back. Several people had turned to stare at us. Sam winked at them and dunked the ball through an imaginary net by the wall clock, then passed the ball back to me. I dribbled around a stack of suitcases and went for a lay-up by a hanging fern. I misjudged and knocked the plant to the floor. What surprised me was that the fronds were plastic but the dirt was real. There was a huge mound of it on the carpet. At the registration desk, the clerk told us the motel was already full and that he could not find our name on the advance reservation list.

"Nebraska sucks eggs," Sam said loudly as we carried our luggage to the door. We spent the night curled up on the hard front seat of the van like boulders. The bony parts of our bodies kept bumping as we turned and rolled to avoid the steering wheel and dash. In the morning, my knees and elbows felt worn away, like the peaks of old mountains. We hadn't touched each other sexually since California.

"So she had big ta-ta's," I said. "She had huge ta-ta's and a bad-breath problem." We had pushed on through the corn, across Iowa, Illinois and Indiana, and the old arguments rattled along with us, like the pots and pans in the back of the van.

"She was a model," he said. He was describing the proprietress of the slender cigarettes and red panties.

"In a couple of years she'll have gum disease," I said.

"She was a model and she had a degree in literature from Oxford."

I didn't believe him, of course, but I felt the sting of his intention to hurt. "By the time she's forty she'll have emphysema."

"What would this trip be like without the melody of your voice," he said. It was dark, and taillights glowed on the road ahead of us like flecks of burning iron. I remembered how, when we were undergraduates attending different colleges, he used to write me letters which said: keep your skirts down and your knees together, don't let anyone get near your crunch. We always amused each other with our language.

"I want a divorce," I said in a motel room in Columbus, Ohio. We were propped against pillows on separate double beds watching a local program on Woody Hayes, the Ohio State football coach. The announcer was saying, "And here in front of the locker room is the blue and gold mat that every player must step on as he goes to and from the field. Those numbers are the score of last year's loss to Michigan." And I was saying, "Are you listening? I said I want a divorce when we get to Virginia."

"I'm listening."

"Don't you want to know why I want a divorce?"

"No."

"Well, do you think it's a good idea or a bad idea?"

"I think it's a good idea."

"You do?"

"Yes."

The announcer said, "And that is why the night before the big game Woody will be showing his boys reruns of the films *Patton* and *Bullit.*"

*   *   *

That night someone broke into the van and stole everything we owned except the suitcases we had with us in the motel room. They even stole the broken radio. We stood in front of the empty van and looked up and down the row of parked cars as if we expected to see another black van parked there, one with two pairs of skis and two tennis rackets slipped into the spaces between the boxes and the windows.

"I suppose you're going to say I'm the one who left the door unlocked," I said.

Sam sat on the curb. He sat on the curb and put his head into his hands. "No," he said. "It was probably me."

The policeman who filled out the report tried to write "Miscellaneous Household Goods" on the clipboarded form, but I made him list everything I could remember, as the three of us sat on the curb—the skis and rackets, the chess set, a baseball bat, twelve boxes of books, two rugs which I had braided, an oak bed frame Sam had refinished. I inventoried the kitchen items: two bread pans, two cake pans, three skillets. I mentioned every fork and every measuring cup and every piece of bric-a-brac I could recall—the trash of our life, suddenly made valuable by the theft. When the policeman had left without giving us any hope of ever recovering our things, I told Sam I was going to pack and shower. A half hour later when I came out with the suitcases, he was still on the curb, sitting in the full sun, his cotton shirt beginning to stain in wing shapes across his shoulder blades. I reached down to touch him and he flinched. It was a shock—feeling the tremble of his flesh, the vulnerability of it, and for the first time since California I tried to imagine what it was like driving with a woman who said she didn't want him, in a van he didn't like but had to buy in order to travel to a possible job on the other side of the continent, which might not be worth reaching.

* * *

On the last leg of the trip, Sam was agreeable and
compliant. If I wanted to stop for coffee, he stopped
immediately. If I wanted him to go slower in thick
traffic, he eased his foot off the pedal without a look
of regret or annoyance. I got out the dictionary. Oper-
ose, ophelimity, ophryitis. He said he'd never heard of
any of those words. Which president died in a bath-
tub? He couldn't remember. I tried to sing to keep
him company. He told me it wasn't necessary. I played
a few tunes on a comb. He gazed pleasantly at the
freeway, so pleasantly that I could have made him up.
I could have invented him and put him on a mountainside terrace and set him going. "Sammy," I said, "that
stuff wasn't much. I won't miss it."

"Good," he said.

About three a.m. green exit signs began to appear
announcing the past and the future: Colonial Williams-
burg, Jamestown, Yorktown, Patrick Henry Airport.
"Let's go to the beach," I said. "Let's just go all the
way to the edge of the continent." It was a ludicrous
idea.

"Sure. Why not."

He drove on past Newport News and over an arch-
ing bridge towards Virginia Beach. We arrived there
just at dawn and found our way into a residential
neighborhood full of small pastel houses and sandy
lawns. "Could we just stop right here?" I said. I had an
idea. I had a plan. He shrugged as if to say what the
heck, I don't care, and if you want to drive into the
ocean that will be fine, too.

We were parked on a street that ran due east
towards the water—I could see just a glimmer of ocean
between two hotels about a mile away. "All right," I
said, with the forced, brusque cheerfulness of a high
school coach. "Let's get out and do some stretching
exercises." Sam sat behind the wheel and watched me
touch my toes. "Come on, Sammy. Let's get loose.

We haven't done anything with our bodies since California." He yawned, got out of the van, and did a few arm rolls and toe touches. "All right now," I said. "Do you think a two-block handicap is about right?" He had always given me a two-block advantage during our foot races in California. He yawned again. "How about a one-and-a-half-block lead, then?" He crossed his arms and leaned against the van, watching me. I couldn't tell whether he had nodded, but I said anyway, "I'll give you a wave when I'm ready." I walked down the middle of the street past houses which had towels hanging over porch rails and toys lying on front walks. Even a mile from the water, I smelled the salt and seaweed in the air. It made me feel light-headed and for a moment I tried to picture Sam and myself in one of those houses with tricycles and toilet trainers and small latched gates. We had never discussed having a child. When I turned to wave, he was still leaning against the van.

I started out in a jog, then picked up the pace, and hit what seemed to be about the quarter-mile mark doing a fast easy run. Ahead of me the square of water between the two hotels was undulating with gold. I listened for the sound of Sam's footsteps but heard only the soft taps of my own tennis shoes. The square spread into a rectangle and the sky above it fanned out in ribs of orange and purple silk. I was afraid to look back. I was afraid that if I turned to see him, Sam might recede irretrievably into the merciless gray of the western sky. I slowed down in case I had gone too fast and he wanted to catch up. I concentrated on the water and listened to the still, heavy air. By the time I reached the three-quarters mark, I realized that I was probably running alone.

I hadn't wanted to lose him.

I wondered whether he had waited by the van or was already headed for Newport News. I imagined him at a phone booth calling another woman collect in California, and then I realized that I didn't actually know whether there was another woman or not, but I hoped there was and that she was rich and would send him money. I had caught my second wind and was breathing easily. I looked towards the shore without seeing it and was sorry I hadn't measured the distance and thought to clock it, since now I was running against time and myself, and then I heard him—the unmistakable sound of a sprint and the heavy, whooping intake of his breath. He passed me just as we crossed the main street in front of the hotels, and he reached the water twenty feet ahead of me.

"Goddammit, Day," I said. "You were on the grass, weren't you?" We were walking along the hard, wet edge of the beach, breathing hard. "You were sneaking across those lawns. That's a form of cheating." I drummed his arm lightly with my fists pretending to beat him up. "I slowed down because I thought you weren't there." We leaned over from the waist, hands on our hips, breathing towards the sand. The water rolled up the berm near our feet and flickered like topaz.

"You were always a lousy loser," he said.

And I said, "You should talk."

Shifting

ANN BEATTIE

Born in 1947 in Washington, D.C., Ann Beattie was educated at American University and the University of Connecticut. She has written three novels: Chilly Scenes of Winter *(1976)*, Falling in Place *(1980), and* Love Always *(1985). Her short story collections include* Distortions *(1976)*, Secrets and Surprises *(1979), and* The Burning House *(1982), and* Where You'll Find Me *(1986). In 1980 she was the recipient of an award in literature from the American Academy and Institute of Arts and Letters. She has taught at Harvard and the University of Virginia.*

"All over America," Beattie writes in a passage from Love Always, *"people were driving around hearing a song and remembering exactly where they were, who they loved, how they thought it would turn out. In traffic jams, women with babies and grocery bags were suddenly eighteen years old, in summer, on the beach, in the arms of somebody who hummed that song in their ear. They ironed to songs they had slow-danced to, shot through intersections on yellow lights the way they always had, keeping time with the Doors' drumbeat." Ann Beattie's characters are passive, troubled men and women who grew up in the 1960s—they came of age during the Vietnam War—and who, now languishing in early middle age, are haunted by missed connections and suspended convictions. Her descriptions are precise, her sentences concrete, and her tone*

*unemotional. This is a bewildered and sensitive genera-
tion of people, and as Beattie charts their manners with
a clear and sympathetic eye, we see how the absence of
desire and urgency often leads to the sad path of least
resistance.*

Ann Beattie lives in Charlottesville, Virginia.

The woman's name was Natalie, and the man's
name was Larry. They had been childhood sweet-
hearts; he had first kissed her at an ice-skating party
when they were ten. She had been unlacing her skates
and had not expected the kiss. He had not expected to
do it, either—he had some notion of getting his face
out of the wind that was blowing across the iced-over
lake, and he found himself ducking his head toward
her. Kissing her seemed the natural thing to do. When
they graduated from high school he was named "class
clown" in the yearbook, but Natalie didn't think of
him as being particularly funny. He spent more time
than she thought he needed to studying chemistry, and
he never laughed when she joked. She really did not
think of him as funny. They went to the same college,
in their hometown, but he left after a year to go to a
larger, more impressive university. She took the train
to be with him on weekends, or he took the train to
see her. When he graduated, his parents gave him a
car. If they had given it to him when he was still in
college, it would have made things much easier. They
waited to give it to him until graduation day, forcing
him into attending the graduation exercises. He thought
his parents were wonderful people, and Natalie liked
them in a way, too, but she resented their perfect
timing, their careful smiles. They were afraid that he
would marry her. Eventually, he did. He had gone on
to graduate school after college, and he set a date six
months ahead for their wedding so that it would take

place after his first-semester final exams. That way he could devote his time to studying for the chemistry exams.

When she married him, he had had the car for eight months. It still smelled like a brand-new car. There was never any clutter in the car. Even the ice scraper was kept in the glove compartment. There was not even a sweater or a lost glove in the back seat. He vacuumed the car every weekend, after washing it at the car wash. On Friday nights, on their way to some cheap restaurant and a dollar movie, he would stop at the car wash, and she would get out so he could vacuum all over the inside of the car. She would lean against the metal wall of the car wash and watch him clean it.

It was expected that she would not become pregnant. She did not. It had also been expected that she would keep their apartment clean, and keep out of the way as much as possible in such close quarters while he was studying. The apartment was messy, though, and when he was studying late at night she would interrupt him and try to talk him into going to sleep. He gave a chemistry-class lecture once a week, and she would often tell him that overpreparing was as bad as underpreparing. She did not know if she believed this, but it was a favorite line of hers. Sometimes he listened to her.

On Tuesdays, when he gave the lecture, she would drop him off at school and then drive to a supermarket to do the week's shopping. Usually she did not make a list before she went shopping, but when she got to the parking lot she would take a tablet out of her purse and write a few items on it, sitting in the car in the cold. Even having a few things written down would stop her from wandering aimlessly in the store and buying things that she would never use. Before this, she had bought several pans and cans of food that she had not used, or that she could have done without. She felt better when she had a list.

She would drop him at school again on Wednesdays, when he had two seminars that together took up all the afternoon. Sometimes she would drive out of town then, to the suburbs, and shop there if any shopping needed to be done. Otherwise, she would go to the art museum, which was not far away but hard to get to by bus. There was one piece of sculpture in there that she wanted very much to touch, but the guard was always nearby. She came so often that in time the guard began to nod hello. She wondered if she could ever persuade the man to turn his head for a few seconds—only that long—so she could stroke the sculpture. Of course she would never dare ask. After wandering through the museum and looking at least twice at the sculpture, she would go to the gift shop and buy a few postcards and then sit on one of the museum benches, padded with black vinyl, with a Calder mobile hanging overhead, and write notes to friends. (She never wrote letters.) She would tuck the postcards in her purse and mail them when she left the museum. But before she left, she often had coffee in the restaurant: she saw mothers and children struggling there, and women dressed in fancy clothes talking with their faces close together, as quietly as lovers.

On Thursdays he took the car. After his class he would drive to visit his parents and his friend Andy, who had been wounded in Vietnam. About once a month she would go with him, but she had to feel up to it. Being with Andy embarrassed her. She had told him not to go to Vietnam—told him that he could prove his patriotism in some other way—and finally, after she and Larry had made a visit together and she had seen Andy in the motorized bed in his parents' house, Larry had agreed that she need not go again. Andy had apologized to her. It embarrassed her that this man, who had been blown sky-high by a land mine and had lost a leg and lost the full use of his arms, would smile up at her ironically and say, "You were right." She also felt as though he wanted to hear what she would say now, and that now he would listen. Now she had nothing to say. Andy would pull himself up, relying on his right arm, which was the stronger, gripping the rails at the side of the bed, and sometimes he would take her hand. His arms were still weak, but the doctors said he would regain complete use of his right arm with time. She had to make an effort not to squeeze his hand when he held hers because she found herself wanting to squeeze energy back into him. She had a morbid curiosity about what it felt like to be blown from the ground—and go up, and to come crashing down. During their visit Larry put on the class-clown act for Andy, telling funny stories and laughing uproariously.

Once or twice Larry had talked Andy into getting in his wheelchair and had loaded him into the car and taken him to a bar. Larry called her once, late, pretty drunk, to say that he would not be home that night— that he would sleep at his parents' house. "My God," she said. "Are you going to drive Andy home when you're drunk?" "What the hell else can happen to him?" he said.

Larry's parents blamed her for Larry's not being happy. His mother could only be pleasant with her for a short while, and then she would veil her criticisms by putting them as questions. "I know that one thing that helps enormously is good nutrition," his mother said. "He works so hard that he probably needs quite a few vitamins as well, don't you think?" Larry's father was the sort of man who found hobbies in order to avoid his wife. His hobbies were building model boats, repairing clocks, and photography. He took pictures of himself building the boats and fixing the clocks, and gave the pictures, in cardboard frames, to Natalie and Larry for Christmas and birthday presents. Larry's mother was very anxious to stay on close terms with her son, and she knew that Natalie did not like her very much. Once she had visited them during the week, and Natalie, not knowing what to do with her, had taken her to the museum. She had pointed out the sculpture, and his mother had glanced at it and then ignored it. Natalie hated her for her bad taste. She had bad taste in the sweaters she gave Larry, too, but he wore them. They made him look collegiate. That whole world made her sick.

When Natalie's uncle died and left her his 1965 Volvo, they immediately decided to sell it and use the money for a vacation. They put an ad in the paper, and there were several callers. There were some calls on Tuesday, when Larry was in class, and Natalie found herself putting the people off. She told one woman that the car had too much mileage on it, and mentioned body rust, which it did not have; she told another caller, who was very persistent, that the car was already sold. When Larry returned from school she explained that the phone was off the hook because so many people were calling about the car and she had decided not to sell it after all. They could take a little money from their savings account and go on the trip if he wanted. But she did not want to sell the car. "It's not an automatic shift," he said. "You don't know how to drive it." She told him that she could learn. "It will cost money to insure it," he said, "and it's old and probably not even dependable." She wanted to keep the car. "I know," he said, "but it doesn't make sense. When we have more money, you can have a car. You can have a newer, better car."

The next day she went out to the car, which was parked in the driveway of an old lady next door. Her name was Mrs. Larsen and she no longer drove a car, and she told Natalie she could park their second car there. Natalie opened the car door and got behind the wheel and put her hands on it. The wheel was covered with a flaky yellow-and-black plastic cover. She eased it off. A few pieces of foam rubber stuck to the wheel. She picked them off. Underneath the cover, the wheel was a dull red. She ran her fingers around and around the circle of the wheel. Her cousin Burt had delivered the car—a young opportunist, sixteen years old, who said he would drive it the hundred miles from his house to theirs for twenty dollars and a bus ticket home. She had not even invited him to stay for dinner, and Larry had driven him to the bus station. She wondered if it was Burt's cigarette in the ashtray or her dead uncle's. She could not even remember if her uncle smoked. She was surprised that he had left her his car. The car was much more comfortable than Larry's, and it had a nice smell inside. It smelled a little the way a field smells after a spring rain. She rubbed the side of her head back and forth against the window and then got out of the car and went in to see Mrs. Larsen. The night before, she had suddenly thought of the boy who brought the old lady the evening newspaper every night; he looked old enough to drive, and he would probably know how to shift. Mrs. Larson agreed with her—she was sure that he could teach her. "Of course, everything has its price," the old lady said.

"I know that. I meant to offer him money," Natalie said, and was surprised, listening to her voice, that she sounded old too.

She took an inventory and made a list of things in their apartment. Larry had met an insurance man one evening while playing basketball at the gym who told him that they should have a list of their possessions, in case of theft. "What's worth anything?" she said when he told her. It was their first argument in almost a year—the first time in a year, anyway, that their voices were raised. He told her that several of the pieces of furniture his grandparents gave them when they got married were antiques, and the man at the gym said that if they weren't going to get them appraised every year, at least they should take snapshots of them and keep the pictures in a safe-deposit box. Larry told her to photograph the pie safe (which she used to store linen), the piano with an inlaid mother-of-pearl decoration on the music rack (neither of them knew how to play), and the table with hand-carved wooden handles and a marble top. He bought her an Instamatic camera at the drugstore, with film and flash bulbs. "Why can't you do it?" she said, and an argument began. He said that she had no respect for his profession and no understanding of the amount of study that went into getting a master's degree in chemistry.

That night he went out to meet two friends at the gym, to shoot baskets. She put the little flashcube into the top of the camera, dropped in the film and closed the back. She went first to the piano. She leaned forward so that she was close enough to see the inlay clearly, but she found that when she was that close the whole piano wouldn't fit into the picture. She decided to take two pictures. Then she photographed the pie safe, with one door open, showing the towels and sheets stacked inside. She did not have a reason for opening the door, except that she remembered a *Perry Mason* show in which detectives photographed everything with the doors hanging open. She photographed the table, lifting the lamp off it first. There were still eight pictures left. She went to the mirror in their bedroom and held the camera above her head, pointing down at an angle, and photographed her image in the mirror. She took off her slacks and sat on the floor and leaned back, aiming the camera down at her legs. Then she stood up and took a picture of her feet, leaning over and aiming down. She put on her favorite record: Stevie Wonder singing "For Once in My Life." She found herself wondering what it would be like to be blind, to have to feel things to see them. She thought about the piece of sculpture in the museum—the two elongated mounds, intertwined, the smooth gray stone as shiny as sea pebbles. She photographed the kitchen, bathroom, bedroom and living room. There was one picture left. She put her left hand on her thigh, palm up, and with some difficulty—with the camera nestled into her neck like a violin—snapped a

picture of it with her right hand. The next day would
be her first driving lesson.

He came to her door at noon, as he had said he
would. He had on a long maroon scarf, which made
his deep-blue eyes very striking. She had only seen
him from her window when he carried the paper in to
the old lady. He was a little nervous. She hoped that it
was just the anxiety of any teen-ager confronting an
adult. She needed to have him like her. She did not
learn about mechanical things easily (Larry had told
her that he would have invested in a "real" camera,
except that he did not have the time to teach her
about it), so she wanted him to be patient. He sat on
the footstool in her living room, still in coat and scarf,
and told her how a stick shift operated. He moved his
hand through the air. The motion he made reminded
her of the salute spacemen gave to earthlings in a
science-fiction picture she had recently watched on
late-night television. She nodded. "How much—" she
began, but he interrupted and said, "You can decide
what it was worth when you've learned." She was
surprised and wondered if he meant to charge a great
deal. Would it be her fault and would she have to pay
him if he named his price when the lessons were over?
But he had an honest face. Perhaps he was just embarrassed to talk about money.

He drove for a few blocks, making her watch his
hand on the stick shift. "Feel how the car is going?"
he said. "Now you shift." He shifted. The car jumped
a little, hummed, moved into gear. It was an old car
and didn't shift too easily, he said. She had been
sitting forward, so that when he shifted she rocked
back hard against the seat—harder than she needed
to. Almost unconsciously, she wanted to show him
what a good teacher he was. When her turn came to
drive, the car stalled. "Take it easy," he said. "Ease
up on the clutch. Don't just raise your foot off of it
like that." She tried it again. "That's it," he said. She

looked at him when the car was in third. He sat in the seat, looking out the window. Snow was expected. It was Thursday. Although Larry was going to visit his parents and would not be back until late Friday afternoon, she decided she would wait until Tuesday for her next lesson. If he came home early, he would find out that she was taking lessons, and she didn't want him to know. She asked the boy, whose name was Michael, whether he thought she would forget all he had taught her in the time between lessons. "You'll remember," he said.

When they returned to the old lady's driveway, the car stalled going up the incline. She had trouble shifting. The boy put his hand over hers and kicked the heel of his hand forward. "You'll have to treat this car a little roughly, I'm afraid," he said. That afternoon, after he left, she made spaghetti sauce, chopping little pieces of pepper and onion and mushroom. When the sauce had cooked down, she called Mrs. Larsen and said that she would bring over dinner. She usually ate with the old lady once a week. The old lady often added a pinch of cinnamon to her food, saying that it brought out the flavor better than salt, and that since she was losing her sense of smell, food had to be strongly flavored for her to taste it. Once she had sprinkled cinnamon on a knockwurst. This time, as they ate, Natalie asked the old lady how much she paid the boy to bring the paper.

"I give him a dollar a week," the old lady said.

"Did he set the price, or did you?"

"He set the price. He told me he wouldn't take much because he has to walk this street to get to his apartment anyway."

"He taught me a lot about the car today," Natalie said.

"He's very handsome, isn't he?" the old lady said.

She asked Larry, "How were your parents?"

"Fine," he said. "But I spent almost all the time with Andy. It's almost his birthday, and he's depressed. We went to see Mose Allison."

"I think it stinks that hardly anyone else ever visits Andy," she said.

"He doesn't make it easy. He tells you everything that's on his mind, and there's no way you can pretend that his troubles don't amount to much. You just have to sit there and nod."

She remembered that Andy's room looked like a gymnasium. There were handgrips and weights scattered on the floor. There was even a psychedelic pink hula hoop that he was to put inside his elbow and then move his arm in circles wide enough to make the hoop spin. He couldn't do it. He would lie in bed with the hoop in back of his neck, and holding the sides, lift his neck off the pillow. His arms were barely strong enough to do that, really, but he could raise his neck with no trouble, so he just pretended that his arms pulling the loop were raising it. His parents thought that it was a special exercise that he had mastered.

"What did you do today?" Larry said now.

"I made spaghetti," she said. She had made it the day before, but she thought that since he was mysterious about the time he spent away from her ("in the lab" and "at the gym" became interchangeable), she did not owe him a straight answer. That day she had dropped off the film and then she had sat at the drugstore counter to have a cup of coffee. She bought some cigarettes, though she had not smoked since high school. She smoked one mentholated cigarette and then threw the pack away in a garbage container outside the drugstore. Her mouth still felt cool inside.

He asked if she had planned anything for the weekend.

"No," she said.

"Let's do something you'd like to do. I'm a little ahead of myself in the lab right now."

That night they ate spaghetti and made plans, and the next day they went for a ride in the country, to a factory where wooden toys were made. In the showroom he made a bear marionette shake and twist. She all envied him his long sweeping turns, with his legs somehow neatly together and his body at the perfect angle. She never saw him have an accident on the ice. Never once. She had known Andy, and they had skated at Parker's pond, for eight years before he was drafted.

The night before, as she and Larry were finishing dinner, he had asked her if she intended to vote for Nixon or McGovern in the election. "McGovern," she said. How could he not have known that? She knew then that they were farther apart than she had thought. She hoped that on Election Day she could drive herself to the polls—not go with him and not walk. She planned not to ask the old lady if she wanted to come along because that would be one vote she could keep Nixon from getting.

At the museum she hesitated by the sculpture but did not point it out to him. He didn't look at it. He gazed to the side, above it, at a Francis Bacon painting. He could have shifted his eyes just a little and seen the sculpture, and her, standing and staring.

After three more lessons she could drive the car. The last two times, which were later in the afternoon than her first lesson, they stopped at the drugstore to get the old lady's paper, to save him from having to make the same trip back on foot. When he came out of the drugstore with the paper, after the final lesson, she asked him if he'd like to have a beer to celebrate.

"Sure," he said.

They walked down the street to a bar that was filled with college students. She wondered if Larry ever came to this bar. He had never said that he did.

She and Michael talked. She asked why he wasn't in high school. He told her that he had quit. He was living with his brother, and his brother was teaching him carpentry, which he had been interested in all along. On his napkin he drew a picture of the cabinets and bookshelves he and his brother had spent the last week constructing and installing in the house of two wealthy old sisters. He drummed the side of his thumb against the edge of the table in time with the music. They each drank beer, from heavy glass mugs.

"Mrs. Larsen said your husband was in school," the boy said. "What's he studying?"

She looked up, surprised. Michael had never mentioned her husband to her before. "Chemistry," she said.

"I liked chemistry pretty well," he said. "Some of it."

"My husband doesn't know you've been giving me lessons. I'm just going to tell him that I can drive the stick shift, and surprise him."

"Yeah?" the boy said. "What will he think about that?"

"I don't know," she said. "I don't think he'll like it."

"Why?" the boy said.

His question made her remember that he was sixteen. What she had said would never have provoked another question from an adult. The adult would have nodded or said, "I know."

She shrugged. The boy took a long drink of beer. "I thought it was funny that he didn't teach you himself, when Mrs. Larsen told me you were married," he said.

They had discussed her. She wondered why Mrs. Larsen wouldn't have told her that, because the night she ate dinner with her she had talked to Mrs. Larsen about what an extraordinarily patient teacher Michael was. Had Mrs. Larsen told him that Natalie talked about him?

On the way back to the car she remembered the photographs and went back to the drugstore and picked up the prints. As she took money out of her wallet she remembered that today was the day she would have to pay him. She looked around at him, at the front of the store, where he was flipping through magazines. He was tall and he was wearing a very old black jacket. One end of his long thick maroon scarf was hanging down his back.

"What did you take pictures of?" he said when they were back in the car.

"Furniture. My husband wanted pictures of our furniture, in case it was stolen."

"Why?" he said.

"They say if you have proof that you had valuable things, the insurance company won't hassle you about reimbursing you."

"You have a lot of valuable stuff?" he said.

"My husband thinks so," she said.

A block from the driveway she said, "What do I owe you?"

"Four dollars," he said.

"That's nowhere near enough," she said and looked over at him. He had opened the envelope with the pictures in it while she was driving. He was staring at the picture of her legs. "What's this?" he said.

She turned into the driveway and shut off the engine. She looked at the picture. She could not think of what to tell him it was. Her hands and heart felt heavy.

"Wow," the boy said. He laughed. "Never mind. Sorry. I'm not looking at any more of them."

He put the pack of pictures back in the envelope and dropped it on the seat between them.

She tried to think what to say, of some way she could turn the pictures into a joke. She wanted to get out of the car and run. She wanted to stay, not to give him the money, so he would sit there with her. She reached into her purse and took out her wallet and removed four one-dollar bills.

"How many years have you been married?" he asked.

"One," she said. She held the money out to him. He said "Thank you" and leaned across the seat and put his right arm over her shoulder and kissed her. She felt his scarf bunched up against their cheeks. She was amazed at how warm his lips were in the cold car.

He moved his head away and said, "I didn't think you'd mind if I did that." She shook her head no. He unlocked the door and got out.

"I could drive you to your brother's apartment," she said. Her voice sounded hollow. She was extremely embarrassed, but she couldn't let him go.

He got back in the car. "You could drive me and come in for a drink," he said. "My brother's working."

When she got back to the car two hours later she saw a white parking ticket clamped under the windshield wiper, flapping in the wind. When she opened the car door and sank into the seat, she saw that he had left the money, neatly folded, on the floor mat on his side of the car. She did not pick up the money. In a while she started the car. She stalled it twice on the way home. When she had pulled into the driveway she looked at the money for a long time, then left it lying there. She left the car unlocked, hoping the money would be stolen. If it disappeared, she could tell herself that she had paid him. Otherwise she would not know how to deal with the situation.

When she got into the apartment, the phone rang. "I'm at the gym to play basketball," Larry said. "Be home in an hour."

"I was at the drugstore," she said. "See you then."

She examined the pictures. She sat on the sofa and laid them out, the twelve of them, in three rows on the cushion next to her. The picture of the piano was between the picture of her feet and the picture of herself that she had shot by aiming into the mirror. She picked up the four pictures of their furniture and put them on the table. She picked up the others and examined them closely. She began to understand why she had taken them. She had photographed parts of her body, fragments of it, to study the pieces. She had probably done it because she thought so much about Andy's body and the piece that was gone—the leg, below the knee, on his left side. She had had two bourbon-and-waters at the boy's apartment, and drinking always depressed her. She felt very depressed looking at the pictures, so she put them down and went into the bedroom. She undressed. She looked at her body—whole, not a bad figure—in the mirror. It was an automatic reaction with her to close the curtains when she was naked, so she turned quickly and went to the window and did that. She went back to the mirror; the room was darker now and her body looked better. She ran her hands down her sides, wondering if the feel of her skin was anything like the way the sculpture would feel. She was sure that the sculpture would be smoother—her hands would move more quickly down the slopes of it than she wanted—that it would be cool, and that somehow she could feel the grayness of it. Those things seemed preferable to her hands lingering on her body, the imperfection of her skin, the overheated apartment. If she were the piece of sculpture and if she could feel, she would like her sense of isolation.

This was in 1972, in Philadelphia.

Say Yes

TOBIAS WOLFF

*Tobias Wolff was born in Alabama in 1945, and grew up in Washington State. He was educated at Oxford and Stanford. Twice awarded the O. Henry Prize for short fiction, his stories have appeared in An-*taeus, *Esquire, Vanity Fair, The Atlantic Monthly, and many other magazines. His books include* In the Garden of the North American Martyrs *(1981), which received the St. Lawrence Award for fiction,* Back in the World *(1985), and* Barrack's Thief, *which was awarded the PEN/Faulkner Award for 1985.*

In the introduction for the collection of short stories he edited, Matters of Life and Death, *Tobias Wolff wrote, "(These writers) speak to us, without flippance, about things that matter. They write about what happens between men and women, parents and children. They write about fear of death, fear of life, the feelings that bring people together, and force them apart, the costs of intimacy. They remind us that our home is built on sand. They are, every one of them, interested in what it means to be human." The same can be said of Wolff's spare, straightforward, and lucid prose. In his acceptance speech for the PEN/Faulkner award he spoke about language and writers: "Language is our meeting place, the sea we all live in. When I watched my children learning to talk I had the sense that they were not so much learning language as being claimed by it, taken into its arms as if it were another parent, and so it is. In*

*the arms of language they will join the family of man.
They will learn what has gone before, and they will
learn what is left to be done. In language they will learn
to laugh, and to grieve, to be consoled in their grief and
to console others. In language they will discover who
they are. It is the common ground of our humanity . . .
But those who take language for their work must accept
the purest solitude as the first condition of their work.
You have to come to it alone . . . Who knows why they
do it? They probably don't know themselves. But I
suspect a reason. My guess is that the unearthly joy of
those moments when they are visited with favor, when
words come alive in their mouths, makes any tempta-
tion to use their lives otherwise seem pale and not worth
thinking about."*

*Tobias Wolff lives with his wife and two sons in
upstate New York and teaches at Syracuse University.*

They were doing the dishes, his wife washing while
he dried. He'd washed the night before. Unlike most
men he knew, he really pitched in on the housework.
A few months earlier he'd overheard a friend of his
wife's congratulate her on having such a considerate
husband, and he thought, *I try*. Helping out with the
dishes was a way he had of showing how considerate
he was.

They talked about different things and somehow got
on the subject of whether white people should marry
black people. He said that all things considered, he
thought it was a bad idea.

"Why?" she asked.

Sometimes his wife got this look where she pinched
her brows together and bit her lower lip and stared
down at something. When he saw her like this he knew
he should keep his mouth shut, but he never did.
Actually it made him talk more. She had that look now.

"Why?" she asked again, and stood there with her hand inside a bowl, not washing it but just holding it above the water.

"Listen," he said, "I went to school with blacks, and I've worked with blacks and lived on the same street with blacks, and we've always gotten along just fine. I don't need you coming along now and implying that I'm a racist."

"I didn't imply anything," she said, and began washing the bowl again, turning it around in her hand as though she were shaping it. "I just don't see what's wrong with a white person marrying a black person, that's all."

"They don't come from the same culture as we do. Listen to them sometime—they even have their own language. That's okay with me, I *like* hearing them talk"—he did; for some reason it always made him feel happy—"but it's different. A person from their culture and a person from our culture could never really *know* each other."

"Like you know me?" his wife asked.

"Yes. Like I know you."

"But if they love each other," she said. She was washing faster now, not looking at him.

Oh boy, he thought. He said, "Don't take my word for it. Look at the statistics. Most of those marriages break up."

"Statistics." She was piling dishes on the drainboard at a terrific rate, just swiping at them with the cloth. Many of them were greasy, and there were flecks of food between the tines of the forks. "All right," she said, "what about foreigners? I suppose you think the same thing about two foreigners getting married."

"Yes," he said, "as a matter of fact I do. How can you understand someone who comes from a completely different background?"

"Different," said his wife. "Not the same, like us."

"Yes, different," he snapped, angry with her for resorting to this trick of repeating his words so that they sounded crass, or hypocritical. "These are dirty," he said, and dumped all the silverware back into the sink.

The water had gone flat and gray. She stared down at it, her lips pressed tight together, then plunged her hands under the surface. "Oh!" she cried, and jumped back. She took her right hand by the wrist and held it up. Her thumb was bleeding.

"Ann, don't move," he said. "Stay right there." He ran upstairs to the bathroom and rummaged in the medicine chest for alcohol, cotton, and a Band-Aid. When he came back down she was leaning against the refrigerator with her eyes closed, still holding her hand. He took the hand and dabbed at her thumb with the cotton. The bleeding had stopped. He squeezed it to see how deep the wound was and a single drop of blood welled up, trembling and bright, and fell to the floor. Over the thumb she stared at him accusingly. "It's shallow," he said. "Tomorrow you won't even know it's there." He hoped that she appreciated how quickly he had come to her aid. He'd acted out of concern for her, with no thought of getting anything in return, but now the thought occurred to him that it would be a nice gesture on her part not to start up that conversation again, as he was tired of it. "I'll finish up here," he said. "You go and relax."

"That's okay," she said. "I'll dry."

He began to wash the silverware again, giving a lot of attention to the forks.

"So," she said, "you wouldn't have married me if I'd been black."

"For Christ's sake, Ann!"

"Well, that's what you said, didn't you?"

"No, I did not. The whole question is ridiculous. If you had been black we probably wouldn't even have met. You would have had your friends and I would have had mine. The only black girl I ever really knew was my partner in the debating club, and I was already going out with you by then."

"But if we had met, and I'd been black?"

"Then you probably would have been going out with a black guy." He picked up the rinsing nozzle and sprayed the silverware. The water was so hot that the metal darkened to pale blue, then turned silver again.

"Let's say I wasn't," she said. "Let's say I am black and unattached and we meet and fall in love."

He glanced over at her. She was watching him and her eyes were bright. "Look," he said, taking a reasonable tone, "this is stupid. If you were black you wouldn't be you." As he said this he realized it was absolutely true. There was no possible way of arguing with the fact that she would not be herself if she were black. So he said it again: "If you were black you wouldn't be you."

"I know," she said, "but let's just say."

He took a deep breath. He had won the argument but he still felt cornered. "Say what?" he asked.

"That I'm black, but still me, and we fall in love. Will you marry me?"

He thought about it.

"Well?" she said, and stepped close to him. Her eyes were even brighter. "Will you marry me?"

"I'm thinking," he said.

"You won't, I can tell. You're going to say no."

"Let's not move too fast on this," he said. "There are lots of things to consider. We don't want to do something we would regret for the rest of our lives."

"No more considering. Yes or no."

"Since you put it that way—"

"Yes or no."

"Jesus, Ann. All right. No."

She said. "Thank you," and walked from the kitchen into the living room. A moment later he heard her turning the pages of a magazine. He knew that she was too angry to be actually reading it, but she didn't snap through the pages the way he would have done. She turned them slowly, as if she were studying every word. She was demonstrating her indifference to him, and it had the effect he knew she wanted it to have. It hurt him.

He had no choice but to demonstrate his indifference to her. Quietly, thoroughly, he washed the rest of the dishes. Then he dried them and put them away. He wiped the counters and the stove and scoured the linoleum where the drop of blood had fallen. While he was at it, he decided, he might as well mop the whole floor. When he was done the kitchen looked new, the way it looked when they were first shown the house, before they had ever lived here.

He picked up the garbage pail and went outside. The night was clear and he could see a few stars to the west, where the lights of the town didn't blur them out. On El Camino the traffic was steady and light, peaceful as a river. He felt ashamed that he had let his wife get him into a fight. In another thirty years or so they would both be dead. What would all that stuff matter then? He thought of the years they had spent together, and how close they were, and how well they knew each other, and his throat tightened so that he could hardly breathe. His face and neck began to tingle. Warmth flooded his chest. He stood there for a while, enjoying these sensations, then picked up the pail and went out the back gate.

The two mutts from down the street had pulled over the garbage can again. One of them was rolling around on his back and the other had something in her mouth. Growling, she tossed it into the air, leaped up and caught it, growled again and whipped her head from side to side. When they saw him coming they trotted away with short, mincing steps. Normally he would heave rocks at them, but this time he let them go.

The house was dark when he came back inside. She was in the bathroom. He stood outside the door and called her name. He heard bottles clinking, but she didn't answer him. "Ann, I'm really sorry," he said. "I'll make it up to you, I promise."

"How?" she asked.

He wasn't expecting this. But from a sound in her voice, a level and definite note that was strange to him, he knew that he had to come up with the right answer. He leaned against the door. "I'll marry you," he whispered.

"We'll see," she said. "Go on to bed. I'll be out in a minute."

He undressed and got under the covers. Finally he heard the bathroom door open and close.

"Turn off the light," she said from the hallway.

"What?"

"Turn off the light."

He reached over and pulled the chain on the bed-side lamp. The room went dark. "All right," he said. He lay there, but nothing happened. "All right," he said again. Then he heard a movement across the room. He sat up, but he couldn't see a thing. The room was silent. His heart pounded the way it had on their first night together, the way it still did when he woke at a noise in the darkness and waited to hear it again—the sound of someone moving through the house, a stranger.

Cooker

FREDERICK BARTHELME

Frederick Barthelme was born in Houston in 1941. He lived for a time in Manhattan, thought of becoming a painter, then returned to Texas to do advertising work. He later studied creative writing at Johns Hopkins University, and became in 1977 the director of the Center for Writers at the University of Southern Mississippi. The author of one book of stories, Moon Deluxe *(1983), he's also written two novels,* Second Marriage *(1984) and* Tracer *(1985). Several years ago when asked about the difficulties in writing a second novel he replied, "You're still out in the middle of nowhere doing something nobody asked you to do, and you suspect, all polite evidence to the contrary, that they didn't ask because they don't want, and if they did want, they'd get it elsewhere."*

Frederick Barthelme's fiction has been called sensitive, spacey, funny, and weird. His protagonists—mostly men—adrift in a world of ever-changing sexual roles, occupy a universe of subdivisions, apartment complexes, fast-food counters, and shopping malls. Their inability to connect—with women, friends, the past—is always vaguely unsettling to them, but rarely anything more. Authentic involvement is not something they enjoy. Mr. Barthelme fashions his stories with a keen ear, an eye for the quirky detail, and an unsentimental warmth for all his characters.

I tell Lily I'm tired of complaining about things, about my job, about the people I work with, about the way things are at home with her, about the kids and the way the kids don't seem to be coming along, about the country, the things the politicians say on television, on "Nightline" and on "Crossfire" and the other news programs, tired of complaining about everybody lying all the time, or skirting the truth, staying just close enough to get by, tired of having people at the office selectively remember things, or twist things ever so slightly in an argument so that they appear to be reasonable, sensible, and thoughtful, tired of making excuses for my subordinates and supervisors alike, tired of rolling and tumbling and being in a more or less constant state of harangue about one thing and another.

Lily, who is sitting on the railing of our deck petting the stray cat that has taken up with us, nods as I talk, and when I stop to think of the next thing I'm tired of complaining about, says to me, "I'm tired, too, Roger."

Our children—Christine, who is eight, and Charles, who is eleven—are in the yard arguing about the hose. Charles has the nozzle tweaked up to maximum thrust, and he's spattering water all around Christine, making her dance to get out of the way.

"Charles," I say, waving at him to tell him to get the hose away from Christine. "Quit screwing around, O.K.?"

"Ah, Dad. I'm not hurting her. I'm just playing with her. We're just playing."

"We are not," Christine says. "I'm not, anyway. I don't want to play this way." She twists herself into a collection of crossed limbs, a posture that says "pout" in a big way.

"Why don't you water those bushes over there?" Lily says, indicating the bushes that line our back fence. "They look as if they could use the water."

I say, "The thing is, I hate all these people. There's

almost nobody I don't hate. Sometimes I see something on TV and I just go into a rage, you know?"

"What things?" she says. "See what things?"

"Somebody says a self-serving thing, I don't know, some guy'll say something about preserving the best interests of something or other, doing the best job he can and all that, upholding standards, and you can look at this guy and tell that what he's thinking is how can he make this sound good, how can he sell this thing he's saying, whatever it is."

"You're talking about the preachers, right?"

"They're all preachers now. They're all holier-than-thou, self-righteous killers. I mean, everybody's a flack these days, they'll say anything just as long as they can keep on making their killings. I see this all the time at work. A guy'll come in and make a big argument for his own promotion, and when he's done I don't even recognize the world he's talking about. Remember that intern we had last fall, kid from Colorado? Then we hired him, right? You know why? Because he made friends with Lumming and what's-his-name, the other guy in production."

"Mossy—isn't that it? Mosely?"

"Something. But when the personnel committee met to talk about this job, Lumming and Mossy didn't say a word about being friendly with this kid. They said he was the greatest thing since sliced bread. It was a clear and simple lie. No question."

"You're complaining about the office," Lily says. "I thought the point of this talk was that you wanted to stop complaining."

"I do, but this stuff is driving me nuts. I don't want to be in a world where this stuff goes on."

"Go to Heaven," Lily says.

"Thanks. That's real interestingly cynical."

"Why not do a little discipline? Ease up." She spins herself off the railing and thumps as her feet hit the deck. "Besides, what would you do if you didn't complain? You wouldn't have anything to talk about."

"You're a charmer," I say. "You're a swell guy. An ace wife and companion."

"Mother of your children," she says, rolling the Weber into place.

"You cooking out here tonight "

"You are," she says. "Therapy."

I don't mind that. In fact, I'm pleased that she's found something for me to do, something to occupy me, take my mind off the office and the things people are doing wrong. I used to be a lot more easygoing than I am now, and Lily, of course, recognizes that. Watching her mess with the grill, I wonder if she doesn't miss that more than anything else. "What am I cooking?" I asked. I should know the answer to this. I helped bring the groceries in from the car, helped her put them away. I have no idea what groceries they were.

"Lamb chops," she says.

This makes me feel better. Lamb chops, and suddenly the world is new, a place of mystery and possibility. Lily and my mother are the only two women on the planet who believe a lamb chop is a reasonable and appropriate thing to cook for dinner. That she wants them barbecued means I get to look up the recipe in the twenty-four-page no-nonsense Weber Kettle cookbook. I say, "We've got lamb chops?"

"Yep." She's redistributing the coals in the Weber, evening them. She squats beside the cooker and wiggles the bottom vent back and forth to release the ashes into the ash catcher, then dumps the ashes over the side of the deck. "I am serving corn and the lima beans, if you're interested."

"I love the lima beans," I say.

"So get cracking."

I go into the storage closet that opens onto the deck. I'm getting the barbecue tools. As I come out of there, I think: I have no desire to touch Lily. I don't know why, but that's what I think. She's not unattractive—in fact, she's quite lovely—but I don't want to touch her. It's not a desperate thing; I'm not thinking how awful it would be. But at the same time it's a clear thing. There isn't any question. She probably doesn't want to touch me, either. I wouldn't blame her. It's been a while since I've been in any kind of shape; I don't even like to touch me. I try to remember the last time we touched—apart from the usual, casual touches that happen without thinking. It's been weeks, maybe months. Not twelve months, but two, maybe.

I arrange my tools—barbecue tweezers and fork, hickory chips, Gulf lighter fluid—on the redwood table, and I think what brought this stuff about Lily to mind was a TV show I watched last night on CNN: a Los Angeles sex therapist answers all your questions after midnight. What struck me was the assumptions this woman made. She managed, without literally specifying, to predicate everything she said on a version of the ideal relationship which was a joke to me: one man and one woman having happy sex together forever. This was the implicit ideal. Now, we all know that's just plain wrong. It'll never happen. And yet here was this woman taking callers' questions, answering with the kind of dull-witted assurance and authority that characterizes these people: Here are the solutions, follow these three easy steps, put your little foot. I got angry watching this program. Somebody called in from Fairfax, Virginia, said sex wasn't interesting, and asked why this woman didn't get real.

I watched for an hour. This woman wore a lot of eye makeup. Not as much as Cleopatra, but plenty, more than enough. She was good-looking—a dark-skin, dark-hair type, but a handful of freckles—but there was something of the born-again about her, that kind of earnest matter-of-factness that makes you want to run the other way. Almost everybody's born-again these days; if you're not born-again you're out to lunch, yours is a minority view, you lose. Anyway, this woman had an easy rapport with the announcer, who was a newsman, and they traded asides, little jokes between callers' questions—he apologized a lot about his hopeless manhood.

I don't make too much of a mess with the cooking, though I'm pretty angry when I bring the chops in and drip lamb juice on the carpet in the living room. But before I have time to get worse, Lily's got the plate of chops out of my hands and is telling me to remember three weeks ago, when I threw barbecue at the kitchen window.

"That was pork," I say. "And I don't know why you feel you have to remind me about it all the time anyway. I cleaned it up, didn't I?"

"Yes, Roger." She's circling the table, dropping lamb chops on the plates. "It took you two hours, too."

"But it was real cool, Dad," Charles says, making a throwing move. "Splat!"

I say, "No, my little porcupine, it wasn't."

"I agree," Christine says. "It was childish." She's repeating what she heard her mother say immediately after I tossed the pork chops.

"How old is she?" I ask Lily. I kiss the top of Christine's head and then take my chair. "If you're real good," I say to Christine, "we can get a dog later, O.K.?" She knows, I think, that this is a joke.

"I think maybe you're trying too hard again, Dad," Charles says. He's taken to adding "Dad" to every sentence. It's annoying.

"Yeah, Dad," Lily says. "Take it easy, would you?" She pinches Charles' ear and turns him to face his dinner.

Charles squirms, trying to get away from her. "Jesus, Mom," he says.

"None of that, kid," I say. I wave my fork at him for emphasis, point it at him, wiggle it.

"Who wants a stupid dog, anyway?" Christine says. She's using an overhand grip on her spoon, shoving the food on her plate around to make sure that nothing touches anything else. She's always eaten this way, ever since she was four. She'll eat all of one vegetable, then all of the next, and so on. I've tried to stop it, but Lily says it's O.K., so I haven't made much progress. She says Christine will grow out of it. I say I know that, but what will she grow into? Lily says I'm a hard-liner.

"You want a dog," I say to Christine. "What are you talking about? All you've said for the last three weeks is how much you want a dog."

"That was before," she says.

"Before what?" Charles says. He turns to me as if we are co-conspirators. "She wants one, Dad. I know she does. She's lying."

"Don't call your sister a liar," Lily says. "Roger, tell him."

"Your mother's right, Charles. Don't call Christy a liar, O.K.? Not nice." I'm just about finished with my first lamb chop. The mint-flavored apple jelly is glistening on my plate. I feel pretty good.

"It's true," Charles says. "What do you want me to do? Do you want me to lie, too?"

Christine is playing with her food, twirling her chop in the clear space she's left for it on her plate. "I wanted a dog," she says, "but now I don't. Can't anybody understand that?"

"I can't," Charles says.

"Eat your dinner, Charles," Lily says. "You can understand *that*, can't you?"

I know I shouldn't tease the kids the way I do—like telling them we can get a dog. It's a standing joke in our house. They know we're not getting a dog. And they know why: Daddy's bad about dogs, about pets in general. Daddy looks at a dog and what he sees is a travel club for ticks and fleas. Try explaining that to a kid. Lily and I used to have big fights about it, but I won. I outlasted her. I'm not proud of it, but it's O.K. I don't mind winning one every now and then. She still thinks I'll come around after a while, but she's wrong about that. I've told the kids they can have fish, but they don't want fish.

So there's a history going on about this dog stuff, in the family, and I tease them about it all the time; it might sound cruel, but it seems to me they ought to understand. You can't always get what you want and all that. It's important that they know what's going on, that once they know no dog's forthcoming, then the dog is fair game. Lily says I'm crazy on this one, that kids don't work the way we do. She says I'm building a horrible distrust. She says it's not smart, that when I'm old and pathetic they'll trick me—tell me they're coming to see me and then not show, or take me out for a drive and slam me into a home or something.

"O.K.," I say. "I'm sorry I brought up the dog. The dog remark was a bad idea. No dog. Christine?"

"What?" She's petulant. "I know," she says.

"I shouldn't have said a thing about the dog, O.K.? I don't know why I did. I'm upset."

"Daddy's upset about the office, sweetheart," Lily says.

"I'm sorry," Christine says.

"He shouldn't take it out on us," Charles says. He turns to me, gives me a real adult look. "You shouldn't, Dad."

I don't think I like the way Charles is turning out. For a time, his early moves toward adulthood, the grave looks and the knowing nods, were charming, even touching. After all, he's a boy, a kid, and it's nice to see him practicing. But it gets old.

"I know that, Charles," I say. "Thank you."

"Well," he says, "I'm just trying to help."

Lily pats his arm. I don't know why mothers always pat their children's arms. It's disgusting. "Yes, Charles," she says. "But Daddy's tired. Let's just be quiet and eat, what do you say? Daddy's had a hard day."

"Another one?"

"That's enough, Charles," she says.

And it is enough. After that, we eat in silence. I

watch Christine, who eats her corn first, kernel by
kernel, then the beans. She doesn't even touch her
lamb chop. When I finish eating, I take my plate to
the kitchen, scrape the used food into the brown paper
bag we keep under the sink—only now it's out on the
kitchen floor in front of the cabinet—and put my plate
under the faucet. I turn on the water for a few seconds
to rinse, then go back through the dining area, stop
behind Lily for a minute, and cross the room toward
the back door. "I'm going to straighten up out here,"
I say. "I may water for a while."

"You're going to water?" Charles says.

"Finish eating," Lily says. "I think your father might
want some individual time."

"What's individual time?" Christine says.

"Don't be dumb," Charles says to her.

What I'm thinking about, out there on the deck, is
that I'm not living the way I ought to be living, not the
way I thought I would be. It's all obvious stuff—women,
mostly. I'm not Mr. Imagination on the deal. A woman
stands for a connection and another way of living,
something like that. So I'm thinking about the woman
on "West 57th," the TV show, and the dewy young
girls in the movies—though you don't see them as
much as you used to—and thinking of the poor ap-
proximations that throng the malls. I'm not thinking
anything *about* these women, I'm only thinking *of*
them.

I put the charcoal lighter back in the storage closet,
finger the hickory chips, think for a minute about
sitting down in there. This closet is about six feet
square, lined with empty cardboard boxes that our
electronics came in; we've kept computer boxes, stereo boxes, TV and VCR boxes, speaker boxes, tape-
recorder boxes. Then I decide to do it, to sit down just
the way I want to, and I go back to the deck and get
one of the white wire chairs and put it in the storage
room and sit down, my feet up on the second shelf of

the bookcase that I bought from Shorehouse so the junk we keep in the storage closet will be more orderly: charcoal, lighter, and chips on the bottom shelf, plant foods and insecticides on the second, plant tools on the third, also on the third electric tools (saw, drill, sander), and accessories on the top. It isn't too bad in there. From where I sit I can see out across the deck to the small lump of forest that borders one side of our lot. She always puts plants out there in the summer, and I look at those—pencil cactus, other euphorbias.

Lily comes out and walks right past the door of the storage closet out to the edge of the deck, looking around for me. "Roger?" she calls. "Roger, where are you?"

"Back here."

She turns and looks at me in the closet. "What are you doing in there, Roger?"

I say, "Thinking about my sins," which is a thing my mother always used to say when I was a kid, that she was thinking about her sins. She didn't have any sins to think about, of course, which is why it was a funny thing to say.

"Why don't you come out of there? Sit out here with me, O.K.?"

I say, "Fine," and pick up my chair and carry it back out to the spot on the deck where I got it.

She closes the storage door behind me. "Now," she says, sitting down on the deck railing. "You've got this nice family, these two kids and everything, this good job, and things are going great, right?"

"Things are O.K."

"Right. And you're complaining all the time about everything."

"Right."

"And you don't want to complain."

"Right."

"So you're like Peter Finch," she says. "In that movie, whatever it was. The one where he went out the window and said he was mad as hell, remember?"

"Sure," I say. "What's the point?"

"Where'd it get him?" Lily says. "He's dead as a doornail. I mean, that's not *why* he's dead, but he is dead. I think there's a lesson in that."

I nod and say, "That lesson would be . . ."

"Take it easy, Greasy," Lily says.

"But everything's wrong now. People'll say anything. Everybody's transparent and nobody minds—like you, for example. Here, now. What you want is for me not to be upset. That's all. You don't care what I'm upset about, you just want me over it."

"Well?"

"In a better world we'd deal with the disease, not the symptom."

"In a better world we wouldn't have the disease," she says.

"Good point."

"Thank you."

Charles comes out of the house carrying a sleeping bag, a yellow ice chest, some magazines, and the spread off his bed. "I'm camping out tonight, O.K.?" he says as he passes us.

I start to say no, but then Lily catches my eye and gives her head a little sideways shake. This means that she has already signed off on things.

"Watch out for spiders," I say.

"There aren't any spiders," Lily says, shaking her head. She smiles at Charles and holds out her arm to him, and he comes over for a kiss, trailing his equipment.

I nod. "That's right. No spiders. I just said that."

"Your daddy's having a hard time," Lily says.

Charles is hanging around in an annoying way, lingering. It's as if he doesn't really want to camp out in the back yard after all.

"I don't care about them anyway," he says. "I play with spiders at school." He waits a second, then says, "Dad, I'm making a tent. Is it O.K. if I use the boards behind the garage?"

I say sure.

*   *   *

It's dark, and we've got a pretty good tent in the yard. I'm in there with Charles. He's reading a car magazine and listening to a Bon Jovi tape on the portable we got him for his last birthday. I've already asked him to turn it down twice, and the second time he went inside for his earphones. It must be midnight. I'm lying on my back under the tent, my feet sticking out the back end of it, my head on one of the three pillows he brought out. The floor of our place here is cardboard, but we've got a rug over that, a four-by-seven thing that Lily and I got at Pier 1 about fifteen years ago. I got it out of the garage, where it's been a couple of years.

The bugs aren't too bad. Both of us rubbed down with Off, so there's this thin, slightly turpentine smell in the air.

I get along well enough with Charles. We're not like some "Father Knows Best" thing, but we do all right. He has his world and I have mine. Looking at him there in the tent, his head hopping with music, his eyes on the magazine, I have an idea what he's about, what it's like for him. I mean, he sees the stuff I see on TV and he believes it, or maybe he believes nothing, or maybe he recognizes that none of it makes any difference to him anyway. I guess that's it. And if that's it, he's right. Let 'em lie. We've got the yard, the bedspread tent, there are crickets around here, and pretty soon a cat will stick its head in the opening at the front of the tent, look us over, maybe even come in and curl up. What goes on out there is entertainment; I'm not saying it won't touch him, but the scale is so big that really it won't. We'll do another Grenada—what a pathetic, disgusting, hollow, ignorant joke that was—but he'll be in school, or doing desk work for some Army rocker, or waiting for his second child. He's just like me, he's out of it. He can get in if he wants to—he can be a TV guy, a reporter, a senator, a staff person. It's America. He can be anything, do anything. I'm stumped.

"What're you doing, Dad?" Charles says.

I keep looking at the top of the tent. "Thinking about you."

"Oh." He waits a minute, then he says, "Well? Is it a mystery or what?"

"It's no mystery," I say, rolling over on my side so I can look at him. He's got the earphones down around his neck. "What're you reading?"

"Bigfoot." He flashes the magazine at me. It's called *Bigfoot*. "The truck, you know?"

"Monster truck," I say.

"Right. It's a whole magazine about Bigfoot—how they got started, what happened, you know. . . ."

"You interested in trucks?" I say. What I'm thinking is, I don't like the way this sounds, this conversation. It sounds like conversations on television, fathers and sons in tortured moments. "Never mind," I say.

"Not really," he says, answering me anyway.

"I don't know why I'm out here, Charles," I say. "Am I bothering you?"

"Not really. I mean, it's strange, but it's not too bad."

"I'm just a little off track today, know what I mean? I think I'm down on my fellow-man—talking weenies everywhere, talking cheaters and liars. I mean, normally it doesn't bother me, I just play through. You do what you can. Pick up the junk and paste it back together whatever way you can."

"Dad? Are you drunk?"

"Nope," I say. "I haven't been drunk for ten years, Charles. There's nothing to drink about." I sit up, crossing my legs, facing him. "I never wanted to have a son—any child, for that matter. You and Christine are Lily's doing, what she wanted. I didn't mind, you see. It's not like I hate kids or anything, it's just that having kids wasn't the great driver for me. You're a problem, you know? Kids are. I don't want to treat you like a pet, but you're small—and, of necessity, kind of dumb. I don't mean dumb, but there's stuff you don't know, see what I mean?"

"Sure," he says.

"It's not stuff I can tell you."

"Dad," he says, "are you sure you're O.K.? You want me to get Mom?" He's up, bent over, already on his way out.

"Well . . . sure. Get Mom."

I lie down again when he's gone. I feel fine, I feel O.K. In a minute Lily's crawling into the tent. "Roger?" she says. "What's going on? Do you feel all right?"

"I'm functional."

Charles comes in long enough to get his magazine and his tape recorder. "I think I'll stay inside tonight," he says.

"I talked to him," I say to Lily.

"Uh-huh." She's got an arm across my chest and she's patting me.

"So long, Sport," I say to Charles as he backs out of the tent.

"Night, Dad," he says.

I'm left there in the tent with my wife. I say, "I'm acting up, I guess."

"A little."

"But that's acceptable, right? Now and then?"

"It's fine," she says.

"It's by way of a complaint, huh? So we're back where we started from."

"Yep."

"It's not a vague complaint in my head," I say. "It's just that it covers everything. There are too many things to list. You start listing things that are wrong and you either make them smaller and sort of less wrong, or you go on forever. You got forever?"

"Sure." She waits a few seconds after she says that; I can feel her waiting. Then she says, "But I've got to go to the mall sometime."

"All right."

She gets up on her knees and twists around so she can lie down on her back alongside me. She takes my right hand in her left. "See there? You're not completely gone. You're O.K. We've just got to take it one thing at a time. We've got to go binary on this one."

To Room Nineteen

DORIS LESSING

Doris Lessing was born in Kermonshah, Persia, in 1919. Her parents were British. In 1924, her family moved to a three thousand-acre maize farm in Southern Rhodesia, where her father, a banker, decided to try his hand at farming. They lived in a mud-walled, grass-roofed house that was isolated by several miles from the nearest white farmers, a solitude that would later make Lessing describe her childhood as "hellishly lonely." When she was seven, she was sent to a Roman Catholic convent boarding school in Salisbury, the capital. After leaving school at the age of fourteen—against her mother's wishes—she earned her living at various secretarial jobs. From then on, she was self-educated. "I had to be," she has said. "The school was no good. I read and when I was interested in something, I followed it up. Whenever I met anyone who knew anything, I would bore them stiff until they told me what they knew." She read, for the first time, those writers who would later influence her own work—Tolstoy, Dostoyevsky, Balzac, Stendhal, and Turgenev. "I think I've always been a writer by temperament," she stated in an interview in 1964. "I wrote some bad novels in my teens. I always knew I would be a writer, but not until I was quite old—twenty-six or seven—did I realize I'd better stop saying I was going to be one and get down to business." During the 1940s in Salisbury, Mrs. Lessing helped to organize a Communist party, a group that admitted both black and white members. In 1949, after a second marriage that ended in divorce, she left Southern Rhodesia for England. Alone with a small child and little money, she published her first novel, The Grass Is Singing, *in 1950, from a manuscript she had brought with her from Africa. In it, she deals with many of the topics that would continue to be important in all her work: men, women, religious injustice, oppression, social class, loneliness, lust. She has written more than twenty books. Among them the five volume* Children of Violence *(1952–1969),* The Golden Notebook *(1962),* Briefing for a Descent into Hell *(1971),* The Summer Before the Dark *(1973),* The Memoirs of a Survivor *(1974),* Collected Stories *(1978), a set of five novels,* Canopus in Argos Archives *(1979–1983),* The Good Terrorist *(1985), and* The Fifth Child *(1988). She has resided in England since 1949.*

This is a story, I suppose, about a failure in intelligence: the Rawlings' marriage was grounded in intelligence.

They were older when they married than most of their married friends: in their well-seasoned late twenties. Both had had a number of affairs, sweet rather than bitter; and when they fell in love—for they did fall in love—had known each other for some time. They joked that they had saved each other "for the real thing." That they had waited so long (but not too long) for this real thing was to them a proof of their sensible discrimination. A good many of their friends had married young, and now (they felt) probably regretted lost opportunities; while others, still unmarried, seemed to them arid, self-doubting, and likely to make desperate or romantic marriages.

Not only they, but others, felt they were well-matched: their friends' delight was an additional proof of their happiness. They had played the same roles, male and female, in this group or set, if such a wide, loosely connected, constantly changing constellation of people could be called a set. They had both become, by virtue of their moderation, their humour, and their abstinence from painful experience, people to whom others came for advice. They could be, and were, relied on. It was one of those cases of a man and a woman linking themselves whom no one else had ever thought of linking, probably because of their similarities. But then everyone exclaimed: Of course! How right! How was it we never thought of it before!

And so they married amid general rejoicing, and because of their foresight and their sense for what was probable, nothing was a surprise to them.

Both had well-paid jobs. Matthew was a subeditor on a large London newspaper, and Susan worked in an advertising firm. He was not the stuff of which editors or publicised journalists are made, but he was much more than "a subeditor," being one of the essential background people who in fact steady, inspire and make possible the people in the limelight. He was content with this position. Susan had a talent for commercial drawing. She was humorous about the advertisements she was responsible for, but she did not feel strongly about them one way or the other.

Both, before they married, had had pleasant flats, but they felt it unwise to base a marriage on either flat, because it might seem like a submission of personality on the part of the one whose flat it was not. They moved into a new flat in South Kensington on the clear understanding that when their marriage had settled down (a process they knew would not take long, and was in fact more a humorous concession to popular wisdom than what was due to themselves) they would buy a house and start a family.

And this is what happened. They lived in their charming flat for two years, giving parties and going to them, being a popular young married couple, and then

Susan became pregnant, she gave up her job, and they bought a house in Richmond. It was typical of this couple that they had a son first, then a daughter, then twins, son and daughter. Everything right, appropriate, and what everyone would wish for, if they could choose. But people did feel these two had chosen; this balanced and sensible family was no more than what was due to them because of their infallible sense for *choosing* right.

And so they lived with their four children in their gardened house in Richmond and were happy. They had everything they had wanted and had planned for.

And yet . . .

Well, even this was expected, that there must be a certain flatness. . . .

Yes, yes, of course, it was natural they sometimes felt like this. Like what?

Their life seemed to be like a snake biting its tail. Matthew's job for the sake of Susan, children, house, and garden—which caravanserai needed a well-paid job to maintain it. And Susan's practical intelligence for the sake of Matthew, the children, the house and the garden—which unit would have collapsed in a week without her.

But there was no point about which either could say: "For the sake of *this* is all the rest." Children? But children can't be a center of life and a reason for being. They can be a thousand things that are delightful, interesting, satisfying, but they can't be a wellspring to live from. Or they shouldn't be. Susan and Matthew knew that well enough.

Matthew's job? Ridiculous. It was an interesting job, but scarcely a reason for living. Matthew took pride in doing it well, but he could hardly be expected to be proud of the newspaper; the newspaper he read, *his* newspaper, was not the one he worked for.

Their love for each other? Well, that was nearest it. If this wasn't a center, what was? Yes, it was around this point, their love, that the whole extraordinary structure revolved. For extraordinary it certainly was. Both Susan and Matthew had moments of thinking so, of looking in secret disbelief at this thing they had created: marriage, four children, big house, garden, chairwomen, friends, cars . . . and this *thing*, this entity, all of it had come into existence, been blown into being out of nowhere, because Susan loved Matthew and Matthew loved Susan. Extraordinary. So that was the central point, the wellspring.

And if one felt that it simply was not strong enough, important enough, to support it all, well whose fault was that? Certainly neither Susan's nor Matthew's. It was in the nature of things. And they sensibly blamed neither themselves nor each other.

On the contrary, they used their intelligence to preserve what they had created from a painful and explosive world: they looked around them, and took lessons. All around them, marriages collapsing, or breaking, or rubbing along (even worse, they felt). They must not make the same mistakes, they must not.

They had avoided the pitfall so many of their friends had fallen into—of buying a house in the country *for the sake of the children,* so that the husband became a weekend husband, a weekend father, and the wife always careful not to ask what went on in the town flat which they called (in joke) a bachelor flat. No, Matthew was a full-time husband, a full-time father, and at night, in the big married bed in the big married bedroom (which had an attractive view of the river), they lay beside each other talking and he told her about his day, and what he had done, and whom he had met; and she told him about her day (not as interesting, but that was not her fault), for both knew of the hidden resentments and deprivations of the woman who has lived her own life—and above all, has earned her own living—and is now dependent on a husband for outside interests and money.

Nor did Susan make the mistake of taking a job for the sake of her independence, which she might very

well have done, since her old firm, missing her qualities of humour, balance, and sense, invited her often
to go back. Children needed their mother to a certain
age, that both parents knew and agreed on; and when
those four healthy, wisely brought up children were of
the right age, Susan would work again, because she
knew, and so did he, what happened to women of fifty
at the height of their energy and ability, with grownup
children who no longer needed their full devotion.

So here was this couple, testing their marriage,
looking after it, treating it like a small boat full of
helpless people in a very stormy sea. Well, of course,
so it was. . . . The storms of the world were bad, but
not too close—which is not to say they were selfishly
felt: Susan and Matthew were both well-informed and
responsible people. And the inner storms and quick-
sands were understood and charted. So everything was
all right. Everything was in order. Yes, things were
under control.

So what did it matter if they felt dry, flat? People
like themselves, fed on a hundred books (psychological, anthropological, sociological), could scarcely be
unprepared for the dry, controlled wistfulness which is
the distinguishing mark of the intelligent marriage.
Two people, endowed with education, with discrimination, with judgement, linked together voluntarily from
their will to be happy together and to be of use to
others—one sees them everywhere, one knows them,
one even is that thing oneself: sadness because so
much is after all so little. These two, unsurprised,
turned towards each other with even more courtesy
and gentle love: this was life, that two people, no
matter how carefully chosen, could not be everything
to each other. In fact, even to say so, to think in such
a way, was banal; they were ashamed to do it.

It was banal, too, when one night Matthew came
home late and confessed he had been to a party, taken
a girl home and slept with her. Susan forgave him, of
course. Except that forgiveness is hardly the word.

Understanding, yes. But if you understand something, you don't forgive it, you are the thing itself: forgiveness is for what you *don't* understand. Nor had he *confessed*—what sort of word is that?

The whole thing was not important. After all, years ago they had joked: Of course I'm not going to be faithful to you, no one can be faithful to one other person for a whole lifetime. (And there was the word "faithful"—stupid, all these words, stupid, belonging to a savage old world.) But the incident left both of them irritable. Strange, but they were both bad-tempered, annoyed. There was something unassimilable about it.

Making love splendidly after he had come home that night, both had felt that the idea that Myra Jenkins, a pretty girl met at a party, could be even relevant was ridiculous. They had loved each other for over a decade, would love each other for years more. Who, then, was Myra Jenkins?

Except, thought Susan, unaccountably bad-tempered, she was (is?) the first. In ten years. So either the ten years' fidelity was not important, or she isn't. (No, no, there is something wrong with this way of thinking, there must be.) But if she isn't important, presumably it wasn't important either when Matthew and I first went to bed with each other that afternoon whose delight even now (like a very long shadow at sundown) lays a long, wandlike finger over us. (Why did I say sundown?) Well, if what we felt that afternoon was not important, nothing is important, because if it hadn't been for what we felt, we wouldn't be Mr. and Mrs. Rawlings with four children, et cetera, et cetera. The whole thing is *absurd*—for him to have come home and told me was absurd. For him not to have told me was absurd. For me to care or, for that matter, not to care, is absurd . . . and who is Myra Jenkins? Why, no one at all.

There was only one thing to do, and of course these sensible people did it; they put the thing behind them, and consciously, knowing what they were doing, moved forward into a different phase of their marriage, giving thanks for past good fortune as they did so.

For it was inevitable that the handsome, blond, attractive, manly man, Matthew Rawlings, should be at times tempted (oh, what a word!) by the attractive girls at parties she could not attend because of the four children; and that sometimes he would succumb (a word even more repulsive, if possible) and that she, a goodlooking woman in the big well-tended garden at Richmond, would sometimes be pierced as by an arrow from the sky with bitterness. Except that bitterness was not in order, it was out of court. Did the casual girls touch the marriage? They did not. Rather it was they who knew defeat because of the handsome Matthew Rawlings' marriage body and soul to Susan Rawlings.

In that case why did Susan feel (though luckily not for longer than a few seconds at a time) as if life had become a desert, and that nothing mattered, and that her children were not her own?

Meanwhile her intelligence continued to assert that all was well. What if her Matthew did have an occasional sweet afternoon, the odd affair? For she knew quite well, except in her moments of aridity, that they were very happy, that the affairs were not important.

Perhaps that was the trouble? It was in the nature of things that the adventures and delights could no longer be hers, because of the four children and the big house that needed so much attention. But perhaps she was secretly wishing, and even knowing that she did, that the wildness and the beauty could be his. But he was married to her. She was married to him. They were married inextricably. And therefore the gods could not strike him with the real magic, not really. Well, was it Susan's fault that after he came home from an adventure he looked harassed rather than fulfilled? (In fact, that was how she knew he had been *unfaithful*, because of his sullen air, and his glances at her, similar to hers at him: What is it that I share with this person that shields all delight from me?) But none of it by anybody's fault. (But what did they feel ought to be somebody's fault?) Nobody's fault, nothing to be at fault, no one to blame, no one to offer or to take it . . . and nothing wrong, either, except that Matthew never was really struck, as he wanted to be, by joy; and that Susan was more and more often threatened by emptiness. (It was usually in the garden that she was invaded by this feeling: she was coming to avoid the garden, unless the children or Matthew were with her.) There was no need to use the dramatic words "unfaithful," "forgive," and the rest: intelligence forbade them. Intelligence barred, too, quarrelling, sulking, anger, silences of withdrawal, accusations and tears. Above all, intelligence forbids tears.

A high price has to be paid for the happy marriage with the four healthy children in the large white gardened house.

And they were paying it, willingly, knowing what they were doing. When they lay side by side or breast to breast in the big civilised bedroom overlooking the wild sullied river, they laughed, often, for no particular reason; but they knew it was really because of these two small people, Susan and Matthew, supporting such an edifice on their intelligent love. The laugh comforted them; it saved them both, though from what, they did not know.

They were now both fortyish. The older children, boy and girl, were ten and eight, at school. The twins, six, were still at home. Susan did not have nurses or girls to help her: childhood is short; and she did not regret the hard work. Often enough she was bored, since small children can be boring; she was often very tired; but she regretted nothing. In another decade, she would turn herself back into being a woman with a life of her own.

Soon the twins would go to school, and they would be away from home from nine until four. These hours, so Susan saw it, would be the preparation for her own slow emancipation away from the role of hub-of-the-family into woman-with-her-own-life. She was already planning for the hours of freedom when all the children would be "off her hands." That was the phrase used by Matthew and by Susan and by their friends, for the moment when the youngest child went off to school. "They'll be off your hands, darling Susan, and you'll have time to yourself." So said Matthew, the intelligent husband, who had often enough commended and consoled Susan, standing by her in spirit during the years when her soul was not her own, as she said, but her children's.

What it amounted to was that Susan saw herself as she had been at twenty-eight, unmarried, and then again somewhere about fifty, blossoming from the root of what she had been twenty years before. As if the essential Susan were in abeyance, as if she were in cold storage. Matthew said something like this to Susan one night: and she agreed that it was true—she did feel something like that. What, then, was this essential Susan? She did not know. Put like that it sounded ridiculous, and she did not really feel it. Anyway, they had a long discussion about the whole thing before going off to sleep in each other's arms.

So the twins went off to their school, two bright affectionate children who had no problems about it, since their older brother and sister had trodden this path so successfully before them. And now Susan was going to be alone in the big house, every day of the school term, except for the daily woman who came in to clean.

It was now, for the first time in this marriage, that something happened which neither of them had foreseen.

This is what happened. She returned, at nine-thirty, from taking the twins to the school by car, looking forward to seven blissful hours of freedom. On the first morning she was simply restless, worrying about the twins "naturally enough" since this was their first day away at school. She was hardly able to contain herself until they came back. Which they did happily, excited by the world of school, looking forward to the next day. And the next day Susan took them, dropped them, came back, and found herself reluctant to enter her big and beautiful home because it was as if something was waiting for her there that she did not wish to confront. Sensibly, however, she parked the car in the garage, entered the house, spoke to Mrs. Parkes, the daily woman, about her duties, and went up to her bedroom. She was possessed by a fever which drove her out again, downstairs, into the kitchen, where Mrs. Parkes was making cake and did not need her, and into the garden. There she sat on a bench and tried to calm herself looking at trees, at a brown glimpse of the river. But she was filled with tension, like a panic: as if an enemy was in the garden with her. She spoke to herself severely, thus: All this is quite natural. First, I spent twelve years of my adult life working, *living my own life*. Then I married, and from the moment I became pregnant for the first time I signed myself over, so to speak, to other people. To the children. Not for one moment in twelve years have I been alone, had time to myself. So now I have to learn to be myself again. That's all.

And she went indoors to help Mrs. Parkes cook and clean, and found some sewing to do for the children. She kept herself occupied every day. At the end of the first term she understood she felt two contrary emotions. First: secret astonishment and dismay that during those weeks when the house was empty of children she had in fact been more occupied (had been careful to keep herself occupied) than ever she had been when the children were around her needing her continual attention. Second: that now she knew the house would be full of them, and for five weeks, she resented the fact she would never be alone. She was already looking back at those hours of sewing, cooking (but by herself) as at a lost freedom which would not be hers for five long weeks. And the two months of term which would succeed the five weeks stretched alluringly open to her—freedom. But what freedom—when in fact she had been so careful *not* to be free of small duties during the last weeks? She looked at herself, Susan Rawlings, sitting in a big chair by the window in the bedroom, sewing shirts or dresses, which she might just as well have bought. She saw herself making cakes for hours at a time in the big family kitchen: yet usually she bought cakes. What she saw was a woman alone, that was true, but she had not felt alone. For instance, Mrs. Parkes was always somewhere in the house. And she did not like being in the garden at all, because of the closeness there of the enemy—irritation, restlessness, emptiness, whatever it was—which keeping her hands occupied made less dangerous for some reason.

Susan did not tell Matthew of these thoughts. They were not sensible. She did not recognise herself in them. What should she say to her dear friend and husband, Matthew? "When I go into the garden, that is, if the children are not there, I feel as if there is an enemy there waiting to invade me." "What enemy, Susan darling?" "Well I don't know, really. . . ." "Perhaps you should see a doctor?"

No, clearly this conversation should not take place. The holidays began and Susan welcomed them. Four children, lively, energetic, intelligent, demanding: she was never, not for a moment of her day, alone. If she was in a room, they would be in the next room, or waiting for her to do something for them; or it would soon be time for lunch or tea, or to take one of them to the dentist. Something to do: five weeks of it, thank goodness.

On the fourth day of these so welcome holidays, she found she was storming with anger at the twins; two shrinking beautiful children who (and this is what checked her) stood hand in hand looking at her with sheer dismayed disbelief. This was their calm mother, shouting at them. And for what? They had come to her with some game, some bit of nonsense. They looked at each other, moved closer for support, and went off hand in hand, leaving Susan holding on to the windowsill of the livingroom, breathing deep, feeling sick. She went to lie down, telling the older children she had a headache. She heard the boy Harry telling the little ones: "It's all right, Mother's got a headache." She heard that *It's all right* with pain.

That night she said to her husband: "Today I shouted at the twins, quite unfairly." She sounded miserable, and he said gently: "Well, what of it?"

"It's more of an adjustment than I thought, their going to school."

"But Susie, Susie darling. . . ." For she was crouched weeping on the bed. He comforted her: "Susan, what is all this about? You shouted at them? What of it? If you shouted at them fifty times a day it wouldn't be more than the little devils deserve." But she wouldn't laugh. She wept. Soon he comforted her with his body. She became calm. Calm, she wondered what was wrong with her, and why she should mind so much that she might, just once, have behaved unjustly with the children. What did it matter? They had forgotten it all long ago: Mother had a headache and everything was all right.

It was a long time later that Susan understood that that night, when she had wept and Matthew had driven the misery out of her with his big solid body, was the last time, ever in their married life, that they had been—to use their mutual language—with each other. And even that was a lie, because she had not told him of her real fears at all.

The five weeks passed, and Susan was in control of herself, and good and kind, and she looked forward to the holidays with a mixture of fear and longing. She did not know what to expect. She took the twins off to school (the elder children took themselves to school) and she returned to the house determined to face the enemy wherever he was, in the house, or the garden or—where?

She was again restless, she was possessed by restlessness. She cooked and sewed and worked as before, day after day, while Mrs. Parkes remonstrated: "Mrs. Rawlings, what's the need for it? I can do that, it's what you pay me for."

And it was so irrational that she checked herself. She would put the car into the garage, go up to her bedroom, and sit, hands in her lap, forcing herself to be quiet. She listened to Mrs. Parkes moving around the house. She looked out into the garden and saw the branches shake the trees. She sat defeating the enemy, restlessness. Emptiness. She ought to be thinking about her life, about herself. But she did not. Or perhaps she could not. As soon as she forced her mind to think about Susan (for what else did she want to be alone for?), it skipped off to thoughts of butter or school clothes. Or it thought of Mrs. Parkes. She realised that she sat listening for the movements of the cleaning woman, following her every turn, bend, thought. She followed her in her mind from kitchen to bathroom, from table to oven, and it was as if the duster, the cleaning cloth, the saucepan, were in her own hand. She would hear herself saying: No, not like that, don't put that there. . . . Yet she did not give a damn what Mrs. Parkes did, or if she did it at all. Yet she could not prevent herself from being conscious of her, every minute. Yes, this was what was wrong with her: she needed, when she was alone, to be really alone, with no one near. She could not endure the knowledge than in ten minutes or in half an hour Mrs. Parkes would call up the stairs: "Mrs. Rawlings, there's no silver polish. Madam, we're out of flour."

So she left the house and went to sit in the garden where she was screened from the house by trees. She waited for the demon to appear and claim her, but he did not.

She was keeping him off, because she had not, after all, come to an end of arranging herself.

She was planning how to be somewhere where Mrs. Parkes would not come after her with a cup of tea, or a demand to be allowed to telephone (always irritating, since Susan did not care who she telephoned or how often), or just a nice talk about something. Yes, she needed a place, or a state of affairs, where it would not be necessary to keep reminding herself: In ten minutes I must telephone Matthew about . . . and at half past three I must leave early for the children because the car needs cleaning. And at ten o'clock tomorrow I must remember. . . . She was possessed with resentment that the seven hours of freedom in every day (during weekdays in the school term) were not free, that never, not for one second, ever, was she free from the pressure of time, from having to remember this or that. She could never forget herself; never really let herself go into forgetfulness.

Resentment. It was poisoning her. (She looked at this emotion and thought it was absurd. Yet she felt it.) She was a prisoner. (She looked at this thought too, and it was no good telling herself it was a ridiculous one.) She must tell Matthew—but what? She was filled with emotions that were utterly ridiculous, that she despised, yet that nevertheless she was feeling so strongly she could not shake them off.

The school holidays came round, and this time they were for nearly two months, and she behaved with a conscious controlled decency that nearly drove her crazy. She would lock herself in the bathroom, and sit on the edge of the bath, breathing deep, trying to let go into some kind of calm. Or she went up into the spare room, usually empty, where no one would expect her to be. She heard the children calling "Mother, Mother," and kept silent, feeling guilty. Or she went to the very end of the garden, by herself, and looked at the slow-moving brown river; she looked at the

river and closed her eyes and breathed slow and deep,
taking it into her being, into her veins.

Then she returned to the family, wife and mother,
smiling and responsible, feeling as if the pressure of
these people—four lively children and her husband—
were a painful pressure on the surface of her skin, a
hand pressing on her brain. She did not once break
down into irritation during these holidays, but it was
like living out a prison sentence, and when the children went back to school, she sat on a white stone
near the flowing river, and she thought: It is not even
a year since the twins went to school, since *they were
off my hands* (What on earth did I think I meant when
I used that stupid phrase?), and yet I'm a different
person. I'm simply not myself. I don't understand it.

Yet she had to understand it. For she knew that this
structure—big white house, on which the mortgage
still cost four hundred a year, a husband, so good and
kind and insightful; four children, all doing so nicely;
and the garden where she sat; and Mrs. Parkes, the
cleaning woman—all this depended on her, and yet
she could not understand why, or even what it was she
contributed to it.

She said to Matthew in their bedroom: "I think
there must be something wrong with me."

And he said: "Surely not, Susan? You look marvellous
—you're as lovely as ever."

She looked at the handsome blond man, with his
clear, intelligent, blue-eyed face, and thought: Why is
it I can't tell him? Why not? And she said: "I need to
be alone more than I am."

At which he swung his slow blue gaze at her, and
she saw what she had been dreading: Incredulity. Disbelief. And fear. An incredulous blue stare from a
stranger who was her husband, as close to her as her
own breath.

He said: "But the children are at school and off
your hands."

She said to herself: I've got to force myself to say:

Yes, but do you realize that I never feel free? There's never a moment I can say to myself: There's nothing I have to remind myself about, nothing I have to do in half an hour, or an hour, or two hours. . . .

But she said: "I don't feel well."

He said: "Perhaps you need a holiday."

She said, appalled: "But not without you, surely?" For she could not imagine herself going off without him. Yet that was what he meant. Seeing her face, he laughed, and opened his arms, and she went into them, thinking: Yes, yes, but why can't I say it? And what is it I have to say?

She tried to tell him, about never being free. And he listened and said: "But Susan, what sort of freedom can you possibly want—short of being dead! Am I ever free? I go to the office, and I have to be there at ten—all right, half past ten, sometimes. And I have to do this or that, don't I? Then I've got to come home at a certain time—I don't mean it, you know I don't—but if I'm not going to be back home at six I telephone you. When can I ever say to myself: I have nothing to be responsible for in the next six hours?"

Susan, hearing this, was remorseful. Because it was true. The good marriage, the house, the children, depended just as much on his voluntary bondage as it did on hers. But why did he not feel bound? Why didn't he chafe and become restless? No, there was something really wrong with her and this proved it.

And that word "bondage"—why had she used it? She had never felt marriage, or the children, as bondage. Neither had he, or surely they wouldn't be together lying each other's arms content after twelve years of marriage.

No, her state (whatever it was) was irrelevant, nothing to do with her real good life with her family. She had to accept the fact that, after all, she was an irrational person and to live with it. Some people had to live with crippled arms, or stammers, or being deaf.

She would have to live knowing she was subject to a state of mind she could not own.

Nevertheless, as a result of this conversation with her husband, there was a new regime next holidays.

The spare room at the top of the house now had a cardboard sign saying: PRIVATE! DO NOT DISTURB! on it. (This sign had been drawn in coloured chalks by the children, after a discussion between the parents in which it was decided this was psychologically the right thing.) The family and Mrs. Parkes knew this was "Mother's Room" and that she was entitled to her privacy. Many serious conversations took place between Matthew and the children about not taking Mother for granted. Susan overheard the first, between father and Harry, the older boy, and was surprised at her irritation over it. Surely she could have a room somewhere in that big house and retire into it without such a fuss being made? Without it being so solemnly discussed? Why couldn't she simply have announced: "I'm going to fit out the little top room for myself, and when I'm in it I'm not to be disturbed for anything short of fire"? Just that, and finished; instead of long earnest discussions. When she heard Harry and Matthew explaining it to the twins with Mrs. Parkes coming in— "Yes, well, a family sometimes gets on top of a woman"—she had to go right away to the bottom of the garden until the devils of exasperation had finished their dance in her blood.

But now there was a room, and she could go there when she liked, she used it seldom: she felt even more caged there than in her bedroom. One day she had gone up there after a lunch for ten children she had cooked and served because Mrs. Parkes was not there, and had sat alone for a while looking into the garden. She saw the children stream out from the kitchen and stand looking up at the window where she sat behind the curtains. There were all—her children and their friends—discussing Mother's Room. A few minutes later, the chase of children in some game came pounding up the stairs, but ended as abruptly as if they had fallen over a ravine, so sudden was the silence. They had remembered she was there, and had gone silent in a great gale of "Hush! Shhhhh! Quiet, you'll disturb her. . . ." And they went tiptoeing downstairs like criminal conspirators. When she came down to make tea for them, they all apologised. The twins put their arms around her, from front and back, making a human cage of loving limbs, and promised it would never occur again. "We forgot, Mummy, we forgot all about it!"

What it amounted to was that Mother's Room, and her need for privacy, had become a valuable lesson in respect for other people's rights. Quite soon Susan was going up to the room only because it was a lesson it was a pity to drop. Then she took sewing up there, and the children and Mrs. Parkes came in and out: it had become another family room.

She sighed, and smiled, and resigned herself—she made jokes at her own expense with Matthew over the room. That is, she did from the self she liked, she respected. But at the same time, something inside her howled with impatience, with rage. . . . And she was frightened. One day she found herself kneeling by her bed and praying: "Dear God, keep it away from me, keep him away from me." She meant the devil, for she now thought of it, not caring if she was irrational, as some sort of demon. She imagined him, or it, as a youngish man, or perhaps a middleaged man pretending to be young. Or a man young-looking from immaturity? At any rate, she saw the young-looking face which, when she drew closer, had dry lines about mouth and eyes. He was thinnish, meagre in build. And he had a reddish complexion, and ginger hair. That was he—a gingery, energetic man, and he wore a reddish hairy jacket, unpleasant to the touch.

Well, one day she saw him. She was standing at the bottom of the garden, watching the river ebb past, when she raised her eyes and saw this person, or

being, sitting on the white stone bench. He was looking at her, and grinning. In his hand was a long crooked
stick, which he had picked off the ground, or broken
off the tree above him. He was absent-mindedly, out
of an absent-minded or freakish impulse of spite, using
the stick to stir around in the coils of a blindworm or a
grass snake (or some kind of snakelike creature: it was
whitish and unhealthy to look at, unpleasant). The
snake was twisting about, flinging its coils from side to
side in a kind of dance of protest against the teasing
prodding stick.

Susan looked at him, thinking: Who is the stranger?
What is he doing in our garden? Then she recognised
the man around whom her terrors had crystallised.
As she did so, he vanished. She made herself walk
over to the bench. A shadow from a branch lay across
thin emerald grass, moving jerkily over its roughness,
and she could see why she had taken it for a snake,
lashing and twisting. She went back to the house thinking: Right, then, so I've seen him with my own eyes,
so I'm not crazy after all—there *is* a danger because
I've seen him. He is lurking in the garden and sometimes even in the house, and he wants to *get into me
and to take me over*.

She dreamed of having a room or a place, anywhere, where she could go and sit, by herself, no one
knowing where she was.

Once, near Victoria, she found herself outside a
news agent that had Rooms to Let advertised. She
decided to rent a room, telling no one. Sometimes she
could take the train in to Richmond and sit alone in it
for an hour or two. Yet how could she? A room would
cost three or four pounds a week, and she earned no
money, and how could she explain to Matthew that
she needed such a sum? What for? It did not occur to
her that she was taking it for granted she wasn't going
to tell him about the room.

Well, it was out of the question, having a room; yet
she knew she must.

One day, when a school term was well established, and none of the children had measles or other ailments, and everything seemed in order, she did the shopping early, explained to Mrs. Parkes she was meeting an old school friend, took the train to Victoria, searched until she found a small quiet hotel, and asked for a room for the day. They did not let rooms by the day, the manageress said, looking doubtful, since Susan so obviously was not the kind of woman who needed a room for unrespectable reasons. Susan made a long explanation about not being well, being unable to shop without frequent rests for lying down. At last she was allowed to rent the room provided she paid a full night's price for it. She was taken up by the manageress and a maid, both concerned over the state of her health . . . which must be pretty bad if, living at Richmond (she had signed her name and address in the register), she needed a shelter at Victoria.

The room was ordinary and anonymous, and was just what Susan needed. She put a shilling in the gas fire, and sat, eyes shut, in a dingy armchair with her back to a dingy window. She was alone. She was alone. She was alone. She could feel pressures lifting off her. First the sounds of traffic came very loud; then they seemed to vanish; she might even have slept a little. A knock on the door: it was Miss Townsend, the manageress, bringing her a cup of tea with her own hands, so concerned was she over Susan's long silence and possible illness.

Miss Townsend was a lonely woman of fifty, running this hotel with all the rectitude expected of her, and she sensed in Susan the possibility of understanding companionship. She stayed to talk. Susan found herself in the middle of a fantastic story about her illness, which got more and more impossible as she tried to make it tally with the large house at Richmond, well-off husband, and four children. Suppose she said instead: Miss Townsend, I'm here in your hotel because I need to be alone for a few hours, above all *alone and with no one knowing where I am*. She said it mentally, and saw, mentally, the look that would inevitably come on Miss Townsend's elderly maiden's face. "Miss Townsend, my four children and my husband are driving me insane, do you understand that? Yes, I can see from the gleam of hysteria in your eyes that comes from loneliness controlled but only just contained that I've got everything in the world you've ever longed for. Well, Miss Townsend, I don't want any of it. You can have it, Miss Townsend. I wish I was absolutely alone in the world, like you. Miss Townsend, I'm besieged by seven devils, Miss Townsend. Miss Townsend, let me stay here in your hotel where the devils can't get me. . . ." Instead of saying all this, she described her anaemia, agreed to try Miss Townsend's remedy for it, which was raw liver, minced, between whole-meal bread, and said yes, perhaps it would be better if she stayed at home and let a friend do shopping for her. She paid her bill and left the hotel, defeated.

At home Mrs. Parkes said she didn't really like it, no, not really, when Mrs. Rawlings was away from nine in the morning until five. The teacher had telephoned from school to say Joan's teeth were paining her, and she hadn't known what to say; and what was she to make for the children's tea, Mrs. Rawlings hadn't said.

All this was nonsense, of course. Mrs. Parkes's complaint was that Susan had withdrawn herself spiritually, leaving the burden of the big house on her.

Susan looked back at her day of "freedom" which had resulted in her becoming a friend of the lonely Miss Townsend, and in Mrs. Parkes's remonstrances. Yet she remembered the short blissful hour of being alone, really alone. She was determined to arrange her life, no matter what it cost, so that she could have that solitude more often. An absolute solitude, where no one knew her or cared about her.

But how? She thought of saying to her old em-

ployer: I want you to back me up in a story with
Matthew that I am doing part-time work for you. The
truth is that . . . But she would have to tell him a lie
too, and which lie? She could not say: I want to sit by
myself three or four times a week in a rented room.
And besides, he knew Matthew, and she could not
really ask him to tell lies on her behalf, apart from
being bound to think it meant a lover.

Suppose she really took a part-time job, which she
could get through fast and efficiently, leaving time for
herself. What job? Addressing envelopes? Canvassing?

And there was Mrs. Parkes, working widow, who
knew exactly what she was prepared to give to the
house, who knew by instinct when her mistress with-
drew in spirit from her responsibilities. Mrs. Parkes
was one of the servers of this world, but she needed
someone to serve. She had to have Mrs. Rawlings, her
madam, at the top of the house or in the garden, so
that she could come and get support from her: "Yes,
the bread's not what it was when I was a girl. . . . Yes,
Harry's got a wonderful appetite, I wonder where he
puts it all. . . . Yes, it's lucky the twins are so much of
a size, they can wear each other's shoes, that's a
saving in these hard times. . . . Yes, the cherry jam
from Switzerland is not a patch on the jam from Po-
land, and three times the price . . ." And so on. That
sort of talk Mrs. Parkes must have, every day, or she
would leave, not knowing herself why she left.

Susan Rawlings, thinking these thoughts, found that
she was prowling through the great thicketed garden
like a wild cat: she was walking up the stairs, down the
stairs, through the rooms into the garden, along the
brown running river, back, up through the house,
down again. . . . It was a wonder Mrs. Parkes did not
think it strange. But, on the contrary, Mrs. Rawlings
could do what she liked, she could stand on her head
if she wanted, provided she was *there*. Susan Rawlings
prowled and muttered through her house, hating Mrs.
Parkes, hating poor Miss Townsend, dreaming of her

hour of solitude in the dingy respectability of Miss Townsend's hotel bedroom, and she knew quite well she was mad. Yes, she was mad.

She said to Matthew that she must have a holiday. Matthew agreed with her. This was not as things had been once—how they had talked in each other's arms in the marriage bed. He had, she knew, diagnosed her finally as *unreasonable*. She had become someone outside himself that he had to manage. They were living side by side in this house like two tolerably friendly strangers.

Having told Mrs. Parkes—or rather, asked for her permission—she went off on a walking holiday in Wales. She chose the remotest place she knew of. Every morning the children telephoned her before they went off to school, to encourage and support her, just as they had over Mother's Room. Every evening she telephoned them, spoke to each child in turn, and then to Matthew. Mrs. Parkes, given permission to telephone for instructions or advice, did so every day at lunchtime. When, as happened three times, Mrs. Rawlings was out on the mountainside, Mrs. Parkes asked that she should ring back at such-and-such a time, for she would not be happy in what she was doing without Mrs. Rawlings' blessing.

Susan prowled over wild country with the telephone wire holding her to her duty like a leash. The next time she must telephone, or wait to be telephoned, nailed her to her cross. The mountains themselves seemed trammelled by her unfreedom. Everywhere on the mountains, where she met no one at all, from breakfast time to dusk, excepting sheep, or a shepherd, she came face to face with her own craziness, which might attack her in the broadest valleys, so that they seemed too small, or on a mountain top from which she could see a hundred other mountains and valleys, so that they seemed too low, too small, with the sky pressing down too close. She would stand gazing at a hillside brilliant with ferns and bracken, jewelled with running water, and see nothing but her devil, who lifted inhuman eyes at her from where he leaned negligently on a rock, switching at his ugly yellow boots with a leafy twig.

She returned to her home and family, with the Welsh emptiness at the back of her mind like a promise of freedom.

She told her husband she wanted to have an *au pair* girl.

They were in their bedroom, it was late at night, the children slept. He sat, shirted and slippered, in a chair by the window, looking out. She sat brushing her hair and watching him in the mirror. A time-hallowed scene in the connubial bedroom. He said nothing, while she heard the arguments coming into his mind, only to be rejected because every one was *reasonable*.

"It seems strange to get one now; after all, the children are in school most of the day. Surely the time for you to have help was when you were stuck with them day and night. Why don't you ask Mrs. Parkes to cook for you? She's even offered to—I can understand if you are tired of cooking for six people. But you know that an *au pair* girl means all kinds of problems; it's not like having an ordinary char in during the day. . . ."

Finally he said carefully: "Are you thinking of going back to work?"

"No," she said, "no, not really." She made herself sound vague, rather stupid. She went on brushing her black hair and peering at herself so as to be oblivious of the short uneasy glances her Matthew kept giving her. "Do you think we can't afford it?" she went on vaguely, not at all the old efficient Susan who knew exactly what they could afford.

"It's not that," he said, looking out of the window at dark trees, so as not to look at her. Meanwhile she examined a round, candid, pleasant face with clear dark brows and clear grey eyes. A sensible face. She brushed thick healthy black hair and thought: Yet that's the reflection of a madwoman. How very strange! Much more to the point if what looked back at me was the gingery green-eyed demon with his dry meagre smile. . . . Why wasn't Matthew agreeing? After all, what else could he do? She was breaking her part of the bargain and there was no way of forcing her to keep it: that her spirit, her soul, should live in this house, so that the people in it could grow like plants in water, and Mrs. Parkes remain content in their service. In return for this, he would be a good loving husband, and responsible towards the children. Well, nothing like this had been true of either of them for a long time. He did his duty, perfunctorily; she did not even pretend to do hers. And he had become like other husbands, with his real life in his work and the people he met there, and very likely a serious affair. All this was her fault.

At last he drew heavy curtains, blotting out the trees, and turned to force her attention: "Susan, are you really sure we need a girl?" But she would not meet his appeal at all. She was running the brush over her hair again and again, lifting fine black clouds in a small hiss of electricity. She was peering in and smiling as if she were amused at the clinging hissing hair that followed the brush.

"Yes, I think it would be a good idea, on the whole," she said, with the cunning of a madwoman evading the real point.

In the mirror she could see her Matthew lying on his back, his hands behind his head, staring upwards, his face sad and hard. She felt her heart (the old heart of Susan Rawlings) soften and call out to him. But she set it to be indifferent.

He said: "Susan, the children?" It was an appeal that *almost* reached her. He opened his arms, lifting them palms up, empty. She had only to run across and fling herself into them, onto his hard, warm chest, and melt into herself, into Susan. But she could not. She would not see his lifted arms. She said vaguely: "Well, surely it'll be even better for them? We'll get a French or a German girl and they'll learn the language."

In the dark she lay beside him, feeling frozen, a stranger. She felt as if Susan had been spirited away. She disliked very much this woman who lay here, cold and indifferent beside a suffering man, but she could not change her.

Next morning she set about getting a girl, and very soon came Sophie Traub from Hamburg, a girl of twenty, laughing, healthy, blue-eyed, intending to learn English. Indeed, she already spoke a good deal. In return for a room—"Mother's Room"—and her food, she undertook to do some light cooking, and to be with the children when Mrs. Rawlings asked. She was an intelligent girl and understood perfectly what was needed. Susan said: "I go off sometimes, for the morning or for the day—well, sometimes the children run home from school, or they ring up, or a teacher rings up. I should be here, really. And there's the daily woman. . . ." And Sophie laughed her deep fruity *Fräulein's* laugh, showed her fine white teeth and her dimples, and said: "You want some person to play mistress of the house sometimes, not so?"

"Yes, that is just so," said Susan, a bit dry, despite herself, thinking in secret fear how easy it was, how much nearer to the end she was than she thought. Healthy Fräulein Traub's instant understanding of their position proved this to be true.

The *au pair* girl, because of her own commonsense, or (as Susan said to herself, with her new inward shudder) because she had been *chosen* so well by Susan, was a success with everyone, the children liking her, Mrs. Parkes forgetting almost at once that she was German, and Matthew finding her "nice to have around the house." For he was now taking things as they came, from the surface of life, withdrawn both as a husband and a father from the household.

One day Susan saw how Sophie and Mrs. Parkes were talking and laughing in the kitchen, and she

announced that she would be away until tea time. She
knew exactly where to go and what she must look for.
She took the District Line to South Kensington, changed
to the Circle, got off at Paddington, and walked around
looking at the smaller hotels until she was satisfied
with one which had FRED'S HOTEL painted on window-
panes that needed cleaning. The facade was a faded
shiny yellow, like unhealthy skin. A door at the end of
a passage said she must knock; she did, and Fred
appeared. He was not at all attractive, not in any way,
being fattish, and run-down, and wearing a tasteless
striped suit. He had small sharp eyes in a white creased
face, and was quite prepared to let Mrs. Jones (she
chose the farcical name deliberately, staring him out)
have a room three days a week from ten until six.
Provided of course that she paid in advance each time
she came? Susan produced fifteen shillings (no price
had been set by him) and held it out, still fixing him
with a bold unblinking challenge she had not known
until then she could use at will. Looking at her still, he
took up a ten-shilling note from her palm between
thumb and forefinger, fingered it; then shuffled up
two half-crowns, held out his own palm with these bits
of money displayed thereon, and let his gaze lower
broodingly at them. They were standing in the passage, a red-shaded light above, bare boards beneath,
and a strong smell of floor polish rising above them.
He shot his gaze up at her over the still-extended
palm, and smiled as if to say: What do you take me
for? "I shan't," said Susan, "be using this room for
the purposes of making money." He still waited. She
added another five shillings, at which he nodded and
said: "You pay, and I ask no questions." "Good," said
Susan. He now went past her to the stairs, and there
waited a moment: the light from the street door being
in her eyes, she lost sight of him momentarily. Then
she saw a sober-suited, white-faced, white-balding little man trotting up the stairs like a waiter, and she
went after him. They proceeded in utter silence up the

stairs of this house where no questions were asked—
Fred's Hotel, which could afford the freedom for its
visitors that poor Miss Townsend's hotel could not.
The room was hideous. It had a single window, with
thin green brocade curtains, a three-quarter bed that
had a cheap green satin bedspread on it, a fireplace
with a gas fire and a shilling meter by it, a chest of
drawers, and a green wicker armchair.

"Thank you," said Susan, knowing that Fred (if this
was Fred, and not George, or Herbert or Charlie) was
looking at her, not so much with curiosity, an emotion
he would not own to, for professional reasons, but
with a philosophical sense of what was appropriate.
Having taken her money and shown her up and agreed
to everything, he was clearly disapproving of her for
coming here. She did not belong here at all, so his
look said. (But she knew, already, how very much she
did belong: the room had been waiting for her to join
it.) "Would you have me called at five o'clock, please?"
and he nodded and went downstairs.

It was twelve in the morning. She was free. She sat
in the armchair, she simply sat, she closed her eyes
and sat and let herself be alone. She was alone and no
one knew where she was. When a knock came on the
door she was annoyed, and prepared to show it: but it
was Fred himself; it was five o'clock and he was calling
her as ordered. He flicked his sharp little eyes over the
room—bed, first. It was undisturbed. She might never
have been in the room at all. She thanked him, said
she would be returning the day after tomorrow, and
left. She was back home in time to cook supper, to
put the children to bed, to cook a second supper for
her husband and herself later. And to welcome Sophie
back from the pictures where she had gone with a
friend. All these things she did cheerfully, willingly.
But she was thinking all the time of the hotel room;
she was longing for it with her whole being.

Three times a week. She arrived promptly at ten,
looked Fred in the eyes, gave him twenty shillings,

followed him up the stairs, went into the room, and shut the door on him with gentle firmness. For Fred, disapproving of her being here at all, was quite ready to let friendship, or at least acquaintanceship, follow his disapproval, if only she would let him. But he was content to go off on her dismissing nod, with the twenty shillings in his hand.

She sat in the armchair and shut her eyes.

What did she *do* in the room? Why, nothing at all. From the chair, when it had rested her, she went to the window, stretching her arms, smiling, treasuring her anonymity, to look out. She was no longer Susan Rawlings, mother of four, wife of Matthew, employer of Mrs. Parkes and of Sophie Traub, with these and those relations with friends, school-teachers, tradesmen. She no longer was mistress of the big white house and garden, owning clothes suitable for this and that activity or occasion. She was Mrs. Jones, and she was alone, and she had no past and no future. Here I am, she thought, after all these years of being married and having children and playing those roles of responsibility—and I'm just the same. Yet there have been times I thought that nothing existed of me except the roles that went with being Mrs. Matthew Rawlings. Yes, here I am, and if I never saw any of my family again, here I would still be . . . how very strange that is! And she leaned on the sill, and looked into the street, loving the men and women who passed, because she did not know them. She looked at the downtrodden buildings over the street, and at the sky, wet and dingy, or sometimes blue, and she felt she had never seen buildings or sky before. And then she went back to the chair, empty, her mind a blank. Sometimes she talked aloud, saying nothing—an exclamation, meaningless, followed by a comment about the floral pattern on the thin rug, or a stain on the green satin coverlet. For the most part, she wool-gathered—what word is there for it?—brooded, wandered, simply went dark, feeling emptiness run deliciously through her veins like the movement of her blood.

This room had become more her own than the house she lived in. One morning she found Fred taking her a flight higher than usual. She stopped, refusing to go up, and demanded her usual room, Number 19. "Well, you'll have to wait half an hour, then," he said. Willingly she descended to the dark disinfectant-smelling hall, and sat waiting until the two, man and woman, came down the stairs, giving her swift indifferent glances before they hurried out into the street, separating at the door. She went up to the room, *her* room, which they had just vacated. It was no less hers, though the windows were set wide open, and a maid was straightening the bed as she came in.

After these days of solitude, it was both easy to play her part as mother and wife, and difficult—because it was so easy: she felt an imposter. She felt as if her shell moved here, with her family, answering to Mummy, Mother, Susan, Mrs. Rawlings. She was surprised no one saw through her, that she wasn't turned out of doors, as a fake. On the contrary, it seemed the children loved her more; Matthew and she "got on" pleasantly, and Mrs. Parkes was happy in her work under (for the most part, it must be confessed) Sophie Traub. At night she lay beside her husband, and they made love again, apparently just as they used to, when they were really married. But she, Susan, or the being who answered so readily and improbably to the name of Susan, was not there: she was in Fred's Hotel, in Paddington, waiting for the easing hours of solitude to begin.

Soon she made a new arrangement with Fred and with Sophie. It was for five days a week. As for the money, five pounds, she simply asked Matthew for it. She saw that she was not even frightened he might ask what for: he would give it to her, she knew that, and yet it was terrifying it could be so, for this close couple, these partners, had once known the destination of every shilling they must spend. He agreed to give her five pounds a week. She asked for just so much, not a penny more. He sounded indifferent about it. It was as if he were paying her, she thought: *paying her off*—yes, that was it. Terror came back for a moment when she understood this, but she stilled it: things had gone too far for that. Now, every week, on Sunday nights, he gave her five pounds, turning away from her before their eyes could meet on the transaction. As for Sophie Traub, she was to be somewhere in or near the house until six at night, after which she was free. She was not to cook, or to clean; she was simply to be there. So she gardened or sewed, and asked friends in, being a person who was bound to have a lot of friends. If the children were sick, she nursed them. If teachers telephoned, she answered them sensibly. For the five daytimes in the school week, she was altogether the mistress of the house.

One night in the bedroom, Matthew asked: "Susan, I don't want to interfere—don't think that, please— but are you sure you are well?"

She was brushing her hair at the mirror. She made two more strokes on either side of her head, before she replied: "Yes, dear, I am sure I am well."

He was again lying on his back, his blond head on his hands, his elbows angled up and part-concealing his face. He said: "Then Susan, I have to ask you this question, though you must understand, I'm not putting any sort of pressure on you." (Susan heard the word "pressure" with dismay, because this was inevitable; of course she could not go on like this.) "Are things going to go on like this?"

"Well," she said, going vague and bright and idiotic again, so as to escape: "Well, I don't see why not."

He was jerking his elbows up and down, in annoyance or in pain, and, looking at him, she saw he had got thin, even gaunt; and restless angry movements were not what she remembered of him. He said: "Do you want a divorce, is that it?"

At this, Susan only with the greatest difficulty stopped herself from laughing: she could hear the bright bubbling laughter she *would* have emitted, had she let herself. He could only mean one thing: she had a lover, and that was why she spent her days in London, as lost to him as if she had vanished to another continent.

Then the small panic set in again: she understood that he hoped she did have a lover, he was begging her to say so, because otherwise it would be too terrifying.

She thought this out as she brushed her hair, watching the fine black stuff fly up to make its little clouds of electricity, hiss, hiss, hiss. Behind her head, across the room, was a blue wall. She realised she was absorbed in watching the black hair making shapes against the blue. She should be answering him. "Do *you* want a divorce, Matthew?"

He said: "That surely isn't the point, is it?"

"You brought it up, I didn't," she said, brightly, suppressing meaningless tinkling laughter.

Next day she asked Fred: "Have enquiries been made for me?"

He hesitated, and she said: "I've been coming here a year now. I've made no trouble, and you've been paid every day. I have a right to be told."

"As a matter of fact, Mrs. Jones, a man did come asking."

"A man from a detective agency?"

"Well, he could have been, couldn't he?"

"I was asking you. . . . Well, what did you tell him?"

"I told him a Mrs. Jones came every weekday from ten until five or six and stayed in Number 19 by herself."

"Describing me?"

"Well, Mrs. Jones, I had no alternative. Put yourself in my place."

"By rights I should deduct what that man gave you for the information."

He raised shocked eyes: she was not the sort of

person to make jokes like this! Then he chose to
laugh: a pinkish wet slit appeared across his white
crinkled face; his eyes positively begged her to laugh,
otherwise he might lose some money. She remained
grave, looking at him.

He stopped laughing and said: "You want to go up
now?"—returning to the familiarity, the comradeship,
of the country where no questions are asked, on which
(and he knew it) she depended completely.

She went up to sit in her wicker chair. But it was not
the same. Her husband had searched her out. (The
world had searched her out.) The pressures were on
her. She was here with his connivance. He might walk
in at any moment, here, into Room 19. She imagined
the report from the detective agency: "A woman calling herself Mrs. Jones, fitting the description of your
wife (et cetera, et cetera, et cetera), stays alone all day
in Room No. 19. She insists on this room, waits for it
if it is engaged. As far as the proprietor knows, she
receives no visitors there, male or female." A report
something on these lines Matthew must have received.

Well, of course he was right: things couldn't go on
like this. He had put an end to it all simply by sending
the detective after her.

She tried to shrink herself back into the shelter of
the room, a snail pecked out of its shell and trying to
squirm back. But the peace of the room had gone. She
was trying consciously to revive it, trying to let go into
the dark creative trance (or whatever it was) that she
had found there. It was no use, yet she craved for it,
she was as ill as a suddenly deprived addict.

Several times she returned to the room, to look for
herself there, but instead she found the unnamed spirit
of restlessness, a pricking fevered hunger for movement, an irritable self-consciousness that made her
brain feel as if it had coloured lights going on and off
inside it. Instead of the soft dark that had been the
room's air, were now waiting for her demons that made
her dash blindly about, muttering words of hate; she

was impelling herself from point to point like a moth dashing itself against a windowpane, sliding to the bottom, fluttering off on broken wings, then crashing into the invisible barrier again. And again and again. Soon she was exhausted, and she told Fred that for a while she would not be needing the room, she was going on holiday. Home she went, to the big white house by the river. The middle of a weekday, and she felt guilty at returning to her own home when not expected. She stood unseen, looking in at the kitchen window. Mrs. Parkes, wearing a discarded floral over-all of Susan's, was stooping to slide something into the oven. Sophie, arms folded, was leaning her back against a cupboard and laughing at some joke made by a girl not seen before by Susan—a dark foreign girl, So-phie's visitor. In an armchair Molly, one of the twins, lay curled, sucking her thumb and watching the grown-ups. She must have some sickness, to be kept from school. The child's listless face, the dark circles under her eyes, hurt Susan: Molly was looking at the three grownups working and talking in exactly the same way Susan looked at the four through the kitchen window: she was remote, shut off from them.

But then, just as Susan imagined herself going in, picking up the little girl, and sitting in an armchair with her, stroking her probably heated forehead, So-phie did just that: she had been standing on one leg, the other knee flexed, its foot set against the wall. Now she let her foot in its ribbon-tied red shoe slide down the wall, stood solid on two feet, clapping her hands before and behind her, and sang a couple of lines in German, so that the child lifted her heavy eyes at her and began to smile. Then she walked, or rather skipped, over to the child, swung her up, and let her fall into her lap at the same moment she sat herself. She said "Hopla! Hopla! Molly . . ." and began strok-ing the dark untidy young head that Molly laid on her shoulder for comfort.

Well. . . . Susan blinked the tears of farewell out of

her eyes, and went quietly up through the house to her
bedroom. There she sat looking at the river through
the trees. She felt at peace, but in a way that was new
to her. She had no desire to move, to talk, to do
anything at all. The devils that had haunted the house,
the garden, were not there; but she knew it was because her soul was in Room 19 in Fred's Hotel; she
was not really here at all. It was a sensation that
should have been frightening: to sit at her own bedroom window, listening to Sophie's rich young voice
sing German nursery songs to her child, listening to
Mrs. Parkes clatter and move below, and to know that
all this had nothing to do with her: she was already out
of it.

Later, she made herself go down and say she was
home: it was unfair to be here unannounced. She took
lunch with Mrs. Parkes, Sophie, Sophie's Italian friend
Maria, and her daughter Molly, and felt like a visitor.

A few days later, at bedtime, Matthew said: "Here's
your five pounds," and pushed them over at her. Yet
he must have known she had not been leaving the
house at all.

She shook her head, gave it back to him, and said,
in explanation, not in accusation: "As soon as you
knew where I was, there was no point."

He nodded, not looking at her. He was turned away
from her: thinking, she knew, how best to handle this
wife who terrified him.

He said: "I wasn't trying to . . . It's just that I was
worried."

"Yes, I know."

"I must confess that I was beginning to wonder . . ."

"You thought I had a lover?"

"Yes, I am afraid I did."

She knew that he wished she had. She sat wondering how to say: "For a year now I've been spending all
my days in a very sordid hotel room. It's the place
where I'm happy. In fact, without it I don't exist." She
heard herself saying this, and understood how terrified

he was that she might. So instead she said: "Well, perhaps you're not far wrong."

Probably Matthew would think the hotel proprietor lied: he would want to think so.

"Well," he said, and she could hear his voice spring up, so to speak, with relief, "in that case I must confess I've got a bit of an affair on myself."

She said, detached and interested: "Really? Who is she?" and saw Matthew's startled look because of this reaction.

"It's Phil. Phil Hunt."

She had known Phil Hunt well in the old unmarried days. She was thinking: No, she won't do, she's too neurotic and difficult. She's never been happy yet. Sophie's much better. Well, Matthew will see that himself, as sensible as he is.

This line of thought went on in silence, while she said aloud: "It's no point telling you about mine, because you don't know him."

Quick, quick, invent, she thought. Remember how you invented all that nonsense for Miss Townsend.

She began slowly, careful not to contradict herself: "His name is Michael" *(Michael What?)*—"Michael Plant." (What a silly name!) "He's rather like you—in looks, I mean." And indeed, she could imagine herself being touched by no one but Matthew himself. "He's a publisher." (Really? Why?) "He's got a wife already and two children."

She brought out this fantasy, proud of herself.

Matthew said: "Are you two thinking of marrying?"

She said, before she could stop herself: "Good God, *no!*"

She realised, if Matthew wanted to marry Phil Hunt, that this was too emphatic, but apparently it was all right, for his voice sounded relieved as he said: "It is a bit impossible to imagine oneself married to anyone else, isn't it?" With which he pulled her to him, so that her head lay on his shoulder. She turned her face into the dark of his flesh, and listened to the blood pounding through her ears saying: I am alone, I am alone, I am alone.

In the morning Susan lay in bed while he dressed.

He had been thinking things out in the night, because now he said: "Susan, why don't we make a foursome?"

Of course, she said to herself, of course he would be bound to say that. If one is sensible, if one is reasonable, if one never allows oneself a base thought or an envious emotion, naturally one says: Let's make a foursome!

"Why not?" she said.

"We could all meet for lunch. I mean, it's ridiculous, you sneaking off to filthy hotels, and me staying late at the office, and all the lies everyone has to tell."

What on earth did I say his name was?—she panicked, then said: "I think it's a good idea, but Michael is away at the moment. When he comes back, though— and I'm sure you two would like each other."

"He's away, is he? So that's why you've been . . ." Her husband put his hand to the knot of his tie in a gesture of male coquetry she would not before have associated with him; and he bent to kiss her cheek with the expression that goes with the words: Oh you naughty little puss! And she felt its answering look, naughty and coy, come onto her face.

Inside she was dissolving in horror at them both, at how far they had both sunk from honesty of emotion.

So now she was saddled with a lover, and he had a mistress! How ordinary, how reassuring, how jolly! And now they would make a foursome of it, and go about to theatres and restaurants. After all, the Rawlings could well afford that sort of thing, and presumably the publisher Michael Plant could afford to do himself and his mistress quite well. No, there was nothing to stop the four of them developing the most intricate relationship of civilised tolerance, all enveloped in a charming afterglow of autumnal passion. Perhaps they would all go off on holidays together?

She had known people who did. Or perhaps Matthew would draw the line there? Why should he, though, if he was capable of talking about "foursomes" at all?

She lay in the empty bedroom, listening to the car drive off with Matthew in it, off to work. Then she heard the children clattering off to school to the accompaniment of Sophie's cheerfully ringing voice. She slid down into the hollow of the bed, for shelter against her own irrelevance. And she stretched out her hand to the hollow where her husband's body had lain, but found no comfort there: he was not her husband. She curled herself up in a small tight ball under the clothes: she could stay here all day, all week, indeed, all her life.

But in a few days she must produce Michael Plant, and—but how? She must presumably find some agreeable man prepared to impersonate a publisher called Michael Plant. And in return for which she would— what? Well, for one thing they would make love. The idea made her want to cry with sheer exhaustion. Oh no, she had finished with all that—the proof of it was that the words "make love," or even imagining it, trying hard to revive no more than the pleasures of sensuality, let alone affection, or love, made her want to run away and hide from the sheer effort of the thing. . . . Good Lord, why make love at all? Why make love with anyone? Or if you are going to make love, what does it matter who with? Why shouldn't she simply walk into the street, pick up a man and have a roaring sexual affair with him? Why not? Or even with Fred? What difference did it make?

But she had let herself in for it—an interminable stretch of time with a lover, called Michael, as part of a gallant civilised foursome. Well, she could not, and she would not.

She got up, dressed, went down to find Mrs. Parkes, and asked her for the loan of a pound, since Matthew, she said, had forgotten to leave her money. She exchanged with Mrs. Parkes variations on the theme that husbands are all the same, they don't think, and without saying a word to Sophie, whose voice could be heard upstairs from the telephone, walked to the underground, travelled to South Kensington, changed to the Inner Circle, got out at Paddington, and walked to Fred's Hotel. There she told Fred that she wasn't going on holiday after all, she needed the room. She would have to wait an hour, Fred said. She went to a busy tearoom-cum-restaurant around the corner, and sat watching the people flow in and out the door that kept swinging open and shut, watched them mingle and merge, and separate, felt her being flow into them, into their movement. When the hour was up, she left a half-crown for her pot of tea, and left the place without looking back at it, just as she had left her house, the big, beautiful white house, without another look, but silently dedicating it to Sophie. She returned to Fred, received the key of Number 19, now free, and ascended the grimy stairs slowly, letting floor after floor fall away below her, keeping her eyes lifted, so that floor after floor descended jerkily to her level of vision, and fell away out of sight.

Number 19 was the same. She saw everything with an acute, narrow, checking glance: the cheap shine of the satin spread, which had been replaced carelessly after the two bodies had finished their convulsions under it; a trace of powder on the glass that topped the chest of drawers; an intense green shade in a fold of the curtain. She stood at the window, looking down, watching people pass and pass and pass until her mind went dark from the constant movement. Then she sat in the wicker chair, letting herself go slack. But she had to be careful, because she did not want, today, to be surprised by Fred's knock at five o'clock.

The demons were not here. They had gone forever, because she was buying her freedom from them. She was slipping already into the dark fructifying dream that seemed to caress her inwardly, like the movement of her blood . . . but she had to think about Matthew first. Should she write a letter for the coroner? But what should she say? She would like to leave him with the look on his face she had seen this morning—banal, admittedly, but at least confidently healthy. Well, that was impossible, one did not look like that with a wife dead from suicide. But how to leave him believing she was dying because of a man—because of the fascinating publisher Michael Plant? Oh, how ridiculous! How absurd! How humiliating! But she decided not to trouble about it, simply not to think about the living. If he wanted to believe she had a lover, he would believe it. And he *did* want to believe it. Even when he had found out that there was no publisher in London called Michael Plant, he would think: Oh poor Susan, she was afraid to give me his real name.

And what did it matter whether he married Phil Hunt or Sophie? Though it ought to be Sophie, who was already the mother of those children . . . and what hypocrisy to sit here worrying about the children, when she was going to leave them because she had not got the energy to stay.

She had about four hours. She spent them delightfully, darkly, sweetly, letting herself slide gently, gently, to the edge of the river. Then, with hardly a break in her consciousness, she got up, pushed the thin rug against the door, made sure the windows were tight shut, put two shillings in the meter, and turned on the gas. For the first time since she had been in the room she lay on the hard bed that smelled stale, that smelled of sweat and sex.

She lay on her back on the green satin cover, but her legs were chilly. She got up, found a blanket folded in the bottom of the chest of drawers, and carefully covered her legs with it. She was quite content lying there, listening to the faint soft hiss of the gas that poured into the room, into her lungs, into her brain, as she drifted off into the dark river.

ℂ **SIGNET CLASSIC** (0451)

SHORT STORY SELECTIONS

☐ **THE RED BADGE OF COURAGE and Selected Stories, by Stephen Crane.**
A pioneer in the realistic school of American fiction, and a forerunner of
Ernest Hemingway, Stephen Crane probed the thoughts and actions of
trapped or baited men fighting the destructive forces in nature, in other
human beings, and in themselves. (515927—$1.50)

☐ **CANDIDE, ZADIG, and Selected Stories of Voltaire.** The savage contempt
with which Voltaire derided the bureaucracies of his day and his gift for
creating exotic panoramas find their perfect merger in these satirical
stories. With ruthless wit, the master of social commentary dissects
science and spiritual faith, ethics and legal systems, love and human
vanity. (523571—$2.50)*

☐ **JUST SO STORIES, by Rudyard Kipling.** Drawn from the wondrous tales
told to Kipling as a child by his Indian nurses, *Just So Stories* creates
the magical enchantment of the dawn of the world, when animals
could talk and think like people. Unforgettable reading for generations to
come. (521803—$2.95)

*Price slightly higher in Canada

Buy them at your local bookstore or use this convenient coupon for ordering.
NEW AMERICAN LIBRARY
P.O. Box 999, Bergenfield, New Jersey 07621
Please send me the books I have checked above. I am enclosing $_____
(please add $1.00 to this order to cover postage and handling). Send check or
money order—no cash or C.O.D.'s. Prices and numbers are subject to change
without notice.

Name_____

Address_____

City _____ State _____ Zip Code _____

Allow 4-6 weeks for delivery.

This offer, prices and numbers are subject to change without notice.